"Francesca-
that you e
etough helevar't u
"Searlet woman" in Sight!

The Witch of Eye

Mari Griffith

Published by Accent Press Ltd 2016

ISBN 9781783759507

Copyright © Mari Griffith 2016

The right of Mari Griffith to be identified as the author of this work has been asserted by the author in accordance with the Copyright, Designs and Patents Act 1988.

The story contained within this book is a work of fiction. Names and characters are the product of the author's imagination and any resemblance to actual persons, living or dead, is entirely coincidental.

All rights reserved. No part of this book may be reproduced, stored in a retrieval system, or transmitted in any form or by any means, electronic, electrostatic, magnetic tape, mechanical, photocopying, recording or otherwise, without the written permission of the publishers: Accent Press Ltd, Ty Cynon House, Navigation Park, Abercynon, CF45 4SN

Map and family tree design by Zoe Foster.

For Megan, Manon and Jessica,
the next generation of young women
who will have to make their way in the world.

House of Lancaster

Blanche of Lancaster — *m* — John of Gaunt — *m* — Katherine Swynford
c.1345-1368   Duke of Lancaster   1350-1403
     1340-1399

Cardinal Henry Beaufort
b.c.1375

John Beaufort
c.1373-1410

Joan Beaufort
Queen of Scotland
b.c.1404

Mary de Bohun — *m* — Henry IV
c.1368-1394   1367-1413

John — *m* — Jacquetta of Luxembourg
Duke of Bedford   b.c.1415
b.1389

Humphrey — *m* — Eleanor Cobham
Duke of Gloucester   b.c.1400
b.1390

Henry V — *m* — Catherine de Valois
1386-1422   b.1401

Henry VI
b.1421

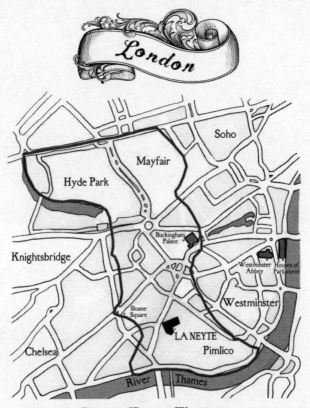

The estate of Eye–next–Westminster
showing the approximate location of the manor house of La Neyte

WHO'S WHO AMONG THE RESIDENTS OF WESTMINSTER VILLAGE

At the Palace
Henry VI, King of England and France
Humphrey, Duke of Gloucester (the King's uncle)
Eleanor, Duchess of Gloucester (Duke Humphrey's second wife)
Cardinal Henry Beaufort (the King's great-uncle)
William de la Pole, Earl of Suffolk (adviser to the King)
Alice de la Pole (his wife)
Canon John Hume (secretary to the Duke)
Magister Roger Bolingbroke (secretary to the Duchess)
William Woodham (a member of the Duke's administrative staff)
Members of the Royal Council

At the Abbey and the Monastery
Abbot Richard Harweden
Thomas Southwell (Canon of Westminster and Rector of St Stephen's Royal Chapel)
John Virley (supplier of inks and vellum to the monastery scriptorium)

Workers on the Eye Estate
William Jourdemayne (the tenant farmer)
Margery Jourdemayne (his wife)
Dairymaids and other farm workers

PROLOGUE

Early summer 1435

'It's going to be beautiful!'

As her husband helped her to alight from the royal barge onto the landing stage, Her Grace the Duchess of Gloucester paused for a moment, shielding her eyes against the sun and looking around her. A short distance away from the riverbank she could see workmen clambering about on the wooden scaffolding that clad the front of a charming manor house. A broad, winding path led up to the entrance.

'Such a heavenly spot,' she murmured, 'here at the water's edge. When the building work is finished, it will be the most beautiful house on the Thames.'

'It will be the most beautiful house in the whole of England!' said Duke Humphrey. 'At least, that's my intention, though I dread to think how much money I have already spent on it.'

'It will be worth every groat,' his wife assured him.

They had journeyed downriver from the Palace of Westminster to inspect the improvements being made to Bella Court, the manor house at Greenwich that the Duke had acquired on the death of his older brother, King Henry V. At present, the building was modest enough, though it benefitted greatly from its picturesque setting on a gentle curve of the river. Weeping willows dipped their long tresses into the water while graceful swans, with downy little cygnets perched snug and safe on their backs, glided serenely on its sunlight-dappled surface. Eleanor smiled as she watched: there was beauty in motherhood throughout the natural world.

Stepping on to dry land, she tucked her hand possessively

i

under her husband's elbow and they began strolling towards the house, their attendants following in their wake.

'Poor Henry,' said the Duke. 'He was really looking forward to taking his ease here, resting and celebrating his victories. He saw Bella Court as a place where he could relax completely.'

'He didn't have much opportunity to do that,' said Eleanor.

'No, sadly, he didn't,' Humphrey agreed. 'The price of his success was that he was forced to spend most of his time in France.'

'With you to help him in subduing the French,' she was quick to point out.

'I could hardly do otherwise. After all, he did save my life at Agincourt. I'll never forget that.'

'Of course. But, d'you know, Humphrey,' said Eleanor as they walked, 'I think it's a pity that Bella Court is such a dull name, because it certainly won't be a dull house, not after we've moved into it. Could we change it, do you think? Perhaps we should give it a French name to honour your brother's memory.'

'That would certainly be appropriate,' he agreed.

'Maison Agincourt, perhaps?'

'Oh, no! Agincourt was the bloodiest of battles, despite Henry's great victory. Our house won't be a place of confrontation, it will be a house where everything is agreeable, enjoyable … pleasing.'

'Pleasing to all the senses?'

'Mmmm,' said Humphrey. 'La Pleasaunce would be better.'

'Oh, that's a delightful name!' Eleanor exclaimed, stopping briefly to hug his arm. 'It's perfect.'

'Yes, isn't it?' Humphrey said, pleased with himself. 'So come, my sweet, let us explore the many delights of our new pleasure palace and see how everything is coming along.'

'I'm so excited about this, Humphrey. When does the architect expect it will be finished?'

'We've made ambitious plans,' Humphrey said, 'so, of course, the building work will take time, probably several months. Then the house must be furnished exactly to our liking. But we will certainly have taken full possession of it come springtime and we should be feeling thoroughly at home here by next summer.'

'In time for my birthday in August?'

'In plenty of time for your birthday. By August, I'm sure we'll feel as though we've lived here all our lives.'

'Then I shall insist upon holding a celebration second to none, a party everyone will remember as the best they ever attended. We will invite your nephew, the King, and everyone who is anyone at court. We'll show them how to have a wonderful day, far away from dreary old Westminster or dull old Windsor. And all in celebration of my birthday!'

Eleanor skipped a step or two in delight, thrilled at the thought of a glittering royal event in the presence of the King, where she was the centre of attention. Walking beside her, Humphrey regarded her rapture with a smile. He knew the work would take time, though teams of builders were already hard at work, extending the existing house and creating a bigger and better structure, as befitted the nobility of its inhabitants. The detailed plans that he had discussed with his architects included tranquil gardens on all sides, as far as the eye could see. These had already been planted so as to be fully mature by the following year and shady river walks were dotted with sweetly scented, rose-covered arbours.

Behind the main building was a spacious tiltyard where an audience of a hundred or more could be seated to watch a joust and, beyond that, two hundred acres of parkland offered the opportunity for sports, hawking and hunting of all kinds. With its soothing architecture, the house would welcome all who visited and the high wall which surrounded the whole estate would ensure complete privacy and safety for the guests. Though it was less than an hour's journey downriver from Westminster, it could have been a hundred miles away.

'This will be an enchanting place,' Humphrey enthused as he and Eleanor neared the imposing main entrance with their guards and attendants following at a respectful distance. 'We'll fill it with good fellowship and with poetry, we'll dance to the finest music. Our discourse will be with astronomers, astrologers, philosophers, writers…'

'And what of entertainments, Humphrey? Will we have masques and dancing?' Eleanor asked, seeing it all in her mind's eye.

'We'll have all manner of entertainments, feasting, singing, jousting. And we shall take pleasure in the talents of the most skilled entertainers, the best poets and musicians.'

'And will you read to me, Humphrey?'

'Of course. What would you like to hear? *Floris and Blancheflour? King Horn? Havelok the Dane?*'

'Yes, maybe. Or perhaps some of John Gower's work? I'm very fond of the *Confessio Amantis*. And you must read me Chaucer's *Parliament of Fowls* on St Valentine's Day. But it doesn't matter which. I love them all!'

'And I love you,' Humphrey said, bending his head to whisper in her ear, 'especially when the happy ending to a romantic story puts you in the mood for a little romance of your own.'

'Humphrey,' she said, stopping for a moment and standing quite still. 'How long do you think it will be before we can use our bedchamber here for its proper purpose?'

'Sleeping, you mean?' he teased her.

'Oh, Humphrey! You know exactly what I mean!'

'Alas, my Lady,' said Humphrey with mock regret, 'but until our love nest is prepared and ready for us, there is little we can do about what we both desire. We will have to wait until tonight, when we have returned to Westminster.'

'You are easily dissuaded, Sir!' Eleanor rebuked him, pretending annoyance by gently smacking his hand. Then, turning her face up to his, she gave him the look he knew so well. Her eyes, a deep shade of grey which darkened towards the outer rim of the iris, took on a sultry quality and the corners of her generous mouth began to twitch in a smile. Then the pink tip of her tongue appeared and traced the arc of her upper lip. He knew the signal.

'There are plenty of secret places in the garden,' she said. 'Surely it is not always necessary to be a-bed!'

'Indeed not,' Humphrey agreed, 'and if you were to dismiss your ladies … and I my gentlemen … we could make the excuse of inspecting the rose arbours!' He freed her hand from where it had been tucked under his elbow and bent to kiss it. Looking at her from under his eyebrows, he slipped his tongue between her fingers and Eleanor gave a throaty chuckle, knowing exactly what he had in mind.

They turned then and, to all outward appearances the epitome of decorum, continued their walk towards the house.

'We can at least inspect the rooms which are to be ours,' Eleanor said. 'I'm very keen to see exactly where they will be. I have plans for them and I don't simply mean choosing furnishings and tapestries.'

What she was really wondering was whether adequate provision had been made for a nursery. She had waited long enough, now she must redouble her efforts to conceive a child, so she would send for Margery Jourdemayne as soon as they returned to Westminster. Surely, Margery would know of some medicine or decoction to do the trick. Perhaps she had a charm or a talisman which would help. Eleanor didn't have any qualms about the dubious nature of such things.

She was becoming desperate.

Part One

The Journey

Love will not be constrained by mastery;
When mastery comes, the god of love anon
Beats his fair wings, and farewell! He is gone!

Geoffrey Chaucer
The Franklin's Tale

CHAPTER ONE

Summer 1435

In the parish of Kingskerswell, Devon

'Try to keep still, my dove.'

Betsy wrung out a cloth in warm water and applied it gently to her daughter's ear. Jenna's gasping sobs drowned out the sound of the kettle simmering on the fire.

'Truth is, I don't know if this is the best thing for a fat ear like this, but perhaps 'twill bring the swelling down.' Betsy's soothing voice belied her fury, her rage at the cruelty of the man. 'What did you do to offend him this time?'

Jenna squirmed in the chair, biting her lip so as not to squeal in pain under the pressure of the warm compress.

'I don't know,' she whispered. 'Really, Mam, I don't know. I'd been talking to Parson Middleton, that's all. Just being polite … but Jake said…'

'Aye, let me guess. He accused you of wanting to warm Parson's bed, I'll wager.'

'Yes,' said Jenna in a small voice. 'Yes, he did. He says I didn't ought to be talking to men like that.'

'Like what?'

'Well, you know, he says I always talk to men like I wanted to lie with them.'

'Take no heed of him. You're just a young woman with a pretty smile and Jake's jealous, that's all, eaten up with it. Some men are like that. They hate seeing other men looking at their wives, but then they beat the wife, as if it was all her fault. Mind you, your Jake's worse than most. It doesn't take great heavy punches like he gives you to keep a wife in her place.

He'd been bibblin' again, had he?'

'Of course. It's always when he's drunk too much that he hits me.'

'And I suppose that stupid Adam Luxton he works for had been paying him in cider.'

Jenna nodded, carefully. 'He often does. Jake says he works better for it. But then he went to the tavern.'

'Before going home? Why?'

'Because Walter the miller's wife has a new babe, a boy, and Walter was in the tavern buying ale and cider for everyone, Jake said.'

'Makes you laugh, don't it?' said Betsy, with a grunt. 'Strutting around the tavern like cocks, as though the hens had nothing to do with it. You'd think they were the ones who went through all the pain. Still,' she sighed, 'it's a woman's duty to bear children and a man needs a few youngsters around the place if he's a farm to run. My Gilbert is very pleased that you're helping with the milking. Saves him having to bend.'

Despite her painful ear, Jenna wasn't going to let her mother get away with that one. 'It's not just helping with the milking, Mam, you know that.' Since Jenna had learned to do the reckoning, she had taken on more and more responsibility for the day-to-day running of the dairy. 'If your Gilbert had to keep account and do the milk tallies himself, he wouldn't like it one bit, would he? It'd keep him away from…'

'You mind your tongue, my girl. It's none of your business what your stepfather does in his own time.' Betsy spoke sharply. The girl should be grateful that Gilbert had taken them in, a young widow and her child. At least they'd had decent food in their bellies and a roof over their heads these last twenty years and never had to beg for scraps from richer folk.

She concealed her irritation by inspecting the swollen ear again. Jenna would have to hide it under a coif or comb her hair over it. No use provoking Jake any further, he wouldn't want a wife with a puffball ear to remind him of his own violence.

The moment of tension had passed. 'Never you mind the old milk tallies,' said Betsy, giving Jenna's shoulders a small hug. 'There are more important things. At least you've got a husband, and your place is to give him a child as soon as you can, before he gets one on another woman. It won't take him long, he's handsome enough.' She began to busy herself, smoothing out the damp cloth she had been using, hanging it to dry near the fire, nodding, smiling, pleased at having suggested a solution to the problem. 'A baby,' she said, 'that's what you need. And pray it will be a boy.'

'It's not for want of trying.' A lopsided smile tweaked the corners of Jenna's bruised mouth and her mother smiled back at her, tender again. Things couldn't be too bad between the pair of them then, she thought. And at least Jake's great ham fist hadn't broken any of her daughter's teeth.

'Aye, the sooner you get yourself with child the better,' she said. 'Perhaps Old Mother Morwenna will know of something to help you. Give Jake a babe or two and maybe he won't beat you so often. Come, my dove, let me help you up. It's best you be getting back to your husband. You don't want to go upsetting him no more.'

***

At sunset, Jenna crossed the bridge over the village stream with reluctant steps and was back at the small, low-roofed cottage she shared with Jake rather sooner than she really wanted to be. She found her husband slumped on the bench near the fire pit, seemingly sober. He sat motionless in the firelight, watching her take off her shawl and hang it behind the door. She had no inkling of his mood: perhaps he was feeling genuine remorse, but he might equally well be seething with temper, struggling to remain calm. Eventually he spoke, his voice low and regretful.

'Sweet Christ, Jenna, I'm sorry. I don't know what comes over me.'

Not trusting herself to speak, she watched him rise and come towards her, flinching as he took hold of her arms and bent to kiss her, recoiling from the stink of stale alcohol on his breath. He stared intently at her then, as though trying to penetrate her mind, his eyes bloodshot in his handsome face.

How she had once loved that face, adored it and lavished exuberant, extravagant kisses upon it, smiling with the pleasure of touching it. Now she felt nothing but an icy calm as she waited for what she knew would come next.

Tears welled in his eyes. 'I didn't mean it, Jenna. You know that, don't you? You know I didn't mean it. I'll never do it again. Never. You do still love me, don't you, Jen? I didn't mean to hurt you. You know that. You know that, don't you, Jen?' He was snivelling now, butting his head against Jenna's neck like a small child begging her forgiveness, making her swollen ear throb painfully. She struggled in an attempt to hold her head away from him and he suddenly tried to take her in a clumsy embrace. Knocked off balance, she stumbled, almost lost her footing and would have fallen had he not tightened his arms around her. Pushing against him with both hands, she tried to break away.

'Stop it, Jake! Stop it! Get away from me. You're not sorry! You weren't sorry the last time it happened and you're not sorry now! Get away from me, Jake!' Jenna was screaming now, pushing him, pummelling his chest. 'Get away from me!'

She was no match for his strength. He overpowered her easily, his arms tightening like iron bands around her, pinning her own arms uselessly against her sides, her hands bunched into limp fists. His eyes narrowed as he realised she was not going to be won over this time. He began to mock her then, as he shoved her roughly towards the straw pallet where they slept on the floor in the far corner, an ugly sardonic smile twisting his face.

'So,' he said, his voice low and threatening, 'you think you can get away from me, do you, you teasing little whore? Well, you can't. You're my wife and there's no bastard on earth can change that. But they can't wait to get their stinking little hands on you. I've watched them going out of their minds wanting to grab your tits, pull up your skirts. It's your fault, you're like a bitch on heat. You set a man's prick alight. But I'm going to have you now, bitch, I'm going to show you … show you how it feels to have a real man screwing you … not a sickly whelp of a man like the Parson … you want it, don't you? You want it, don't you, bitch!'

Jenna whimpered hopelessly as he pushed her down onto

4

their mattress then dropped to his knees, roughly shoving her skirt up over her thighs, forcing her legs apart. He was inches taller than she was and as strong as an ox, his powerful body honed by years of labour in the fields. She could only pray that this time he wouldn't leave her skin raw and bleeding, her mind blank with shame and horror.

***

Jenna lay on her back for a long time after Jake had violated her, praying for merciful sleep. His arm lay heavy across her body, pinning her down, and she dared not move for fear of disturbing him. Over the sound of his snoring, she heard a tomcat yowling in the darkness outside the cottage and she pitied the poor queen that would soon have to endure the pain of his selfish penetration. Managing to turn onto her right side so that the weight of her own head on the pillow wouldn't put unbearable pressure on her swollen left ear, she slowly became aware that, with her damaged ear uppermost, she could hear neither the tomcat's yowling nor Jake's snoring with any clarity. It was as though she had pulled the pillow over her head – but she hadn't.

Dear God, if Jake had damaged her hearing, what would he do next? Would it always be like this for her, treading on eggshells for fear of annoying him, never knowing when his mercurial temper would flare up? Would she live in terror of her own husband for the rest of her life? And would she have to work her fingers to the bone on her stepfather's farm each day? She always avoided being alone in the dairy with the dirty old bastard her mother had been so grateful to marry and when there was no alternative but to work alongside him, she tried hard not to mind his drooling leer and his groping hands, if only for her mother's sake.

Why did men behave so oddly towards her? In all honesty, she reflected, if her stepfather hadn't made her so nervous, perhaps she wouldn't have been so keen to marry Jake, though she had to admit she had thought herself madly in love with him. She should have given herself time to get to know him better, time to discover the jealous temper simmering perilously close to the surface, ready to explode into violence as soon as it was fuelled with drink. How stupid she had been to fall so unquestioningly in love with a beautiful face.

Nothing was likely to change. If God spared her and she was still alive twenty years hence she would be just like her mother, her back bent with hard work, her face lined with worry. She could see no choice but to go on living with Jake, lying passively under the bulk of him at night, waiting until he grunted his satisfaction then heaved himself off her and began snoring like a bull. Did she really want a child as a result of these bestial couplings? Her mother's assertion that a baby would be the answer to her problems was of no comfort to her and in any case, although she didn't want to admit it to Betsy, she had already been to see Old Mother Morwenna to ask her advice. And to pay for it.

The wise woman of the village had been unexpectedly sympathetic. They talked companionably over a glass of small beer, sitting at the table where the toothless old crone concocted her herbal remedies for everyday ailments, coughs and colds, aches and pains, making medicines to cure constipation or aid conception. Amid much sighing and tut-tutting, Old Mother Morwenna pointed out that failure to conceive did not always mean the woman was barren.

'Look at the Dynhams, up at the Manor,' she said in her cracked, high-pitched voice. 'Those men couldn't beget a son to save their lives, not for all their money and their fancy ways. That's why the house and the land kept reverting to the King. Yes, for want of an heir. I'm old enough to remember it. Can you believe that? Eh? Can you? Do you know how old I am? Eh? Well, in truth, I'm not sure myself. But I do remember my own mother saying that one or two of the Dynhams' widows went on to have fine broods after their husbands died.'

She patted Jenna's arm with her bony hand. 'So it could easily be your man's fault that you have no little ones, my dove. Mind you,' she added with a cackle, 'you'd be a fool to tell him so!'

Before she left Morwenna's cottage, Jenna had parted with half a groat in payment for a phial of something viscous and brown which the old wise woman assured her would resolve the situation if she drank a third of it exactly mid-way between her menses on three consecutive months. But the phial had remained hidden under the eaves, unopened, while Jenna looked for some sign that things were going to change between her and Jake before she swallowed its vile-looking contents.

Nothing did change and she was forced to the conclusion that nothing ever would. Sooner or later, she would have to overcome her squeamishness and drink the thick, sticky brown liquid in the hope of conceiving a child. Yet in her heart she knew a child wasn't the answer: she couldn't bring a little one into the world to have its bones broken by a drunken father.

Besides, she had no absolute guarantee that Old Mother Morwenna's brown liquid would have any effect because, wise woman or not, her potions were not infallible. She had not been able to cure whatever had ailed Alice, Jenna's best friend since childhood. Jenna and Alice. They had been a pair of mischievous little rascals with a deep affection for each other, as close as sisters. Jenna and Alice did everything together, playing games, laughing, singing or running errands for their mothers. They loved nothing better than their weekly visit to the parsonage where Parson Middleton, then an enthusiastic, forward-thinking young clergyman, did his best to teach a group of the village children the rudiments of reading and reckoning.

But tonight, as Jenna lay sleepless beside her snoring lout of a husband, Alice lay silent in six feet of cold earth from whence, a year ago, a stony-faced Parson Middleton had committed her immortal soul to God's keeping. Gripped by an agony of belly cramps and vomiting, Alice had derived no benefit from Old Mother Morwenna's decoction of seeds of quince. Undeterred, the old wise woman had intoned some incantations above the bed where Alice writhed in agony, but to no avail. In desperation, her anxious parents had summoned the leech doctor from Newton Abbot, scraping together enough money to pay his extortionate fee. He took the money willingly enough before shaking his head and muttering that 'right side sickness' was beyond his help because it was the will of God.

In unendurable pain, poor Alice died, leaving her mother, her father and her dearest friend to mourn her and wonder what sin they had committed that was sufficiently grave to cause such a loss. How had they offended God so much that He took Alice away from them?

Jenna passed a restless night. The sensation of falling from a great height would convulse her from the brink of slumber until, finally, she abandoned all thought of sleep and slid carefully from under Jake's arm. In the last glow of the dying embers, she lowered herself gingerly down onto the bench by the fire pit, muscle by aching muscle, until she found a moderately comfortable position.

As she sat, she took stock of her situation. In time, she realised, she could become a vexed and resentful old woman, cowed by her husband's callousness, the teeth knocked from her head and deaf as a post from his blows. While she was still comparatively young, her most precious possession was a lively mind in a God-given healthy body, something Alice would never have again.

By the first light of dawn, Jenna had made her decision. She would get as far away as she possibly could from Kingskerswell and all it stood for. No matter what it took, she would get away from Jake.

And there would be no going back.

CHAPTER TWO

Midsummer 1435

William Jourdemayne, dependable and honest, excelled in his work as the tenant farmer on the manorial estate of Eye-next-Westminster but, in his wife's opinion, that was not enough. It infuriated her that he seemed perfectly content with things as they were.

It had taken some persuasion on Margery's part to get her husband to do what she wanted of him. Though impatient to put her plans in motion, she had realised the value of investing her time and energy over several weeks in pleasing him in every way she could, being warmly receptive towards him in their bed and readily agreeing to help him with the quarterly accounts for Abbot Harweden. She was eventually rewarded with the key to a small room just off the manor farmhouse kitchen for her own exclusive use.

Once Margery took possession of the room, she had cupboards moved into position against three of the walls and filled them with pots and pans, jugs and funnels, bottles and ewers, pestles and mortars. There were small bowls for mixing her ingredients and bigger bowls for washing her utensils; she was scrupulously clean in her work. Above the cupboards were several high shelves where, in a series of small locked coffers, she kept the secret ingredients she used in her recipes. Bunches of summer herbs for winter use were strung up to dry above the hearth while their seeds were stored in meticulously labelled boxes. Beneath the window, a sturdy table was positioned where the light was good and next to that, fixed with great care to the wall, was a large mirror. The mirror had been an indulgence on Margery's part; William would have been appalled if she'd been entirely truthful about the cost of it, but she had paid for it herself out of money she'd saved from selling her wares so she didn't think it any of her husband's business to question her purchase. Next to the mirror was a hook for her apron, but that apron was now tied around her slim waist as she worked at the table.

Raising a phial to her lips, Margery tasted a drop of liquid which was sharp and bitter on her tongue. Good, that was about the right consistency, and the correct balance of myrrh resin to strong, sweet white wine. She couldn't afford to make mistakes with anything as expensive as myrrh. Reaching for a small flask containing an infusion of mint leaves in boiled water, she tested the temperature of the liquid by letting a little of it drip onto the inside of her wrist. Judging it to have cooled to blood heat, she then held the flask up to the light and measured into it precisely ten drops of the tincture of myrrh, shaking the two gently together, watching the mint infusion become opaque and milky as the two liquids blended.

'Mmm,' she murmured, satisfied, setting the flask down on the table. 'Good. That should do the trick.'

Had Margery been a man, she would certainly have been a noted apothecary, but she had to be satisfied with her reputation as a wise woman, secure in the knowledge that the skills that her mother had handed down to her had commercial potential. As word of those skills spread, it pleased her to realise that people were prepared to pay considerable sums of money for what she sold them. There was profit in presenting these old remedies and decoctions in such a way that they appeared to be something entirely new, something different and exciting to help a woman realise her dreams of beauty and desirability and thus her chances of marriage. Margery possessed a shrewd intellect. She recognised vulnerability in other women. And she took advantage of it.

Fitting a pewter funnel into the neck of a small bottle, Margery carefully poured into it some of the tincture of myrrh she had just made, it was her favourite remedy for easing the pain of toothache. If she was careful, there would be enough to fill six of these bottles and each one would sell for a penny. Sixpence in all and it had cost her one penny to purchase the myrrh from her spice merchant. That meant a good profit for her, since white wine was easy enough to come by and spearmint grew in profusion alongside all the other herbs in her little physic garden between the farmhouse and the nearby brook. Spearmint was such a rewarding herb: Margery loved it for its usefulness in doing everything from treating a lady's greasy hair to keeping moths and mice at bay.

Methodically, she washed and dried the utensils she had been using and replaced them in a cupboard before setting out for the Palace at Westminster for another appointment with Lady Northumberland. At least she had found time today to stock up on the tooth tincture for the Duchess of Gloucester who was almost certain to need some very soon. She was becoming more and more demanding these days. Margery was very pleased about that.

***

A young man sat at the head of the long table in the library at the Palace of Westminster, flanked by two very much older men.

'The problem, Sire,' said the Earl of Suffolk, 'is that the French are as wily and dangerous as snakes. The Dauphin will do anything to challenge the English right to the French throne and establish himself as King of France.'

The man sitting opposite the Earl was wearing the deep scarlet cassock of a cardinal and exuded an air of authority when he spoke.

'In confidence,' he said, 'and within these four walls of course, I'm beginning to think we would be better off without them. I must confess to feeling heartily sick of the whole burden of France around English necks. The conflict has gone on for far too long and it's costing us dear. Too many fine young Englishmen dead, too many children orphaned. There's little to be gained from holding on to France just to avoid losing face. We'd be well rid of it.'

'Not everyone agrees with you,' the Earl pointed out. 'You'd be hard-pressed to get the Duke of Gloucester to share your opinion.'

'I'm afraid my nephew and I agree about very little these days,' said Cardinal Beaufort. 'Though I would feel more kindly disposed towards him if he would only be prepared to see sense about France.'

'But, to be fair,' protested the young man who was sitting between the two, 'perhaps he is merely concerned about me and my duties towards France. After all, I am the sovereign king of both countries. And I take my responsibilities very seriously.'

'And as members of the Council, Your Highness,' the Earl of Suffolk assured him, 'we take our responsibilities towards you very seriously and we would –'

'I'm sure the King does not need to be reminded of our loyalty,' interrupted Cardinal Beaufort. 'He knows we have always had his best interests at heart. But for the sake of both king and country, we must decide carefully what to do for the best. And this is now an urgent matter.'

Though sumptuously dressed, Henry appeared an unlikely king. He was quite a pleasant-looking boy, with plentiful brown hair, but his eyes held a peculiarly dull expression and his pallid skin often erupted into small, yellow pustules.

Henry VI, King of England and France, was thirteen years old and young for his age.

The Earl of Suffolk, as Steward of the Royal Household, was an adviser to the adolescent monarch. 'I understand, Your Highness, that His Holiness the Pope has requested this conference,' he said.

'Congress,' corrected Beaufort, 'an altogether bigger gathering, to be held at Arras, in Burgundy, and I have committed myself to attending. Philip of Burgundy will be there, of course, with a large French delegation, no doubt.'

'And will Pope Eugene attend?' asked the King.

'No, he won't. His Holiness has informed us that the interests of the Vatican will be represented by two cardinal mediators. They will both be senior men, you can depend upon it.'

Suffolk looked up from the papers on the table in front of him. 'And is the Dauphin himself to be present?'

'Very probably,' said Beaufort. 'As we know, he will do

anything or go anywhere to press his claim to the throne. He seems to have gained a great deal more confidence since the so-called Maid of Orléans went into battle on his behalf and succeeded in getting him crowned.'

'Not that we acknowledge a coronation brokered by a witch,' said Suffolk.

Cardinal Beaufort nodded without comment. He himself had interrogated Joan of Arc in France four years ago and had witnessed her death, tied to a stake above a huge fire in the marketplace at Rouen, burning in agony. The sight still invaded his dreams. Joan had died for her religious conviction that the Dauphin Charles was the rightful heir to the French throne.

Looking suddenly startled, the King swung round in his chair to face the Cardinal. 'But if the Dauphin will be there, then shouldn't I, too, attend this Congress at Arras?'

'I would advise against it,' said Beaufort, aware that Henry, still scarcely more than a child, would be unlikely to contribute anything of any significance to such an important gathering.

'Good,' said the King, clearly relieved, 'because I really cannot understand why we must have all this squabbling. The French throne is mine! I have been crowned in Paris. I am God's anointed King of France. Why is there all this bad feeling? I don't understand why we cannot all live together in peace.'

'I'm afraid, Your Highness,' said the Earl of Suffolk, 'that your mother's French relatives are a good deal less peaceable than you are, and there are several French nobles who have cast doubt on the English claim to the throne of France ever since the Treaty of Troyes, when your parents were married. I really can't imagine why it pleases them to acknowledge the Dauphin Charles their king: he's such a dreadful little man.' Suffolk looked suddenly embarrassed, aware that in speaking his mind, he had possibly overstepped the mark. 'Forgive me, Your Highness,' he said with remorse, 'I know the Dauphin is your mother's brother, but he is entirely devoid of her charm.'

The King looked wistful for a brief moment then hardened his expression. 'I understand that my French uncle granted a charter to the University of Poitiers not long ago. So, surely, he must be a decent man at heart, a man who encourages learning.' He paused, looking wistful. 'And I would like to follow the Dauphin's example when I'm older. I, too, will endow a school or a college one day.'

'Very laudable, Your Highness,' said the Earl of Suffolk. The two adults exchanged surreptitious glances. Though inclined to be pompous beyond his years, there were times when the King appeared even more of a child than he really was. The finest tutors had done their best in the schoolroom to acquaint the boy with all that had gone before. They taught him the history of conflict between France and England and the way in which his father, King Henry V, had brought the enemy to heel with a string of successes in battle and sealed the agreement by marrying the daughter of the old French king. Yet his son showed no interest at all in anything save the study of theology and the celebration of religious ritual. King Henry VI seemed unlikely to follow in the footsteps of his illustrious father on the battlefield or anywhere else. But these were early days and he was still very immature. Things could change.

'Of course,' the Earl of Suffolk went on, 'the other thing we must consider is Your Highness's own betrothal to a French princess as a way of consolidating our position.'

'My ... betrothal?' The young King's expression was suddenly mutinous. 'Surely that will not be a subject for discussion at the Congress of Arras?'

'Possibly,' said Suffolk, 'though the English delegation may not choose to introduce it. It could, however, prove a strong weapon in their armoury and they should be absolutely certain of our English policy on that or on any other subject that crops up.'

'Then,' said Cardinal Beaufort, 'since I shall be leading the delegation, we need to discuss our English tactics in great depth before I leave for France in a few weeks. I must be well briefed. We live in troubling times.'

***

Cows were such gentle creatures, with their friendly faces and their big eyes, long-lashed and inquisitive. But their backsides

14

were something very different, scrawny and dung-encrusted with thin tails swishing in an endless, fruitless attempt to keep the flies off the rumps that swayed from side to side as they walked. Jenna walked behind them, pleased that the drove would soon arrive at its overnight pasture.

Following six dairy cows and three hundred and ninety-five bullocks in procession for three weeks was an experience she would never be likely to recall with pleasure, though she revelled in her intense feeling of flight towards freedom. Droving was properly a masculine profession and women were not normally permitted to accompany a drove. Perhaps that was why she had become fond of those six other females walking just ahead of her, Daisy, Bluebell, Poppy, Matty, Molly and Meggy, the cows whose milk was sold along the way to defray the drovers' expenses. We girls should stick together, Jenna thought with a wry smile.

There had been four hundred bullocks originally, the drovers told her, before the wolves came in the night. Three animals had been killed outright, despite the best efforts of the drove dogs to keep the wolves at bay, and the drovers had to finish off the two poor mauled creatures that had been left for dead. The edible remains of the carcasses were sold off as stewing bones for the poor of the parish and they buried the loyal dog that had given its life for the herd under a hedge by the roadside.

It was a month since Jenna had walked out of her stepfather's dairy quite early one morning, casually, as though simply on an errand. Knowing Jake was cutting hay for Adam Luxton, she didn't expect him home until his day's work was done, so she would not be missed for several hours. She walked on calmly until she had reached the outskirts of the village, trying not to attract anyone's attention, willing herself not to run. After half a mile she retrieved a small canvas sack containing a few of her belongings, carefully hidden in the hollow trunk of an old oak. Then she quickened her pace until she had put a good eight miles between herself and her old life.

Never once did she look back.

In the following weeks, while doing her best to appear casually inconspicuous, Jenna moved from farm to farm in search of work. She had left home with no particular plan in mind beyond simply getting as far away from Kingskerswell and from Jake as she possibly could, terrified that he might try to pursue her, scared of meeting anyone she knew.

She was lucky. At the height of summer, with the haymaking season in full swing, farmers were desperate to take on extra hands to work in the fields. Jenna found she could earn as much as two or three pence a day as long as she was prepared to put in long, back-breaking hours, raking and baling, winnowing, helping to build ricks and load hay wains. More often than not, she had enough pennies in her pocket to buy herself the share of a straw mattress in a hay loft. She didn't often have to sleep under a hedge.

In her desperation to get away, Jenna had made no real plan for her journey, nor had she thought about a destination until she found herself three days' work on a farm in Honiton. On the third day, she and the other casual workers crowded round the farmer's two daughters who had brought the usual plain fare of bread, cheese and small beer out to the hayfield for the workers' midday dinner. They also brought news of an approaching cattle drove which would be stopping overnight and, said the two girls, mischievous eyes shining in anticipation, the drovers would be sure to liven things up in the barn that evening.

Well before nightfall, a dozen drovers on horseback, together with their dogs, had herded four hundred head of cattle into their overnight pasture. At sunset, with work finished for the day, food and small beer were laid out on a long trestle table in the big barn. The drovers mingled with the farm hands and casual labourers, their shouts and laughter loud on the evening air. Someone produced a tabor and began beating out an accompaniment for a piper and a fiddler who were playing a popular dance tune, while one of the stable lads shook a handful of gravel in a wooden box to the rhythm. Bets were being laid on whether a drover or a farm hand would win the wrestling contest which would take place later in the roped-off area in the corner.

Sitting on a hay bale, munching bread and cheese, was a tall man sporting a jaunty sprig of rowan in the hat which he had pushed to the back of his head, revealing a face sunburned to the colour of autumn beech leaves. His dark eyes lit up when he caught sight of Jenna and he jumped down off the bale of hay to introduce himself to her. Doffing his hat with exaggerated politeness, he told her his name was Robin Fairweather and he was the Head Drover. For all the world as though they were both at a very noble gathering, he begged for the pleasure of having her join him in the dance. Jenna was already smiling as she placed her hand in his.

They danced easily together and talked companionably throughout the evening though Jenna, painfully conscious of the need to be careful, was wary of telling Robin anything much about herself. Nevertheless he gathered, little by little, that she had been unhappy in her last employment and wanted to try her luck somewhere other than in Devon. Jenna thought London might suit her purpose: she knew little about it but she'd heard it was a very big town. It was, he agreed, nodding. Oh yes, London was very big, and full of opportunities for a bright girl like her, and he should know: this drove was heading for a village just outside London and he often took cattle there. But, he pointed out, there was one drawback: it was nearly three weeks' walk away from Devon.

A sudden idea hit Jenna like a kick from a mule. 'Could I ... would you ... permit me to travel with you?'

'No,' said Robin, curtly, turning aside. 'Under no circumstances. Droving is men's work. Women get in the way. They distract the men. Besides, it isn't seemly.'

'I won't get in the way, I promise. And I give you my solemn word that I will behave in a proper manner.'

'No. I said no. If you once stepped out of line you could ruin my reputation. I could lose my job.'

Jenna sat quietly. She was well aware that only men of the greatest integrity and honesty would be put in charge of a big cattle drove like this one. Robin Fairweather was certain to be well-respected in his home village, probably from a good family. Just the kind of man, in fact, to whom she could entrust her safe conduct. She couldn't let this opportunity pass. Just as she was about to speak again, to beg him to take her on, he cut across her.

'If ... and I mean if ... I were to allow you to travel with us there'd be no flighty, fancy nonsense with the men. You would have to promise me. Is that clear?' His face was stern but there was still that twinkle in his eye.

'I promise,' said Jenna with great solemnity. 'I shall behave like a nun.'

'Huh! That guarantees nothing. Nuns are often no better than they should be!'

'Very well, then – I shall behave like a decent, respectable Devonshire woman.'

'In that case,' said Robin, 'you may travel with us. If you're quite sure you want to.'

'Clear and sheer,' Jenna said. 'I was never so sure of anything in my life.'

Having relented, Robin assured her that though no one could offer her complete protection from the many dangers on the road, she would be safer with the drove than she would be on her own. The animals were being taken to a stock farm on the outskirts of London, he told her, in the village of Westminster where the bullocks would be grazed and fattened up for a few weeks before being sold in the livestock market at Smithfield.

'Sleep on it,' advised Robin. 'And if you still want to go through with it, be ready at cockcrow. I want to be on the road as soon after daybreak as we can. I haven't got time to waste.'

Should she join them? Would she be putting herself at risk? It was difficult to think rationally in the festive atmosphere of the barn: by now, small beer had given way to stronger ale, and the wrestling match was well under way, the favourites being cheered to the rafters.

Jenna spent the remainder of the evening veering between her conviction that the idea was a good one and nervous apprehension at venturing into the unknown – but she also realised that the last place Jake would think of looking for her was in the middle of a cattle drove. It was no use dithering, she had to make a decision because this could be the best opportunity she would ever have. And she knew what

Alice would have done.

Jenna left with the drove when it moved out shortly after dawn the next morning.

***

The Duchess of Gloucester had a feeling of delighted anticipation on the one hand and disturbing anxiety on the other. These conflicting emotions had been brought about by an urgent request from the King for the Duke and Duchess to attend him at the palace at their earliest convenience and, while Eleanor was always eager to be in the presence of her husband's royal nephew, something had set an alarm bell sounding in her head. She had no idea why they had been sent for. Neither, it seemed, had her husband.

Yet again, niggling disquiet had dragged Eleanor out of a shallow, fretful slumber, to the sound of her own aching teeth grinding against each other. She had been through a whole bottle of Margery Jourdemayne's tincture of myrrh in a single week. It often amazed her that her restlessness didn't wake Humphrey but there was nothing of the alert soldier about her husband when he was in his bed. He slept like a man with no conscience and now, lying on his back, he was snoring fit to wake the dead. There would be no more sleep for Eleanor that night.

Admittedly, Humphrey was not at his most attractive at moments like this: the passing years had not been kind to him, and the excesses of his table and his liking for Burgundy wine had thickened his waist. But his wife was able to look beyond the slackly open mouth, the stained teeth and the smell of stale drink and still be grateful that he was her husband because he was unquestionably a duke of royal blood. It was all Eleanor cared about. She smiled in the darkness, marvelling at the remarkable change in her circumstances since she had first come to court thirteen years ago, a confidently pretty twenty-one-year-old, eager to seize her opportunities.

Her father, Sir Reginald Cobham, a minor knight entirely without influence, owned only a very modest estate in Kent, so no daughter of his could have expected to marry well. Without the advantages of high birth, the young Eleanor had spent several vigilant weeks assessing potential husbands and planning her strategy with care. Hers was a two-pronged attack: she wanted to re-establish her family's failing status and, more than anything, she wanted a titled husband for herself. Her dark hair, sinuous grace and startling grey eyes often turned heads, though the only heads that interested her were those that wore coronets. Aiming high, she had begun with the King's uncle and set out to entrap John, Duke of Bedford, brother of the late King Henry V.

John of Bedford was a tall man with a round face and a ready smile. In Eleanor's critical analysis of what he had to offer, he seemed pleasant enough, but by no stretch of the imagination could he be called handsome: his hairline was receding and, in her opinion, his nose was rather too hooked. His major advantage was that he was next in line to the throne and unmarried. Though she tried to catch his eye at every opportunity, not even at her most coquettish could she manage to attract his attention, much less strike up any kind of conversation with him. He seemed entirely unmoved by her, even slightly irritated, but, as a knight of the realm, his innate chivalry would not permit him to be rude to a lady. Instead, he was icily polite.

His younger brother Humphrey, Duke of Gloucester, was an entirely different kettle of fish. Tall, lithe and aware of his own smooth good looks, he flirted outrageously with Eleanor from the moment they met. He would look at her with his intense brown eyes before bending his head to kiss her hand, then he would press his lips to her fingers for a moment too long, giving her hand a gentle squeeze. On one occasion he slipped the tip of his tongue between her fingers, making his meaning perfectly plain.

Thrilled by his attentions, Eleanor would laugh her tinkling laugh, smiling and fluttering her long, dark eyelashes at him. She would have been ready to fall into Humphrey's bed at the first suggestion, except that it was already occupied by his wife.

But a woman of Eleanor Cobham's calibre would not allow herself to be deflected from the chase by a small detail like that.

She meant to have her Duke and would stop at nothing to achieve her ambition. As it happened, the Duchess Jacqueline was brought to bed of a stillborn child a few weeks later and was in no position to pleasure her husband. With his wife thus inconveniently indisposed, Humphrey, being the man he was, felt entitled to seek gratification elsewhere. He fell, like a ripe plum off a tree, into Eleanor's inviting arms.

There were plenty of opportunities for the pair to be together since Eleanor had become one of the Duchess Jacqueline's ladies, though she spent a great deal more time with her love than she did with his wife. It wasn't long before tongues began to wag. Unable to claim rights of ownership over his Dutch-born wife's extensive lands in the Low Countries, the mercurial, selfish Humphrey quickly tired of the unfortunate Jacqueline and, within a few months, he had readily agreed to the annulment of their marriage on the grounds of its illegality.

No sooner was Duke Humphrey free than he married his Kentish concubine. The subject of bitter criticism and the victim of cruel jokes, she managed to survive the finger-pointing and malicious gossip, and her persistence brought her triumph in the end. On her marriage she became the wife of one of the most significant, powerful men in England, though she never took her position for granted and was at pains to please her husband at every opportunity. When she was with him, she hung on his every word and laughed appreciatively whenever he said something clever. Away from him, she spent hours with her seamstress, demanding the creation of ever-more-lavish gowns, or with her maid, patiently trying new and attractive ways of dressing her hair.

Her meetings with Margery were more covert but no less regular. Mistress Jourdemayne was a constant source of face creams, soaps, powders and perfumes but, over the years, she had also provided Eleanor with potions and decoctions which she claimed would attract and keep a lover. Once Eleanor had trapped her man and married him, she began to demand medicines to help her conceive a child, preferably a son. Margery had promised to do all she could to help her.

21

The Duchess spent even longer than usual on her appearance during the morning that followed her sleepless night. Now, standing tall and elegant beside her husband, she smiled winningly at the young King as he received them both in the Throne Room of the Palace of Westminster. His Royal Highness bestowed a dazzling smile on them.

'Come,' he said, 'let us find a private corner where I can tell you something in great confidence. No one else must know!' He grinned at them conspiratorially as he led them towards the far corner of the big room. When they were safely out of earshot of the handful of courtiers who were in constant attendance on him, the King turned excitedly towards them.

'I have made an important decision,' he whispered, looking from side to side to ensure he wasn't overheard, for all the world like a child sharing a secret in the nursery, 'and I do hope it will please you both.' The Duke and Duchess glanced uncertainly at each other as the King went on. 'Now, if you, Uncle, were not already a member of the most chivalrous Order of the Garter, I would want to make you one as a token of my esteem. Of course, I shall be fourteen years old come December and expect to take more decisions myself after that, as is right and proper. But, my noble uncle, I do wish to mark your excellent service to the Crown.'

'That is most kind of you, my Lord, but there is no need...'

'Let me finish, Uncle,' said the King. 'Now, since you are already a Garter Knight, I cannot confer that honour upon you so I have decided instead to invite you, Aunt Eleanor, to become a Lady of the Garter. As your King, this honour is solely within my gift and I think it entirely appropriate.'

'An admirable idea! Excellent!' said Humphrey, clearly delighted.

It took all Eleanor's self-control to remember where she was. Astounded, she wanted to shout out loud, to lift her skirts and cavort around the big room, singing at the top of her voice. The King appeared to notice nothing, pleased with himself for having made a decision independently of the Council.

'Of course,' he went on, as confidingly as before, 'the Garter ceremony will not be held until next May, and the announcement of the names of the new recipients of the honour will not be made public until St George's Day in April. That is more than six months hence, so I must ask you both to keep the secret until then. I do hope you won't find that too arduous. Of course, some administrators will need to know, including my esteemed great-uncle, Cardinal Beaufort, since he is Prelate of the Order.' He paused. 'Are you pleased?' he asked.

Beaming, Humphrey turned to his wife. 'Are you pleased, my dear?'

Eleanor had recovered her composure. 'More pleased than I would ever have thought possible,' she said slowly.

She was to become a Lady of the Garter. This was the ultimate accolade.

'Come,' the King was saying from somewhere in the distance. In her imagination, Eleanor was already wearing a white silk gown under the dark blue velvet mantle of the Order, its badge pinned prominently to the wide sash draped over her shoulder, people smiling, women curtseying to her, men congratulating her and saying how lovely she looked. She had to concentrate hard to bring herself back to the present and listen to what the King was saying.

'...let us call for some wine to celebrate my decision. I know, my Lord Uncle, that you are partial to a glass of Burgundy wine from time to time.'

The next few minutes passed in a daze for Eleanor. She would have liked to sit for a moment while she came to terms with what she had just been told, but the King and the Duke remained standing, so she contented herself with another winning smile. King Henry's announcement today was the absolute endorsement of her position as Humphrey's wife and, until the King himself was married, she was indisputably the first lady in the land. If only she could give her husband a child, she would be unassailable.

***

The decision to join the cattle drove had been made instinctively, but the nearer they drew to London, the more pleased Jenna felt that she had obeyed that instinct. It felt right and she seemed to have found a genuine, dependable friend in Robin Fairweather.

Conversation between them was sporadic as they walked side by side behind the herd with Mallow, Robin's dog, at their heels. Leading his horse by the bridle, Robin was keeping an eye open for any bullock that might decide to loiter and graze the grass verge. If he spotted one, he would thrust the horse's bridle into Jenna's hand while he and Mallow went after the miscreant to round it up, Robin smacking its rump with his withy stick to persuade it to change its mind.

The air was filled with the barking of dogs, the shouts of the men, the lowing and blowing of animals disinclined to move any faster and the clopping of their metal-shod hooves on the dry, stony clay of the drove road. Flanking the long line of cattle, keeping them on track, a dozen men on horseback rode back and forth, calling to each other and whistling commands to their dogs. They needed to get the bullocks safely to their destination: they were valuable animals.

'Westminster isn't far from here,' Robin said, as they trudged past yet another village green. 'It won't be long before we get there.'

'How far is Westminster from London?'

'Just outside. Near enough for the King to be in the city when he has to and still be in his own bed come nightfall.'

'The King!' Jenna was wide-eyed.

'Yes, the King. His Royal Highness King Henry VI,' Robin was smiling at Jenna's innocence. 'He lives in Westminster, too.'

'But not on the farm!'

He roared with laughter. 'No! No, of course not. Not on the farm, though there is a fine manor house on the estate where I'm sure he would be very comfortable. No, the King has a grand palace all of his own with servants and great lords and ladies to look after him.'

Jenna was quiet for a long time, taking in this unexpected information.

'Will I see him?'

'Who, the King?' Robin laughed again. 'Unlikely. He

doesn't go walking around the village streets in Westminster. He lives in the palace. But it's quite close. We're making for the Manor of Eye-next-Westminster, the demesne which belongs to the monastery.'

'The what?'

'The demesne. We'd call it a barton back in Devon. It's a big estate.'

'That's a strange name.'

'What is? Demesne?'

'No, not that. The other one. The Manor of whatever you said.'

'The Manor of Eye? Yes, Eye is the old name, apparently. Eybury is the name of the home farm, though the estate is still known as Eye. It's a huge place, must run to a thousand acres, perhaps more. And there are always droves of cattle coming and going. Sheep, too, but mainly cattle. I bring bullocks up from Devon four times a year.'

Jenna watched the swaying bovine backsides for a moment. 'They're all looking very thin,' she said.

'Not surprising,' said Robin, 'think how far they've walked. It's nigh on two hundred miles.' He grinned at her. 'You're not so fat yourself after walking all that way! How are you feeling?'

'Oh, a bit leary.'

'Weary?'

'No, leary. I could do justice to some bread and cheese. What are you laughing at?'

Robin was chuckling. 'You're going to have to lose your Devon accent if you want to make yourself understood,' he said. 'They don't use words like "leary" round these parts. They'd say "hungry". You'll have to start using the right words, or you'll never find work. You might not even get anything to eat!'

Jenna laughed, too. She and Robin had become good companions during the course of the journey, easy with each other, and she was pleased by that and very grateful. As he pointed out to her several times, the only reason he'd allowed her to travel with them was that she was a good Devon girl and she should not be traipsing around the countryside on her own,

25

looking for casual work on farms. The other men had been quite respectful towards her too, once Robin had lain down the ground rules on that first morning back in Honiton. Their business was to get the animals to Westminster without mishap.

'Not far now,' Robin said. 'Journey's end is in sight.'

'The girls will be glad of the rest.'

'Aye, they will, and so will the bullocks. They'll get a couple of weeks' rest on Eybury Farm, on rich pasture down by the river Thames. It's good and green at this time of year and not too wet, even though it's clay soil. They'll fatten up nicely.'

'And then they'll be killed.'

Robin shrugged. 'That's what happens.'

It was pointless getting fond of animals, Jenna thought, they were only there for the convenience of people. So she had been surprised the first time she'd heard Robin calling the six dairy cows his 'girls'. But Robin was a surprising man, a no-nonsense, responsible head drover with a concern for the herd in his charge and a great affection for his dog, Mallow. Mallow? That seemed strange to Jenna, too: dogs were usually given names like Trojan or Holdfast.

'Why Mallow?' she had asked him a few days ago.

'Why not? It's a pretty plant, she's a pretty bitch.'

The black and white cattle dog was no prettier than any other bitch, Jenna thought, but her devotion to Robin was obvious and she had an endearing habit of nuzzling her long nose under his hand until it moved to stroke her head or tickle her ears.

So there was a soft side to his nature, but cattle were cattle, the commodity he traded in. The bullocks would bring a good profit when they were slaughtered, enough to make it worthwhile for men like Robin Fairweather to spend their lives on the drove roads, satisfying the needs of city folk who had no room to keep animals or grow crops of their own but still needed food in their bellies. Droving was hard, dangerous work: Mallow wasn't just there to herd the animals, she had to protect her master, too.

***

26

The sun, low in the sky, was to their backs when the drove arrived at Eybury farm. Robin had sent one of the men on ahead to warn the tenant-farmer to expect them and now the animals had come to a halt, some cropping the grassy bank, the drovers waiting to be told which field they were to use as pasture.

'I told you we'd get here by dimmet-time,' Robin said with a smile in his eyes.

'And we did,' said Jenna, wondering why he was so amused.

'This time of day is called "evening" in these parts, or sometimes "dusk".'

'Not dimmet?'

'No. They'd probably think you meant dinner-time,' he said, 'so you'd get nothing to eat. Well, I did warn you!' Jenna groaned at him but took the advice to heart.

'Hey, Robin!'

He turned at the shout and waved. Two young cowherds were running up the lane towards them, withy sticks in hand, ready to help round up the animals and head them off into the field.

'Seth, you young dog! How are you? Piers, I'll swear you've grown since I last saw you!'

'Good to see you, Robin,' panted Seth. 'The neats are to go here in the upper meadow, Master Jourdemayne says. We'll drive 'em down to the lower meadow tomorrow, when he's had a chance to move the sheep. They've not been moved since they were sheared three weeks ago.'

'Three weeks ago! A bit late in the year for shearing, wasn't it?'

'Aye, it's all been a bit late this year, what with the weather and everything, and then the shearers said the stars were all wrong for shearing so they wouldn't do it. Said it would bring bad luck. The Master could do with a bit more help, truth to tell. We're on the go from dawn 'til dusk.'

'No peace for the wicked,' Piers grinned, pushing open a wide gate just as an errant bullock made a break for freedom.

'*Whoa!*' Seth shouted. 'You pesty bastard of a bullock! *Hoop ha!*' He sprinted nimbly up the bank to head off the animal, smacking his withy stick on its rump. '*Hoop ha!*' he whooped again. 'You ain't goin' nowhere but in that field, my old mate. *Hoop ha!*' Mallow, knowing what was expected of her, circled behind the bullock, barking and snapping at its heels to drive it back in the right direction. Once it was safely through the gate, the others, nose to tail, began to trot obediently behind it into the meadow, tempted by the prospect of sweet pasture and even sweeter rest. The drovers and their dogs stood by to deter any other wanderers.

Jenna had been watching this activity from a distance, not wanting to get in the way. It was only after he had looped the gate back on to the gatepost that Seth spotted her and gave a low whistle.

'A woman!' he said, surprised.

'Yes, a woman,' agreed Robin, smiling. 'Haven't you seen one before?'

'Aye,' Seth laughed, 'I've seen a few in my time. But not many as pretty as this one. Not drovin' no neats, anyhow.'

'I broke the drovers' code for once and let her travel with us because she needed looking after. This here's Jenna,' Robin introduced them then gave Jenna a broad grin. 'Neats is the name for cattle hereabouts,' he explained, his eyes sparkling with amusement. 'I told you you'd have to learn a lot of new words if you want to find work in Westminster. They don't speak proper English, like what we do in Devon!'

Piers laughed at that, but Seth looked hard at Jenna, sizing her up. ''Lookin' for work, are you?' he asked. 'What sort of work? Most girls seem to want to work up at the palace for the gentry. Is that what you want?'

'The palace!' Jenna was astounded. 'What would I do in the palace?'

'Well, there's kitchen jobs, for scullions and so on. You don't need fancy ways for those.'

'Jenna's a dairymaid,' said Robin firmly. 'That's what she's told me.'

'Yes,' Jenna agreed. 'I'd like some dairy work if I can find it. Is there any going round here?'

Seth whistled through his teeth. 'Aye, there might be. We've got our own dairy herd to milk twice a day. Then, if the drovers bring any cows along with the fatstock herds, we've got to look after them, too. And that's without all the other work we've got on the farm. So when we're busy, Master needs extra people who know what they're doing. You should go and ask him. He's in there,' he said, jerking his head towards a wooden building a little further along the lane. 'He's just finishin' off milkin' the last of our own neats.'

Jenna looked at Robin for approval. 'What do you think?'

He shrugged. 'You're the one who needs the work,' he said. 'And William Jourdemayne is the Master hereabouts, the man you need to see. You might as well go and ask. You're none the worse.'

'I will,' said Jenna, 'thank you. And Robin, thank you for all your kindness. I won't forget you.'

'You won't have a chance to forget me,' Robin smiled. 'Even if I don't see you again before we start for home, I'll be back with another herd in nine or ten weeks, an even bigger one, with animals to fatten up for the Christmas market. So I'll see you around Martinmas, if you're still here.'

'If I am, I'll look out for you, for old time's sake. Look after the girls for me!'

'Oh, Jenna,' he called after her, 'the girls will need milking later. Will you tell Master Jourdemayne? And tell him I'll be expecting the usual tankard of ale later on.' He paused. 'Good luck to you!' he added, watching as she set off down the lane. 'And God's blessings.'

CHAPTER THREE

Jenna hesitated at the open door of the byre until her eyes became accustomed to the gloom and she could make out the shapes of empty cattle stalls. She could still hear the muted shouts of the drovers and the barking of dogs in the distance but it was very quiet in here, and very big.

'And what can I do for you?'

The questioner's low voice was muffled against the flank of a dun cow as his fingers pulled rhythmically at her teats. After a moment, the cow turned her head and regarded Jenna with an inquiring expression in her dark eyes as though she, too, expected a reply. Milk, squirting into the wooden pail beneath her udder, made the only sound in the warm byre.

'Well? What can I do for you?'

'Beg pardon, sir?'

The man's voice came again, louder this time and with a note of tetchiness. 'I said, what can I do for you?'

All Jenna could see of the big man who was crouching awkwardly on a three-legged milking stool was the back of his head. She had an impression of strands of grey in dark hair, powerful shoulders. She swallowed, suppressing a sudden wave of anxiety, but she really needed this job. If she said nothing she would likely gain nothing and that was not the way to start the rest of her life. She cleared her throat.

'If it please you, Master Jourdemayne,' she said. 'I heard from Robin the Drover that you might be looking for someone to help with the milking and the running of the dairy.'

William Jourdemayne eased himself up from the low stool, stretching his cramped back as he stood. 'Off with you, then, my beauty,' he said, giving the cow's rump a gentle slap to move her on, deftly removing the pail before she kicked it.

'So,' he turned towards Jenna, wiping his hands on a clean

31

rag, 'you're looking for work, are you? And Robin's told you I might be wanting some help around here. True enough. I wouldn't be doing the milking if we weren't short of cowmen. I've got better things to do. What's your name?'

'Jenna, sir. Jenna Harding.'

'Hmm. And can you milk a cow, Jenna Harding?

'Oh, yes, master. I have done it a thousand times.'

'Good. And what about dairy work? Have you any experience of that?' He raised his dark eyebrows as he looked down at her.

'Yes, sir, in my stepfather's dairy, ever since I started to work as a child. And I am now four-and-twenty years old.'

'Four-and-twenty, eh! Is that so? Well, an older woman could be an advantage, I suppose, someone experienced who knows what she's doing. Have you anyone to recommend you? Someone in Chelsea, perhaps? Knightsbridge?'

'No. No one in any village hereabouts, sir,' she replied, 'though you could ask several people in Kingskerswell and I'm sure they would vouch for my honesty.'

'Kingskerswell? And where might that be?'

'Down Devon way, sir. Not far from Exeter.'

'Ah, so that's your accent; you're a Devonshire lass. Well, that's clever of you, Mistress Harding,' William laughed, showing teeth which were still white and even, though Jenna judged him to be above thirty years old. 'Do you think I'm going to go all the way to Devon to find someone to recommend you? Eh? Or could Robin recommend you?'

'No, sir. I have only recently met Robin. So you must take my word for it,' she said quietly. 'And I'm jonnack.'

'I thought you said your name was Jenna?'

'It is, sir. I'm sorry. I meant I'm jonnack, I speak the truth.'

He looked down at her again from under his eyebrows, his dark hair falling forward, blue eyes sizing her up. He was amused, but he had no wish to embarrass her.

'No,' he said, 'you don't look like a liar. But I have only your word about your experience. What do you know of milk tallies? Could you keep account?'

'Oh, yes, sir. I was nearly always the one who did that. And

I was responsible for the cheese and butter, depending on the tally of milk.'

'Didn't your stepfather keep account?'

'Yes, sir, to start with. But not after the parson in our village had taught some of us to reckon up numbers and to read a few words.'

'You'll be telling me next that you looked after the hens as well!'

'I did, sir, geese too. The eggs fetched a good price.'

'Then why, in Heaven's name, did you leave? Seems to me you had good employment.'

'I did, sir.'

William didn't quite know what to make of this girl – this woman, rather. Her gaze was disarmingly steady, as though she was challenging him to ask her what had brought her here to Eye-next-Westminster. Perhaps she was one of the drover's women? His friend Robin been known to boast of his conquests after a few tankards of ale; perhaps he wanted to keep this one here in Westminster, away from his respectable family in Devon. But, even if she wasn't the drover's woman, no doubt it was all to do with some man. It usually was, especially with the pretty ones, and this one's eyes were as sweet and brown as chestnuts under her linen coif. And she had an appealing little way of cocking her head to one side when he questioned her, as though anxious not to miss anything he might say, eager to please. She was clearly intelligent and she looked strong, too, as though she wasn't afraid of hard work. If she was telling the truth – and he had a shrewd idea she was – then she'd be an asset to the dairy at Eybury Farm.

But the dairy was rightly Margery's responsibility. As his wife, her place was at his side, helping him to run the farm, not putting him in the position of having to do any of the milking himself. That was women's work. If Margery did run the dairy, as she was supposed to, then he wouldn't need to employ anyone like this woman. Nor have to pay for the privilege.

'Well,' he said, 'we sometimes have a vacancy for a dairymaid, but the running of the dairy is my wife's responsibility, so I'll speak to her first. Come back tomorrow.'

'Thank you, Master Jourdemayne,' said Jenna, disappointed. 'I'll be here at first light. Do you think your wife might…'

'I said I'd speak to her. If she wants to take you on, I'll let you know tomorrow.'

'Thank you, sir,' Jenna said again. She was about to drop a curtsey when she remembered Robin saying that William Jourdemayne was no more than a tenant farmer, for all that he had complete responsibility for managing Eybury as a stock farm. So she simply took her leave of him and had turned to walk away when he called after her.

'Have you somewhere to sleep tonight?'

She hesitated, unsure of his meaning, buying time. 'I beg your pardon, sir?'

'I said have you somewhere to sleep tonight? The drovers always sleep in the big barn, but there's plenty of room in the hay loft. Make up a pallet for yourself and sleep up there if you want. At least you'll have a roof over your head. Don't worry, two or three of the younger girls sleep up there, too. You won't be on your own, so the stable lads won't trouble you. They'll feel my belt on their backsides if they do.'

He smiled at her and she smiled shyly in return. He seemed a decent man and he did offer the realistic prospect of good, honest work which she knew she could do and do well. If there was a job – and she hoped there was – she resolved to do it to the very best of her ability.

***

The Duchess Eleanor had a niggling toothache again. Mercifully, the tooth was quite a long way back in her lower jaw so, even if it should become discoloured and unpleasant to look at, it wouldn't show when she smiled or laughed her tinkling laugh. Nothing about her should ever appear unpleasant. She never forgot that her beauty had made her what she was today.

Hers had not been an easy position to achieve but she was still, even after seven years of marriage, the same beautiful woman her husband, Humphrey, Duke of Gloucester, wanted in his bed. That was all that mattered. Turning her head from side to side, she inspected her reflection in the ornate ivory-backed mirror on her dressing table, admiring the ruby earrings which had been a gift from her husband's nephew, the King, pleased by the effect of their dark fire against a wing of her raven hair.

But the tooth still throbbed in her jaw. Pushing the mirror aside, she picked up the bell on her table and rang it. A young woman, scurrying in from the next room, dropped a hurried curtsey.

'Sarah, fetch me Mistress Jourdemayne,' said Eleanor. 'And be quick about it.'

'Yes, Your Grace. Where will I find her?'

'How should I know? Just find her. Go to the farm first and see if she's at home. Tell her I must see her.'

'What if she isn't there, Your Grace?'

'Then find her husband. He'll know where she is. Tell her I am plagued by the toothache and Canon Southwell has had no success in curing it, so she must attend me immediately.'

'Certainly, Your Grace.'

'And Sarah!'

'Your Grace?'

'Not a word to anyone, do you hear? Not a single word.'

'Naturally, Your Grace. Not a word. Will there be anything else, Your Grace?'

'No, nothing else. Now go, Sarah, and don't loiter, gossiping with your friends. Go directly to the Manor of Eye and find Mistress Jourdemayne. It isn't much more than a mile, it shouldn't take you long.'

'Yes, Your Grace.'

The girl backed hastily out of the room with her head bowed, groping behind her for the door handle rather than daring to turn her back on her royal mistress. Once the door had closed, Eleanor rose and went to her *prie-dieu* in the corner. She knelt on the richly embroidered cushion, bent her head on her clasped hands and prayed fervently to St Apollonia for deliverance from the infernal ache in her tooth. If the saint failed her, Margery had better be able to produce some tincture to ease the pain.

***

35

Having dismissed the young Devonshire woman, William picked up a besom, checked that the twigs around the base of its long handle were securely tied and began sweeping up. He shouldn't have to do this, but there never seemed to be anyone else available. The truth of it was that he needed more help: the monks were expecting far too much for what they paid him. It was all very well for men of God to be at their devotions seven or eight times a day and saying endless masses for the souls of the dead, but they should show a bit more concern for those who were trying to wrest a living from the heavy clay soil of Westminster. If he wasn't employed by a huddle of celibate monks, William reflected, there'd be sons and daughters of the family to swell the workforce but, as it was, there were fewer than thirty farmhands employed on the whole thousand acres of the demesne. There were sixty cows to be milked twice a day, and that was without having to look after the fatstock for market. Then there were back-breaking days in the fields, ploughing or reaping, stock-proofing fences or mending walls. He was grateful the sheep looked after themselves for most of the year, now that there was no longer any danger from wolves in the district. Moreover, sheep yielded a good-quality meat and their wool returned a handsome profit for the monastery.

The monks themselves did little or nothing that William could see, beyond wielding a desultory hoe in the Abbot's garden from time to time before scuttling back to the chapel at the first note of the chapel bell. Or so it seemed to William. But William had too much to do.

He went outside and, shooing an indignant brown hen out of his way with the besom, he began brushing away mud and straw with long, rhythmic strokes, sluicing down the cobbles with pails of water from the big water butt in the corner of the yard.

'I could do that for you.'

She hadn't gone. Jenna Harding stood outside the door of the byre, watching him with concern. 'Let me help,' she said. 'It will pay for my night's lodging. And, if your wife will agree to employ me, then I might as well start today as start tomorrow.'

'But ... but clearing out the yard would be no part of your duties.' Surprised, William let her take the besom away from him without demur. 'Your work would be in the dairy.'

'But looking after the hens would be part of my duties, too, and I felt sorry for that poor creature you shooed out of your way,' Jenna said with a shy smile. 'I almost feel responsible for her! Her eggs could be worth four silver pence a year to you.' She started sweeping the wet cobbles methodically, hoping he didn't think her too disrespectful.

Bemused, William watched her. Yes, he'd been right. He had a feeling this one was going to be a good worker and, to be honest, he could really do with another willing pair of hands to help around the farm, especially since his wife was so busy elsewhere.

Still, perhaps Margery was right to say she was far better employed in selling dreams to fine ladies of fashion, rather than working her fingers to the bone in a draughty dairy. One day, she promised, she would make enough money to buy him a holding of his own, making him the equal of his older brother Robert in Acton. Then he'd be grateful to her and he could take on all the dairymaids he wanted.

Margery was always one for grand ideas. A clever woman, too. William had to admit that Margery seemed popular with the fine ladies up at the palace and they did pay absurd amounts of money for what she sold to them. Her eyes lit up with laughter when she came home and regaled him with stories about which great ladies had paid ridiculously high prices for her creams, her lotions and perfumes. Gentlemen, too, for whom toothpicks, ear scoops or tweezers were absolutely essential aids to grooming. Yes, Margery was undoubtedly clever.

He shook his head and brought his attention back to the woman who was still sweeping the yard with great diligence and skill.

'Thank you, Mistress Harding,' he said. 'It's kind of you to do that.'

'Oh, tut, that's nothing,' she said, straightening up. 'It's a pleasure. And please … call me Jenna.'

'Not jonnack?'

She laughed, delighted to realise that William Jourdemayne had a sense of humour to rival Robin's.

'No, not jonnack. Jenna will do very nicely, thank you!'

'Very well, Jenna,' he said. 'And I don't think I need trouble my wife to make a decision in your case. Consider yourself hired.'

***

Margery made sure the linen squares were scrupulously clean before packing them up with the order. It would be stupid to run any risks with Lady Northumberland's eyes for the sake of re-using a small pad of folded linen. She crossed the kitchen floor to the fire where a pan full of blue liquid was boiling ferociously, and judged it to have reduced by half since she had placed it on the hob.

'Come in,' she called, mildly irritated by a knock on the outer door.

'Excuse me, mistress.'

Margery frowned. 'Yes, Hawys, what is it?' she said, wrapping a cloth around her hand before removing the pan of liquid from the fire and placing it on the hearthstone to cool. She straightened up. 'Speak up, girl. Is there a problem in the dairy?'

'It's Kitty, Mistress Jourdemayne. The child has a terrible belly-ache and I wondered…'

'Has she been sick?'

'Yes, mistress, twice.'

'Then it's probably something she's eaten.'

'Well, yes, mistress, but I wondered whether you would be able to come down to the dairy to give her something to aid it?'

'No, I'm far too busy. Make her an infusion of sweet camomile. That will help.'

'And where would I…?'

'Wait there.' Margery went into her own room and closed the door to the kitchen. Really, these women didn't seem capable of doing anything for themselves. Camomile was such

38

a well-known cure for a stomach upset and it wasn't difficult to make an infusion of it. Reaching for a coffer on the shelf, she took out a rough handful of dried camomile flowers and put them into a clean linen bag.

'Here,' she said as she returned to the kitchen. 'Make the child an infusion of these in boiling water.'

'Will I boil up the water here, mistress?'

'No, Hawys, I'm busy here, you'll have to take it to the brewhouse. And, remember, let the infusion cool before she drinks it. That should do the trick.'

'And what if it doesn't, mistress?'

'It will,' said Margery, becoming impatient. 'Now, Hawys, I suggest you get back to the dairy as soon as you can. There's always more than enough work to do.'

'Yes, mistress. Thank you, mistress.'

The kitchen door closed behind Hawys and Margery turned her attention back to the saucepan. She tested the temperature of the blue liquid with a cautious finger. Her Ladyship must suffer dreadfully from pinkeye if her constant demand for Margery's decoction of cornflowers was anything to go by. Her maid had come to the farm yet again this morning to buy a bottle of it for her mistress and Margery didn't have any of the decoction made up, so the job was urgent.

Her Ladyship wanted some yarrow, too, to settle her stomach, though Margery was not sure it was the best remedy for the wind. Generally she preferred tansy but Lady Northumberland swore by the efficacy of yarrow and was rumoured to take it after every meal. And she was always prepared to pay good money for it, so why argue? If it meant a higher profit, that suited Margery very well.

But there was one problem. William said there was a big cattle drove coming up from Devon this afternoon. This meant all hands were needed to settle the animals and see to the milking so there wouldn't be anyone available to deliver the order for her. She'd simply have to deliver it herself: she couldn't let a good client down, she dared not. The word would spread around the palace that she was not reliable, so there was no other option. What with one thing and another, she certainly didn't have time to go wandering down to the dairy to attend to that child, whatever her name was.

But at least William wouldn't be getting under her feet tonight, not with the Devon drovers staying in Westminster for a day or two before returning home. He'd probably be in the ale house with his friend Robin Fairweather. It's what they usually did.

***

The loft above the stable was much like many others where Jenna had slept during her journey from Devon, fragrant with stored hay and still retaining the warmth of the departed day. She stuffed hay into the canvas sack she'd brought with her, pleased that it seemed fairly clean: it would make a dry, comfortable pallet. She shook it vigorously then laid it flat and levelled the hay inside it before lying down. There were two other women already fast asleep in the gathering darkness, exhausted after a hard day's work. Next to her, a much younger girl was still awake, wide-eyed in the gloom and apparently hungry for information about this newcomer to the farm.

'So, whereabouts in Devon are you from?' she asked.

'Kingskerswell,' Jenna answered shortly. She didn't want to be quizzed.

'And where might that be, then?'

'If I told you, you'd be none the wiser. What about you? What's your name?'

'My real name is Keturah.'

'That's nice. It's in the Bible, isn't it? Wasn't she one of Abraham's wives?'

'Yes, but I don't care who she was. I hate my name. It's horrible. Most people call me Kitty. I'd rather that.'

'Then that's what I'll call you. Kitty. My name's Jenna.'

'Jenna? That's a strange name!'

'It's from Cornwall.'

'Is that in Devon?'

'Well, down that way.'

'I wouldn't know anyway, like you said. We get drovers here from Devon sometimes. There's one called Robin who comes here quite often.'

'Yes, I know, I walked part of the way with him.'

'With Robin! Oh, you're so lucky! He's lovely. I think I'm going to marry him when I grow up.'

'Oh, really? Does he know that?'

'No, not yet. I haven't told him. But I expect I'll tell him soon.'

Jenna smiled to herself in the half-darkness. This little girl sounded very young, ten or eleven years old perhaps, or less, still young enough to think all her problems would end at the altar. She'd learn soon enough that they didn't.

'I'm tired now, Kitty. I'd like to thank St Christopher for keeping me safe on the journey and then I'm going to go to sleep. I have work to do tomorrow!'

'Where did you sleep when you were travelling?' Young Kitty wanted to know everything.

Jenna sighed. 'Well,' she said, turning on her side, her back towards her persistent interrogator, 'I mostly slept in hay lofts like this one. Under a hedge once or twice.'

'It's a good thing it was summer,' Kitty observed, nodding sagely to herself.

'Yes, it is, for lots of reasons. There was plenty of work to be had and the field workers always got fed. And I sometimes earned enough to pay for a share of a straw mattress. But nobody ever kept me awake like you're doing. Now, Kitty, I really want to get to sleep.' Jenna yawned exaggeratedly, feigning a tiredness she didn't really feel. But she was not yet ready to confide in Kitty, or anyone else for that matter.

Kitty was not to be deflected. She inched closer to Jenna and leaned on one elbow, still determined to talk. 'You'll like it here,' she said in a confidential tone. 'The monks keep themselves to themselves and Master Jourdemayne is ever so nice, for all that he's very fussy about keeping the dairy clean. No one likes his wife though – we call her Old Mother Madge – so it's as well we don't see much of her.'

'Why is that?'

'She spends a lot of time up at the palace. She makes creams and ointments and things like that and sells them to the gentry up there. I've heard tell she makes a tidy living at it, so she's away quite often. Mind you, there was a time when she was away for a couple of months. But that was different.' She waited: surely curiosity would get the better of Jenna.

'Don't you want to know why?' she asked, after a long pause.

'Oh, all right then. Why?'

'She was in prison!' Kitty said, dropping her voice dramatically.

Jenna twisted herself up to face her. Now it was her turn to be wide-eyed.

'In prison! Really? What had she done?'

'Well, it was never really proved, but I just remember it. Not many people do these days, because it was … oh, I don't know, a good few years ago. But I remember my mother saying she came out of prison in May. The ninth, I think it was. Or perhaps it was the tenth. Mind you, my mother's dead long since, so I could be misremembering. But I can just remember her coming home to the farm, even though I was only a very, very little girl. I remember I was ever so frightened…'

'Kitty!' By now, Jenna was shaking Kitty's arm. 'What had she done? What was she accused of?'

Kitty paused again, a little too long, for the greatest dramatic impact.

'Tell me, Kitty!'

Kitty took a deep breath and composed herself.

'Witchcraft,' she whispered in the darkness.

CHAPTER FOUR

September 1435

September was one of the busiest months of the year on the monastery's manor farm. The harvest was barely home when Michaelmas was upon them. Hiring fairs were in full swing and not only were the quarterly rents due to be paid, but Abbot Harweden would also want to see the accounts for the whole year, and reckoning was not one of William Jourdemayne's greatest talents. He hated doing it so much that he always found something else to do instead, putting it off until the very last moment, then becoming agitated about it. So he was more than grateful the new dairymaid had proved her claim to be able to keep account. Surprisingly, she appeared to be quite at ease with reckoning.

For her part, Jenna had been delighted to help, pleased to be entrusted with the responsibility of helping the Master in this way, even though she had only been working at the farm for little more than two months. Though the old days at Kingskerswell were slipping further and further into memory, she would always be able to use the skills she'd learned under the enthusiastic tuition of Parson Middleton. She could read moderately well, but her real talent was for figures and she was easily able to add up simple numbers in her head. But these days, when it came to more complicated calculations, she relied on using an abacus. Since she had never had occasion to use one before arriving at Eybury farm, it had taken more than a little determination to master the techniques required. But, having been shown the basic principles, she could now achieve correct answers to the most complicated calculations with impressive speed and unfailing accuracy.

In the small room behind the brewhouse which served as the tenant-farmer's office, she sat across the table from the Master, a small frown of concentration on her forehead and a quill pen held awkwardly in her hand. The abacus lay on the table to one side and she was checking a column of figures on an accounts roll in front of her, her lips moving silently.

William watched her for a moment. 'I do appreciate you doing this, Jenna,' he said. 'I confess it doesn't come easily to me.'

Jenna looked up from her work. 'That's all right, master,' she said, 'though it's much more difficult reckoning than I'm used to. The milk tallies are easy compared with this. But it does make sense eventually.'

She took a breath, hesitated a moment, and then spoke again. 'You know, master, looking at what you've got here, I'm sure we could do better with the hens and geese. I do know about those. Each hen should be laying enough to give you four silver pence a year at market and if you were to buy another four dizzen –'

'Dozen?'

'Yes, four dozen hens, that would be a profit of one hundred and ninety-two pence a year for the farm, not for the monastery. The monks keep their own hens up there to provide for the refectory.'

'Haven't got time for hens,' William said.

'But … just another three or four dozen birds…'

'Neats are our main concern,' he said, 'then sheep. We only keep hens to provide eggs for the kitchen.'

'Well, I'd look after them for you, and maybe I could take the extra eggs to market in Chelsea each week. Young Kitty could help me. It would teach her a bit of responsibility.'

'Perhaps, one day,' William said. 'We'll see.'

That seemed to be an end to it. But William's expression softened. 'By the way,' he asked, 'how is Kitty? I haven't seen her lately.'

'Kitty seems very happy,' Jenna said, putting the abacus away tidily in its box. 'She'll make a fine dairymaid when she's a bit older.'

'Her mother was a good dairymaid. And if Kitty is half as good as Elizabeth was, she'll do well. Perhaps she'll be nearly as good as you are.'

Jenna smiled. She'd had to concede the argument about hens, but it didn't really matter. William Jourdemayne was an agreeable man, easy to work for and appreciative of what she did. She was settling in well at Eybury Farm and beginning to forget the reasons why she had fled her old life – though she was still a little hard of hearing in her left ear, so she could never forget Jake.

'Oh,' said William, remembering suddenly, 'talking of hens and geese, I meant to ask you whether we had a nice fat goose to send over to the manor house? Abbot Harweden likes to stay at La Neyte for a few days after the day of Obligation and we always send over a Michaelmas goose for him. I'm afraid it slipped my mind this year, with being so busy.'

'I fattened up a few stubble geese after the harvest, master, as it happens. So I'll pick out the best of them for him. Just as long as you don't ask me to kill it.'

'Don't worry,' said William, 'I'll do that.'

'It should taste good with an apple stuffing. I'll send a bag of apples over to the Manor with the bird. A bunch of sage, too, and some onions.'

'Don't,' said William, laughing. 'You're making me feel hungry and there's an hour to go before dinner!'

'I'm sorry, master. I didn't mean to do that.'

She had almost slipped back into the old ways, planning a meal, thinking about cooking for a man and enjoying the prospect of doing so. She must guard against that, however much the thought pleased her.

***

With his Michaelmas duties discharged for another year, Abbot Harweden was delighted to spend a few days relaxing in the manor house on the Eye estate. La Neyte was very much more comfortable and luxurious than his accommodation in the Westminster monastery, or in any other property where the monks had invested their wealth. It gave him the best of both worlds, since it offered close proximity to the monastery combined with all the advantages of a quiet country retreat. An elegant, moated manor house, it boasted fine gardens, an orchard and a well-stocked fish pond. A small permanent staff saw to his worldly needs and the manor house itself was less than half a mile from the Thames. A fast wherry could whisk him the short distance downriver to the Westminster steps in next to no time, which meant he could return to his monastic duties within an hour, should the need arise.

His neighbours at La Neyte were the tenant-farmer William Jourdemayne and his wife who lived only a few hundred yards away at Eybury Farm. They seemed a quiet couple, tending to keep themselves to themselves except when there was some aspect of farm business to be discussed or the quarterly accounts were to be presented for his inspection. Then, at Michaelmas, they would spend a day together going over the figures for the whole year.

It was also a Michaelmas tradition that Abbot Harweden, as titular head of the Manor of Eye-next-Westminster, was presented with a nicely fattened goose for the midday dinner.

Today, he had invited a guest to join him. His friendship with Thomas Southwell, a Canon of Westminster and Rector of St Stephen's Royal Chapel, was the result of many years in the service of the church and of the royal family. The two often ate companionably together.

'This goose is excellent, Richard,' said Thomas Southwell between mouthfuls.

'I'm glad you're enjoying it,' said Abbot Harweden. 'There are great advantages in having a stock farm attached to the monastery. One never has an empty trencher and we don't lack for butter or cheese. Or milk, of course. But it's many a long year since I've had a Michaelmas goose as good as this one.'

'What is your tenant like? What's-his-name, Jourdemayne, the stockman. Is he good?'

'Seems a very capable fellow, I must say. He manages the farm extremely well, keeps the stock in good shape. He has even balanced the books for this quarter, though his book-keeping isn't always perfect.'

'A man of many parts!'

'Indeed. I had my concerns about his paperwork, as I say, but he seems to have found someone to help him with that. The profits on our surplus produce run satisfyingly high and the needs of the monastery are amply met. The farm provisions the kitchen here at La Neyte, too. Why do you ask?'

'Because I met Jourdemayne's wife not so long ago,' said Southwell casually, breaking off a piece of bread from the loaf on a board between them. 'She's not in the first flush of youth, but she's a fine-looking woman.'

'You're not meant to notice things like that, Thomas,' the Abbot rebuked him gently with a smile. 'You're a man of the cloth.'

Southwell tried his best to look pious. 'Quite so. Her looks were a matter of complete indifference to me, of course. But she does seem very intelligent for a farmer's wife.'

'She's a clever woman,' said Abbot Harweden, 'and no mistake. She's as shrewd and clever as any wise woman I've ever come across.'

'A wise woman, eh? Ever made use of her services?'

'No. Well, not in any official capacity, of course, but she was … er, able to help me with a … shall we say … a certain painful embarrassment a year or so ago. She sold me an unguent of lesser celandine … pilewort, as she called it. It did the trick. I still use it occasionally when the need arises, and she keeps me supplied.'

'Painful things, piles,' observed Southwell, soaking up the last morsels of goose gravy on his platter with the remaining bread. 'Pilewort's the best thing for them. I always prescribe it.'

Abbot Harweden grimaced and nodded in agreement. 'Apart from that, I hardly ever see her. So, tell me, where did you meet her?'

Thomas Southwell took a long draught of wine then set his goblet down on the table. 'She was among some ladies in attendance upon the Duchess of Gloucester. I was waiting to see Her Grace who wished to consult me on a small medical matter.' Southwell took an inflated pride in his role as personal physician to the Duke and Duchess. 'Of course, I was able to give Her Grace the correct advice. And she was very grateful,' he added, nodding his head in affirmation of his statement.

'Is there any pie in which you do not have a finger, Thomas?'

'The more pies, the merrier,' Southwell replied, smiling. He was a man comfortably full in his clothes who appreciated the fact that the Abbot kept a good table.

'Well, there's a pie to follow this,' said Abbot Harweden, 'a sweet one, of apples and blackberries with honey. But do go on, Thomas. Why was Margery Jourdemayne in attendance on the Duchess?'

'She wasn't,' said Southwell, 'she was in an ante-room, showing her wares to some of the ladies of Her Grace's household. Gentlemen, too.'

'And were you tempted to buy anything?'

'Indeed not! I went about my own business and I minded it, too!'

'So why should you be so interested in Mistress Jourdemayne and her abilities?'

'Because Her Grace has been troubled by a painful tooth but claims to have derived great benefit from Mistress Jourdemayne's tincture of myrrh, implying that it was rather more efficacious than my own tincture.' The Abbot hid a smile as Canon Southwell went on. 'As far as I can see, there's no evidence of a worm in the tooth itself but, of course, I like to explore every avenue in finding new ways of advising the Duchess on matters pertaining to her health. I thought there might be areas in which the Jourdemayne woman and I could pool our knowledge to Her Grace's advantage.'

'Well, I suppose it's possible,' the Abbot said, sounding doubtful. 'But be careful. I should warn you that she got two clerics into trouble some years ago.'

Canon Southwell raised his eyebrows in a query. 'Really? In what way?'

'By getting ideas above her station,' Abbot Harweden replied. 'She spent more time than she should have consorting with a friar of the Holy Cross and a man by the name of John Virley. He was one of our monastery clerks at the time, which is why I remember the case.'

'Virley?' said Southwell. 'I believe I know him. Isn't he the one who supplies the scriptorium with vellum and inks and so on?'

'Yes, that's the man. Of course,' the Abbot went on, enjoying the opportunity to impart a titbit of gossip, 'both men should both have known better. If they hadn't encouraged her, they wouldn't have been arrested for associating with her. That's why they spent a whole winter in prison.'

Southwell was agog with interest. 'Prison! But, surely they would have known she had a reputation as a wise woman?'

'Perhaps they did,' the Abbot said with a shrug. 'But Mistress Jourdemayne must have flattered her way into their company, to learn from them in order to improve the products she sells to the ladies of the court. She's an ambitious woman.'

Canon Southwell, himself more ambitious than most, was quiet for a moment. The Abbot glanced at him. 'Thomas, do have a little more of this excellent goose,' he said.

Southwell's face brightened. 'Thank you, Richard, I will. Indeed,' he added, picking up his knife, 'I thought you would never ask!'

***

The pale sunshine of early autumn lingered over the Westminster countryside for several more days: plump blackberries still dotted the hedgerows, sloes had ripened to a cloudy blue on the blackthorn and there was little sign of the winter to come. A distant curlew called plaintively from the river as Margery, on her way to the palace to attend her most important client, made her way along the Willow Walk which skirted La Neyte, then followed the path alongside the stream for the short distance down to the Thames. If she ignored the whistles and catcalls from the wherrymen in their boats, it would be pleasant enough to walk along the river bank on a day like this.

She put her heavy basket down for a moment, slipped off her cloak and draped it over her arm. There was nothing to be gained by rushing and getting too hot: looking cool and calm was part of Margery's game and it would never do to appear otherwise to anyone she might encounter, be they wherrymen, royal household servants or courtiers. Wiping her face with her kerchief, she took a deep breath before picking up her basket and resuming her walk towards the river and thence to the palace.

She expected to find the Duchess Eleanor languishing in her bower, bemoaning the unseasonal warmth or some imagined malady, or demanding to try some new lotion or perfume. So Margery was surprised to be shown into an ante-room by a footman whom she didn't know and told to wait until she was called. This was highly unusual since she made it her business to be on friendly terms with most of the royal servants, even managing to smile when they occasionally called her Madge, a name she loathed. Whereas she would normally be ushered through to see her client almost immediately, today she was kept waiting for the better part of an hour while footsteps came and went and voices were raised in the next room. Despite straining her ears, she was not quite able to hear what was being said.

At last, the doors swung open and Margery was bidden to enter. The Duchess of Gloucester was alone, standing in the centre of the room, an elegant figure in a gown of blue samite, her dark hair caught up in jewelled cauls on either side of her pale face. Clasping and unclasping her hands, she was clearly agitated.

'Margery! Where have you been?' she demanded.

'I came as soon as I received your message, Your Grace, but I was told to wait until you were ready to see me.'

'Yes, yes,' said the Duchess, nodding impatiently. 'My Lord Duke was here. He has just received some … some … news.' She paused for a moment. Margery thought she looked stunned, surprised, as though someone had slapped her.

'I trust it was nothing untoward, Your Grace?'

'I'm afraid it was. It … it wasn't exactly unexpected, but it has altered things quite considerably.'

Eleanor of Gloucester stood with her eyes closed, trying to compose herself. Margery waited: it wasn't her place to ask any

50

further questions. The Duchess started shaking her head as though to ward off a flying insect before opening her eyes and looking at Margery, who raised her eyebrows in an unspoken enquiry.

'Yes, it was bad news, I'm afraid … for my husband … his brother, John of Bedford, has died. News has just come through from France.'

'I'm very sorry to hear that, Your Grace. Please allow me to express my sympathy.'

'Thank you.'

'His Grace the Duke of Bedford was your husband's older brother, was he not?'

'He was, yes, a year older than my husband.'

'Was it sudden, Your Grace?'

'Er, no. John had been ill, we knew that. But it has still come as quite a shock for my husband. For both of us, of course.'

'Yes, Your Grace, I'm sure it must have. If I might ring for some hot water, I could make you an infusion of camomile and lemon balm. It will help to calm you.' Margery opened her medicine coffer, taking out two small linen bags of herbs which were packed in beside the bottles of tooth tincture – but the Duchess seemed to have forgotten all about her toothache. She ignored Margery's suggestion and began pacing up and down again.

'There will be a memorial of some kind here at Westminster,' she said, 'the monks will arrange all that. No doubt Cardinal Beaufort will insist on conducting the memorial service, it would be typical of him to want to play the grieving uncle. But the funeral has already taken place in the cathedral at Rouen. A very grand affair, by all accounts.'

'I'm sure that is only right and proper, Your Grace,' said Margery. 'As Regent of France the Duke of Bedford must surely have been given a funeral fit for a king. I understand he was very highly thought of.' She was aware that the Duchess Eleanor had stopped her pacing up and down and was now standing very still.

'Margery!'

Margery looked up from her medicine coffer, saying

nothing.

'Margery!' the Duchess said a second time. 'You know what this means, don't you?'

Margery did not reply. She knew exactly what it meant, but she also knew the simple statement had to come from her client, not from her. She waited.

Eleanor raised her hand to her mouth, her fist clenched, trying to stop her lower lip from trembling.

'It means, Margery, that the Duke – my husband – is now next in line to the throne. Now that his older brother has died, my husband is the King's heir.' She spoke very slowly, sounding calm, but clearly needing to keep a lid on feelings that were simmering perilously, threatening to come to the boil.

Margery seemed to be expected to say something. 'And should anything happen to His Highness the King … Heaven forfend, of course,' she said, crossing herself hurriedly, 'your husband, His Grace the Duke, would … would make a very fine king – he would be wise, and just – and if I may be so bold as to say so, Your Grace, you would make him a fitting consort.'

'Queen,' said Eleanor with great emphasis. 'I would be the Queen of England.'

'Yes, Your Grace, you would be the Queen of England.' Margery hesitated for a moment then added, 'unless, of course…'

'Unless what?'

'Well, unless, that is … did the Duke of Bedford not leave a widow?' Margery immediately realised she had said the wrong thing, but she could not retract her words, much as she regretted having uttered them. Her client did not need to be reminded that, if the Duke of Bedford had left his young widow pregnant, then a male child of that union would become the heir to the throne, taking precedence over her own husband, the Duke of Gloucester.

The Duchess's grey eyes were like flint. 'No,' she said. 'No mention has been made of that. She's just a chit of a girl, only seventeen years old when John married her. I doubt he even bothered to take her virginity, knowing how he felt about his first wife, Anne of Burgundy, God rest her soul.' Eleanor crossed herself hurriedly. 'No,' she went on, 'John was nearly old enough to be Jacquetta's grandfather, so there was no love involved. He only married her to keep the peace in France and the Low Countries. It was entirely political. Everyone knows that.'

Margery was wary of making another unguarded observation, but felt she was expected to say something.

'So, Your Grace, if *she* is not with child, then – and I'm sure you will pardon my impertinence – you should do everything possible to make sure you are.'

'Exactly,' said the Duchess. 'If Jacquetta is not with child, then nothing will stop my husband inheriting the throne if the King should die without issue. But,' she added, her voice almost inaudible, 'he will need legitimate sons of his own to follow him, in order to secure the succession.'

She suddenly grabbed Margery's wrist, her face contorted with emotion. 'You will help me give Humphrey a child, won't you, Margery? By whatever means. It is my dearest wish. God knows, we've been married long enough to have had four children by now. So it's up to you. You've helped me in the past – you must help me now. You must!'

Margery Jourdemayne nodded. This was going to be a far greater challenge than finding an effective tooth tincture.

'I will do everything I can, Your Grace,' she said.

CHAPTER FIVE

Twelfth Night, January 1436

Occasional peals of rowdy laughter punctuated the cheerful atmosphere in the Great Hall at the Palace of Westminster. Against the constant background clatter of pewter and plate, a bagpipe droned from the minstrels' gallery and four fiddlers played a dance tune to the steady rhythm of the tambour. Garlands of holly hung on the walls, kissing boughs were suspended above every table and the great Yule log which had been kept burning slowly throughout the twelve days of Christmas was finally disintegrating into white ash in the hearth. Twilight faded into velvet darkness outside the castle and rush lights and wax candles sparkled to light up the scene inside where noble lords and ladies had assembled to celebrate the final event of the Christmas festival with the young King. Though the court had only recently emerged from the period of official mourning for the death of John of Bedford, it would have been impossible to restrain the high spirits induced by freely flowing wine and the music of the dance. Tomorrow would mark the Feast of Epiphany, when Christian decorum would again be the order of the day, but Twelfth Night was given up to feasting and celebration.

'One hundred and sixty-four!' said Eleanor in triumph, looking up from something that lay on the table between her pewter platter and her husband's.

'One hundred and sixty-four what?' Gloucester asked, leaning towards her to catch what she was saying above the din in the hall.

'One hundred and sixty-four pearls. Can you believe it, my Lord? Is that not uncommonly generous of His Highness the King?'

'Indeed it is,' said Humphrey, 'and it seems clear to me that my young nephew's generosity means he is nearly as fond of his uncle as he clearly is of his aunt. As he should be, sweet Nell,' he added, squeezing her thigh under the table, 'because you are a very lovely, very clever woman to be able to count up to so high a number. I am impressed!'

Eleanor's eyes gleamed dark in the candlelight. 'I'm glad of that,' she whispered, leaning close to him, pushing her ample breast against his arm. 'I would impress you even more were we not surrounded by so many people.' Humphrey's hand slid further up her thigh with easy intimacy. She giggled and put her mouth to his ear. 'Humphrey, do be careful!'

'Why? Are you wearing mistletoe in your garter again, Nell?'

Eleanor smiled. 'That is for you to discover, my Lord,' she murmured, and gently bit his earlobe. Humphrey, well aware that mistletoe aided conception, anticipated the night ahead with relish: his voracious sexual appetites were always more than adequately satisfied by a wife so desperate for a child. He gave her thigh a playful pinch.

The Duchess of Gloucester was at her brightest and best on this glittering occasion. She and her husband were among King Henry's principle guests and were seated with the fourteen-year-old monarch on the royal dais. He had given them both the most generous of New Year gifts. Eleanor had received a gold brooch, set with a diamond and five large pearls, from which hung three little pendants adorned with smaller pearls and rubies. He had presented Humphrey with a tablet of gold bearing an image of Our Lady, decorated with six diamonds, six sapphires and, by Eleanor's excited reckoning, no less than one hundred and sixty-four pearls. Eleanor caught King Henry's eye as he was finishing his last mouthful of roast swan. She smiled at him, making a great show of lovingly stroking the new gold brooch she was wearing with pride.

The King gave her a shy smile in return and immediately dropped his eyes, not wanting to appear to be staring at the bodice of his aunt's gown, where the brooch was so prominently pinned.

The adolescent monarch was at a vulnerable, suggestible phase in his life, acutely aware of embarrassing changes taking place in his own body and troubled by his lack of control over his physical reactions to women. He was prone to blushing furiously. Only last week, he had felt compelled to cancel a performance being given at court by a group of jongleurs as part of the Christmas celebrations, because a woman dancer was scantily dressed in a costume which left nothing to the imagination. The King tried his best not to look at her and yet his eyes were drawn inexorably to the soft curve of her voluptuous breasts, swaying hypnotically to the rhythm of the dance.

The gift of the brooch had clearly pleased his aunt. It was easy enough, he thought, to give gifts. All it required was enough money to pay for them. Perhaps he should have given that money to some cause where it would really make a difference, to the building of a new church, perhaps, or to endow a school. The Duchess could so easily lose the brooch if she was careless with it and all the money that had been spent on it would have no meaning.

This worried him. He was quite fond of his Aunt Eleanor because she sometimes made him laugh, but he also knew she could be very frivolous. Moreover, the Earl of Tankerville, one of the older boys being educated with the King in the royal schoolroom, had dropped heavy hints that the Duke and Duchess had known each other intimately before their marriage, describing their imagined activities in shocking detail and using words Henry had never heard before. Henry was appalled by this information and refused to believe it was true. Surely, no uncle of his, no chivalrous royal duke, could behave in that way! The young Earl had simply laughed and boasted that, since he himself was betrothed to Antigone, the Duke of Gloucester's natural daughter, he had inside knowledge of the affair. He also claimed Antigone was a chip off the old block when it came to pleasurable dalliance.

Henry was glad his uncle was now safely married to the Duchess, their union sanctified by the church. He had no idea what actually went on between a man and a woman in the privacy of their bedchamber, but he was quite sure it was immoral and sordid unless it had God's blessing. And he was quite certain he would never be able to do it, whatever it was, with or without approval from on high.

***

In the barn, the Twelfth Night celebration was in full swing. Abbot Harweden's traditional contribution to the feast for the estate workers on the monastery's manor farm was the gift of a wild boar, a heavy beast, which had cost ten shillings and taken several hours to roast on the spit in the farmhouse kitchen. Its head, decorated with holly, now graced a large wooden platter in the centre of the long table at the top end of the barn. The fresh green apple in its mouth gave it a jaunty look belied by the puckered, shrunken lids which covered its dead eyes. Such an animal should satisfy the appetites of thirty or so estate workers but, just in case more wassailers should arrive than were expected, Mistress Jourdemayne had also provided a fat goose which should easily feed another twenty.

Though she had been here at the farm for six months by now, Jenna had seen very little of her employer's wife and still felt nervous about her. Kitty had said they called her the Witch of Eye or Old Mother Madge. But she wasn't really old, so what did that mean? Was she really a witch? She certainly wasn't snaggle-toothed and Gib, the farmhouse cat, was just there to catch mice. He was hardly a witch's familiar. Surely a witch would have warty skin or a hairy lip? Jenna's occasional glimpses of Mistress Jourdemayne had shown her to be a perfectly attractive woman, apparently quite well suited to be her employer's wife. And Master Jourdemayne was a decent man with a ready smile, not at all the kind of man who would have married a witch.

In fact, anyone less like a witch than Margery Jourdemayne was difficult to imagine. Tonight, she was wearing a close-fitting dark red gown under a sleeveless mantle of brown wool to keep out the cold in the draughty barn. Her long fair hair, plaited and coiled on either side of her face, was held in place by a plain white linen fillet. A casual observer might be forgiven for assuming she was at least the wife of a minor knight, rather than a tenant farmer. She had something about her, an air of easy breeding, though her complexion was marred by fine lines which would become wrinkles within a few short years. And she looked tired.

Her husband looked tired, too. The day-to-day routine of the farm made few concessions to the celebration of Twelfth Night. The cows still needed milking twice a day, the stock had to be fed and the eggs collected. It had been a day much like any other for William, except for the traditional pouring of ale around the trees in the lower orchard, but that had to be done, of course, to ensure a good crop of apples in the coming year. As soon as the ceremony was over, William had returned to the farmhouse to clean himself up for the feast, though his leather jerkin, for all that it had been dressed with neatsfoot oil, was still only a leather jerkin and it had seen better days.

'It's all very grand, isn't it?' said Kitty, who was sitting next to Jenna on a bench at the far end of the barn with a gaggle of excited scullions and dairymaids. 'I love Twelfth Night, it's wonderful! We shall have the plum cake in a moment, then we'll see who will be king and queen for the night.'

'I think Mistress Jourdemayne looks like a queen already, don't you, Kitty?' said Jenna. 'She's sure to get the slice of cake with the pea in it.'

'Then Master Jourdemayne had better get the slice with the bean in it,' said Kitty, nodding her head knowingly. 'Because Mistress Jourdemayne wouldn't like it if anyone else came to sit next to her to be the king. She's very high and mighty. She won't talk to everyone.' Kitty had opinions about such things.

Jenna had rather taken the youngster under her wing since coming to work at Eybury Farm. Having first encountered her in the dimpsy half-light of the hay loft, she hadn't realised quite how young Kitty was, and Jenna's heart went out to the child when she realised she was entirely alone in the world.

Kitty's earnest little face clouded over as she told Jenna her story, or as much of it as she could remember. She had never known her father and her mother had died, though Kitty didn't know what had ailed her. If it hadn't been for Master

Jourdemayne being so kind, she said, she would have had to ask the monks to take her in like a foundling. But she had been allowed to stay on at the farm, doing all manner of small menial tasks around the place, earning her keep after a fashion. She was devoted to Master Jourdemayne but still missed her mother, she said, even though she'd died a long time ago.

Listening to Kitty, Jenna felt a sudden, unexpected longing to see her own mother again. Admittedly, they hadn't always seen eye to eye, but she knew Betsy had loved her in her own awkward way and she'd always been there to bathe Jenna's childhood wounds and dry her tears. She would have got on with her mother perfectly well if only her stepfather could have kept his clammy hands off her while she was growing up…

Jenna shuddered at the thought. Not long after Gilbert had married her mother, she had been alone with him one day when he suddenly pulled her onto his knee, put his arm around her, and began stroking her cheek. Then, with a strange smile on his face, he told her that if she made him feel very happy, he would let her have a puppy of her own. And he had a puppy, too, he said, a nice little puppy with a wet nose and a waggly tail and he'd let her stroke it if she'd like to. By now, he was fiddling with something under his jerkin and the bewildered child sensed somehow that what he was doing was wrong.

But this was her new stepfather, the man who would be taking the place of her dead father. He was kind, Betsy said, and Jenna should be grateful to him for taking them both in and giving them a home. But her real father had never done anything like this and the six-year-old Jenna felt very frightened. She wriggled as her stepfather's grip tightened more firmly around her until, suddenly desperate to get away from him, she summoned all her strength and kicked him hard on the shin with her alderwood clog. His face flushed and he recoiled in pain. Seizing her opportunity, she scrambled down from his knee and fled, hiding behind the barn until her heart stopped hammering. She knew instinctively she could never tell her mother what had happened. And she never did.

'Ooooh, look!' Kitty suddenly squealed, nudging Jenna out

of her memories. 'Look! Here's the plum cake. Now the fun will begin!'

Slabs of plum cake were being brought in on trays and grabbing hands reached out on all sides, everyone wanting to have a chance to become King of the Bean or Queen of the Pea for the evening. It meant a seat at the top table and a complete reversal of roles where the workers could lord it over their masters for once and the masters would have to do what they were told. It was an annual opportunity not to be missed.

William Jourdemayne regarded his slab of cake warily. He was a man who respected those who worked for him, but he didn't relish the prospect of being ordered about by any of them. They had been drinking far more strong ale than they were accustomed to and the younger ones, certainly, would abuse the privilege of being king for the evening. He raised his piece of cake to his mouth and bit down on something hard. A dried bean! Good. So there would be no dilemma, no having to obey stupid commands from the young farmhands. He was still the man who gave the orders, still the king, even if only King of the Bean.

But who would be his queen? Not Margery, by the look of it because there was a sudden commotion among a group of young women at the end of the room.

'Oooooh!' shrieked Kitty. 'It's you, Jenna! You have the pea! You are to be Queen of the Pea!'

Jenna had spat out a small, hard pea and was staring at it as it lay in the palm of her hand. She really didn't want this, in fact the last thing she wanted was to sit at the top table, behind that repulsive boar's head, with everyone looking at her. She had done her best to remain inconspicuous since running away from Kingskerswell and she just wanted to sit in a corner and watch everyone else enjoying Twelfth Night. She certainly did not want to be the centre of attention.

'Here she is!' carolled Kitty. 'Here's the Queen of the Pea. Queen Jenna!'

Excited hands pushed Jenna towards the top table as Margery Jourdemayne rose from her seat with a distant smile.

'Sit down, girl,' she said quietly, gesturing Jenna to take her own place at the table. 'And do try to stop my husband falling asleep!'

'I beg your pardon, mistress?'

Over the excited hubbub in the barn, Margery repeated, 'I said try to stop my husband falling asleep. He's exhausted.'

William Jourdemayne rose to welcome the flustered, self-conscious Jenna, taking her hand and showing her to the place at the table so recently vacated by his wife. He was being kind, but Jenna's cheeks were flaming. She would have given her eye teeth to be elsewhere.

'Well met, Queen Jenna,' William greeted her. 'Don't feel nervous. You'll soon settle down and get used to giving orders. And you'll find it's a great deal more agreeable than taking them, I promise you!' He smiled. 'I'm the King of the Bean, by the way.'

Jenna smiled back at him. 'Yes, I realise that,' she said, still flushed with embarrassment, but grateful that he had tried to put her at her ease.

'Here,' said William, reaching for a nearby jug, 'a goblet of Lamb's Wool for the wassail.' He poured a generous measure of spiced ale with cream and apples into her goblet. Then he turned and banged on the table with the handle of his knife.

'My Lords, Ladies and gentlemen,' he began, raising his glass, 'pray be upstanding to drink the health of Her Royal Highness, Jenna Harding, who is to be crowned Queen of the Pea. Wassail!'

'Wassail! Wassail!' The cry echoed around the barn and now the two young cowherds, Seth and Piers, were approaching the top table, marching in time to clapping and whooping calls from all sides, each bearing a crudely fashioned crown of entwined withies, one decorated with holly for the king, the other trimmed with ivy for the queen. They skirted around the table to place the crowns clumsily on William and Jenna's heads then, giggling, Seth held a large sprig of mistletoe over the two of them. Piers, almost doubled-up with his hand over his mouth, was finding it difficult to contain his laughter, embarrassed by causing discomfiture to the Master.

'I'm sorry, Jenna,' said William, 'but I'm afraid the King of the Bean has to kiss the Queen of the Pea. It is expected.' He leaned towards her as a great cheer went up from everyone in the room. It was the first time Jenna had felt a man's mouth on her own since she had fled from Jake's bruising caresses but William's lips as they brushed hers fleetingly, felt as light as thistledown.

Surprised and blushing furiously, she pulled back from him just as Geoffrey the Carpenter, who had been declared Lord of Misrule for the evening's festivities, leaped in front of them, waving an inflated pig's bladder on the end of a beribboned stick.

'By your leave, Your Highnesses?' Geoffrey had grabbed Seth by the scruff of the neck and was bouncing the bladder balloon on his head. 'Your loyal subjects wish to indulge themselves in a thrilling game of Hoodman Blind, with young Seth here as the first hooded man. Do we have the permission of Your Gracious Persons so to do?'

William looked at Jenna and raised his eyebrows. 'Well, my Lady?' he said. 'Shall we grant our royal permission for the game?'

'I think we might, my Lord,' Jenna replied, beginning to enter into the spirit of the occasion and doing her best to sound regal and haughty. 'Yes, I think we might.'

William raised his hand to give his blessing to the game and the Lord of Misrule turned the wriggling Seth's hood around to the front of his head then pulled it up over his face so he couldn't see a thing. William watched their antics with an indulgent smile on his face. Plough Monday would be here soon enough and they'd all have to buckle down once again to the daily grind of life on the farm. They might as well relax and enjoy themselves while they had a chance.

The party disrupted into a scuffle of young farm hands, boys and girls, giggling and squealing in anticipation of spinning Seth around in circles several times before letting him go to stagger, disorientated around the barn, trying to catch one of them. Amid the hubbub, the King of the Bean turned to the Queen of the Pea and raised his goblet again, gazing at her over the rim with an enquiring lift of his eyebrows.

'Is everything to Your Highness's liking?' he asked.

Jenna smiled and inclined her head graciously. 'Indeed, it is, my Lord.'

It was the start of a topsy-turvy evening of great merriment and, after a while, Jenna quite forgot her misgivings about being Queen of the Pea. What she couldn't dismiss from her mind was the thrill of William Jourdemayne's lips brushing hers.

***

This Christmas had been busier than the Abbot of Westminster had ever known it. Back in October, he had assisted Cardinal-bishop Henry Beaufort at the memorial service for the Duke of Bedford and soon afterwards there had been all that dreary business of negotiating the realignment of the Paddington stream to make more water available to the monastery. With Advent came the pressure of the extended Christmas festival itself, quite the busiest period in the Christian calendar, so he was feeling very tired by the time he reached La Neyte for a few days' relaxation – perhaps because he was getting old or, perhaps, because the young King was very demanding.

Of course, Abbot Harweden approved of the fact that His Highness was ardently devout, but despite the opportunity to worship in the royal chapel of St Stephen's as often as he wished, the King still seemed to want to attend Mass in the Abbey very frequently. And each time he did, it was expected that the Abbot would entertain the royal visitor and provide a sumptuous meal for him and his entire entourage. The King brought all his youthful energies to his Christian worship but the Abbot, so much older than his monarch, felt very drained.

After several days of relaxation at La Neyte, and for the first time in many weeks, he was beginning to feel reinvigorated, he was not even slightly irritated by the distant sounds of seasonal revelry which were quite audible on the early evening air. The Jourdemaynes were clearly holding the traditional Twelfth Night celebrations for the estate workers in the barn. Abbot Harweden preferred to dine quietly with a friend or colleague and, again, his companion was Thomas Southwell. They knew the Feast of Epiphany on the morrow would be a busy day for them both.

'They do seem a noisy crowd down at the home farm this evening,' observed Southwell between mouthfuls of beef stew. 'I can hardly hear myself chew! Incidentally, Richard, this stew is excellent.'

'You're always so appreciative, Thomas,' smiled the Abbot. 'My cook loves to hear the kind things you say about the food here at La Neyte.' He paused while Southwell continued to chew with enthusiasm, then leaned back in his chair, his fingertips together. 'It doesn't seem like three months since we last ate together, Thomas,' he said. 'So, tell me, how was the season of goodwill for you? Were you at St Stephen Walbrook? I didn't see you here at Westminster.'

'Yes, I was here,' replied Southwell. 'It is still not possible to use St Stephen's because of the building work, but it's going to be a magnificent church when it re-opens.'

Abbot Harweden nodded approvingly. 'It's always good to know of improvements to places of worship. So, you were here at Westminster? You were very quiet about it.'

'I also attended some services at Southwark,' said Southwell, wiping grease from his mouth, 'I made a point of it. It's always a pleasure to hear Cardinal Beaufort preach a sermon. I try to attend St Mary Overie whenever he is there.'

'Indeed, his addresses are always excellent,' agreed the Abbot. 'It's just a pity his political manoeuvring is not always so skilful these days. He's getting old, like the rest of us.'

'A great pity. And he was always so successful at these things in the past. It's a shame that the whole English delegation stormed out of the Congress of Arras last September then had to come home with their tails between their legs.'

'Yes, very unfortunate,' said Abbot Harweden.

The Abbot was as aware as anyone else that the Congress of Arras had been a near disaster. Cardinal Beaufort and the English delegation had done their best to reach a peaceful agreement with the Duke of Burgundy, but the Frenchman proved himself a wily negotiator. He was clearly determined to rid France of her English overlords so that his cousin, the

Dauphin, could legitimately call himself King Charles VII of France. To that end, the two had recently signed a treaty, pledging their absolute loyalty to each other.

'It seems,' observed the Abbot, 'that they're both pressing very hard to break the cordial relationship between France and England.'

'Cordial relationship?' Southwell snorted. 'Hardly that. Our young King may rule over both countries, but it has never been a "cordial relationship".'

The Abbot sighed. 'I would like to take refuge in the Epistle to the Romans, Thomas,' he said. '"If God is for us, who can be against us?"'

'The French,' replied Southwell grimly. 'No doubt about it. Though Her Grace the Duchess of Gloucester confided in me that her husband thinks it imperative that France should be kept under English rule.'

'Not so Cardinal Beaufort,' said the Abbot, 'especially since everything went so dreadfully wrong at Arras. And I do tend to agree with him. Perhaps we ought to make a clean break away from France and let the wretched country fend for itself. Where exactly do you stand on the issue, Thomas?'

Southwell, soaking up beef gravy with his bread, wore a frown of concentration. 'I'm not at all sure,' he said. 'Not at all.'

The Abbot regarded his companion with cynical amusement. He knew Southwell would always sit firmly astride the fence, not taking sides with one or the other until he was certain who would win the argument.

Beaufort and Gloucester were both very influential men and Canon Southwell had ambition. He would always want to side with the winner.

***

King Henry disliked the feeling of having grease on his hands and beckoned his ewerer to bring him a bowlful of water. As he rinsed away the last slimy traces of roast swan and dried his fingers carefully on the proffered towel, he looked around him at the excited, happy faces of the revellers seated at the table on the royal dais, enjoying the last merry celebration of the long Christmas festival. These were his close family and there were few enough of them. His father's only remaining brother, the Duke of Gloucester, was listening with rapt attention to something his wife was saying and Henry heard the Duchess laugh delightedly, a laugh which started on a high, fluting note and tinkled down the scale like a peal of little silver bells. He liked that.

Catching his eye, his aunt Eleanor made a great show of stroking the new brooch once again and he snatched his eyes away from her, only to find his cousin, the seventeen-year-old Antigone, waving her hand excitedly to attract his attention. Humphrey's natural daughter was seated between her brother, Arthur Plantagenet, and her fiancé, the Earl of Tankerville.

'Your Highness!' she called to him, 'This time next year I shall be a Countess!' Antigone, rather a strident young woman, seemed hardly able to wait to marry the Earl. In Henry's opinion, Tankerville was welcome to her, though he nodded, smiled and kept his uncharitable thoughts to himself.

The only face that was missing, the dear face he wanted to see more than any other, was his mother's. The Dowager Queen Catherine should be here on the royal dais, watching the dancing, her slim fingers tapping the table to the rhythm of the music. She loved music and always charmed everyone when she sang the songs of her native France in her pretty Parisian accent. But she was spending Christmas in the country and no one but her son seemed to care that she wasn't in Westminster; no one even mentioned her name.

At least Henry now knew the reason why she wasn't here, and he was the only person seated at the table who knew the truth.

When he was younger, the King had been very distressed by his mother's frequent absences from court and he had prayed earnestly that she was not ill. Then he reasoned with himself that she was probably still mourning his father's death. Or maybe his mother disliked him and couldn't bring herself to say so? Perhaps she was disappointed that he wasn't growing up to resemble his late father. He had been told many tales of his father's bravery and of the high regard in which the people had held him. Henry really, really wanted to grow up to be resolute and steadfast like his father and he had always wanted to please his lovely, gentle mother. But he was afraid she didn't care for him.

It had been with very mixed emotions that he'd learned the real reason for her absences. Far from mourning the death of her husband, as Henry had imagined, she had at last confided in him that she had married again, in secret this time, and she made him swear not to divulge the secret to anyone. The only other person at court who knew the truth of her situation was Henry's great-uncle, Cardinal Beaufort.

Henry had been deeply shocked, hurt and resentful that his mother preferred to be in the country with her new husband, Owen Tudor, rather than at Windsor with her son. But she explained to him that the marriage had to be kept secret because, as her Clerk of the Wardrobe, Tudor was a servant in her household. He was also Welsh and therefore had no rights under English law. He could be hanged if anyone ever found out about it. So Henry must promise never to tell anyone.

At first Henry had found it very difficult to understand why his mother had lowered herself to associate with a servant. Then she told him of Tudor's great kindness towards her when, as a French woman at the English court, she had felt lonely and vulnerable. They had fallen in love, but were forced to keep their relationship a secret because of a parliamentary statute which threatened terrible punishment for any man who married the dowager queen without the express permission of the King. Henry really wanted his mother to be happy and said he would readily give his permission for the marriage, but she told him that it wasn't as easy as that and one day she would explain it all to him. For the moment, all he needed to know was that the statute had been drawn up by none other than Henry's own uncle, the Duke of Gloucester, so his mother and her new husband deemed it wise to stay away from court, rather than arouse the Duke's suspicion and face the threat of Owen Tudor's possible execution. The Duke still knew nothing of the marriage and neither did the Duchess.

Of course, Henry would never let his mother down in any way, but she had entrusted him with an enormous secret and it was very, very difficult to keep it to himself. Sometimes he felt his head would burst with the effort, especially now he knew he had two younger brothers. Henry, who had thought himself an only child, was tremendously excited by the knowledge. He knew their names were Edmund and Jasper. Edmund and Jasper! When he was on his own, he would say the names quietly to himself, rolling them around his tongue, savouring them. He whispered those names in his prayers each night and entreated God to be kind to them. Edmund and Jasper. What did they look like? Did they look like him? Or did they take after their father, Owen Tudor? Edmund and Jasper. He wished he could spend time with them, teach them to ride, help them with their reading, worship with them in St Stephen's Chapel or in the Abbey Church of St Peter. It wasn't fair that he should be constantly alone. He ached to have his other, secret family with him here at Windsor, sitting on the royal dais, eating roast swan, enjoying the games, the music and the dancing, not hiding away in the country at Bishop's Hatfield. What was the point in being King of England and France if he couldn't have what he really wanted?

The burden of the secret was almost too much to bear and he was relieved to be able to talk about it to the one other person who knew it, his great-uncle Henry Beaufort. Beaufort had warned him strongly against saying anything to anyone, particularly the Duke of Gloucester. He had been at great pains to stress that the King's uncle was a dangerous, devious politician. He pointed out that, by forcing the Royal Marriage Bill through parliament to prevent the Dowager Queen from re-marrying and having more children, Gloucester's main motivation was to strengthen his own claim to the throne.

His Highness should wait, said Beaufort, biding his time and looking forward to the day when he was old enough to make his own decisions. Then he could welcome his half-brothers to court and no one could gainsay him.

Henry was aware that there was no love lost between the Cardinal and the Duke but, of the two, his instinct was to trust his great-uncle Henry Beaufort. So, though it was all he could do to stop himself blurting out the truth, Henry knew he must keep the exciting secret of his half-brothers to himself and, whatever happened, he must never, ever, tell his uncle of Gloucester, nor his aunt, the Duchess Eleanor.

CHAPTER SIX

Spring 1436

'May Day tomorrow,' said Jenna, expertly slapping a ball of butter into a rectangular shape between two wooden butter paddles. 'It'll soon be summer and then we'll have trouble keeping the dairy cool.'

'Well,' said Jane, 'it's a lot better since Master Jourdemayne diverted the stream to run through it last year. It makes it a lot easier to clean out, too.'

'Cold feet are my problem when I'm in here,' Hawys said, with a scowl, 'they've been frozen solid all winter.'

'They don't have to be Hawys,' said Jenna. 'If you're shrammed with cold, you can always try stuffing stinging nettles in your shoes.'

'Ugh! I'll put up with the cold feet, thank you! Shall I pass you the butter stamp, Jenna?'

'Please.' Jenna added the butter to a tray of similar yellow rectangles, each lying on a dock leaf, then began stamping each one with the imprint of the farm before wrapping the leaf around it.

'Oooh, I *love* May Day!' exclaimed Kitty, pirouetting around her butter churn and humming a little dance tune. 'I wonder who will be Queen of the May! Will it be you, do you think, Jenna?'

'I doubt it,' Jenna shook her head. 'I've already been a queen once this year, remember. I was Queen of the Pea. I won't be May Queen as well. Perhaps it will be Hawys.'

'Oh, it won't be me,' said Hawys dismissively. 'May Day,' she grimaced, 'already! And my Seth still hasn't said a word.'

'Perhaps he won't,' Jenna said, 'and don't waste your time grieving over that. Marriage isn't all it's made out to be. Or so they say,' she added.

'I can't see any alternative, and I'm not getting any younger.' Hawys wasn't exactly sure of her age, but thought she was about nineteen years old. To Hawys, that meant her chances of marrying were decreasing rapidly.

Jenna said nothing. Kitty had told her that the other dairymaids were itching to know whether she was a maiden, a wife or a widow, but she didn't intend telling them. That was none of their business. She steered the conversation away from the subject.

'Has Seth built the fires for the neats yet, Hawys?'

'What? The Beltane fires?'

'Yes, of course.'

'But what have they got to do with the neats?'

The longer Jenna lived in Westminster, the more she realised that things were often done quite differently here. Back home in Devon, the custom was to build two big bonfires with space between them wide enough to walk the cows through. It kept them safe from harm for the rest of the year.

'Weren't they frightened?' Hawys wanted to know.

'Well, yes, I suppose they were a bit frightened, but there was always somebody leading them so they were safe enough, really. They're such sweet beasts, but they don't think for themselves. They'll follow wherever they're led.'

'True enough,' Hawys agreed. 'If they had minds of their own, they wouldn't let us anywhere near them, much less let us take their calves away from them so we can have their milk.'

'And use the calves' rennet to make cheese. Poor creatures. It's not much of a life for them. There's no sound quite as sad as a cow lowing for her dead calf.'

'That's motherhood for you,' said Jane. 'No bond is as strong as a mother's love for her little one, even if the little one has four hairy legs and a tail!'

As the other dairymaids laughed, Jenna caught sight of Kitty's stricken face. 'This isn't getting the butter churned,' she said briskly. 'Come on, Kitty, let's hear you sing "Come, Butter, Come." It's one of your favourites, isn't it? Or would you rather sing "Summer is a-Coming In"?'

Kitty shook her head mutely then said in a small voice, 'No thank you, Jenna.'

'Come on, Kittymouse,' said Jenna, before the youngster could start moping for her mother again. 'Come and help me. We need to take this skimmed milk down to the pigsties, then we'll go to the cow shed and get some more milk for the setting dishes. The cows are back in full milk again now they've got good grass to eat so there's bound to be some milk to be separated overnight. We might as well bring it back with us. Here, help me on with this yoke, please.'

Kitty was immediately diverted from her peevishness. 'I'll take the yoke, Jenna! Let me! Oh, please! Let me!'

'No, Kitty. It's far too heavy for you. Just hang the buckets on it for me, please.'

'Oh, but Jenna, I could carry it, really I could.'

'Perhaps I'll let you carry it someday, Kitty, but not until you've grown a bit more. The pails would be dragging on the ground if you carried them!'

Kitty gave in and they began to make their way towards the pigsties, Jenna with the wooden yoke across her shoulders, trying not to jolt the buckets of skimmed milk which hung on either end of it. Kitty pranced along beside her, singing a springtime song about ewes bleating for their lambs and cows lowing for their calves, having forgotten her brief moment of misery. Jenna joined in, beginning the melody a phrase later than Kitty, each of them holding her own tune and both singing at the tops of their voices.

***

Kitty was the very picture of a happy little girl, thought William Jourdemayne as he watched them coming towards him. She and Jenna had clearly taken to each other and if Jenna was assuming the role of substitute mother for Kitty, well, perhaps Kitty was responding in kind. William had no idea whether Jenna had ever had a child of her own, it was none of his business, but he was a man who liked children and he thought any youngster would be privileged to be brought up by a woman like her.

He was rounding up the younger farmhands to come and

help in the Lower Acre where thieving crows were pestering the men who were trying to finish off the late sowing of barley. The birds were brazen enough to perch on the hats of the scarecrows, eyeing their opportunities. Youngsters with catapults were the best way of keeping the birds at bay while the men got the job done. William always tried to include Kitty in activities like this. Her mother, Elizabeth, had been one of his best dairymaids – it was the least he could do.

'Master Jourdemayne!' Kitty called to him. 'We're going to see the pigs, to take them some skimmed milk. They like that.'

'And making enough noise about it, too,' William smiled. 'Mind you don't scare them! I'll have another little scaring job for you to do in a moment.' Then he turned to Jenna.

'How are things going at the dairy, Jenna?' he asked. 'I haven't seen you for several weeks. I haven't had time to check the milk tallies…'

'You can trust me, master. I promise I wouldn't cheat you.'

'I know that. But we did say we'd arrange to get in some more chickens, didn't we? Something young Kitty here can help you with. We should think about it soon.'

'Oh, yes, master, yes, whenever you wish. But it was only a suggestion. Thank you, master, thank you,' Jenna answered, a little flustered and not sure what to say next, conscious of the way he was looking at her, trying not to meet those blue eyes of his. Kitty was tugging at her hand.

'Kitty and I are off to the shippon,' Jenna said, 'after we've been to the sties.'

'The where?'

'Oh dear, I'm sorry. I've done it again! The cowshed … er … the byre. A shippon is what we call it in Devon. I'm sorry … I didn't mean to…'

Concerned by her confusion, William put his hand on her arm. 'Please, don't worry. It's just that it sounded more like something you'd see on the river. And the Thames is back in that direction!'

'Ooooh,' Kitty laughed, 'Master Jourdemayne thought you meant a ship, Jenna!'

Jenna barely heard her. The touch of the Master's hand on

her arm had unsettled her and she knew that a strong blush was spreading up from her neck and suffusing her face. She stared at her shoes in embarrassment while William determinedly kept up a normal conversation.

'Well, Kitty,' he said, 'there are different names for different things all around England. When you're as well-travelled as Jenna is, then I'm sure you'll learn a few more words for things. Now then, Kitty, you know what a catapult is, don't you?'

'Yes, of course I do,' said Kitty, nodding in the way she always did. 'Would you like me to come and stone the crows for you, Master Jourdemayne?'

'Yes, I would,' he said. 'Most of the other children have started work already. But that's only if Jenna can spare you, of course. Can you spare her, Jenna?' He looked down at Jenna, his eyebrows raised, his dark hair falling forward.

Jenna's heart hadn't quite resumed its normal beat and his direct gaze didn't help a bit. Kitty, standing beside him, was looking up at her in excited anticipation of spending the day with her friends.

'Can I go, Jenna? Please?'

'Mmmm, well, I'm not sure whether I can spare you,' Jenna frowned exaggeratedly and shook her head, teasing. 'We need you in the dairy.'

'Oh, please, Jenna!' Kitty tugged at her hand again.

'Oh, all right then. Of course you can, Kittymouse. How could I refuse either of you anything!'

At last, her eyes met William's and, smiling, he gave her a broad wink and she smiled back at him, part of a friendly conspiracy. They were entirely unaware that they were being observed.

From a distance, Margery, on her way home after a frustrating afternoon at the palace, trying to please the vain and empty-headed ladies of the court, saw her husband with the new dairymaid and one of the farm children. They didn't notice her and she didn't call to them or attract their attention in any way. She merely stopped for a moment, watching them thoughtfully as they laughed together, completely engrossed in their cheerful teasing. Then she frowned. This must be discouraged.

***

Canon Thomas Southwell really had to steel himself to travel south of the river to Southwark with its dirty stews and taverns. He was making the journey today only because the Bishop of Winchester was in residence at Southwark Palace, but having to cross London Bridge with all its rowdy activity of shops, huddled together against the clinging stink of the Thames below, was almost more than Southwell's elevated, ecclesiastical nose could bear.

For him, Westminster was the place to be. It was where decisions were made and Thomas Southwell dearly loved being among the decision-makers.

But needs must cross the Thames this morning, since there was royal business to discuss with Henry Beaufort who, in his capacity as Bishop of Winchester, held the office of Prelate of the Order of the Garter. The Dean of Westminster was responsible for the organisation of the Garter ceremony itself so Southwell, as a Canon of St Stephen's Westminster, had volunteered to take charge of several details ahead of next week's ceremony. In fact, these were minor, inconsequential things which could probably have been left until the day of the ceremony but Southwell, bursting with self-importance, thought they merited immediate discussion with His Grace and had requested a meeting with him. Southwark Palace was within view. He was nearly there.

For Southwell, it was a perfect excuse.

For Beaufort, it was an unwelcome interruption. He had a lot on his mind. Things seemed to be going from bad to worse in France since the untimely death of the Duke of Bedford. While he was alive, the Duke had managed to control the volatile French. Now, things had the potential to turn quite ugly. Not for the first time, Beaufort heartily wished that England had never been encumbered by the wretched country.

It worried him greatly that the Duke of Gloucester was keen to keep France under English control. Henry Beaufort had nothing but contempt for his arrogant nephew. And now the King had impetuously invited his flibbertigibbet of a wife to become a Lady Member of the Order of the Garter! Beaufort had little time for the Duchess, either.

His Highness had made another of his impulsive gestures in issuing the invitation to the wretched woman. Rather than take the advice of his ruling Council as he had always done hitherto, the young King appeared to be flexing his royal muscle by making more and more decisions for himself these days and they were not always the right decisions. Still, he couldn't remain a child for ever; he would have to start making decisions some time. Perhaps the earlier the better, thought Beaufort on reflection, because the King's decisions would then take precedence over whatever Gloucester decided and that would bring the arrogant Duke down a peg or two. If only the King could be persuaded to withdraw from France, then life would be a great deal more agreeable for everyone. Everyone, that was, except Gloucester. And Henry Beaufort couldn't give a damn about Gloucester.

Southwell bustled into the room and took the seat offered him. 'Of course, it is a very great honour for Her Grace,' he enthused, as he settled himself comfortably, 'is it not, my Lord?'

Beaufort was not at all sure that he liked this pompous little priest. He grunted non-committally.

'As perhaps you know, my Lord, I have the honour to serve Her Grace in an advisory capacity as her personal physician and I have observed that His Highness the young King appears very fond of his aunt. So it is right and proper that she should be honoured. She is, after all, the highest-ranking lady in the country.'

Beaufort raised his eyebrows. 'She ranks below Her Royal Highness the Dowager Queen Catherine,' he pointed out.

'Ah, the Queen. Yes, of course. But Her Royal Highness has chosen to absent herself from court. She surely cannot expect the King to honour her under the circumstances.'

'Perhaps not,' said Beaufort. 'But then again, perhaps she doesn't seek honour; it may not be important to her.' He kept his own counsel on the subject of the Queen. He had a great fondness for the widow of his late nephew, King Henry V, and would never spread malicious gossip about her. She had enough problems of her own, poor woman, without incurring the disapproval of this bumptious little man. He needed to steer the conversation away from Queen Catherine.

'Sir Thomas Grey has been approved a Knight of the Garter this year,' he said. 'It's about time: Sir Thomas doesn't get any younger. Can't be far off fifty and it's well known that he acquitted himself admirably at Agincourt.'

'So I understand,' said Southwell, who made a habit of learning everything he could about influential people. 'And you must be pleased,' he went on, 'that your nephew is to be honoured this year!'

Beaufort's stony expression immediately softened. 'Edmund,' he said, smiling. The son of his late brother was the nearest he would ever come to having a son of his own and he was immensely proud of him. 'Yes, indeed. A fine, upstanding young man. And you're right, Southwell, I am pleased and proud of him, of course.'

'He clearly takes after his uncle!'

Southwell had found that a little flattery would often grease the delicate mechanism of making an impression on powerful people. He had his eye firmly fixed on a bishop's mitre as soon as he could acquire one and Henry Beaufort was a man with influence. It was worth keeping on the right side of him.

On the other hand, like everyone else, he was aware of the open enmity between Beaufort and the Duke of Gloucester. Henry Beaufort was without doubt the most important prelate in England; Gloucester was Protector of England and an authoritative member of the King's Council. He was also heir to the throne. These two formidable characters might personally be at daggers drawn, but Southwell intended to keep on the right side of them both and, this morning, he needed to impress Cardinal Beaufort. He took a sheaf of important-looking sheets of parchment from the scrip he carried.

'These are my plans for the ceremony, my Lord Bishop,' he said. 'I have brought them along for your approval.'

Beaufort yawned.

***

Silk. The sheen on it, the heavenly feel of it! Standing perfectly still, Eleanor felt a purely sensual pleasure in the way it draped over the elegant contours of her body. A royal seamstress knelt on the floor of Eleanor's dressing room, adjusting the length of the heavy white silk gown which the Duchess would wear under a dark blue cloak at the Garter ceremony on the fifth of May.

The seamstress sat back on her heels and looked critically at the hem which she had been tacking in place. 'There, my Lady,' she said as best she could with half a dozen pins between her pursed lips.

'There, Your Grace,' corrected Eleanor without looking at her.

Removing the pins from her mouth, the seamstress got awkwardly to her feet. 'Yes, of course, Your Grace. I'm so sorry. May I ask whether the shoes you are wearing now will be the shoes you will wear at the Garter ceremony?'

'No, of course not. I shall have new ones, shoes of the finest pale leather, and the cordwainer promises to deliver them this afternoon. I can hardly wait to try them on. Why do you ask about my shoes?'

'Because, Your Grace, depending on the height of the heels, they could make a slight difference to the final depth of hem required.'

'So why didn't you say that in the first place?'

'Yes. I'm sorry, my L … er, Your Grace. But might I suggest I leave the final adjustment of the hem until such time as you feel comfortable in your new shoes? Then every detail will be perfect.'

'Oh, very well,' said Eleanor with a sigh, waving her away. 'Go now. Leave me. And tell Sarah to come and help me out of this gown.'

'Very well, my Lady.'

'Your Grace,' Eleanor corrected absently as the seamstress curtseyed and left the room, rolling her eyes heavenward as soon as the door was safely closed behind her.

By re-adjusting the mirror on her dressing room table, Eleanor was able to see almost all of the unfinished gown. Yes, the irritating woman was quite right; it was important that every detail must be perfect. Since the Dowager Queen had absented herself from court, the Duchess of Gloucester was the first and foremost lady in the land and all eyes would be upon her.

She stepped back and twirled slowly, humming to herself, smiling coquettishly at her own reflection, pleased by what she saw. She was a person of importance, wife of the heir to the throne of England.

Bending very close to the mirror, she turned her head from side to side and, analytically, noted that her skin was good, with very few wrinkles – she had Margery Jourdemayne's compound of egg and powdered lily root to thank for that. It was worth every penny she paid for it. Her hair was still quite dark, too, with hardly a trace of grey but, more than anything, her bright eyes shone with all her old zest for life.

Straightening up, she ran the palm of her hand over the fabric of the sumptuous gown, smoothing it over the sinuous curve of her full breasts, her hips, her too-flat belly. If only her hand could trace the contour of a mound there, but hers was still like the flat belly of a virgin.

This overwhelming need to give her husband a child was proving more frustrating with every passing month and her chances of conceiving receded with every successive year. She would be thirty-five years old come summer and, however she looked at it, time was running out. What distressed her most was the realisation that the failure lay fair and square at her own doorstep because Humphrey had succeeded in getting other women with child. No, there was no question of his virility, and Eleanor had to grit her teeth whenever she heard that spoilt little brat Antigone call him 'Father'.

Antigone Plantagenet. What a ridiculous name for a young woman at the English court! It was neither one thing nor the other, neither Greek nor French. The child had probably been named on a stupid whim of Humphrey's when he was going through a classical phase. He would never talk about the mother of his children, dismissing the whole affair as a mere liaison, a

80

dalliance with a woman he had met in France during the years of occupation which followed Agincourt. So much for a dalliance, thought Eleanor: it didn't require an abacus to calculate that it must have lasted at least two years if it survived two pregnancies. Both children had been acknowledged by their father and were living in his household, and all she knew was that they had been born in France. The stern expression on Humphrey's face warned her not to ask any more questions.

Eleanor had been more than pleased when Antigone had married the young Earl of Tankerville three months ago. It had been rather a grand wedding, graced by the presence of the King who was the bride's first cousin. The bride's father and his wife were naturally among the chief guests and it thrilled Eleanor to ride beside her husband through the streets of London in the bridal procession, being gawped at and cheered by the crowds. But as soon as the wedding was over, she could hardly wait for the young earl, who was the seventh Lord Powys, to take his new countess to the family's ancestral home in Montgomeryshire. She was heartily glad to see the back of Antigone and, with luck, she might never have to see her again. Montgomeryshire was in Wales and no one ever went there unless they had to. Good riddance!

Humphrey's other child was a boy named Arthur. To Eleanor, that was a far more acceptable name and at least Arthur was a folk hero to whom the English could lay some claim. No one enjoyed hearing the tales of the heroic King Arthur more than Eleanor did.

'Enter!' she called, in response to a knock at the dressing room door. 'Ah, Sarah, there you are at last. What took you so long?'

'I'm sorry, ma'am,' said her maid, dropping a curtsey. 'You see, I was mending a rent in your …'

'I'm sorry, *Your Grace*,' Eleanor snapped. 'For Heaven's sake, Sarah, how many more times must I correct you! Oh, no matter,' she said, turning her back on her maid, 'now you're here, you can help me out of this gown. Then put it to one side. Carefully, mind!'

'Certainly, Your Grace.'

***

The fact that the Westminster monastery was so near Eybury farmhouse was a mixed blessing. It meant on the one hand that Abbot Harweden was sufficiently close to take almost too much of an interest in the daily working of the farm, but it also meant that the monastery bell, ringing the hours of Divine Office throughout the day, was a reliable means of knowing the time. The bell had just rung the hour of Compline, the final Office of the day, as William Jourdemayne crawled into bed.

'I have to be up early tomorrow morning,' said his wife, pulling her shift over her head. 'I'll be out and about before dawn if I'm to collect enough Beltane dew for Her Grace to use before the Garter ceremony next week. She's heard it's beneficial for the complexion so I've promised I'll get her some. She'll pay a decent price for it.'

William muttered something incomprehensible as he moved over in their bed to make room for her beside him.

'Mind you,' Margery added, snuffing out the candle, 'the Duchess wouldn't know the difference if I bottled up a few drops of water from the stream. I could do that, if you like, then we could stay in bed.'

Blessed darkness at last meant the promise of sleep for William after the back-breaking work of sowing the barley. But it was not to be.

'She's an attractive woman,' Margery said after a few minutes.

Why was it, he thought, that just as he had begun drifting towards that nebulous no-man's land between wakefulness and sweet oblivion, Margery decided to hold a conversation? It was one of her more exasperating habits.

'Who is? The Duchess?' he asked from the depths of the bed, determinedly keeping his eyes closed so that he could drift back into no-man's land again, as soon as he was allowed to.

'No, the Queen of the Pea,' said Margery. 'Joanna.'

'The Queen of the Pea? But that was Twelfth Night. Months ago. Anyway, her name isn't Joanna, it's Jenna,' said William, still keeping his eyes firmly closed. 'Jenna Harding. It's a

82

Cornish name, I believe, but she's from Devon.'

'You seem to know a lot about her!'

'Of course I do, Margery. I gave her the job.'

'As dairymaid?'

'As dairymaid. You were not available at the time. Now, are you going to let me get to sleep?'

'Yes. If you want.'

There was a pause, during which William allowed his mind to drift. There was a big drove coming in from Devon tomorrow afternoon and though it was always good to see Robin Fairweather, he knew he'd keep him up late tomorrow night, talking good-naturedly over more pitchers of ale than was good for either of them, so he needed all the sleep he could get tonight.

'She's wasting her time in the dairy.'

William sat up, wide awake. 'What do you mean, wasting her time! She is by far the best dairymaid we've ever had at Eybury, she's efficient, she's thorough, she's clean. She keeps tally as well as any scholar would…'

'Is she better than … what was her name … Elizabeth?'

'As it happens, yes, she is.'

'And you like her!'

'Well, of course I like her. Why would I not like her? She does her job well, earns her keep. She's never late, she's agreeable, she has taken Elizabeth's young daughter under her wing, she gets on well with the other girls…'

'Quite a paragon!'

'Well, if you want to put it like that, yes, I suppose she is.'

'I'll wager she couldn't pleasure you as well as I can.'

Oh, so that was it. Margery always teased him when she wanted him to pleasure her: getting him riled about something would also often get him aroused. After twelve years of marriage he usually recognised all the signals she sent him, whether of approval or disapproval, spoken or unspoken. He should have realised. She wanted him to take her and bring her to her point of ecstasy quickly and efficiently.

Which was exactly what he did: he was, after all, a normal vigorous man. It was only after she had achieved her objective and was lying satisfied beside him that he spoke again.

'We haven't done that for a long time,' he said.

'No,' she agreed, 'we haven't.'

'Then why tonight?'

Margery hesitated for a moment before replying. 'Sometimes it's necessary,' she said, turning onto her side.

She could have said something kinder than that, something about wanting him, loving him, perhaps. William lay awake for some considerable time, buffeted on a sea of emotions. It wasn't so much that Margery had hurt his feelings in using him for her own sexual gratification, she had done that before. It was more the fact that during all the time he had been making love to his wife, the face in his mind's eye had belonged to another woman, and at the height of his passion, it was all he could do not to call out her name.

***

The good weather held for the remainder of the week, cool but dry and, high above the round tower of Windsor Castle, the royal standard fluttered in a light breeze. On this May morning, the day of the Garter ceremony, Windsor was full to capacity for the celebration of one of the most important days in the royal calendar.

Eleanor had looked forward to the occasion like a small child to her saint's day. She had been awake since before dawn, watching through the slatted shutters of the window as the sun came up, cherishing the thought that today she would become a Lady Companion of the Garter. It was an honour given only to the most noble ladies in the land, the wives of the twenty-four knights – never more than that number – who were the King's most esteemed, most chivalrous cohorts. Humphrey had been a Garter Knight since he was ten years old, having been given the honour by his father, along with his three older brothers, exactly thirty-six years ago. Now, as his wife, Eleanor was to be honoured with the ultimate prize, the King's public endorsement of her relationship with his uncle.

Seated in St George's Chapel as the ceremony began, Eleanor's attention wandered until she found herself looking at the King who was sitting near the altar, his mild brown eyes devoid of any expression, his small pink rosebud mouth unsmiling. He was simply staring straight ahead. Perhaps he was moved in a spiritual way by the ceremony, but she thought it unlikely. He seemed to be stifling a yawn, though, since his deep commitment to his religion was well-known, perhaps his mind could be somewhere more celestial. But, for a privileged young man on the threshold of his adult life, there was not an iota of vitality in him. How much more dynamic Humphrey was than his nephew, she thought. How much more vigorous he would be in the governance of the realm, how much more inspiring, how much better loved by his people. Her husband was his nephew's heir, but he would make a far, far better King.

She held, in that overwhelming moment, the knowledge that there could be one more prize, the greatest, the most glorious, the most glittering of all prizes which might yet be hers, should anything happen to King Henry. She also knew that such ideas were evil and treasonous and that the chapel of St George, the mother chapel of the Order of the Garter, was the last place in which she should allow herself to entertain such thoughts. *Honi soit qui mal y pense* was the motto of the Order, it was inscribed on the silver Garter Badge which she wore so proudly on her shoulder. *Shame on him who thinks this evil.*

Nevertheless, in her heart of hearts, the possibility of her one day becoming Queen was a niggling little nugget of evil that would not go away.

CHAPTER SEVEN

June 1436

'Jenna? Where is Jenna Harding?'

The dairymaids looked up from their work, startled at the interruption. Jane and Hawys were churning butter and Kitty was skimming the cream from the setting dishes, the shallow bowls of yesterday's milk. They all knew that Mistress Jourdemayne's infrequent visits to the dairy usually heralded trouble. They glanced guiltily at each other as the woman they always called Old Mother Madge among themselves stood in front of them, her face a study in expectation.

'Well? Where is Jenna Harding? She works here, doesn't she? So where is she?'

Kitty cleared her throat and spoke up. 'She isn't here, Mistress Jourdemayne. She's delivering cheese up to the monastery.'

'When will she be back?'

'I don't know, mistress. It's not long since she went, but she should be back by dinner-time.'

'Very well. You're Kitty, aren't you?'

'Yes, mistress.' Kitty nodded emphatically.

'Well, Kitty, please remember that when Jenna comes back, you must tell her to come up to the farmhouse to see me. I will be working in my physic garden this morning. After that, I will be in my room. Tell her to be sure to knock and not to barge in.' Margery Jourdemayne turned swiftly on her heel with the air of a woman who had little time to waste.

The dairymaids had been rooted to the spot. Now they turned to each other wide-eyed and started chattering like sparrows.

'Oh, I wonder what Jenna's done!'

'Do you think she's in trouble?'

'If she's in trouble, perhaps she'll have to leave!'

'But if she leaves, I'll have to learn to do the reckoning again … and I'm hopeless at it!'

Kitty's heart was like lead. If Jenna lost her job in the dairy, perhaps she would want to go back to Devon. Kitty had no idea where Devon was but she knew it was a very, very long way away, at least a month's walk. Jenna had said so that very first night in the hay loft, such a long time ago. Jenna seemed to have been here at Eybury Farm for ever and, for Kitty, if she left now it would be like losing her mother all over again. She put down her skimming spoon and wiped her hands on her apron.

'Hawys, will you carry on with this skimming for me, please? I must go and find Jenna and tell her she could be in trouble.'

'Yes, go and find her, Kitty. And go quickly!'

Kitty almost tore off her apron in her hurry. Slamming the door of the dairy behind her, she ran as fast as her legs would carry her in the direction of the monastery, careful to keep off the beaten track. She had no business to be away from the dairy at this time of day so she needed to keep out of sight. Wherever she could, she ducked behind the protective cover of trees and boundary hedging, bent almost double as she ran. She didn't want Jenna to bump into the Mistress by accident; she had to find her first and warn her that Old Mother Madge wanted to see her. It must be something very urgent, Kitty thought. She prayed under her panting breath that Jenna was not in any real trouble.

Kitty had run nearly all the way to the monastery before she spotted Jenna and was almost breathless when she reached her.

'Kitty! Whatever is the matter? What are you doing here?'

'Oh, Jenna,' Kitty gasped, 'I had to come! I had to find you. Something terrible has happened!'

'Something terrible! What, in Heaven's name? Has there been an accident?'

Jenna's mind painted an instant picture of the Lower Acre.

The men were second-ploughing the fallow field today and anything could have happened: ploughshares could be awkward things to handle and they were always kept very sharp. She clutched Kitty's arm.

'Kitty, for Heaven's sake, tell me! What's happened to Master Jourdemayne?'

'Master Jourdemayne? No, no, not Master Jourdemayne. It's Mistress Jourdemayne … she's the one!'

'Oh! Oh … well, what's happened to her? Has she had an accident?'

'No, I never said anything about an accident. But she wants to see you. This morning. What have you done, Jenna? Will Old Mother Madge put a spell on you? Will you be going back to Devon?'

'Put a spell on me! What nonsense! Why? Has someone told you I'll be going back to Devon?'

'No, no, but I'm afraid you will.'

They were at cross purposes, Jenna realised. Nevertheless, she felt mightily relieved that there hadn't been an accident.

Now she needed to calm Kitty down and a little teasing wouldn't go amiss.

'Kitty,' she said, tweaking Kitty's nose, 'you're being a little alkitotle.'

'A what?'

'A silly little elf. I'm sure there's no need to worry. Now come, tell me exactly what has happened.'

Jenna felt annoyed with herself for her instinctive reaction. Even if anything had happened to William Jourdemayne, it wouldn't be any business of hers. She took hold of Kitty's shoulders and gently turned her back in the direction from which she had come. 'Now then, Kittymouse, take it slowly, my dove, and tell me everything. From the beginning.'

Kitty gradually got her breath back as they walked and, bit by bit, she related the story of Margery Jourdemayne's peremptory visit to the dairy. It didn't seem to Jenna that this was anything to worry about, though she was intrigued to find out why she had suddenly become of interest to her employer's wife, having largely been ignored by her in the past.

'You know, Kitty, I can't imagine why Mistress Jourdemayne should want to see me but I'm sure it's nothing to worry about. She has no reason to put a spell on me and, even if she did, she wouldn't have to see me in order to do it, she could curse me from anywhere. And, as far as I know, Master Jourdemayne hasn't complained about my work in the dairy. That's all that matters. Perhaps the Mistress just wants another pair of hands to help out in the farm kitchen. Or they might need me in La Neyte. It could be anything.'

'Oh, I do hope you're right.'

'I'm sure I am. C'mon, Kittymouse, I'll race you back to the dairy!'

Lifting her skirts with one hand and trying to keep the linen coif on her head with the other, Jenna began to run. Kitty had already lost her ribbon and her unruly hair was tumbling down her back as she did her best to keep up. But she didn't care; she was laughing aloud with the relief of knowing that her friend would not abandon her.

**

Shearing was hot work at the best of times, but necessary so that the sheep could be relieved of their heavy woollen coats before the summer sun reached its zenith. And they seem glad to be rid of them, too, William thought as he watched another ewe trotting away from the shearing bench where a shearer had divested her of her thick fleece before setting her back down on her feet. Her lamb, some four months old by now and nearly as big as its mother, scampered dutifully behind her, recognising her from her indignant bleating despite the dramatic change in her appearance.

Sheep were becoming more and more a part of the monastery farm's business, though that was not William's choice. He was a man who took delight in cattle. On the low-lying, clay soil of the riverside pastures, sheep were prone to foot-rot and moving the flock further up to the drier meadows towards Knightsbridge or Hyde made no apparent difference. In any case, they had to be brought back down to the river at this time of year to be dipped and washed before shearing. Apart from these considerations, sheep looked after themselves well enough, and it was years since anyone had seen a wolf in these parts, so there was hardly any need for more than one shepherd. Perhaps he felt as he did because he infinitely preferred beef to lamb on the platter, not that he had the chance to eat either very often. Fine flesh was for the Abbot's table, not the tenant farmer's.

Abbot Harweden was keen to expand the existing flock. The price of wool was at an all-time high and not expected to drop. Moreover, he wanted to develop the cheese-making side of the farm's output and was keen to explore the potential market for sheep's cheese. He had summoned William to a meeting at La Neyte to discuss the issue. William had asked Tom the shepherd to come with him because Tom knew a great deal more about sheep than he did himself.

'P'raps the Abbot thinks he could get to be as rich as Cardinal Beaufort,' said Tom with a short laugh, as he and William trudged along the Willow Walk towards La Neyte for their meeting with Abbot Harweden.

'Well, if he does, he's picked the right time to do it,' said William. 'They tell me wool is trading very well in the international markets these days. So he's doing the right thing. Mind you, he's got a very long way to go before he comes anywhere near to what Beaufort's worth. Richest man in the country, isn't he?

'So they say. Even richer than the King.'

'Well, they say he doesn't mind sharing what he's got. At least, not when it comes to putting his money behind the men who fight in France. That's what I've heard.'

'I've heard that, too,' said Tom as they approached the imposing entrance to La Neyte. 'He can't be that greedy, then.'

Before he took his seat in the Abbot's study, William felt in the pocket of his leather jerkin for a sample of the wool from a sheep which had been shorn that morning.

'It's good enough,' said Abbot Harweden, taking it from him and pulling the strands knowledgeably between his fingers, testing their resilience, 'but I believe we can do better than this.'

'The colour is good,' said Tom. 'Nothing wrong with the colour.'

'Indeed not,' agreed the Abbot. 'It's a good, clean white.'

'And it's the first cut,' added William. 'So it's long. The men Tom hires in know what they're doing with shears. You won't get any chopped-up bits of wool from them.'

'I appreciate all that,' said the Abbot, 'but I'm anxious for us to try something a little different. I'm told the best fleeces come from Herefordshire nowadays, from Leominster. They're softer, silkier. They fetch a good price.'

'That'll be the Ryeland sheep, then,' Tom nodded in agreement.

'That's not the name I've heard,' said the Abbot. 'I thought they were called Lemsters.'

'They are,' agreed Tom. 'Lemster Ore. It's a nickname. They're from Leominster and they're as good as gold to a farmer.'

'Then we must acquire some as soon as we can,' said the Abbot. 'I dare say we can enquire of the drovers whether we can do that easily.'

'Robin Fairweather will know,' said William. 'He's bringing four hundred head of bullocks up from Devon next week so I'll ask him. The drovers all know each other so he's bound to know someone from the Welsh borders, up Hereford way. I'll ask him.'

'I'd be grateful,' said Abbot Harweden. 'When he arrives, tell him to come and see me up at the monastery to discuss the matter, would you, Master Jourdemayne?'

'Certainly, Father Abbot.'

'Well, thank you. That will be all for the moment, gentlemen,' said the Abbot in dismissing them but, just as Tom and William were about to leave the room, he called William back.

'Yes, Father Abbot, what can I do for you?'

Abbot Harweden dropped his voice and beckoned William to come a little nearer.

'Mistress Jourdemayne, your good wife – I trust she is well?'

'Indeed, Father, she enjoys excellent health.'

'Sadly, the same is not entirely true of me,' said the Abbot. 'I have been suffering lately from the same miserable discomfort which has plagued me for some time.'

'I'm sorry to hear that.'

'I'm not greatly indisposed, you understand, not as long as I have an adequate supply of the salve which your wife kindly provides me with. It does seem to be the most efficacious unguent I have tried. I wonder whether you would be kind enough to ask her to bring some to me while I'm here at La Neyte?'

'Certainly, Father Abbot. Will she know what it is?'

'Oh, yes. She will know. Just ask her for my usual salve. And I would like it as soon as she can let me have it.'

'I'll tell her. Will that be all, Father?'

'Yes, there's nothing else at present. Things seem to be running smoothly. You have even construed the accounts in good time. Your good wife must be a great help to you. Good day to you, Master Jourdemayne. And thank you.'

'Thank you, Father.' William inclined his head towards the Abbot and took his leave. He said nothing about the fact that his good wife had not construed the accounts for many a long month. That job had now been taken over by Mistress Jenna Harding.

Abbot Harweden shifted in his chair, trying to find a more comfortable position. Still, it wouldn't be long now before he'd be able to do something about it. He didn't know what secret ingredient differentiated Margery Jourdemayne's pilewort unguent from Thomas Southwell's but, whatever it was, he knew which he preferred; Mistress Jourdemayne's was infinitely superior. In the Abbot's opinion, her herbal remedies were excellent. When she came to see him, he would ask her about his indigestion, too, and the constant dull pain in his stomach. Perhaps she would have something to cure that. That Jourdemayne fellow was very fortunate in his wife.

***

William didn't like the threatening look of the rain clouds

gathering in the west. If hay was allowed to lie overnight and it chanced to rain, it would soon go mouldy and be rendered useless for winter fodder. The hay must be kept dry at all costs. All the available farmhands were needed to load it onto the cart and take it up to the big barn for storage. This meant the dairymaids would have to take over the milking tonight so that the men could get the job done. That's how it was with farming.

He could have sent one of the men up to the dairy with a message but, always glad of an excuse to call in there himself, William hoped none of the dairymaids would guess the real reason for his visit. The truth of it was that his path hadn't crossed Jenna's for a month or more, even though she had a disconcerting habit of invading his dreams. But this was a legitimate excuse to see her. He put his head around the door of the dairy.

'Hello, ladies!'

'Master Jourdemayne!' Kitty was always delighted to see him.

'Well now, young Kitty. How are things going?'

'We're very busy, master, we're trying to make a new kind of cheese.'

'Really? And why are you doing that?'

'It's Jenna's idea, master. It's a cheese they make down in er … er … where she comes from…'

'Devon,' said William. 'You know about Devon, Kitty, it's where Robin the Drover comes from.'

'Oh, yes. That's right. Well, Jenna says their cheese is better than our cheese because they knead salt into the whey. So we're trying it.'

'Really?' said William, his eyebrows raised. 'I look forward to tasting it. And where is Jenna?'

Suddenly evasive, Kitty wouldn't meet his eye. 'I … I'm not sure, master.'

Hawys wasn't so reticent. 'She's gone up to the farm,' she told him.

'Has she? And do you know why?'

'She's gone to see Mistress Jourdemayne,' Hawys said. 'Mistress came looking for her.'

Unaware that he was scowling, William nodded curtly to the dairymaids and turned to leave. What on earth could Margery want with Jenna?

'Thank you,' he said as he left. That was all.

***

On her way to respond to Mistress Jourdemayne's command, Jenna stopped for a moment as she walked past the physic garden, admiring its meticulous neatness. White pebbles divided rows of healthy plants into twelve sections and small wooden markers identified sturdy seedlings. Nets were stretched between poles over the more vulnerable plants to provide protection from birds and the whole was overseen by a splendid scarecrow which, much to Jenna's amusement, was wearing what looked like an old leather jerkin of William Jourdemayne's: Jenna could have sworn she'd seen him wearing it only last week. Though she was no stranger to physic gardens, she had never seen one quite as well-maintained as this. Not one of the plants within its tidy confines looked as though it would have the temerity to grow out of line.

Walking on past the well and around the corner to the back of the farmhouse, she lifted the latch on the big oak door into the kitchen. It was silent, in that after-dinner lull when the food has been eaten and the debris cleared away. Jenna listened but could hear nothing other than the sound of a dog under the table contentedly gnawing on a bone, though she didn't always trust her hearing nowadays.

She called out, 'Is there anyone at home?'

'Is that you, Jenna?'

'Oh, yes, Mistress Jourdemayne.'

A door off the kitchen opened and Margery Jourdemayne beckoned her to enter.

'Come in, Jenna, come in.'

'Thank you, mistress. Forgive me for shouting, but Kitty said I must knock at your door and not barge in. And I wasn't sure which door it was.'

'Quite right. No one comes into this room under any circumstances, other than by my invitation. Now, I expect you

95

wondered why I wanted to see you.'

Jenna nodded, trying not to stare around her at a room the like of which she had never seen before. It was laid out just as meticulously as the physic garden and it was plain to see that the same organisational skills were behind it. Jars and bottles were stored away neatly on shelves: and there were so many of them! Why on earth did her employer's wife need such things? There were books, too, at least three of them as far as Jenna could see.

Margery was watching her. 'I'll explain all this in a moment,' she said. 'But first, why not make yourself comfortable? I have a proposition to put to you which you might find interesting. Please ... do sit down.'

She had clearly prepared for this interview: two small wooden cups and a jug stood on the table with a bench positioned nearby. As Jenna seated herself, Margery Jourdemayne poured small beer into both cups then she, too, sat down.

'Now,' she said again, 'I expect you're wondering what this is about?'

'Well, yes, mistress,' said Jenna, 'I am. I hope it has nothing to do with the standard of my work.'

'No, not in a critical sense,' said Margery. 'In fact, my husband often tells me that you are quite the best dairymaid he has ever employed.' Jenna felt a rush of pleasure at that and hoped her cheeks weren't burning.

'But I think you're wasting your time.' Her words immediately wiped the smile off Jenna's face.

'Oh, I'm sorry, mistress. But ... I ... I rather enjoy working in the dairy. Did you want me to work elsewhere on the farm?'

'No. I don't want you to work on the farm: not at all.'

'You want me to leave?' Jenna's heart was thudding.

'No, I do not want you to leave. On the contrary. Look ...' Margery leaned forward, her elbows on the table, her cup cradled between her hands and her eyes fixed compellingly on Jenna's face. 'Women like us need to understand each other, we both have a little learning and we're both prepared to work hard. Now, I know you're a good worker because my husband keeps telling me you are, so you must be: he won't tolerate slovenliness. And I've seen the figures. Yes, yes,' she went on, putting her cup down, her hand on Jenna's arm now, to stop her interrupting, 'let me finish. Yes, I am able to read as much as I need to and I can construe the accounts as well as any other woman, or any man come to that. I have made it my business to learn.' She paused. 'You're not surprised?'

'No, not at all, mistress. But it's a rare thing.'

'Indeed. You know, you and I are probably the only two people on the entire farm who are able to read. William has a little learning, but not very much, though he's fairly good at reckoning. But he always used to rely on me to check his figures at the end of each month before he showed them to Abbot Harweden. He doesn't do that now, of course, since he has you working in the dairy, keeping the milk tallies. But, no, this has nothing to do with that.'

Jenna waited until Margery spoke again.

'Well now, Jenna, as you might have heard, I run a small enterprise of my own outside the farm and I'm pleased to say it has become very successful of late. In fact, I need an assistant to help me. Which is why I wanted to have this talk with you.'

Jenna hesitated. 'Were you thinking of me as an assistant, mistress?'

'Assistant, apprentice, call it what you will but, yes, that's exactly what I'm thinking.'

Jenna suddenly felt protective of William. She had so often seen him frown over a particularly difficult set of figures. Who would help him if she didn't?

'But … but that would mean Master Jourdemayne would have to find someone else to do the milk tallies.'

'He'll manage. He can go back to doing them himself until he can teach one of the others to replace you. I, on the other hand, need very specific help as a matter of urgency and it could take me a long time to find someone – a woman – with your precise qualities. Up until now, I have been able to manage on my own, but these days I find Her Grace the Duchess of Gloucester is making more and more demands on my time and I cannot let her down. That would be most disloyal.'

'No, of course not, mistress. You wouldn't want to do that.'

Jenna didn't know what to think. This had come as a great surprise. On the one hand, Mistress Jourdemayne was telling her how good a dairymaid she was and, on the other, she was suggesting that she should leave the dairy. But Jenna didn't want to leave the dairy.

'I ... I don't know what to say, mistress,' she said, hesitating.

'Then say you'll give it a try,' said Margery. 'Look ... let me give you an idea of what I do, let me show you some of the things I make, creams, ointments and the like.' She rose from the table and went to the shelves, taking down half a dozen phials and jars. Setting them down in front of Jenna, she took her seat again.

'Here,' she said, picking up a small flask of greenish liquid, 'this is an infusion of nettle seeds in vinegar. It does wonders for dandruff. And this? Well, this is Hungary Water, simply made with rosemary, but it's critical to use exact quantities in its preparation. Now, this is tooth powder but beware, because this ...' she held up a small pot full of what looked like white dust, 'this is powdered cyclamen root to whiten the face. No good mixing those two up: they look exactly the same but they do quite different things. So they have to be labelled because it's crucial that you can identify which is which. That is why I couldn't take on an assistant who could neither read nor write. You can do both and that's a rare talent. Your abilities could take you a long way. You don't have to work your fingers to the bone in a dairy for the rest of your life.'

Jenna hesitated, buying time. 'It all looks very complicated, mistress. I don't think I could ever learn it all.'

'On the contrary, I think you could. Of course, you would need to start slowly as you learn the techniques involved, but I don't think it would take you long. You're an intelligent woman and it would save me having to do everything associated with the business. Then, later on perhaps, you could keep account for me, or perhaps ...', and here she paused, 'perhaps you would prefer to come up to the palace with me to help me sell my wares.'

'The palace! Oh, but, Mistress Jourdemayne, I couldn't! I would have to wear fine clothes to go up to the palace. And I have none.'

'Not yet perhaps, but nothing is impossible. I have a fardel of cloth I bought at St Bartholomew's Fair. That was last year but the cloth is still perfectly good. It wouldn't take long to make you a very fine kirtle.'

Jenna paused, mildly shocked. She needed a moment to take it all in. The few clothes she possessed had been bought at second hand from the fripperer in Newton Abbot and now Mistress Jourdemayne was talking about a brand-new kirtle. How things had changed! She was being offered the chance of a lifetime, an opportunity which was given to few. She would be working in a scrupulously clean environment and given the chance of wearing pretty clothes. Even going to the palace, perhaps, and mingling with beautiful ladies and grand gentlemen. She might even catch a glimpse of the King himself!

Margery Jourdemayne was smiling at her, reading her thoughts as she took in the possibilities she was being offered.

'So, would you like to try it for a few weeks?'

Jenna hesitated. 'No. No, thank you, mistress. Really, I can't. I'd be letting the Master down. He really needs us all in the dairy. There's such a lot of work to do.'

'Oh, don't worry about Master Jourdemayne,' said Margery, waving her hand airily, as though brushing away a fly. 'I'll settle it with him. He'll be perfectly agreeable to you doing it for part of the time.'

Given this assurance, Jenna didn't hesitate. 'Then yes, mistress, I would like to try it very much. As long as you're sure the Master will agree. And thank you for considering me.' Then she paused uncertainly. 'Would I still be sleeping over the brewhouse? I don't think young Kitty would forgive me if I went away and left her.'

'Yes. My plan is that you'll be working here in the farmhouse every day, in this room, not in that freezing cold dairy. But you'll still be sleeping in the dormitory with the other women, so Kitty needn't worry. She hasn't seen the last of you. Though I don't know why you concern yourself with the child.

There are hundreds like her.'

'I've become fond of her, that's all. She hasn't had a very happy life.'

Margery shrugged. She didn't much care about the bond of affection between Jenna and the little orphan. She was only too pleased to have found an obviously intelligent apprentice who could read sufficiently well to follow a recipe and was capable of reckoning; an attractive woman, neither too young nor too old, who was sufficiently pretty to please her aristocratic male clients without alienating the ladies of the court, making them aware of their own deficiencies. And she had the smooth, unmarked skin which was often typical of dairymaids – but the ladies would be quite ready to believe it was entirely thanks to her regular use of Margery's face cream. That would be good for business.

Jenna's voice interrupted her thoughts. 'Perhaps, mistress, I could start the day in the dairy, rather than let the Master down. Then, when you need help, I could come up here to lend a hand and learn a little more about your skills.'

Margery stood, gathering up the two wooden cups on the table. 'Very well,' she said, 'we'll try it like that for a while. But only so long as you don't tire yourself too much. You dare not make mistakes if you're working for me.'

'I'll do my very best, mistress,' Jenna promised. 'And if it gets to be too much, perhaps one of the other girls can take over my work at the dairy.'

'Good,' said Margery. 'Then that's what we'll do.' She intended to make the work so irresistible that Jenna would never want to go back to the dairy. She'd square it with William and he'd soon forget the girl.

'Out of sight, out of mind.'

Though she muttered the words under her breath, it was nevertheless Margery's fervent hope.

Part Two

Apprentice

Get wisdom, get understanding ... Forsake her not, and she shall preserve thee: love her, and she shall keep thee.

Proverbs 4:5-6

CHAPTER EIGHT

July 1436

'The Abbot didn't want to tell me he suffered from piles!' said William a week or so later, as he and Robin Fairweather sat on a bench outside the Thames-side tavern at the sign of The Swan, watching the setting sun and enjoying a relaxing mug of ale together after the day's work. He laughed. 'As if I couldn't guess! He had a face as long as a fiddle.'

'Painful things, piles,' agreed Robin. 'Or so they tell me. Mercifully, I've never suffered from them. So Margery has a fail-safe cure, has she?'

'She does seem to have a gift for making preparations which have the desired effect.'

'A clever woman, your wife.'

William paused before responding. 'Yes,' he said. 'Sometimes a bit too clever.'

Robin's eyebrows rose questioningly. 'Do I detect a note of marital discontent?'

'To be honest with you, I could do with a bit more help from her,' William admitted. 'She's a capable woman; she's got every attribute needed to be a good wife.'

'But?'

'But she's spending more and more time with her fine clients up at the palace, getting fancy ideas. Margery's changed, Robin.'

'Oh, surely not that much!'

'Well, she doesn't seem to want to have anything to do with the farm any more. Won't settle for what she's got. Between you and me, things haven't been the same between us since I got her bailed out of that bit of bother six years ago, after she'd got mixed up with those clergymen, Virley and Ashwell.'

'You'd think she'd have been grateful for that.'

'She doesn't seem to be. And, God knows, it cost enough. But she never used to be like this, not when we were first married. She liked me well enough in those days.'

'Perhaps she married you thinking she could change you somehow, to get you round to her way of thinking. A lot of women do that, they tell me. A daft idea.'

'Yes, it is, isn't it? Then again, perhaps I'm too set in my ways.'

''Nothing wrong with you, William. You're a good man.' He looked thoughtful for a moment. 'Is she making plenty of money with this enterprise of hers?'

'So she says. Not that I ever see any of it. She says she's saving for our future. She thinks we should have land of our own, rather than being at the beck and call of the monastery for our living. My brother Robert has his own farm in Acton. Margery thinks I should have one, too.'

'So, if she's spending so much time up at the palace, how are you managing? Who is baking? Brewing? Cleaning? Cooking? Generally running the place?'

'Oh, we get by,' said William, noncommittally, 'we manage.' He didn't add that he was beginning to rely more and more on the help which was unstintingly given by Jenna and always with good grace.

Robin might have been reading his mind. 'Tell me,' he said, 'how is Jenna Harding getting on? I was thinking about her only the other day. A pleasant woman. Attractive, too. It's nigh on a year since she came up with our drove from Devon and I've hardly seen her since.'

'She seems well,' said William. 'In fact, she's settled in nicely. All right, I'll be honest, she's a great help. She gets on well with the other girls, keeps an eye on the younger ones. She's persuaded me to buy four dozen more hens. She runs the dairy for me, she's even come up with a new recipe for sheep's cheese, just because I mentioned that the Abbot wants to try it. And she's always willing to take a turn at … well, anything, really.'

'She'll make some man a great wife one day,' said Robin, 'particularly if she's as good in bed as she is at all those other things.'

William nodded, feeling his face begin to flush a dark red. He often thought along broadly the same lines. His friend looked at him shrewdly.

'William,' he said, 'are you sure you don't want to tell me something? Believe me, I can be the very soul of discretion and I'm hardly likely to blurt out your secret to all and sundry. I was never a blabbermouth. '

'Oh, it's … it's nothing. Really.'

'Come on, William. It's Jenna, isn't it? That's why you've gone as coy as a milkmaid.'

William sighed heavily. 'There's nothing to be gained by talking about it,' he said. 'It's my cross to bear. It's just that I can't get her out of my mind. She just arrived here, with you, looking for work. I know nothing about her, she just shuts up like an oyster when anyone asks about her previous life. She won't tell anyone about herself, not anyone. And yet I want to know everything about her, why she came here, what drove her out of Devon – made her leave her home and the good job she had …'

'And, above all, you want to know whether there's a man lurking somewhere in the story, yes?' Robin's eyes never left his friend's face.

'Yes, that more than anything,' said William.

'You're in love with her, aren't you, you old dog!'

'Something like that,' William said, nodding his head slowly and reaching for his tankard. He took a deep draught of ale and wiped his mouth on the back of his wrist. 'Yes, I am in love with her, God help me.'

***

There was something about Roger Bolingbroke that made the Duchess of Gloucester want to laugh and yet the last thing she wanted to do was hurt his feelings. He was a gentle creature but the sight of him always reminded her of a timid creature bending down to look more closely at something, much like an animal she had seen illustrated in one of Humphrey's books, perhaps *The Travels of Sir John Mandeville*, she couldn't quite remember which: her husband had so many books. But she did remember the creature was called a *jarraf* or something like that. Bolingbroke, a tall, gaunt man with a stooped back, had an extraordinarily long neck and seemed to peer down benignly from a great height, his precious spectacles perched on the bridge of his pointed nose.

He was very proud of the spectacles: they had been made in Southwark by a resourceful craftsman who had copied the Florentine design. To protect them from damage, Bolingbroke kept them in a little padded leather bag suspended from his belt so they were always conveniently to hand. He freely admitted he would never have been able to afford to buy anything so precious had he still been trying to eke out a living as a Magister at the University of Oxford. But since his appointment to the household of the Duke of Gloucester, such a wondrous thing as a pair of spectacles was within his grasp. He was deeply grateful.

Humphrey, himself a man of considerable learning, was anxious to surround himself with knowledgeable, cultured men who would always be available for debate or discussion. To this end, he had appointed Roger Bolingbroke to the position of personal clerk to Her Grace the Duchess. Bolingbroke was delighted by this, since his Oxford students were often tardy in paying him the modest fees he charged them for their education. Far better to work in the service of a patron, especially one as wealthy as the Duke of Gloucester. A priest by training and profession, Bolingbroke would have preferred to serve his patron in the capacity of personal chaplain but that position was already held by John Hume, a rather belligerent man who was nevertheless a highly respected canon of both Hereford and St Asaph.

So Bolingbroke contented himself with the more modest position and in many ways this suited him very well, allowing him ample time to pursue his own academic interests. The job itself could hardly be described as arduous, in fact he attended Her Grace only once a day, usually after the mid-day dinner, for a private meeting in order to assist her with her correspondence.

'Was there anything you wished me to write for you today, Your Grace?' he asked now, laying out parchment and ink. 'Might I assist you with a letter to His Grace the Duke, perhaps, now that he has left for France?'

'It is possibly a little early for that, Magister, the Duke has only been gone a matter of days. Perhaps we would do better to write to him when there will be more news from home to give him.'

'Does he expect to be gone for long, Your Grace?'

'I hope not. He said he expects to expedite his duties in France without undue effort. With God's help, of course,' she added, crossing herself, 'though, according to the horoscope that Canon Southwell cast for my husband before he left, all the signs and portents point towards a great success in Calais and an early return home.'

'*Deo volente,*' agreed Bolingbroke. 'It seems the Duke clearly deserves his excellent reputation as a military leader, my Lady. Not that I have much understanding of these things.'

'You don't need to understand them, Magister,' said Eleanor, smiling. 'Your expertise lies in your knowledge of astronomy and astrology and my husband values such knowledge very highly.'

'As you say, Your Grace, he does. And he can easily hold his own in discussing these subjects with us. In fact…'

'Yes, Magister?'

'In fact, Your Grace, your noble husband did tell me before he left for France last week that if his commitments and responsibilities would permit such a thing, then he would try his best to locate a specific scientific instrument which would help me in my work.'

'Indeed? I know nothing of this.'

'Of course, it may not have been possible. He will have many responsibilities … leading the army … that sort of thing … though I don't know exactly what that entails. But I imagine he would have messengers and other minions who would be able to hunt out such things as these on his behalf…'

'Such things as what, Magister?'

'Well, His Grace did say he would do his best to find an astrolabe. There are very fine scientific instruments being made in Paris at present, from what I understand...'

'An astrolabe?' Eleanor had heard of such a thing, but was not exactly sure what it was. 'Is that to do with stars?'

'Indeed, Your Grace, the word is derived from the Greek. How perspicacious of you! That is exactly what it is.'

Roger Bolingbroke was often surprised by Eleanor. She gave the impression that she was a rather silly woman, obsessed with fashion and self-aggrandisement, but he suspected that under those elaborate headdresses, the jewelled cauls or the padded hennins, lay the shrewd mind of a woman who knew exactly what she wanted and would learn anything she needed to help her achieve her ends. The Duke was a cultured, well-read man; the Duchess made sure she could talk to him on his own level, or something very close to it. Bolingbroke respected that.

What he understood less well was the depth of Her Grace's single-minded motivation. She leaned forward, her face alert and interested. 'I very much hope, Master Bolingbroke, that my husband will succeed in acquiring this wonderful instrument. Tell me, exactly what does it do?'

Bolingbroke's eyes squinted excitedly behind the lenses of his spectacles. 'It's difficult to know where to begin an exact explanation, Your Grace, though if you wish to learn about it at your leisure, you would be wise to acquire a copy of a treatise on the subject which Master Geoffrey Chaucer wrote some forty years ago for his young son, Lewis. It seems the boy was anxious to learn how to use one. Sadly, the treatise is incomplete: Master Chaucer's intention was to write it in five sections, but he only completed two of them. The remaining three are sketches of what he intended.'

'A pity,' said Eleanor. 'But two-fifths of a treatise is better than none.'

Bolingbroke was all enthusiasm. Never had he had such a charming, intelligent, interested pupil. 'Of course,' he went on, 'should your husband, the Duke, be fortunate enough to find an appropriate astrolabe in France, one designed for this latitude, then I shall be delighted to demonstrate it to you myself and explain it in detail.'

'What might you use it for?'

'For calculating many, many things, Your Grace. An astrolabe enables the user to tell with accuracy the positions of celestial bodies, the sun, the stars and planets. Naturally, navigators make much use of it for this reason, but it is also invaluable to mathematicians, as well as to astronomers and astrologers. For example, it can help greatly in casting horoscopes...'

'Horoscopes?' Eleanor interrupted, suddenly more interested. 'Could you cast more accurate horoscopes by using this ... this astrolabe? Could you do that for me?'

'Indeed, Your Grace. But I would need to know a little more about you than I do at present, for example, your date of birth.'

'Oh, that need not be a secret, Magister, at least, not if it is to be used to cast my horoscope. In fact, my birthday happens to be very soon, at the end of next month. Should my husband return from Calais in good time – and I pray he will – I plan to combine a birthday party with a wonderful welcome home for His Grace at La Pleasaunce, our manor at Greenwich.'

'Delightful, Your Grace, I'm sure.'

'It will be a joyous occasion, of course, a time of relaxation and celebration. And that is very appropriate since my husband's own birthday occurs not long after mine, in September. If things go according to my plan,' she went on confidingly, 'I'm hoping to persuade His Highness the King to make the river journey to Greenwich so that he can join us!'

Bolingbroke's face lit up. 'The King, eh? What an honour! I'm told His Highness believes that a good education provides the foundation for a rewarding life. It must please him greatly that you and His Grace the Duke set such a good example in this regard.'

'It's kind of you to say so, Magister. After all, the ink of the scholar's pen is as crucial to a civilised society as the blood of the martyr.'

The little homily tripped easily off Eleanor's tongue: it was not a personal philosophy of hers, just something she had once heard Humphrey say. Bolingbroke stood, open-mouthed for a moment. She had astounded him yet again.

'Quite so, Your Grace, quite so. And for that reason it would give me great pleasure if, when I have finished writing it, you would permit me to dedicate my most recent book to you. Would you be so kind as to allow that?'

'Why, of course, Magister! I should be delighted and I look forward to reading it. What is the subject of your book?'

'Geomancy, Your Grace.'

'Geomancy! How … interesting.'

'Yes, isn't it?' Bolingbroke enthused. 'It is so important that new buildings should be sited in the most auspicious places for the ultimate good of those who will use them and live in them. Geomancy is crucial in this regard. I feel very strongly about it. Don't you agree, Your Grace?'

'Er, yes, of course,' said Eleanor, her smile not quite reaching her eyes.

'Then dare I cherish the hope that you will enjoy reading the book? I confess, Your Grace, it would have been twice as difficult to write were it not for the new spectacles. My academic work is very much easier now I'm able to see so much better.'

'No doubt that will save His Grace a fortune on candles.'

She was pleased to have a book of any kind dedicated to her, though she would have preferred it to be one of chivalric romance.

***

Jenna's new shoe had rubbed a blister on the back of her heel and she would gladly have given the price of the pair to be able to change them for her comfortable old alderwood clogs. Not that she had paid for the shoes. They, together with the clean linen coif she wore and her modest kirtle of blue broadcloth, had been provided by Mistress Jourdemayne. Margery stood next to her in the ante-room outside the Duchess Eleanor's private withdrawing room and glanced sideways at her. Jenna was anxiously chewing her lip.

'She won't eat you!' Margery said, nudging her.

'I'm sorry,' said Jenna, 'but I can't help it. I'm terribly

nervous. I've never met a real Duchess before.'

Straight-faced, Margery whispered, 'Just try to imagine her with no clothes on.'

Jenna gasped. 'I couldn't do that! She's the wife of a Duke!'

'Women are all the same under the skin. We all want the same, need the same things. It's only down to the difference in circumstances.'

The door to the Duchess's room opened and her maid came out.

'Her Grace is ready to see you,' she announced, then she added in a quiet voice, 'you'd better have something interesting to show her. She was with Magister Bolingbroke and Canon Southwell. That's why you had to wait. It's more than my life's worth to interrupt her when she's with those two.'

'We can always come back –' Margery began, but Sarah gave her a conspiratorial wink.

'They've gone, now,' she said, 'and she's not too bad today. So if there's something you want, I'd strike while the iron is hot, if I were you.'

'Enter!'

Hearing the note of authority in the Duchess's voice, Jenna thought her heart would stop in her chest. Now she was really going to see the famous Duchess of Gloucester, the most important woman in the country. Suddenly, she would have given anything at all to be anywhere else in England, even back in Kingskerswell.

'Good afternoon, Your Grace,' Margery was saying as they entered the room. 'I trust you're well.'

'Well enough, thank you, Margery,' said the Duchess, 'though my tooth still troubles me occasionally. And who have we here?'

'My new assistant, Your Grace,' said Margery. 'May I present Mistress Jenna Harding?'

Jenna was grateful for the opportunity to curtsey. Margery had spent some considerable time in teaching her how to drop down elegantly, one foot behind the other, and how to bow her head low in front of the Duchess.

'Get up child, and let me see your face.' As Jenna rose to her feet, the Duchess looked at her more closely. 'Ah, not so much a child. You're older than I first took you to be.'

The Duchess, too, appeared older than Jenna had imagined. There were fine lines around her eyes and some strands of grey in the dark hair which was just visible under the ornate crispinette on her head.

'I didn't want to employ some young chit of a girl, Your Grace,' said Margery. 'Anyone whom I entrust with the interests of my clients has to reliable and mature. It wouldn't do to have some silly little assistant who would make mistakes in her reckoning and couldn't read a recipe.'

'You can read, can you?' The Duchess sounded surprised.

'Yes, a little, my Lady.'

'A little, Your Grace,' Eleanor corrected her. 'That's a rather unusual thing, isn't it? And where did you learn to read?'

'Oh, I don't read well, my ... er ... Your Grace,' Jenna stuttered nervously, 'just a few words, mostly in Latin. Parson Middleton ... he was our parson back home ... taught us the alphabet so that we could read a little of the Bible.'

'Your parson, you say. Yes, of course. He would have taught you to read the scriptures. How interesting. My husband, the Duke, is very keen that everyone should learn to read, as is his nephew, the King. Of course, that is impossible: books are far too expensive for most people.'

Jenna didn't know whether she was expected to say anything in reply and was grateful when Margery stepped in.

'Jenna is quite skilled and quick to learn. She will be able to look after the business when I have to be elsewhere.'

The Duchess ignored her. 'You have a very fine skin,' she observed, looking intently at Jenna. 'I can't see a single pock mark. Do you use any of your mistress's preparations?'

'She is devoted to my marigold face cream,' said Margery swiftly, before Jenna could open her mouth. 'I tested the new recipe on her before presenting it to you, Your Grace. As you can see, it has had an astonishing effect. That is the reason why I wanted to see you. I thought you would be interested in trying it for yourself.'

Jenna's jaw dropped. Margery had never let her anywhere

near the marigold face cream other than to package it. She had certainly never tested it on her. That was a blatant lie, though the telling of it seemed not to bother Margery in the slightest. Still talking, she had hold of Jenna's chin and was turning her head from side to side so that her flawless complexion caught the light.

'You will observe, Your Grace, the fine texture and colour of the skin, the slight translucence and, rather surprisingly, an amazing lack of wrinkles for a woman who is ... how shall I put it? Not exactly in the first flush of youth. That is entirely due to my marigold face cream.'

Margery's face betrayed nothing. Astounded at the entirely false claim her mistress had made, Jenna, her chin still held rigid between Margery's thumb and forefinger, swivelled her eyes from one face to the other as both women peered at her, examining her skin very closely. She had always had a good skin, it was not uncommon in dairymaids, but she knew better than to say so.

'Where are you from?' the Duchess demanded to know as Margery finally released Jenna's chin. 'What is your accent?'

'I am from Kingskerswell in the county of Devon, Your Grace.'

'Kingskerswell?' The Duchess thought for a moment. 'I've heard that name before. Is that not the seat of the Dynhams? Not far from Exeter? I know Sir John Dynham, I have met him. He accompanied the Duke on his campaign in Calais. Yes, that's right. Sir John provided the army with several men-at-arms and a large company of archers. The Duke was very grateful to him. Well, well. What a small world we live in. Kingskerswell. It's an unusual name.'

'That's because the manor often reverted to the King in times gone by, Your Grace, for the lack of heirs to inherit it.'

Jenna almost jumped out of her skin when Margery gave her a hard, warning pinch in the skin above her elbow. Glancing at her, Jenna could see Margery's bland, fixed smile as she faced the Duchess. Yes, of course, she should never have mentioned heirs or the lack of them, not to the Duchess. She knew what the situation was. She could have kicked herself. 'Of course,' she added hurriedly, 'the Dynhams also own the manor of Nutwell.'

'Yes, yes, but it's Kingskerswell that interests me particularly. There's something in the back of my mind … why does it make me think about teeth?'

'Teeth?' Margery interrupted, laughing nervously. 'Teeth! Well, I can't imagine why that should be, Your Grace.'

'I … I think I know why, Your Grace,' said Jenna, deeply relieved that her careless reference to a lack of heirs to the Dynhams' manorial estates appeared to have escaped the Duchess's notice. 'Perhaps Sir John Dynham mentioned St Apollonia, who is honoured with a fine window of stained glass in the parish church.'

'Oh, yes! St Apollonia, yes, of course, that's it. Yes, Sir John did mention that, now I come to think of it. It must have been in response to something I said about my troublesome tooth. I'm afraid I talk about it rather too often.' The Duchess gave a little laugh and the tension went out of the situation. 'St Apollonia. Of course. That's it. I frequently pray to the dear saint to bring me relief from the toothache.'

Margery turned to Jenna. 'Do you, perhaps, know someone who could intercede with the saint on the Duchess's behalf?'

'I … er … well, I'm not sure Mistress. Perhaps Parson Middleton…'

'No, there is no need to bother your Parson Middleton. When I need relief from the pain, Mistress Jourdemayne's tincture works perfectly well for the moment. But perhaps that is something we might think about one day.'

She turned away now and began to address herself to Margery. 'For the moment, Margery, before I bid you good afternoon, I'd like you to arrange to deliver a consignment of the new marigold face cream to me as soon as possible, within the week, before my husband and I leave for La Pleasaunce.'

'Certainly, Your Grace. In the meantime, I will leave this jar of it with you and Jenna will make the delivery in a few days.'

Jenna was listening to this exchange without really hearing it. All she could think of was that Margery Jourdemayne was a liar, a woman who was prepared to tell the most blatant of lies for the benefit of her business interests.

The Duchess was waving her hand imperiously. The interview was clearly at an end. Jenna and Margery both curtseyed very low to their royal client.

***

'All up!' the cry went out and William pulled the skiff around quickly. He was no great oarsman, but needs must for Swan Upping. It was one of his responsibilities and swans were valuable creatures, so a record had to kept of their numbers. This was the best time of year to do it, when the cygnets were still young and easy to handle, though the parent swans could give a man a very nasty peck if he wasn't careful. A nest had been spotted on shore and it was time to count the inhabitants.

The Manor of Eye-next-Westminster bordered the waters of the Thames along so much of its length that the Monastery, as a major landowner, could claim ownership of the swans that nested on its banks. Abbot Harweden was rightly proud of these stately, feathered status symbols and was anxious to have them counted and marked to identify them as Monastery property.

Though he complained gruffly about having to undertake this annual chore, William really quite looked forward to it. It always happened, along the entire length of the river, on a specific day in the third week of July so the weather was almost invariably kind to the Swan Uppers and, after the essential work of the farm had been attended to, the estate workers who were not manning the boats strolled down to the river in holiday mood and crowded along the shore. Now they watched as half a dozen skiffs slowly manoeuvred towards the swans' nest, forming a circle around it from which neither the cob nor the pen nor any of their cygnets could escape.

It was all very new to Jenna. She had never seen Swan Upping before and, standing on the bank where she had a good view of what was happening, she was having the necessity for it solemnly explained to her by Kitty.

'It looks awfully cruel, doesn't it, Jenna? But you mustn't worry because it's all right really,' she explained. 'The baby swans just have to have nicks cut in their beaks so everybody knows who they belong to. It doesn't hurt them.'

'But didn't you say they all belong to the King?'

'Well, yes, most of them do, but special people like Abbot Harweden are allowed to have some swans. That's why Master Jourdemayne has to count them for him.'

'Why? Can't Abbot Harweden count?' asked Jenna, teasing.

'Yes, of course he can count! He's probably very good at counting.' Kitty was all indignation until she realised Jenna was joking. 'Oh, Jenna! Abbot Harweden is ever so clever at all sorts of things, but he's very busy. And Tom the Shepherd said he'd heard the Abbot wasn't very well. He's got a pain in his belly. But the swans still have to be counted.'

'I've never tasted swan,' Jenna mused. 'I wonder what it tastes like. Have you ever eaten swan, Kitty?

'No, of course I haven't. It's only very important people who can have swans for their dinner. And you mustn't steal them or steal their eggs.'

'I wasn't intending to,' said Jenna, watching in fascination as William shipped his oars and reached out of the skiff. He made a huge lunge for a big swan which suddenly reared up out of the water, flapping its wings and hissing angrily. Almost losing his footing, William grabbed the bird from behind and managed to haul it into the boat. He held it, still struggling and hissing, while Gilbert the Carpenter tied its legs together to hobble it and prevent it escaping. Wading thigh-deep through the water, Gilbert then lugged the bird towards the shore where he set it down on the bank to be counted and marked along with the others already there. Together in a row, the white, adult birds with their downy brown cygnets in front of them, quietened down, seeming resigned to whatever fate awaited them.

It had been quite an entertainment and Jenna smiled down at Kitty, to share the moment with her. But Kitty was nowhere to be seen.

'Kitty!' Jenna called. 'Kitty! Where are you? Hawys, have you seen Kitty anywhere?'

'She was here a moment ago,' said Hawys. 'She won't have gone far.'

Jenna felt uneasy. Kitty wasn't a stupid child, but Jenna

didn't like to think of her going too near the water. It wasn't that she was unused to water, she was learning to wash her clothes in it from time to time just like everyone else, but it was probably quite cold, despite the July heat and, if it was thigh-deep for Gilbert the Carpenter, then it would be waist-deep for Kitty. Anxiously, Jenna moved further up the river bank where she could get a better view of the whole stretch of water.

And then she saw her, just a little way off to the right, crouching on some stones at the water's edge. Her wayward hair had escaped its ribbon and was dangling in the river as she bent over something with rapt attention. Jenna called out to her.

'Kitty! Kitty, be careful. Come away from the water.'

'Oh, Jenna! Come quickly. Come and help me. I've caught one of the babies!'

Kitty had something in her hands and, as she turned to beckon to Jenna, so a fluffy brown ball fell from her grasp to the surface of the water, righted itself and started swimming furiously away from her, towards the middle of the river.

'No, Kitty! Let it go. Let it go. You'll never reach it!'

Kitty was engrossed in trying to catch the little creature.

'Kitty! Kitty! Come back!'

Kitty had waded into the water, her hands cupped in front of her in an attempt to reach the cygnet when she stumbled, lost her footing and fell headlong with a scream, her arms flailing above her head.

Without stopping to think, Jenna scrambled towards the water, looking around wildly for help, but no one seemed to have heard Kitty's screams.

'William! William!' Desperation lent volume to Jenna's voice and, in calling to him, she instinctively used the name she had for him in her private thoughts. No more 'Master Jourdemayne': he was William, the man she needed.

'William! For God's sake, William!'

Hearing his name, William turned in the boat and saw the little girl floundering helplessly, trying to find her footing but unable to right herself and nearly out of her depth. He grabbed an oar and shoved it hard against the bank to give more impetus to the skiff then began to row strongly towards the spot where

Kitty was in the water, screaming loudly, with Jenna wading out towards her. By now, several people on the riverbank were crowding down towards the water's edge, craning their necks to see.

'Don't panic, Kitty, I'm coming. Kitty, don't scream!' The water felt like heavy syrup around Jenna's legs and she tried to pull her skirt up and away from it. From the other direction, William was rowing towards them as though the eternal repose of his soul depended on it.

The child was still struggling to regain her footing but failing miserably when William brought the skiff around behind her. He shipped the oars, leaned out and caught her around the waist, pulling her strongly towards him. Kitty was crying and coughing up river water as he hauled her into the skiff just as he had hauled in the big white swan a few moments earlier. When Jenna reached the skiff, Kitty was lying on her back in the bottom of the boat with William kneeling over her.

'Turn her,' Jenna ordered, 'let her cough until she has got rid of all the water from her mouth.'

William managed to turn Kitty on to her side where she retched and coughed while Jenna, standing waist-deep in the river, reached out over the side of the skiff, to rub her back, soothing and calming her. 'Hush, Kittymouse, you're all right now. You're safe, my dove. We've got you safe. Just relax, there's a good girl. Hush, hush, Kittymouse. Hush now.'

'Well,' said William, leaning back on his haunches, 'that was nearly very nasty indeed. What on earth was she doing in the river?'

'Trying to catch a cygnet, I think, to help the Swan Uppers,' said Jenna, close to tears. 'Thank God you were here, William. I don't know what I would have done if…'

She realised she'd called him William without thinking.

'Oh, I'm sorry, master!' Her hand flew to her mouth. 'I didn't mean … that is … I'm so sorry, I shouldn't have been so familiar.'

He shook his head slowly before replying. 'Oh, Jenna, please. Let's not pretend. William is my name and I would be very pleased and proud if that is what you would call me.' He watched her as she continued massaging Kitty's back in silence, broken only by the child's distraught sniffling. When she looked up at him, he said, 'But you know, don't you? You must know how I feel.'

Jenna looked away again, confused. Her mouth was pulling involuntarily at the corners and she was in the grip of an emotion she couldn't name. She didn't know whether she wanted to smile or weep. There were certainly tears in her eyes, but her heart was thudding slowly with something that felt very akin to elation. She hardly trusted herself to speak.

'Yes. Yes, I do know,' she said quietly. 'Thank you. Thank you ... William. But I don't think ...' she looked down at Kitty, 'I don't think we should be talking like this. Not here. Not in front of –' She broke off as Gilbert the Carpenter waded up to the prow of the boat, to see if he could help.

The sniffling and retching on the floor of the skiff had subsided into a quiet sobbing as, with infinite gentleness, William lifted up the soaking, shivering Kitty and handed her to Gilbert, who took her weight.

'There, there, girl,' Gilbert muttered, comforting her, 'we'll soon have you home. Soon have you nice and dry.' He began wading back towards the shore, cradling Kitty in his strong arms. Jenna trailed close behind them through the water while William anxiously watched the little cavalcade.

At a safe distance from the boat, a fluffy brown cygnet regarded the scene with evident interest.

CHAPTER NINE

August 1436

The atmosphere in the scriptorium in the north cloister of the Westminster monastery was one of quiet industry, the silence broken only by the droning voice of a monk who stood behind a lectern in one corner, reading aloud from the writings of St Benedict. At each of the ten carrels in the big room monks in dark habits, their tonsured heads bent over their work, were illustrating and copying manuscripts for use in psalters, missals, books of hours and bibles.

The materials they needed for their work were provided by John Virley, who ensured a steady supply of vellum, parchment, quills, coloured inks and gold leaf. When the work was done, he would then collect the pages of manuscript which the monks so painstakingly produced and collate them correctly before taking them away to Walbrook to be bound and covered. It was a service he provided for several of London's monasteries, nunneries and priories.

Virley was an intelligent, educated man who could well have realised his early ambitions within the church had it not been for two things: he was reluctant to forgo the pleasures of the flesh and commit himself to taking holy orders and then, some six years previously, he had been plunged into disgrace. He had earnestly repented his sins at the time and was granted absolution. Nevertheless he hadn't returned to the monastic life.

One thing he knew with absolute certainty was that he would not overreach himself ever again nor crave a position above his station in life. And though it pleased him to be at liberty to consort with women, he would never again have anything to do with any women who might, by any stretch of the imagination, be accused of witchcraft: women like Margery Jourdemayne.

It was thanks to the woman he still thought of as the Witch of Eye that he and his colleague, Friar John Ashwell, had spent many months incarcerated in the dungeons beneath Windsor Castle. Ashwell, a gentle friar of the Order of the Holy Cross, was an affable man, inclined to believe the best of everyone. He had introduced John Virley to Margery Jourdemayne, a woman skilled in the use and preparation of herbs. Virley had been charmed to meet her. In truth, he had been quite smitten with her.

Judged by any yardstick, Margery was an attractive woman, fair-haired and small-waisted. But the most attractive thing about her was her enthusiasm, her desire to learn from both the friar and the cleric, two men whose education and scholarship were vastly superior to hers. She was eager to know about the rudiments of mathematics, about reading, writing and improving her vocabulary. Wanting to learn everything she could, with her quick mind and natural intelligence she made an able pupil, absorbing knowledge from her willing teachers as a cloth might soak up spilt milk. Though she resisted John Virley's physical overtures, she made her admiration for both men quite plain and they were flattered by her attention; they never questioned the wisdom of associating with her.

Margery's contribution to their mutual pool of knowledge was the skill with plants that she had learned from years of assisting her own mother. She imparted age-old secrets of how each plant might best be used for the healing of ailments. She showed them which medicinal herbs would improve the health of the eyes, the belly, the chest, skin and nails and every other part of the body, as well as which plants fought infectious diseases or eased the pains of childbirth. They in turn taught her what they knew of astrology, showing her how to identify celestial bodies in the night sky. They explained how it was possible to cast horoscopes and predict the future by observing the positions of the stars in their individual orbits, then marrying these observations with what was known about astral influences at the time of a person's birth.

That was their undoing. Margery, thrilled by her association with men of learning, had been unable to resist boasting to her neighbours in Westminster and to her husband's family in Acton about her eminent friends. Nobody was ever quite sure how the King's Council got to know of the association between the three, but the Westminster community was a small one, representing the full spectrum of society from the highest nobility at the palace to the humblest farm labourers on the monastery's Eye estate, so it could have been anyone. Whoever it was, some blabbermouth reported the unusual fact that a woman of low social standing was consorting with men of learning.

The members of the Royal Council, ever mindful of the dangers posed to the person of the young King by sorcerers, enchanters, necromancers and soothsayers, were very alarmed to learn of Margery Jourdemayne's connection with Ashwell and Virley. They immediately demanded the arrest of all three, on the assumption that if any respectable clerics willingly associated with a so-called 'wise woman' who was the wife of a mere cowherd, then she must be a sorceress who had them in her thrall. Margery was called a 'python enchantress' by her accusers and though in pleading her case at her trial she used all the long words she had so recently learned, they impressed no one and did nothing to save her. In the chill of a November morning, the three alleged sorcerers were taken into custody and imprisoned.

John Virley well remembered that long, harsh winter in the dungeons underneath Windsor Castle. He remembered the numbing cold, the dirt and discomfort, the rats, the greasy, inedible food. He vowed then that one day someone would pay for those lost months in his life. He hadn't been guilty of anything more sinful than consorting with the wrong people. No, the wrong *person*. The friar was an inoffensive soul, but the same could not be said for the Witch of Eye. Virley swore that one day he'd have his revenge on her.

In the following May, the three miscreants were taken to back to Westminster, this time to appear before an ecclesiastical court. Examined again on charges of sorcery, Friar Ashwell and John Virley were first reminded of their duties and responsibilities as men of the church and then discharged. They were required to sign a bond, which prohibited them from indulging in any further activities of this kind. They were both only too pleased to do so.

Margery Jourdemayne was also made to give her word that she would refrain from sorcerous activity. She was further warned that should she ever violate the law again, she would be shown no mercy and would suffer the most severe punishment. It helped her cause, Virley recalled, that her husband was among a group of men who managed to raise the sum of twenty pounds between them, to provide recognisance on her behalf.

He hadn't seen her since then, nor had he any wish to. He had even avoided contact with Friar Ashwell, though he'd heard that the friar had accurately forecast a lunar eclipse, a blood moon, a year after his sojourn in the Windsor Castle dungeons. Virley was pleased to know that Ashwell had not abandoned his interest in astronomy, but did sincerely hope his old friend practised his science in a more circumspect way these days.

For his part, Virley kept a very low profile and minded his own business. He'd had enough imprisonment for one lifetime though memories of it were fading, particularly when he was out in the fresh air and plying his trade in and among the many religious foundations in the city of London on a pleasant, sunny afternoon like this.

He couldn't mistake the rotund figure of the man walking towards him: the portly priest was a familiar figure in Westminster.

'Canon Southwell,' he greeted him. 'Well met! A good afternoon to you, sir.'

Southwell couldn't avoid the man. He had often seen Virley in and around the cloisters at Westminster, distributing supplies of ink and parchment, keeping the intellectual wheels of the monastery turning with quiet efficiency. Since Virley was not a person of any great significance, Southwell had never had much to do with him, but he couldn't pretend he didn't know him.

'Master Virley, is it not? And what brings you here to the fair parish of St Stephen Walbrook this fine day?'

'The necessity to have a manuscript bound' said Virley. 'There are some very well-established leather workers near the tannery. They have the best choice of fine-quality leathers for book binding and they're very reliable. And not too costly.'

'A significant book?' asked Southwell.

'A treatise,' said Virley, 'and, yes, most significant. It is a copy of Master Geoffrey Chaucer's treatise on the astrolabe, God rest his soul.' John Virley closed his eyes briefly and crossed himself before continuing. 'Not recent, of course, but it is an excellent treatise, from what I understand, if not entirely complete. Though I have not had the opportunity of reading it myself.'

'And for whom has it been copied?'

'For Her Grace, the Duchess of Gloucester. She is a woman with an enquiring mind, it seems. I understand Her Grace insisted it should be copied by the monks of Westminster as a matter of urgency, since she wishes to read it before her husband returns from France. Several of the brothers postponed their work on other projects in order to comply with Her Grace's request.'

As he spoke, he was opening a scrip, which he wore suspended across his body, the better to protect its contents from pickpockets and cutpurses. 'Look,' he said, extracting the leather-bound manuscript, 'see how beautifully it has been finished, feel the quality of the binding.'

'Indeed,' said Southwell, taking the treatise into his hands and examining it closely. 'A thing of great beauty. The quality of the tooled design on the leather is quite exquisite. It's for Her Grace the Duchess of Gloucester, you say?'

'It is. I shall deliver it to the palace tomorrow.'

Here was an opportunity. Canon Southwell had no pressing business here in Walbrook this afternoon. As Rector of St Stephen's, the purpose of his visit had been to check on the progress of work to rebuild the parish church, after which he had planned to purchase a fine fat capon from a merchant he knew in the Poultry. But he had already visited the church and he could forego the pleasure of a tasty spit-roasted fowl for tomorrow's dinner and make do with something else.

'As it happens, Master Virley,' he said, 'I am bound for the palace this very afternoon. In fact, I have an appointment to see

Her Grace on a private matter. Perhaps you know I have the honour to advise her as her personal physician. I could deliver the treatise into her own hand. Would you like me to undertake that small errand for you? It's no trouble at all, and I'm sure you want to get back to Westminster at your earliest convenience.'

It would have been churlish to refuse Southwell's offer and yet Virley knew it was his own responsibility to deliver the book. Still, there was the very attractive widow of a cordwainer who lived a few streets away, quite close to the church of St Benet Sherehog, whom he hadn't visited for some time, and he didn't have to get back to Westminster immediately. So, why not?

'I would, indeed, be grateful to you, Canon Southwell.'

'It will be my pleasure, Master Virley.'

***

'She wants to see you.'

'And by "she", I assume you mean Her Grace the Duchess of Gloucester, do you, Sarah?'

'Yes.'

'Then accord Her Grace her correct title!'

'I'm sorry. I meant no disrespect.' Sarah, the Duchess's maid, was becoming more than a little tired of trudging back and forth between the Palace of Westminster and the farmhouse at the Manor of Eye. It seemed as though the Duchess couldn't do anything these days without consulting Margery Jourdemayne.

'And what does Her Grace wish to see me about?' inquired Margery.

'I dunno,' said Sarah. 'She sent you this.'

Margery had little time for a slipshod attitude, whether it occurred in a person's speech, dress or behaviour. She snatched the folded piece of parchment from the maid's hand.

'It's a list of what she wants, I expect.'

It wasn't. Eleanor had sent a short note in her own handwriting. It was unsigned and there was no salutation.

Please attend me immediately. I have something I wish to

discuss. Send S. back with two bottles of Hungary water so as not to arouse suspicions.

'Can you read, Sarah?' asked Margery.

'No, mistress,' said Sarah.

'You should learn,' said Margery. 'You'd be surprised how useful you'd find it.'

'No, mistress. It's too difficult.'

'That depends on how much you want to learn. I'd recommend you to try,' said Margery, knowing that Sarah never would. She moved a simmering pot of broth off the kitchen fire and dropped the note onto the glowing embers beneath it, watching until she saw it burn: you couldn't be too careful. She replaced the pot and wiped her hands on her apron.

'Now, the Duchess needs some Hungary water. Wait there while I fetch some and when you get back to the palace, tell Her Grace I will attend her within the hour.'

It pleased Margery greatly to realise that she was becoming so indispensable to the Duchess Eleanor, but when she discovered why she had been summoned to see her, she was both surprised and gratified. Her Grace was beaming delightedly.

'Have you heard the news, Margery?'

'The news, Your Grace?'

'Yes, Margery, the most wonderful news!' The Duchess clapped her hands together in delight. 'My noble husband has raised the siege of Calais and he is on his way home!'

Margery answered Eleanor's beaming smile with a smile of her own. 'Why, that's excellent news, Your Grace! You must be very happy at the prospect of his return.'

'What do you imagine, Margery! Of course I am delighted. More delighted than I can say. He has amply proved his point that France should remain under English rule.'

'So Calais is still an English town.'

'Indeed it is. And the King is so grateful that he is to hold a ceremony at Westminster to welcome his uncle home.'

'Most appropriate, Your Grace –'

'And then, Margery, I have decided that we will have a party at La Pleasaunce to celebrate both my husband's success in

France and my own birthday!'

Margery was beginning to wonder why she'd been sent for with such urgency. 'Would you like me to help you in any way with your plans for your celebrations?' she asked.

'Yes, Margery, I would. I want you to be among the guests at the party at La Pleasaunce, to … er … mingle with them.'

'How kind!' beamed Margery. 'Thank you. I'm very grateful to Your Grace…'

Eleanor cut across her. 'I've got a job for you to do.'

'A job, Your Grace? What kind of job?'

Eleanor hesitated for a moment, as though she was deciding exactly how to explain to Margery what she had in mind. 'I want you to use your womanly wiles,' she said. 'Not a word to anyone but … I suppose what I have in mind for you is a little bit of, well … sophisticated spying.' Margery waited while Eleanor appeared to think carefully how to phrase what she was about to say. 'As I said,' she went on, 'the party will be in celebration of two things – my birthday, and His Grace the Duke's return from the very successful siege of Calais.'

'Both are greatly worth celebrating, Your Grace.'

'Indeed. I plan to invite His Highness the King to join us on this occasion. His uncle, my husband, is so very fond of him. I will also invite his mother, the Dowager Queen Catherine, who is presently at court. That's a rare thing these days and I would dearly love to know the reason why she stays away so much.'

'The King himself, Your Grace? And the Dowager Queen? And am I really to be among the guests?'

'No, of course not, Margery. Don't be ridiculous. I want you to be among those *serving* the guests. You know the kind of thing. Someone who circulates constantly with glasses of wine or with sweetmeats on a platter, making sure there's no one with an empty goblet, no one in need of a chair, mopping up spills, calling for a footman if one is needed. You know the kind of thing.'

'Why, yes, Your Grace. But … what of the usual staff? Won't they resent my presence?'

'I don't care whether they do or not. No, I want you to be there for a very specific purpose.' Margery raised her eyebrows.

'I want you to listen,' the Duchess went on. 'Just that. I want you to glean any information you can, keep your ears open for gossip, the kind of thing people say to each other in unguarded moments when they imagine that servants are deaf. It is stupidity itself to do that, of course. Something I've never done.'

'There is wisdom in what you say, Your Grace. But what if I hear nothing of interest?'

Eleanor shrugged. 'Then you hear nothing. However, I am curious to know why the Dowager Queen stays away from court for long periods at a time. So make sure you look after her needs before anyone else's. As I say, don't worry if you learn nothing. I'd rather you were honest with me and tell me that you heard no gossip at all than that you should make something up, just to satisfy me.'

'I would never dream of doing that, Your Grace. You know I would never lie to you.'

'Good. So, I can count on your help?'

'Always, Your Grace. I will report back anything I hear or see.'

'And you will keep any such information to yourself, of course.'

'Naturally, Your Grace. I shall be the very soul of discretion.'

***

The hero's welcome home was an occasion of pure triumph for Eleanor. Londoners had always liked and admired the man they called Good Duke Humphrey and his popularity had never waned. Sitting beside him in the carriage, smiling and waving at the cheering crowds, Eleanor basked in his reflected glory as they rode together at the centre of a procession through cobbled streets thronged with well-wishers. Running alongside, bare-footed urchins whooped and shouted, trying to keep up with the horses, excited by all the pomp and ceremony accorded to the Duke and his cohorts as they rode out of the city and towards Westminster where a grand reception awaited them.

Descending from the carriage outside the palace, Eleanor

placed her hand on her husband's arm, straightened her back and tilted her chin as they turned towards the entrance. She thrived on the adulation, the applause, the shouts of the crowd as they lined the route to welcome their favourite back from France. News of his triumph had spread like wildfire among Londoners and by now, everybody knew that the Duke of Gloucester had raised the siege of Calais and the French town was safely back in English hands. This was how it should be. The French should know their place and be kept in it. Hurrah for England and St George! Long live Good Duke Humphrey!

Inside the palace, with the shouts of the crowd still ringing in her ears, Eleanor's eyes sparkled as she moved towards the throne room with her husband, her hand still resting lightly on his arm. Gathered there, and politely applauding their arrival, were the noble lords of England and their ladies, bejewelled and sumptuously attired, who were attending the King's reception for his uncle.

On the ornate throne at the end of the room sat King Henry himself. As the Duke and Duchess entered the throne room, he rose and slowly descended the steps from the dais to stand, waiting until they reached him.

'Your Graces are both most welcome,' he said in a monotone. 'My noble Lord Uncle, I speak not only for myself but for the whole of England when I say that our gratitude knows no bounds. The whole country is deeply in your debt. You are, indeed, the bravest and noblest of Lords.'

The Duke bowed from the waist and Eleanor executed a faultlessly elegant curtsey: she had been rehearsing it for a week. When the Duke straightened up, the King came towards him, stood on tiptoe, then reached up to kiss his uncle gravely on each cheek before extending his hand to help his aunt to her feet.

She gave him her most dazzling smile, but there was no answering smile in the King's eyes. They were as blank as buttons. He was looking very dispirited today, she thought. He had delivered his short speech of welcome mechanically, with little enthusiasm, and he seemed to have a few more pimples than usual. He looked whey-faced, rather unwell. It was such a pity he couldn't be a bit more charismatic, more popular with his people, like his uncle.

Suddenly, incongruously, she remembered the astrolabe. In all the fuss and excitement of the last few days, she had completely forgotten to ask Humphrey whether he had managed to find one in France. She really must ask him, and at the first opportunity. Canon Southwell had brought her Master Chaucer's treatise as soon as the monks had finished copying it, effusively denying that he had gone to any trouble at all in doing so, and she had been able to skim quickly through it while she awaited her husband's homecoming. By now she had an idea what an astrolabe looked like and understood at least something of the instrument's capabilities. A little tutoring from Magister Bolingbroke would teach her more of what could be done with it.

She wondered what fate it would reveal to her. Perhaps she could learn to use the astrolabe herself, to foretell her own future, her husband's future, even the King's future. After all, if her husband's nephew was as unwell as he looked today, maybe he really was ill. And if that was the case, well, she should at least prepare herself mentally for the prospect that Humphrey might one day inherit the throne, together with all the implications of what that meant for her.

It was possible. He was next in line, after all.

CHAPTER TEN

Early September 1436

It wasn't so much a meeting of superior ecclesiastical intellects, as a reunion of old friends. Cardinal Henry Beaufort sat at one side of the table in the elegant dining hall of the Bishop of Winchester's London residence at Southwark and his friend John Kemp, Archbishop of York, sat opposite him. Between them lay the remains of a roast pheasant with golden leeks and onions boiled in saffron. The two men were now thoroughly enjoying a cherry pottage.

'It's good to be back in England,' said Archbishop Kemp. 'I seem to spend my life going back and forth to France and I don't think French food is all it's made out to be. Give me a good English roast any day of the week.'

'Which is your favourite?' asked Henry Beaufort.

'Oh, I don't have a preference: beef, venison, pheasant, pork, chicken. Really, I don't mind which.'

'Not mutton?'

'I always find mutton a little greasy,' said Kemp, 'unless it has a sprig or two of mint in the pan.'

'I agree,' said Beaufort, wiping his mouth with his napkin. 'The best part of a sheep is its fleece. That's worth a good deal of money these days.'

Kemp gave his friend a shrewd look. 'And you should know that better than most people,' he said.

Beaufort smiled without rancour. It was a well-known fact that he, the richest man in England, had made a substantial part of his wealth off the back of the humble sheep, he wouldn't deny it.

'Yes,' he agreed, 'the wool trade has done well by me.'

He didn't need to elaborate. After spooning up the last

delicious morsel of cherry pottage, he laid his napkin on the table and leaned back in his chair.

'Have you ever noticed, John, that we always use the English name for the live animal but, more often than not, we'll use the French word for the meat or the cooked dish?'

'Do we?'

'Yes. Think about it: pig becomes pork when it's cooked, a cow becomes beef, deer becomes venison, sheep becomes mutton, chicken becomes poultry. Odd, isn't it?'

'It's not the only odd thing about France. I'm heartily sick of the sight of the place, though I suppose I shall have to keep going back there until we've achieved some measure of peace.' Archbishop Kemp had been a member of several peace delegations in recent years, including the previous year's disastrous Congress of Arras.

'Hasten the day,' Beaufort agreed. 'We both set so much store by achieving success at Arras, didn't we?'

'We did, as did every other member of that delegation. And its failure only served to bring Philip of Burgundy closer to his kinsman and support the Dauphin's claim to call himself King Charles VII of France.'

'We'd be well rid of the damned country.'

'Well, Henry, don't tell your nephew Gloucester that! Especially not now that he seems to have brought Calais into line. He's like the cat that got the cream, from what I understand. The party he and his wife threw a week ago was the most ostentatious gathering the country has ever seen.'

'So vulgar!' said Henry Beaufort with disdain. 'And so typical of the pair of them, Humphrey and that dreadful woman he married. I take it you didn't receive an invitation to join them?'

The Archbishop gave a short laugh. 'What do you think, Henry? And I wouldn't have gone anywhere near La Pleasaunce, even if I had. I'd have made any excuse not to go. His Highness the King was there though, or so I'm told.'

'He seems quite fond of his awful aunt, though I can't imagine why. But then, she's always trying to butter up him, make him laugh. Such unbecoming behaviour.'

John Kemp smiled. 'Well, he's still just a boy, of course. Probably misses his mother when she's away from court so much, though I'm told she was with him at the Gloucesters' party, so I expect they both enjoyed it.'

Beaufort was silent for a moment. He knew exactly why the Dowager Queen Catherine chose to stay away from court but he wasn't at all sure how much Archbishop Kemp knew about her situation. If Kemp was aware of Catherine's clandestine marriage to Owen Tudor, he had never said anything about it, not even to his old friend. Best let sleeping dogs lie.

'You could be right,' was all he said.

***

Roger Bolingbroke could hardly contain himself as he watched his employer unwrap an object which had been packed with considerable care. The astrolabe had been delivered from France while the Duke and Duchess were in La Pleasaunce. Now that they had returned to Westminster, he would see the wondrous instrument at last. He had spent most of the night on tenterhooks of excitement and was awake before dawn.

'Of course,' said the Duke of Gloucester, 'I have come across several of these before and, indeed, I have read Master Chaucer's treatise on the subject, as far as it goes. Incomplete, but very interesting.'

'I think the Duchess was a little disappointed to realise the work was unfinished, Your Grace. Perhaps I should not have recommended it to her. I'm so sorry.' For some reason, Roger Bolingbroke seemed to feel the need to apologise on behalf of Geoffrey Chaucer. The Duke of Gloucester had that effect on him.

They were sitting together at a fine oak table in the Library at the Palace of Westminster. It was an elegant room, its high walls hung with tapestries, a fire of pine logs piled high in the hearth and, on the floor, a finely knotted woollen carpet of Persian origin, brought back from the Crusades. Bolingbroke was not accustomed to such luxury. What impressed him most was the number of books which almost filled the shelves along one wall. There must have been a hundred or more, sumptuously bound volumes which had belonged to the late King Henry V or his brother John of Bedford and were now owned by Humphrey of Gloucester. How wonderful, Bolingbroke thought, to be rich enough to afford such an extensive library.

The Duke removed the last of the wrapping cloths and set a brass astrolabe on the table alongside a decanter of Burgundy wine. Gloucester's wineglass stood beside it, half empty: Magister Bolingbroke had yet to touch his. Adjusting the spectacles on the narrow bridge of his nose, Bolingbroke was almost sniffing the air in anticipation.

'Here it is,' said the Duke, 'an astrolabe made in the Paris workshop of Jean Fusoris, the greatest manufacturer in France. It has been made according to my instruction that it should be designed specifically for use at this latitude, here in London. This astrolabe, Magister, is the best that money can buy.'

Once he had got over his initial, speechless wonder at the sight of the instrument, Bolingbroke was effusive in his thanks. 'It was most kind of you to remember your promise, Your Grace. I really did not expect that you would bring anything as fine as this back from France. It will help me immeasurably with my work. I don't know how I can ever repay you.'

'You must not think of repaying me, Magister,' said the Duke. 'Just use it to further your academic research. I will be happy enough with that.'

'I don't know how I would have managed to do any work at all if I had stayed in Oxford,' said Bolingbroke, 'I would never have been able to afford such a wonderful instrument as this. Neither would I have been able to buy my spectacles. You are most generous!'

Humphrey nodded and smiled condescendingly. It pleased him to think that England's finest scholars were indebted to him. The expense of housing them under his roof or entertaining them at his table or even buying them spectacles was nothing compared with the way they enhanced his reputation. It was a fine thing to be a patron of such men. After all, his grandfather, the great John of Gaunt, had been Chaucer's patron: it was a tradition well worth maintaining. He looked up as the door opened.

'Ah, there you are, Nell, my sweet,' he rose to greet his wife as she entered the room accompanied by two of her ladies. 'I'm glad you could join us. Magister Bolingbroke is inspecting his new astrolabe and says he's delighted with it. I'm sure he can't wait to demonstrate it to you.'

Gloucester was pleased at the interruption: enthusing over fine scientific instruments was all very well, but there were other things in a man's life.

'My Lord,' Eleanor gave her hand to Humphrey to be kissed and his lips lingered warm on her skin for a moment before his tongue probed between her fingers, making her smile. The significance of the covert gesture was not lost upon her, though the deed itself would have to wait until later. She turned to Bolingbroke.

'Good morning, Magister. So, this is the famous astrolabe. At last!'

Bolingbroke had risen to offer her his chair and she sat, her eyes widening as she looked at the astrolabe for the first time. It was an odd-looking instrument, the size of a pewter dinner plate, engraved with symbols around its outer rim. Eleanor could see that it actually consisted of five brass discs, each as thin as vellum, fretted with open work in places and highly polished. The discs, mounted one above the other, were held together with a pivoted pointer enabling each one to rotate freely and allowing the user to align the engraved symbols on each disc. On closer inspection, she saw that these symbols were letters of the alphabet, degrees of the compass, zodiac signs, the names of stars and planets, days of the week, months of the year, and equinoxes. Here too were all the saints' days and holy days. So much information! How would she ever learn how to use such a thing?

'It looks very difficult to understand, Magister,' she said.

'Not really, Your Grace. It's a matter of familiarity, and having a little knowledge of the spheres.'

Eleanor looked up as her maid, Sarah, slid quietly into the room through the half-opened door and whispered to one of her ladies.

'Yes, what is it?' Eleanor disliked interruptions.

The Lady Anne crossed the room and bent down to murmur something in Eleanor's ear.

'Very well, tell her I will receive her shortly,' Eleanor said, 'it will do her no harm to wait.' Then, turning once more to Bolingbroke and her husband, she added, 'I'm so sorry, I'm afraid I will have to leave you. Someone needs to see me as a matter of urgency. Well, Magister, it will take me some considerable time to master this instrument, but I certainly look forward to having my first tuition from you. Could we arrange it for next week, do you think?'

'I'm sure we can, Your Grace. I will arrange it with Canon Hume.' Bolingbroke bowed to Eleanor as she rose, took her fond leave of her husband and left the room, her ladies trailing behind her in an elegant swish of skirts.

Though Eleanor had not identified her visitor, Humphrey made the assumption that it was Margery Jourdemayne, since he knew she was one of the few people whom Eleanor would see without a prior appointment. The woman was always calling on his wife, pressing her to try this face cream or that hand lotion. Still, he didn't think it could do much harm – women would always want to buy creams and lotions and such things to enable them to attract and keep a man. He understood that well enough and he was glad Eleanor still wanted to please him. He considered himself fortunate among men, having an attractive wife to pleasure his body and men of science to stimulate his intellect. He resumed his seat next to Roger Bolingbroke.

'Now, Magister,' he said, 'where were we?'

**

The Duchess of Gloucester had been very surprised by the urgent tone of the Lady Anne's whispered message that Margery wanted to see her on a matter of great importance.

'You'd better have a good reason for this, Margery,' she said without preamble as the woman rose from her seat in the ante-room to the Duchess's private apartment. 'Why couldn't you wait until your appointment? I was in a meeting with His Grace the Duke and two of our advisers on important business.'

'I'm sorry to disturb you, Your Grace, but I have a good reason for doing so. This has been my first chance to see you since your return to Westminster. And I have discovered something very interesting I thought you should know.'

'Which is?'

'Well, if you remember, Your Grace, you asked me to attend your reception at La Pleasaunce and pay particular attention to the needs of the Dowager Queen Catherine.'

'Yes, yes, of course. So did you find out anything? Tell me. I need to know.'

Eleanor was becoming agitated now, standing a little too close to Margery, examining her face closely.

'As you instructed, Your Grace, I spent as much time as I could in waiting on her and she did ask me to find her a chair and a glass of wine when she said she was feeling faint. She was clearly very uncomfortable.'

'Well, yes, it was hot in that pavilion.'

'It wasn't merely the heat which was affecting her.' Margery paused, to gain the maximum impact for the statement she was about to make. 'Your Grace, the Dowager Queen Catherine is pregnant.'

'What!' The Duchess stood stock still, open-mouthed, astounded. 'Pregnant! How can she possibly have become pregnant?'

'Presumably, Your Grace, in much the same way as any other woman becomes pregnant.' Margery could have bitten her tongue – Her Grace's nerves were very raw on the subject of pregnancy, but fortunately she appeared not to have noticed the *faux pas*.

'Yes, but ... but by whom? Has she married while she's been away from court? Surely not! We'd have known. But then who ... not Edmund Beaufort ... there was a rumour. But no, it can't be, not now. He's in France. Besides, he's married to Eleanor Beauchamp and she's breeding like a rabbit by all accounts.' She looked stunned. 'Margery, how do you know that the Dowager Queen is pregnant? Did she tell you?'

'Oh, no, Your Grace. She didn't need to. I could tell by

looking at her. She was showing all the signs. Despite the cut of her gown I could see that she's … well, she's thick in the waist and there were shadows under her eyes. Her face was blotchy, too. It's always easy to tell, especially in the summer. Yes, I would say she has a baby due in about four months. I thought you should know.'

'Are you *absolutely* sure, Margery?'

'As sure as I can be, Your Grace. I would stake my reputation on it.'

'Dear God. I'll never be able to tell Humphrey.'

Eleanor slumped into a chair. She had never been so shocked in her life. She felt faint at the thought of what she had just heard: faint and sick to her stomach. Could this be true? If it was, then it changed everything. If the Dowager Queen was having a child, it would be the King's half-brother or sister. She needed to think carefully before she said a word to Humphrey, if indeed she could ever bring herself to tell him. His fury would know no bounds. She must think … think … think …

She needed time on her own, without Margery Jourdemayne or anyone else anywhere near her.

She waved her hand to dismiss Margery and then paused.

'Oh, Margery … there is something very important you must do for me.'

'Your Grace?'

'Find out who the father is.'

***

The party at La Pleasaunce was deemed to have been a huge success, attended by everyone who was anyone at the English court and graced by the presence of His Highness the King and his mother, the Dowager Queen Catherine. Half a dozen of Eleanor's ladies were still happily gossiping about it a week later, having gathered to spend the afternoon with the Duchess in her boudoir, taking light refreshments and listening with enjoyment while Eleanor sang to the accompaniment of the psaltery. She had a charming voice.

The delightful idyll was shattered when the door opened and the Duke of Gloucester stormed into the room, scattering his wife's ladies with no apology for disturbing them. Clutching their embroidery hoops, their musical instruments, poetry books and board games, they picked up their skirts and made a hasty retreat. His Grace clearly did not want them there. He had a face like thunder.

'Humphrey, whatever's wrong?' Eleanor's heart sank: her husband must have found out what she herself already half-knew.

'Wrong! What's wrong? I'll tell you what's damned well wrong. My late brother's bitch of a widow is wrong. The whole damned country is wrong! Everyone has been keeping me in the dark and I will not tolerate it! I will not be made a fool of!'

'Humphrey, Humphrey, calm down a little and tell me who you're talking about.'

'Who do you think I'm talking about? I said my late brother's bitch of a widow, didn't I? Well, that's who I meant. The sainted Catherine. The little French *vache* who pretends butter wouldn't melt between her soft thighs! That's who I'm talking about! The Dowager Queen Catherine!'

Eleanor was very alarmed. Her husband's handsome face was suffused with blood and beads of sweat stood out on his forehead.

'Come, Humphrey, please sit down and tell me what has happened.' Eleanor rose and went to the small occasional table against the wall where she always kept a tray with a flask of Burgundy wine and two goblets, in case he should call on her during the day. She poured a generous measure and handed it to him. She was even more alarmed when he shook his head in refusal and buried his face in his hands.

'I knew nothing about it!' he said. 'Nothing! There was a conspiracy of silence. No one told me!'

'Told you what?'

He took his hands away from his face and looked at her. 'She has married,' he said flatly. 'The Dowager Queen Catherine has married.'

Eleanor's hand was shaking violently. She put down the goblet very carefully then, tense as a bowstring, she perched herself on the edge of the seat next to her husband. So, it was true. She hadn't quite believed it. And she certainly hadn't been able to bring herself to tell her husband what Margery had told her: she would have been too terrified. But now, it seemed, he had found out for himself. Eleanor swallowed hard before she responded.

'Married? Who has she married? When? She can't possibly have married without your knowing … without the King's permission. She can't possibly be married.'

'Well, she is. It seems she has been married for a number of years. It must be the best-kept secret in the history of England.'

'But Edmund Beaufort has married Eleanor Beauchamp, so who …' she left the sentence unfinished.

'Oh, Edmund Beaufort has nothing to do with this. She must have let people assume she was interested in Beaufort as some sort of distraction.'

'So, who …' Again her question hung in the air.

'Does the name Owen Tudor mean anything to you?'

Eleanor stopped and thought. There was no one by that name at court. No one she knew of anyway. 'No,' she said. 'Is he some foreign dignitary?'

'Oh, he's foreign, all right. He's Welsh. One of those filthy, uncouth, war-mongering bastards from beyond the border. But he is certainly no dignitary. He's her servant. Her Clerk of the Wardrobe, no less.' Humphrey started laughing now. 'I ask you – a clerk on her household staff! And she has married him! Has she gone mad? She *must* have gone mad! She must have been screaming for a man – any man – to pleasure her. To satisfy her carnal appetites. I knew it. Like mother, like daughter – and her mother was an absolute slut. Queen Isabeau was the greatest whore in Europe!' His voice was rising, a note of hysteria in it.

'Humphrey!'

'Well, she was. Isabeau had her poor mad husband locked up and then hopped into bed with his brother, Louis. And Louis wasn't the only one. It's a fact. Everyone knows it. And, dear God, how many children did Isabeau have? Thirteen at the last count. She must have been screwing every night of the week!'

Eleanor turned her face away from her husband. He had

142

struck a raw nerve. 'Well, it doesn't sound as though *she* needed to wear mistletoe in her garter,' she said in a small voice.

Humphrey was suddenly contrite and he reached out to put his hand on her arm. 'Oh, I'm sorry, my sweet Nell,' he said. 'I shouldn't have said that. That's man's talk, soldier's talk. It has no place in a lady's boudoir. I'm so sorry.'

Eleanor managed a tight little smile as she gave her husband's hand a forgiving pat. There was a question she had to ask him but not just yet because she dreaded hearing the answer.

'It's all right, Humphrey,' she said. 'Try not to upset yourself any further. I'm sure there's something that can be done. There's a law against dowager queens re-marrying, isn't there?'

'There is,' said Humphrey. 'I got it through Parliament myself when I thought she was behaving like a dockyard cat on heat with young Edmund Beaufort. Yes, there most certainly is a law and it deals very harshly with any man who presumes to marry a dowager queen without the express permission of His Highness the King.'

'And the King knows nothing about this?'

'No. Yes. Oh … I don't know. I expect he does. Everyone seems to know about it. Except me, of course. It's a conspiracy, I tell you. I'll get Suffolk to deal with this Tudor fellow. He can send some of the big brutes in the royal guard to seize him and teach him a lesson he won't forget. The Welsh bastard can kick his heels in Newgate for a couple of months. That will cure him of his ardour!'

'Well, perhaps there's no great harm done as long as … as long as …' She hesitated. 'Humphrey, this … Tudor, and the Queen Catherine … his wife … do they have a child?'

There, the question was out.

'Oh, yes. A few. Well, I'm not sure how many, but there are certainly two boys. Five or six years old … I don't know – but that's how long it's been going on! They'll have to be put away, of course, while we decide what to do with them.'

'Put away?'

'Oh, you know, a convent or something like that. Not the Tower anyway.' He kissed her cheek. 'Poor, soft-hearted Nell. The little ones will come to no harm, if that's what you're worrying about.'

It was decidedly not what she was worrying about. Far from it. She couldn't give a tinker's damn what happened to the children. All she knew was that Queen Catherine had succeeded in giving birth to two sons, something she herself would have sold her soul to do. But more than that, the boys were the King's half-brothers and if anything should happen to him, it would not be difficult to establish that they were of the blood royal: they could even prove a threat to Humphrey's own claim to the throne. So, the further the children were sent away, the better. The King might forget about them; he could be quite absent-minded.

Humphrey would have to deal with the problem of the Queen's children. For Eleanor, it had now become imperative for her to find a way of giving her husband a son as a matter of extreme urgency. If anything should happen to the King, his heir must have a legitimate heir of his own, for the sake of the dynasty.

As soon as Humphrey had left the room and she was sure he was out of earshot, she picked up a little bell and rang it several times with increasing impatience. She paced the room, her hands clenched at her sides, her breath coming in short gasps until Sarah came hurrying into the room. Her face a mask of fury, Eleanor rounded on the girl, gripping her arm.

'Sarah,' she said, 'go to the Eye estate at once and get me Mistress Jourdemayne. Now. This instant. Bring her back with you. It is very, very urgent that she attends me immediately.'

As soon as her mistress's back was turned, Sarah rolled her eyes to the ceiling at the prospect of yet another trip to Eybury farmhouse.

CHAPTER ELEVEN

February 1437

Cardinal Henry Beaufort cherished his memories of the woman whose mortal remains were being laid to rest on a bitterly cold, grey morning. Harsh winter winds, blowing in off the leaden waters of the Thames, found their way under the great door of Westminster Abbey and cut like knives through even the warmest clothes: he felt grateful for his thick woollen hose and the sturdy leather boots on his feet, but his fingernails were blue with cold and his hands were almost too numb to hold his rosary.

The fact that he had never married did not mean he was not an admirer of women, far from it, and the Dowager Queen Catherine whose coffin now lay on a catafalque below the high altar was one woman for whom he had always had a great affection.

He first met her as a young bride when his nephew, King Henry V, brought her home to England after their wedding in France. He'd been instantly captivated by her beauty, her vitality and her quintessentially French charm. When custom dictated that her husband the King did not attend his wife's coronation, it had been Bishop Beaufort who had been her guide and mentor for the occasion. Only sixteen short years ago, on a February day nearly as cold as this one, the Princess Catherine de Valois had been crowned Queen of England by Archbishop Henry Chichele in a solemn, dignified ceremony here in the Abbey, enthroned no more than a yard or two away from where her coffin now lay. The irony of that brought a lump to his throat. But he also remembered the sheer pleasure of sitting on her right at the sumptuous banquet which followed the coronation, enchanted by her attempts to express herself in English and captivated by her delight at seeing the edible sweet subtleties which decorated the high table in her honour. It had been on that day that she had begun to call him 'My Lord Uncle' and though he had been awarded a Cardinalate since then, her name for him had always been one of his most cherished titles.

He doted on her and rejoiced when she gave birth to her husband's son and heir. When she was widowed so pitifully soon afterwards, he mourned with her and did his best to offer her comfort and solace. He even allowed himself the small hope that she might find consolation in the arms of his nephew, Edmund, though that wasn't to be. Nevertheless, they remained friends, even when she confided in him the potentially ruinous secret of her clandestine love for Owen Tudor. Seeing her from time to time in the years that followed, he rejoiced with her when she found happiness with the young Welshman and he patted their children's heads with avuncular pride. He kept Catherine's confidences for many years without ever once betraying her. She was delightful. He was beside himself with sorrow when she became another of the legion of women who had made the ultimate sacrifice in childbed. Life could be intolerably hard on women.

Seated near Cardinal Beaufort among the official mourners at the funeral were the Duke and Duchess of Gloucester. Eleanor knew it would be bone-chillingly cold in the Abbey, so she had given some considerable thought to the mourning weeds she would wear for the occasion. For warmth, she had ordered a cloak of fine black worsted to be lined with coney but edged with miniver, aware that soft white fur near the face was very becoming. Though she would do her best to give the impression that she was enduring great sorrow, she made sure the hennin on her head, richly embroidered with beads of Whitby jet, had a veil which could be drawn across to hide her face, should her mask of sadness begin to slip.

The royal mourners were seated close to the catafalque, which bore Queen Catherine's coffin. Though she tried hard not to look at it, Eleanor's eyes were inexorably drawn to the

Queen's funeral effigy, which lay on top of the coffin, a figure of hollowed-out wood, dressed simply in a square-necked red gown and with its hands joined in prayer. Wooden feet in gold-coloured slippers peeped out from under the hem of the gown and rested on a small carved lap dog. Under a jaunty coronet of base metal, a lifelike wig was nailed to the effigy's head, but its painted blue eyes were dull, devoid of any expression. It looked very unlike the real Catherine, whose shrouded body lay hidden inside the coffin, embalmed with sweet-smelling herbs and unguents to disguise the odour of decaying flesh.

Eleanor was disturbed by the death of an attractive, vibrant woman of her own age, lovely enough to have ensnared a king and charming enough to have enslaved a lover to warm the cold bed of her widowhood, a man with whom she then found a love deep and precious enough to run the risk of a secret marriage. Catherine's beauty had brought her great joy and excitement in her lifetime.

But no more. Death was the end of beauty, the end of opportunity, the end of love. Death was ugly and Eleanor would rather not be reminded of it.

The Queen's short life had not been without purpose: within two years of her first marriage, she had achieved all that was expected of her by producing a male heir to the English throne. Now, fifteen years later, a great scandal had emerged as it became known that the Queen had given birth to five other children, fathered by her lover Owen Tudor and born in secret. The first two children had been a girl then a disabled boy, neither of whom would have been any real threat to Eleanor's ambitions. But then there had been two more boys, Edmund and Jasper, now six and five years old respectively, both sturdily healthy and growing fast. The last child was the sickly girl who had died with her mother in childbed, that blood-soaked sphere of pain and anxiety which Eleanor both craved and dreaded in equal measure.

Duke Humphrey had ordered that the two healthy boys be dispatched like foundlings to the convent at Barking in Essex and put in the care of the Abbess. At least this meant they weren't being given the opportunity to charm anyone at court.

Eleanor prayed that their half-brother the King would forget their very existence. It was possible: he was often away in a daydream.

King Henry was here in the Abbey, of course, Queen Catherine was his mother after all. He had seen very little of her since graduating from the nursery to the schoolroom, but he was doing his best to control his obvious distress. Otherwise, this funeral ceremony was a sham, thought Eleanor. Apart from the immediate royal family, most members of the congregation were here in the Abbey because they thought they should be. Hardly anyone present had known Queen Catherine in her last years. Not even the Queen's husband, Owen Tudor, was there to mourn his wife: he had been incarcerated in Newgate jail since last October, at Humphrey's command.

It was just as well the whole dreary saga had come to its gloomy conclusion today. With luck, nothing more would be heard of the late Queen, her husband or her sons. *Requiescant in pace.*

Dry-eyed, but with respectfully bowed heads, the Duke and Duchess of Gloucester stood together as Abbot Harweden intoned the final prayer in the requiem mass. Standing behind them, Cardinal Beaufort felt a warm tear run down the crease alongside his cold nose and he wiped it away as Queen Catherine's soul was committed to its eternal salvation and her earthly remains to their final resting place in the vault of the Lady Chapel.

The Edward Bell in the tower began to ring out a single, desolate note.

***

Borne on the easterly wind, the sombre tolling of the bell could be heard faintly a mile away at Eybury farmhouse. Working at her table, Margery Jourdemayne well knew who was being buried today – indeed there could not have been many people who didn't know, since the royal court and the entire village of Westminster were still buzzing with gossip about the Dowager Queen's secret love affair with her Clerk of the Wardrobe, their covert marriage and the children whose existence few people had known about until very recently.

Standing opposite her mistress, Jenna crossed herself and prayed silently not only for the Queen but for Alice. She still remembered Alice in her prayers.

Before the intrusion of the Edward Bell, Jenna had been crossing off the items on a list then packing them carefully into a coffer on the table. 'The funeral bell sounds so sad,' she said. 'Poor woman. Do you know how old the Queen was, mistress?'

'She must have been about thirty-five or thirty-six. Around the same age as the Duchess Eleanor, I believe.'

'And did you ever see Her Highness?'

'I did on one occasion, last summer at Greenwich, during a reception at La Pleasaunce which the Duke was giving to celebrate the Duchess's birthday and his own victory at the siege of Calais.'

'Really? I didn't know you attended the Duchess at Greenwich.'

'I don't, normally, but she asked me to help with waiting on the guests. So, yes, I did see Queen Catherine on that one occasion. She was a very fine-looking woman.'

'But not one of your customers?'

'No, never that. She didn't need me to beautify her.'

Jenna looked down at the coffer she was packing: it was nearly full of Margery's expensive perfumes and beauty aids, among them toothpowder, brazilwood chips, tincture of myrrh, the marigold face cream, Carmelite water and a salve for the lips.

'Not like the Duchess of Gloucester, then,' she said.

Margery allowed herself a wicked grin.

'The Duchess of Gloucester is convinced she needs what I sell her and that suits me very well. As long as she wants the Duke in her bed and takes an interest in her appearance in order to keep him there, I will never be out of pocket. Though, to be truthful, she is a perfectly attractive-looking woman in her own right.'

Jenna made no comment. Her respect for her mistress had been dealt a serious blow when she realised that Margery Jourdemayne was a liar and she was still uncertain about the morality of what her mistress was doing and the excessive profit she made. It cost Margery very, very little to make lotions, tinctures, and creams on her farmhouse table. Her ingredients came from her own physic garden or from the wild hedgerows around the farm. St John's Wort, celandine, dandelions, thyme, elderflower, lavender, rosemary and many other plants all had their uses and Margery did a roaring trade with her face cream, made to a special recipe of her own which combined rose petals and beeswax. The alternative version she made for the exclusive use of the Duchess of Gloucester blended marigold flowers with the rose petals in combination with several other secret ingredients, including the root of the marsh mallow. It produced an even richer cream and now Her Grace would use nothing else.

What set Margery's preparations apart was the care she took in presenting her products for sale. Her creams were potted up into the prettiest little ceramic pots sealed with wax, while her lotions and tinctures were funnelled into elegant glass bottles with stoppers and finished off with bows of coloured ribbon. They were a joy to use and graced the dressing table in many an elegant lady's bedchamber. Margery bought her supply of combs, scissors, ear scoops, toothpicks and tweezers very cheaply from itinerant tinkers, then wrapped them carefully in leftover scraps of satin and lace from the royal sewing rooms and packaged them in individual small wicker baskets or boxes decorated with painted roses. These she sold on to the gentry, men and women, for ten times what she had paid the tinkers. She had no scruples about doing this: as she said, as long as people were vain, had faith in the efficacy of her products and enough money to pay the extortionate prices she charged, then they had only themselves to blame. Besides, she wanted the kind of life for William and herself that William's brother Robert and his wife enjoyed in nearby Acton – and if she waited for William to make money, then she would have to wait until hell froze.

'Her Grace has placed a large order this time,' Jenna observed, wrapping a tablet of fine Bristol soap. 'When does she want this delivered?'

'Last week! You know what she's like. Sarah is supposed to be collecting it this morning. She's late, though; she should have been here by now. How far are you from finishing it?'

'Nearly there, mistress. I just need to pot up one more jar of the special face cream.'

'Good,' Margery said. 'Sarah isn't normally late. She daren't be, she says, because Her Grace worries. She's constantly anxious and takes it out on her maid.'

'She's anxious? Why?'

Margery paused in the act of pounding spices in a mortar and considered her answer. 'She's starting to panic, poor soul. At her age, she's living on borrowed time. She's beginning to lose her looks, not to mention her chances of childbearing.'

Jenna continued her packing in silence for a moment, remembering what Old Mother Morwenna had once said.

'Could the fault lie with the Duke?' she asked.

'No. It can't possibly be the Duke's fault. He fathered at least two bastards long before he met her, and his daughter, Antigone, has just given him a grandson – so that probably makes the Duchess even more desperate. Her husband is a grandfather before he's a father – a legitimate one, that is. No wonder she's going mad with frustration.'

Margery put down her pestle and mortar and wiped her hands on her apron before asking, 'What makes you think it might be the Duke's fault?'

'Oh, it was just something our local wise woman once said to me, a long time ago back at home in Devon. I had a … well … I haven't told you, but I had a very unhappy marriage and my mother thought my husband was angry because he had no children. She had some idea that a child would make things better between us. But, as things were, I really didn't want to have his children.'

Margery had never encouraged Jenna to talk about her past and had been wise enough not to probe. But now that her new assistant had confided in her, she felt at liberty to be nosy.

'I can understand that,' she said in a conversational tone, 'and I tend to agree. Why go through all that agony if it doesn't achieve anything? And child-bearing is very aging. Once you start having children, you might as well bid farewell to opportunity. You know, I often think a woman's main problem is that she has both a womb and a brain. Society dictates that her womb is the more important of the two. But I'm not sure that's true.'

Jenna listened to this cynical viewpoint with disbelief. 'Really, mistress? But – surely it's a woman's place to bear children!'

'That's because women are the only ones who *can* bear children. If men could, imagine the fuss they'd make!'

Jenna laughed. 'So that will always keep us in our place.'

'It will. But just think, Jenna: Eve was the first to eat from the Tree of Knowledge, not Adam. The woman, not the man. So why can't women use their knowledge?'

'Eve was tempted by the Devil. What she did was evil,' Jenna protested, worried at having her beliefs challenged.

'And women have been made to pay for it ever since.' Margery picked up her pestle again and started pounding the contents of the mortar with renewed vigour. 'I can't see that knowledge is a bad thing for women. And any woman with half a grain of common sense knows she can run rings around a man ... and very often does!'

Jenna forced a smile, not wanting to become embroiled in an argument. 'Old Mother Morwenna said much the same thing. She said it could well be Jake's fault that I was barren, but I'd be a fool to tell him so.'

'That's the biggest insult to any man's pride. You were wise not to say anything about it.'

They had broached a subject of great interest to Margery, who wanted to explore every avenue in her quest to find a solution to the Duchess of Gloucester's predicament.

'Did the wise woman give you anything to help you conceive?' she asked.

'Oh, yes. But it looked so vile, I never took it.'

'And do you still have it?'

'Yes, I do. It was expensive – Mother Morwenna charged me half a groat for it, so I wasn't going to leave it behind in Devon.'

It had been nearly two years since Jenna had brought the brown liquid with her to Westminster. Perhaps it had curdled or dried up, she had never opened it so she had no way of knowing. But she had no need of it any more, not now that she no longer needed to please a husband. So perhaps she could make her money back by selling the bottle to Mistress Jourdemayne. And she could always find a use for half a groat.

Margery was watching her face, reading her mind.

'A penny for your thoughts,' she said. 'And a whole groat for your medicine if you're prepared to sell it to me. That's half as much again as what you paid for it. Quite a handsome profit!'

'Are you sure, mistress? It's quite old by now. It might have dried up!'

'Let's cross that bridge when we come to it. But importantly, Jenna, do you remember how Old Mother What's-her-name told you to take it? What dose she recommended?'

Jenna smiled. 'Morwenna,' she said. 'I'm fairly sure it was three times a day. Yes, that was it, over three consecutive days exactly half way between my menses.'

'Three times a day, over three consecutive days ...' Margery was repeating the words, committing them to memory, 'exactly half way between the menses. Well, that should be simple enough. So, will you sell it? You could buy a fardel of very pretty broadcloth and pair of shoes and you'd still have change from a groat.'

It didn't take Jenna long to give in to temptation. 'Thank you, mistress,' she said with a broad grin. 'I'll go and fetch it for you. It's in the dormitory.'

Margery felt pleased with herself. If the tincture was still usable, it shouldn't be too difficult to identify what was in it. And it was high time to try out something new on the Duchess. She felt for the small leather pouch she always wore at her waist. Aware it could make her a target for cutpurses, she kept it tightly closed at all times, its drawstring knotted securely and tied to her belt. The bulk of her money was elsewhere and she was most certainly not going to tell anyone where that was, but there were always a few loose coins in her pouch. She undid the drawstring now and counted out four silver pennies.

If Jenna's medicine did the trick, the investment of a groat would be nothing compared with the financial reward she could expect to receive from a grateful, pregnant Duchess. Perhaps she and William would be able to buy that farm rather sooner than she had planned.

***

Leaving the Abbey after the funeral, small groups of sombrely dressed people gathered outside the Chapter House. The King and other members of the royal family and their attendants were following Abbot Harweden in a subdued procession towards the monastery, where they had been invited to a funeral repast after the requiem mass. Those who had not been included in the invitation stood, awaiting their carriages, talking in muted voices, their breath a ghostly mist on the cold air. Cardinal Beaufort stood waiting with them, one foot tapping impatiently on the first step of the mounting block. Canon Southwell spotted him there and came bustling up, pink with pleasure at the opportunity of cornering him in a position where he was unlikely to move away.

'It was such a great pleasure to see you again, Your Grace, despite the sadness of the occasion,' he said, forced to step to one side when the Cardinal's valet approached and proceeded to help his master buckle on his sword under his heavy woollen cloak. 'I must say,' Southwell went on, standing on tiptoe and talking over the valet's shoulder, 'I thought Abbot Harweden conducted the service this morning with just the right degree of deference.'

'Deference? Deference to whom?' demanded Beaufort.

'Well, to His Highness the King and to you. And ... and of course, to His Grace the Duke of Gloucester,' said Southwell obsequiously.

Beaufort didn't like this plump pigeon of a parson any better now than he had a year ago when he'd been obliged to work with him in planning the Garter ceremony. 'Harweden knows he should defer only to Almighty God when he's conducting a requiem mass,' he said shortly, 'or any other mass, if it comes to that. You would do well, sir, to follow the King's example. His Highness made a gesture of great humility this morning when he insisted that every man in church should remove his sword, thereby demonstrating his own belief that the Almighty is greater than any mortal man. That is something we would all do well to remember when we are in God's house, whoever we are.'

There was an embarrassed pause as Southwell realised he'd said entirely the wrong thing, then the Cardinal went on, 'But we do have reason to be grateful to Abbot Harweden for providing the royal mourners with a good dinner. It's a pity I can't stay to partake of it.'

'A great pity, indeed,' agreed Southwell, 'there must be many demands on your time.'

He moved to one side to allow a groom to lead a large black stallion into position in front of the mounting block, holding its bridle while the Cardinal put his foot in the stirrup and swung himself over into the saddle like a man with little time to waste. As it happened, Beaufort had no engagements at all for the remainder of that day, but he would do anything to avoid sitting down to eat at the same table as his nephew Gloucester.

Southwell felt the need to get back into the Cardinal's good books again after his sacrilegious gaffe. 'So, fare you well, my Lord,' he said, stepping back smartly as the huge horse began tossing its mane and pawing the ground, 'and may Almighty God grant you a safe journey home.'

Beaufort curtly nodded his acknowledgement and pulled his horse's head around without another word, striking out for London Bridge and thence to Southwark, the men of his guard guiding their horses to close protectively around him for the journey.

Southwell watched them ride away then he turned and, smiling and inclining his head in greeting here and there as he went, made his way towards the refectory where the royal mourners had gathered for a warming glass of mulled wine as they waited for the meal to be served.

This was an impressive gathering of the English aristocracy and Southwell took a moment to assess his opportunities.

Hearing a tinkling laugh behind him, he turned to see the Duchess of Gloucester smiling delightedly as she extended her hand to be kissed by the elderly Lord Tiptoft. Southwell wasn't at all surprised to hear her laugh, he hadn't really expected her to be in the least bit saddened by the sombre mood of the occasion. He had been her personal physician and adviser for long enough to have a shrewd knowledge of what motivated Her Grace. Joining the fringes of the group, he waited until she noticed him.

'Canon Southwell!' That silvery voice. 'How are you?'

'I am well, thank you, Your Grace,' he replied with a bow as she came towards him. 'As are you, I trust? But we meet on a sad day and it is difficult, is it not, to be unmoved by this morning's requiem mass. It is a distressing occasion.'

The Duchess Eleanor re-arranged her expression. 'Dear Catherine,' she sighed, 'such a very great loss for all of us in the royal family, particularly for His Highness the King. He is so young, too young to have lost both his parents. It is as well for him that he has my husband to advise and protect him.'

'Indeed, Your Grace. The Duke of Gloucester is known to be a very considerate uncle to His Highness,' said Southwell. 'Everyone at court is aware of that.'

'What was that?' Duke Humphrey turned towards them. 'Someone mentioned my name?'

'I was saying, by your leave Your Grace, that you have proved yourself a loyal and caring protector of His Highness the King. It is a fact widely recognised at court.'

The Duke smiled and inclined his head in acknowledgement of the compliment, though he recognised it for what it was. He had never been able to warm to Canon Southwell and he couldn't really understand why Eleanor set such store by what he said. She had remarked only last week that Southwell had cast a profoundly auspicious horoscope for her and she had been very pleased by that. From what Humphrey knew of him, Southwell was much like any other churchman, well versed in the disciplines of theology, astrology and medicine, a man worthy of respect for his scholarship. But much as Humphrey admired a fine intellect and a sound education, that didn't mean he had to like the man. He turned away again.

Neatly snubbed, Southwell nevertheless smiled at the Duchess. 'And I'm sure the Duke relies heavily on you, Your Grace, for support in his care for the King.'

'We both have His Highness's welfare close to our hearts,' replied Eleanor with a wintry smile, beginning to move away. Aware that her husband had no great wish to talk to Southwell, she was a shade less inclined to continue her own conversation with him.

'Your Grace!' Southwell raised his voice slightly, then dropped it conspiratorially when she turned back to him. 'Your Grace, I have been talking to Master Bolingbroke – as you know, *your* welfare is what is very close to *our* hearts – and he tells me that he has recently been using the new astrolabe to make a particular study of your astral chart …'

Now he had Eleanor's full attention. She leaned towards him and whispered, 'He's using the astrolabe? Really? Are the stars particularly propitious for me at the moment?'

'It seems so, Your Grace. Master Bolingbroke wondered whether we three might have a meeting about it sometime next week so that we can check a few facts with you before we complete our study of your current astral influences.'

'Indeed, Canon Southwell. I look forward very much to hearing what you have to say. I will ask Canon Hume to arrange a meeting for us. I trust you would be prepared to travel south of the river for such a meeting? Master Bolingbroke will be going to Greenwich with our other staff when my husband and I return there in a few days.'

'Your Grace, it will be my pleasure to attend you there and I will count it no distance at all.'

'Thank you, Canon Southwell.' Eleanor turned away from him again to join another group of people where Duke Humphrey was the centre of attention, just as Abbot Harweden entered the room to summon his guests to take their seats in the upper chamber where the midday dinner was about to be served. Tantalising smells drifted up from the monastery kitchen and Southwell, thinking that, generally speaking, he had done a good morning's work, savoured his imminent reward.

The King was known to enjoy a dish of Alows of Beef. Southwell, too, was very partial to it and the evidence in his nostrils suggested that neats from the Eye estate had provided the main ingredient for yet another excellent meal.

CHAPTER TWELVE

July 1437

There had been some research to do before Margery was able to offer the new tincture to the Duchess. Trying her best to avoid what William saw as her duties on the farm, she had spent hours poring over her precious books in the hope of finding some clues about the formulation of the tincture. It was a time-consuming, difficult process because Latin had never been her strong suit. Someone like John Virley might be ready to help her, but she immediately rejected that idea. It would have been different if they had parted the best of friends after their last association, but they hadn't. Quite the opposite, in fact.

None of this studious activity had improved her relationship with her husband, but she couldn't run the risk of making her client ill. Margery's two-pronged objective was to help the Duchess conceive a child so that she herself could become the wife of a landowner when William bought his own farm. It was a long-term strategy. There was no use rushing things.

Her text books yielded very little information to help her so there was nothing for it but to try and work out the ingredients of Old Mother Morwenna's tincture for herself. Again, she opened the bottle and inspected it closely. There was nothing recognisable about it, in fact there was no aspect of it which looked at all familiar. She held it up to her nose. Curiously, it had no obvious, recognisable smell. She inserted her little finger into the neck of the bottle and, withdrawing it, looked at the liquid on her fingertip then licked at it with a cautious tongue. The taste was piquant, spicy, not at all unpleasant but impossible to identify.

This was outside her experience. Jenna had brought it with

her from Devon, so perhaps it came from some plant or herb which only grew in the south-west. Or might the decoction be derived from a seaweed? She was familiar with bladderwort but this might be something else. Was it samphire, perhaps? Impossible to obtain in Westminster though common enough on some sea shores. Or could it perhaps be Lady's Mantle? The root was known to stop all bleeding and aid conception but, try as she might, she couldn't get it to grow readily in her own physic garden.

The sound of the latch being lifted on the outside door to the farmhouse kitchen startled her. Then voices, men's voices, a calm female voice above the sound of loud wailing.

'Bring her in here.' That was Jenna. 'Put her down there on that bench. Careful! Keep her weight off that foot. I'll fetch the mistress, she'll know what to do.'

Hurriedly, Margery replaced the stopper, put the bottle of tincture back in a coffer and locked it before opening the door into the kitchen to see what was going on. Seth and Piers were struggling in from outside, carrying the Duchess of Gloucester's maid between them. Sarah's arms were around their necks and they lowered her down gently onto the bench near the fire. Her skirt was covered in mud up to her knees and she was crying piteously, in obvious distress. Jenna was trying to soothe her.

'Why, Sarah!' said Margery, closing the door to her own room. 'What on earth has happened to you?'

Sarah's sobs grew even louder.

'She fell, mistress,' said Seth. 'Slipped in some mud. Piers and me found her in the ditch. She couldn't move.'

'She's probably broken her leg,' said Piers, gloomily.

'No, she hasn't,' Jenna said briskly. 'You'd soon know if she had. But she's certainly turned badly on her ankle. It's very swollen already.'

'All right, I'll take charge of this,' said Margery, pushing up her sleeves. 'Thank you, boys, you can go back to your work now. I'm sure Sarah is very grateful to you for rescuing her.'

Sarah gulped her thanks, turning a pathetic, tear-stained face towards them as they left. At least she had stopped the caterwauling noise she'd been making when they brought her in. Jenna fetched a stool and propped Sarah's leg on it while her mistress gently removed the girl's hose and shoe. Examining the distorted, badly swollen ankle, Margery frowned and drew a sharp breath between her teeth.

'Yes, that's bad,' she said. 'Poor Sarah. I'm afraid you aren't going to be walking on that for at least a few weeks, possibly more.'

'But I've got to get back to Her Grace! She's in a foul temper and she'll be furious if I don't take the order back for her. She has to have everything in good time...'

'Don't be silly, child,' Margery interrupted. 'We don't know whether you've broken that ankle and there's no way of telling until I've brought the swelling down. Jenna, fetch me the arnica balm, please. It's on the third shelf, right-hand side.'

'The arnica, mistress? But I thought...'

'Just fetch it, Jenna. We'll worry about how it's to be paid for later. Besides, having Sarah injured in this way will be very inconvenient for the Duchess. We must do our best to cure her.'

It seemed most unreasonable to Jenna that Mistress Jourdemayne was more concerned about Her Grace's inconvenience than she was about Sarah's obvious pain. But in fact, a plan was forming in Margery's mind, a plan which depended very much on ensuring that Her Grace was *not* inconvenienced.

'Now, Sarah,' she said in a comforting tone as Jenna went off to fetch the balm, 'I'm going to make you a hot, sweet infusion of camomile to calm you down and relax you. And don't worry about the delivery.'

'But the Duchess...'

'Jenna can take Her Grace's order up to the palace. You certainly won't be able to walk. And I think it's better for you to stay here and let me look after you until you can put some weight on that foot, then we'll have to get someone to take you back to the palace on a cart.'

'But she'll kill me! You don't know her. When she's upset about something, she gets very angry and she takes it out on me. I must get back.'

'I think I know Her Grace quite well, Sarah,' said Margery,

pouring boiling water onto some dried camomile flowers. 'And she certainly won't be pleased if you can't walk. You wouldn't be much use to her, now would you?'

'But what –'

'Don't worry. Just leave it to me. Now, tell me, why is the Duchess so upset?'

'Oh, the palace is full of gossip. They've just heard the Duchess of Bedford has had a baby girl. She's to be called Elizabeth.'

'Don't you mean the Duke of Bedford's widow, Sarah? The Lady Jacquetta is no longer the Duchess of Bedford. She relinquished that title when she married Sir Richard Woodville. So it's hardly important that she's had a baby, especially a girl.'

'No, I know, mistress, but everyone is saying they hadn't been married a decent time before the baby came. It's disgusting, they're saying.'

Margery hid a smile. 'Yes, it is, isn't it?'

It was no wonder the Duchess of Gloucester was upset, she thought. Here was yet another woman who had produced a baby with the apparent ease of a cat having kittens. Margery would have to redouble her efforts on behalf of her client.

When Jenna came back with the pot of arnica balm, Margery began to apply it to Sarah's swollen ankle. The patient made a little yelping sound and winced in pain.

'It's all right, Sarah, this balm will soothe it and then I'll bind it for you. We might need to call the bone-setter to look at it, but I'll have to reduce the swelling first. At least the skin isn't broken. Try not to move.'

She turned to where Jenna was hovering nearby, watching, wondering what she could do to be helpful.

'Jenna, you'll have to take the order up to the palace without delay and you must ask if you can see the Duchess personally, to explain to her what has happened.'

'But … but, mistress, I can't do that. She'll never agree to see me.'

'Well, you do have something very personal to deliver to her. And you've met her already. She won't eat you. Remember?'

Jenna nodded. True, the Duchess hadn't eaten her. If anything, Jenna had felt a little sorry for her: she was rather a pathetic, vulnerable figure in her desperate longing for a child. But even so…

'Oh, please, Jenna,' said Sarah, wincing again as Margery applied some pressure in binding up her damaged ankle. 'Please, Jenna, please take the order to her. Otherwise I'll be sure to lose my job.'

'In fact, Jenna,' said Margery, 'I'm sure the Duchess would take it kindly if you suggested to her that you could take over Sarah's duties for a week or so until her ankle has healed, rather than putting Her Grace to the trouble of finding someone else. She won't want to be inconvenienced.'

Jenna's eyes widened in alarm. 'Oh, mistress, I couldn't possibly do that! I wouldn't know what to do … where to start…'

'It's easy,' said Sarah. 'You just have to keep watching her, clearing up after her, washing her small linens, anticipating what she wants and staying out of her way when she's with the Duke. And always remember to call her "Your Grace". She's very fussy about that!'

'But I wouldn't know how to dress her hair, or that sort of thing. I … I don't really know what a Lady's maid is supposed to do.'

'Just do what she tells you,' Sarah said, 'and don't worry about her hair. She always wears a headdress, so you've just got to work out how to pin it up underneath. And she leaves her hair long at night because that's how the Duke likes it.'

'Go and put on your good clothes, Jenna, and then go up to the palace,' said Margery. 'And be prepared to stay on there for a few days if the Duchess wants you to. Sarah can finish her drink and I'll finish packing up the order for you to take with you.'

'But, mistress …' Jenna was making hopeless little gestures with her hands, letting them fall to her sides, feeling that she had absolutely no part in what was going on, feeling manipulated.

'Now,' said Margery, 'we don't want the Duchess to think

you're slovenly. You have a job to do. You must do it properly and you must look the part. So, first help me get Sarah up to the dormitory and then go and wash your face and tidy yourself up.'

Jenna swallowed hard. This would be without doubt the most demanding job she'd ever been called upon to do and she wasn't at all sure she was equal to the challenge: and yet she had a better chance of making a success of it than Alice had. She never lost sight of that.

It was pointless dithering. She would do it, and she would do it well.

Between them, the two managed to manoeuvre Sarah as far as the women's dormitory above the brewhouse where, under the calming influence of camomile laced with powdered Valerian root, she almost immediately fell asleep on Jenna's pallet. Mistress Jourdemayne went back to the farmhouse to finish the Duchess's order, leaving Jenna to make herself as presentable as she could.

Packing a few necessities into a drawstring bag, Jenna frowned at the thought of what Kitty would make of it all. Inquisitive little Kitty would be certain to bombard Sarah with questions. And when she herself returned to the loft over the brewhouse – whenever that might be – Kitty's questioning would no doubt reach new peaks of persistence.

***

Within sight of the palace, Jenna stopped for a moment to slip her feet out of her old alderwood clogs and into the new leather shoes she had bought with some of the money her Mistress had paid for the tincture. Margery had urged her to wear the new ones around the farmhouse from time to time so that her feet could get used to them, but Jenna never had. Now she regretted ignoring the advice, but clogs would have been entirely inappropriate footwear for a Lady's maid in the grand surroundings of the palace so there was nothing for it.

It was as well that she had already been to the palace with Margery, otherwise she would have had no idea where or how to approach it. Now she found her way confidently to a small door in the southern wall.

'I wish to see Her Grace, the Duchess of Gloucester,' she said when she was challenged. The guard who blocked her way regarded her with disdain.

'And who might you be, then?' he asked. 'And what might the likes of you be wanting with Her Grace?'

Jenna was aware that no guard worthy of the name would allow her access to the Royal Palace just for the asking, but she disliked this man's lofty, dismissive attitude. Still, there was nothing to be gained by being haughty with him.

'I have a personal message for Her Grace from Mistress Margery Jourdemayne. Please be good enough to let me pass.'

'Oh, Old Mother Madge,' he said with a genial smile. 'Why didn't you say so?'

Jenna was indignant. 'My employer's name is Mistress Jourdemayne and I'll thank you to remember that. I could report you to the Duchess, you know.'

'Yes, but you won't, will you?' he said, giving her a huge wink as he opened the fortified gate for her to enter. 'Come on … come in. Everybody round here knows Old Mother Madge. Bit of a laugh, really, the way the Duchess and her are such big mates.'

'Where will I find Her Grace?' Jenna snapped. 'That is all you need to tell me.'

As she followed the guard's directions, she was challenged several times, but every time she mentioned her employer's name it was as though a magical key opened the door for her and she was allowed in without further questioning. Margery Jourdemayne was clearly a frequent and well-known visitor to the Duchess's private apartments in the palace.

Her Grace was anxious. 'What's the matter?' she said as soon as Jenna was shown in to her presence. 'What's wrong? Where's Sarah?'

'I'm afraid Sarah has met with an accident, Your Grace,' Jenna replied nervously. 'She tripped and fell into a ditch while she was on her way to the farm this afternoon. She has hurt her ankle very badly and Mistress Jourdemayne says she'll have to stay at Eybury farmhouse until she can put her weight on it. She can't walk. She won't even be clopping for at least a week.'

'Won't be what?'

'I'm sorry, Your Grace. Clopping. Er, limping.'

'Oh! And what am I supposed to do in the meantime?' demanded the Duchess. 'How am I supposed to manage?'

Jenna was appalled though her expression didn't change. How could anyone be so selfish?

'Well, Your Grace,' she said, 'I have brought your order and Mistress Jourdemayne has suggested that perhaps you could make use of my services until Sarah has recovered. That is if you would like to. I'm very willing to try to help. It is an emergency, after all.'

'But would you be able to do what Sarah does for me? Are you prepared to fulfil the duties of a lady's maid? Dressing my hair? Looking after my clothes? Washing my linens? I demand the best possible service.'

'I believe I can, Your Grace, and I am certainly willing to do my best.'

'Well, I suppose you're quite nicely spoken, even if your accent is a little strange. And you're tidily dressed. So we'll just have to see if your best is good enough,' said the Duchess. 'As you say, it is an emergency. Mind you, I won't tolerate any bad manners, dirty hands, anything like that. And if I see you picking your nose …! Very well then, if you learn to speak proper English, we'll see how you get on. You can begin by folding those clean linens and putting them away in the linen press. And be very careful how you fold them. I don't want them creased.'

Jenna was already beginning to see why Sarah was so terrified of upsetting the Duchess. It would be difficult to remember that under the haughty, demanding, supercilious exterior there was a vulnerable woman who had become aware that the opportunities life had offered her in the past would not be there for much longer. Margery had already identified that. The Duchess was growing old, she was probably frightened for her future, certainly more frightened of that than Jenna was of her. The pity was that her servants had to bear the brunt of her uncertainties.

It was bad enough, thought Kitty, that when Jenna had spent all her time working with the Mistress, the job of running the dairy had devolved to Hawys. Kitty didn't like that one bit, but at least Jenna had still slept in the women's dormitory, so she saw her each night when work was done. But nowadays, she didn't even see her at night because, since Sarah had fallen and Jenna had gone up to the palace instead of her, Sarah was sleeping on Jenna's pallet and Jenna was staying away altogether.

Kitty really missed her. She hoped it wouldn't be long before she came back and she'd be able to wish her good night before settling down to sleep. Jenna would always ask her what she had been doing during the day and how things were in the dairy. Master Jourdemayne, Kitty told her scornfully, was trying to teach Hawys to do the milk tallies but Hawys wasn't very good at it and the Master did his best, but he did get cross occasionally. Jenna's conscience pricked her at hearing that but it was as well she didn't see much of William these days. Her feelings for him hadn't diminished in the slightest.

'Hush, Kittymouse,' she would say, putting her finger on Kitty's little tip-tilted nose, to silence her. 'Don't criticise. I'm sure Hawys is doing her best. And don't imagine that you won't have to do the milk tallies yourself one day, young lady. So it's important to learn how to count. You watch what Master Jourdemayne teaches Hawys and try to learn.'

Kitty nodded. Jenna had only to suggest something to her and the youngster would do it immediately, just to please her. Kitty had come to love Jenna dearly and could be quite scornful of Hawys. Hawys had a whining voice and she always seemed to be complaining about something. Still, once she and Seth were married, then she probably wouldn't whine so much. Why was it, Kitty wondered, that women moped around the place, thinking about men. In her opinion, men were far too noisy and she couldn't think of any man who would make her happy, even when she grew up. Oh, except Robin the Drover of course.

Then again, Kitty wasn't sure she still wanted to marry Robin and anyway, he was probably far too old for her. He couldn't really be expected to wait until she was old enough to marry him, she realised that. No, what Robin needed was someone who was pretty and kind and lots of fun to be with, someone nearer his own age. Someone like Jenna. Yes, that would be the ideal thing and, though they didn't know it yet, she intended to bring the two together so that they could be married and live happily ever after.

She had been thinking along these lines for several weeks, though she'd said nothing to Jenna, not until she had formulated her plans for the pair. And never having told Robin she was going to marry him in the first place, there was no point in telling him that she wouldn't mind if he married Jenna instead. Anyway, she hadn't seen him for at least three months, though she knew that as soon as the shearing was over, he would arrive. He would be bringing a big drove of cattle as he always did around harvest time. So he could be here any day.

In the meantime, she watched carefully every time Master Jourdemayne tried to teach Hawys to calculate the butter yield from the day's milk and make a note of the figures. Kitty was surprised that Hawys seemed to find it so difficult since she herself had already learned to count up to twelve. This meant the Master could now entrust her with collecting the eggs from the new hens and sorting them by the dozen, though he said she was not quite old enough to take them to market on her own so Jane, one of the other dairymaids, always went with her.

The latch was lifted on the dairy door and the women looked up from their work.

'Hello, ladies,' William Jourdemayne greeted them with a wide smile. The dairymaids giggled.

'How do you feel about a bit of extra work tonight?' They groaned in unison.

'Now come on, ladies, it's not so bad. And I'll let you off doing the milk tallies, Hawys.'

'Well, that's a relief anyway, master,' Hawys said. 'What's the extra you want us to do? The milking?'

'Yes, as usual, please, Hawys. We're always short of time when we're harvesting and there's a big drove coming in this afternoon and it will need all the available men to handle it, so we could do with some help to get our own neats milked and settled. We'll have a look at the tallies tomorrow.'

'Ooooh, Master Jourdemayne, is Robin the Drover coming today?'

'No, Kitty, not today. This drove's coming in from Wiltshire. Why?'

'Oh, nothing, Master,' said Kitty airily, 'it's just that if it was Robin, then I should have to find Jenna to tell her, that's all.'

'Why would she need to know?'

'Because she's going to marry him.'

'Is she?'

'Oh, yes,' said Kitty, nodding emphatically. The other dairymaids sniggered among themselves but said nothing. They knew Kitty of old.

William was caught entirely off guard. It couldn't be true! Was the child lying? She could be a very fanciful little girl, so she probably was. But maybe she wasn't and he didn't want to appear stupid by challenging her in front of the other dairymaids. He could feel the blood draining from his face. He'd been trying to avoid being alone with Jenna so, of course, he knew nothing about this. And now she was marrying Robin Fairweather! Why hadn't someone told him? Why had Robin never said anything? And why, why in Heaven's name, did he feel so dismayed? It was nothing to do with him.

'Are you all right, master?' Kitty sounded anxious.

'What? Yes. Oh, yes. I'm fine, Kitty. Don't worry. All right then, run along. Just remember about the milking tonight and, Hawys, I'll see you tomorrow.'

He should have found another dairymaid by now, of course he should, ever since Jenna first went to work for Margery. But he hadn't found anyone to replace her yet, not that he'd really been looking. He still hadn't quite accepted that she was not going to return to her job in the dairy. But, if what he had just heard was true, she never would.

William didn't know how he managed to get out of the dairy without making a complete fool of himself. Kitty's earnest little face haunted him and her words repeated themselves like an

169

evil litany in his brain.

'Because she's going to marry him … to marry him … to marry him … because she's going to marry him…'

As if he didn't have enough to worry about today. The drove was a bigger one than usual and it was expected within the hour. And Piers the cowherd was ill with some sweating, vomiting sickness though, thank God, there were no buboes in his armpits so it wasn't the Plague. With luck, none of the other men would go down with it, whatever it was.

'Because she's going to marry him … to marry him … to marry him…'

Damn it! He couldn't get rid of that accursed rhythm. What was he thinking about?

'To marry him … to marry him…'

His hands were bunched into fists at his sides as he strode the Willow Walk towards Eybury farmhouse, the sound of his footsteps underscoring that damnable rhythm. How could Robin be such a cheat, so two-faced as to let William confide in him and all the while…?

'To marry him … to marry him…'

No, it couldn't be true, it couldn't. And yet it must be. Kitty had been so confident. His heart was pounding. He must calm down. This was nothing to do with him, this business of Jenna and Robin. He had no right to feel anything. Jenna could marry whom she pleased. After all, he was married to Margery so what right had he to be concerned about what Jenna did?

'To marry him … to marry him … because she's going to marry him…'

It didn't matter. He wouldn't say a word. And he'd stay away from the ale-house because ale loosened tongues and he didn't want to talk about it. It was none of his business.

And he had no reason to feel so … so bereaved, so betrayed.

***

A week of waiting hand and foot on the Duchess of Gloucester had brought Jenna to the conclusion that, given the choice, she would infinitely prefer farm work to the duties of a lady's maid. She had always taken pride in the responsibility of running a dairy, making butter and cheese, milking the cows, looking after the poultry, covering the fire at night, helping in the fields at harvest time or wherever else she might be required. But being at one selfish woman's beck and call, carrying heavy pails of water for her bath, caring for her clothes, washing her linens, helping her dress, obeying every little whim and fancy, fetching and carrying all day and every day was not a life she cared for, despite the fact that the Duchess pronounced herself delighted with Jenna's work and with her demeanour.

In taking over Sarah's duties, Jenna had expected be called upon to trudge back and forth to Eybury farmhouse fairly often with messages for Margery Jourdemayne, though this was the first afternoon on which the Duchess had asked her to do so. Jenna was only too ready to do the Duchess's bidding because it gave her an opportunity to do something very important to her. It gave her the chance to see Kitty.

Jenna had been sent to the Duchess's aid at such short notice last week that she hadn't given Kitty much thought before she left and she bitterly regretted the fact. The child was vulnerable and had come to depend on Jenna more and more. She should have made time to see her before she left, to explain that she wasn't deserting her, to help her understand the reasons why she had to go away. She had no wish to destroy Kitty's growing, but still fragile, confidence in other people.

Pushing open the door of the dairy, Jenna was surprised to realise that it must be at least two months since she had last been inside it. Nothing seemed to have changed, though after working in the warmth of the farmhouse, she had forgotten quite how cold the big room could be, even at the height of summer, with the diverted stream trickling through the centre of it, keeping the temperature down. With their backs to her, Hawys, Jane and the other dairymaids were pounding the butter in their churns and gossiping. No one noticed her at first.

'Hello, ladies!' she called, in imitation of the way William Jourdemayne always greeted them.

'Jenna!' Kitty screeched when she saw her, jumping up and down in her excitement. 'Jenna, Jenna, Jenna! Look, it's Jenna!'

'Yes, it's me,' said Jenna, laughing as Kitty flung herself at her.

'Well!' said Hawys, her hands on her hips. 'Who looks every inch the fine lady in her new kirtle? And what brings you here, madam? If I may be so bold as to ask.'

'Yes, where have you been, Jenna?' Kitty demanded. 'Hawys said you were up at the palace. Have you come home, Jenna? You're never going back to the palace, are you? Are you, Jenna?'

'Yes, I am, Kitty. I have to. That's what I came to tell you. And I may have to stay there for a few weeks. Perhaps even longer.'

'Oh,' Kitty's face fell. 'Why?'

'Because I'm going to look after the Duchess instead of Sarah, while Mistress Jourdemayne looks after Sarah until her foot gets better.'

Hawys nodded in Kitty's direction. 'She misses you,' she said.

'Well, it can't be helped,' said Jenna. 'I'm sorry, Kittymouse. I'll come back as soon as I can. But the Duchess needs me while Sarah gets over her accident.'

'Sarah says she can be very nasty, that Duchess,' Jane said, wrinkling her nose.

'Well, maybe. But I think I can manage to look after myself, Jane, thank you. Anyway, I only looked in to let you all know what was going on. And I don't want to start off on the wrong foot by being late back and keeping the Duchess waiting. So, I can't stay. Come here, Kittymouse. Give me a kiss, then I must go.'

Jenna kissed the top of Kitty's head then had to detach the child's arms which were clamped firmly around her waist as though she would never let her go.

'Come now, Kitty. You be a good girl and do what Hawys tells you. I'll be back as soon as I can. Goodbye for now, my dove. Goodbye, everyone! Goodbye!'

There: that was done. Pulling the door of the dairy closed behind her, Jenna felt her conscience was salved though she couldn't bring herself to look back and wave. The sight of

Kitty's devastated little face would have weakened her resolve. One day, Kitty would have to grow up and realise that she couldn't have everything her own way in this life, but not just yet. Not wanting to incur the Duchess's displeasure by taking too long in running her errand, Jenna walked briskly back towards the farmhouse to collect the items she wanted before returning to the palace.

'Well met!' called William Jourdemayne, coming towards her. 'So there you are.'

'Master Jourdemayne!'

'William,' he corrected. 'Don't you remember?'

'Yes, yes, of course. I'm sorry, er, William.' There was no avoiding him. She wasn't even half way to the farmhouse yet and here he was, blocking the path, an unfamiliar expression on his face. She was startled, flustered. He was the last person she wanted to see. Not because she didn't want to see him: she did want to see him. Very much. Too much.

William had never seen Jenna wearing anything other than her plain, dark workaday clothes: an apron, a coif covering her hair and a shawl over her shoulders if the weather was cold. Now her hair was plaited becomingly in coils over her ears and held in place by a white linen filet. She wore a new broadcloth kirtle in a light shade of green. To William, she looked enchanting.

'You, er … you're looking well, Jenna,' he managed. 'You look as though you're going somewhere very special.'

'Mistress Jourdemayne thought I should have some new clothes to wear since things will be very different from now on. I can't just…'

'Oh, so you *are* going to marry Robin! Why didn't anyone tell me? I didn't think you and he –' He broke off, seeing the incredulous expression on her face.

'Marry Robin? Who, Robin Fairweather? No, I'm not going to marry Robin, nor anyone else for that matter. Whatever gave you that idea?'

'It … it was something young Kitty said,' he muttered, embarrassed.

'Kitty! Oh, William, Kitty is always marrying people off to

each other. But only in her imagination. You shouldn't have believed her.'

'No. No, of course not. You're right. And Robin had never said anything. Thank God for that. I couldn't have borne it if ...' his voice trailed off before Jenna could quite catch the rest of the sentence. He had never felt so stupid in his life.

'No, I'm not marrying anyone,' she said. 'I'm working for the Duchess of Gloucester. That's why I need better clothes, so I can attend her at the palace. It may not be for very long but Mistress Jourdemayne thought it was a good idea, well, certainly while Sarah's ankle is still too painful to stand on.'

'It's broken,' he said shortly. 'Sarah's ankle is broken and the bone-setter wasn't able to do much about it. That's what Margery said.'

'Oh. I see. Then ... it will be some time before it heals. If it heals. She won't be able to walk on it. I suppose I could be gone for some time...'

William remained silent for a long moment, looking intently at her, shaking his head slightly in disbelief.

'But Margery said you only went there to help out. Surely you're not planning to stay there any longer, are you? You should have more sense than that.'

'Why, yes. I have to stay. Mistress Jourdemayne says...'

'No you don't, Jenna, you don't *have* to do anything you don't want to do, whatever Margery says.'

He reached out to grip her arm, pulling her off the path and into the secluded shelter of an old oak tree's spreading branches.

'Listen to me, Jenna. Margery told me what happened but you don't have to stay at the palace any longer. Listen to me. Look at me, Jenna! You don't have to go. They'll soon find somebody else to look after Her bloody Grace the bloody Duch –'

'Master!'

William was beside himself now, his mind in a turmoil. Jenna wasn't going to marry Robin, of course not. Robin would have said something. He should never have been so ready to believe a fanciful child. But she was going to go to the palace and for William that was just as bad. Feeling his temper rising within him, he turned away and pounded his clenched fist on the wide trunk of the oak. Then he turned back and challenged her.

'Jenna, why do you want to go to the palace? Tell me. Why are you and my wife prepared to spend your lives fawning over vain, empty-headed women like that damned Duchess? Margery is forever talking about her. "The Duchess says this ... Her Grace wants that ..." No, Jenna. No! They're selfish, shallow people. The Duchess and people of her ilk think of nothing but themselves.'

'I don't...'

'Yes, but I don't want you to be beguiled by them, taken in by them because of who they are, because of their ... their fame, because they appear to be important people.' He was gripping her arms now, looking intently into her face. 'That's what frightens me. You'll lose sight of your values, the real things in life, the important things. Please don't go to the palace, Jenna. I don't want you to go!'

'*You* don't want me to go? But what ... what has it got to do with you?'

'Everything, for God's sake. I love you, Jenna. Surely you must know that by now? I love you!'

'But, master ...' Jenna's protest was silenced by William's lips on hers. The last time he had kissed her, on Twelfth Night, his lips had felt as light as thistledown: but not this time. This time, his arms were around her and the yearning passion in his kiss shook her to the depths of her soul.

Terror engulfed her. Trying desperately to pull away from him, she screwed her eyes tight shut and hunched her shoulders, trying to raise her arms to protect her head, holding herself rigid against what must come next: the force, the cruelty, the brutality.

'Jenna, Jenna, my love,' William's pleading voice came from somewhere beyond the tight band of her instinctive defence. 'Jenna, look at me! Please, look at me.'

Lowering her arms slowly and opening her eyes, she looked into William's face, so close to her own, and saw there an expression of great tenderness.

'William!' Her voice was barely above a whisper.

For months, she had managed to keep her feelings bottled up though in her heart she knew that what made her rise from her pallet every morning was the hope of seeing him; her day did not begin until she was certain he still inhabited her world. She had refused over and over again to believe she was in love with him, but she could no longer deny the truth.

Now his arms were around her again, holding her close to him in an embrace, gentle but so vital that it took her breath away and she found herself responding ardently to his clear desire for her with her own need for him. Here was the man she wanted. Her memories of Jake and his dominant, brutish abuse of her body were obliterated and there was nothing of selfishness in this embrace between two people whose feelings for each other were overwhelming. The force which drove their passion was neither possession nor lust. It felt very much like love.

Then, for Jenna, it seemed as if a sudden darkness descended. William abruptly took a step back, away from her, leaving her swaying slightly, her head reeling. His arms fell slackly to his sides and in the total silence which followed, she was aware only of the heavy drumming of her own heart.

When the birdsong began again, she opened her eyes. William was standing in front of her, his head bowed, his body slumped, as though he had given in to something inevitable, something inescapable and now regretted it.

'I'm sorry,' he said. 'I shouldn't have done that.'

'That's … that's all right, master.'

It was a foolish thing to say.

'I had no right. I cannot make demands of you, Jenna, I don't own you. You are not my wife. If you choose to go to the palace, it has nothing to do with me. Nothing at all. You must do what you want to do.'

Among the leaves of the oak tree, a blackbird started singing joyously above their heads. It was some time before William spoke again.

'Go then, my dearest girl, if you must. I cannot hold you

here. I have no right to. Go to the palace, Jenna, but don't be dazzled by the people you meet. They're not worth it. Go now, please, just go. And may God go with you.'

There was nothing to be said after that. William stood to one side for Jenna to pass, then stood watching her as she began to walk away from him, back to the path and on towards the farmhouse. Jenna stared resolutely in front of her, desperately trying to keep her quivering mouth closed and her lips in a straight, determined line. She was almost overwhelmed by the instinct to turn around and scream her love for him, her need of him. There could be no denying that she was deeply in love, but with another woman's husband. No good would ever come of it and she dared not lose control.

They both knew where Jenna's destiny lay. It was not in the dairy at the Manor of Eye-next-Westminster. It was not with Robin. It was not with William: it was with William's wife. And there could be no going back. Not now.

They'd been so engrossed in each other that neither of them noticed a small, dumbfounded face watching them from behind a hawthorn bush, a little way down on the other side of the path.

Kitty had just learned her first lesson in growing up.

CHAPTER THIRTEEN

April 1439

In the Duchess of Gloucester's dressing room, Jenna was putting away the last of the clothes her mistress had been wearing during the visit to Woodstock and Stonesfield with her husband. Now all the members of the ducal household were back at court in the Palace of Westminster and things were returning to normal.

Jenna knew that many women would envy her the job she now did, working within the opulent surroundings of the Palace of Westminster, rarely having to venture out into the winter rain or summer sun, keeping her skin pale and her hands soft. But she found the work unrewarding. Apart from the travelling, which she did enjoy, the daily routine was tedious and thankless. In her heart, she even envied Sarah, despite the fact that she would never walk normally again. At least Sarah had been given the chance to stay on at Eybury Farm where she managed to be surprisingly useful, given that most of the work she did could be done while sitting rather than standing.

At the palace, after a few initial mistakes, Jenna had settled down very quickly to perform the tasks expected of her in her new role. Her everyday duties included looking after Her Grace's personal needs, washing her clothes and underwear, dressing her hair, cleaning her shoes, helping her into her gowns and doing anything else she might require. The Duchess began to rely more and more on Jenna's abilities and her common sense. In expressing her satisfaction, she would show occasional flashes of generosity and Jenna benefited from gifts of cast-off clothes. Among her favourites was a dark red houppelande of the finest worsted cloth, the sleeves trimmed with miniver.

At first, she had protested that she couldn't possibly accept such a gift because, in any case, she wouldn't be allowed to wear it in public. She risked being arrested by the Sheriff's men for contravening the Sumptuary Laws.

'Oh, nonsense!' said the Duchess, waving her hand dismissively. 'The Sumptuary Laws merely protect the interests of persons of quality. And absolutely no one at court is wearing miniver these days, it is completely *passé*. The vogue is for marten. And I think I shall soon set a trend for sable. I do *so* enjoy doing that and seeing other women doing their best to imitate me. So stupid! No doubt you will soon see the humblest of housewives lining their hoods with miniver for warmth, just because I no longer wear it. You should accept the houppelande and be grateful.'

Nevertheless, Jenna never wore the sumptuous garment in public. Whenever she visited Eybury Farm to collect supplies of Margery's cosmetics for the Duchess, she always dressed in an entirely circumspect way. She had no desire to flaunt her new position in life, not in front of any of her old friends and colleagues and she certainly would not have taken the risk of running into William dressed like that. Not after the bitter warnings he had given her about how her work at the palace could turn her head and change her attitudes.

She couldn't think back to that encounter under the oak tree without remembering how, when she had walked away from him, she could barely see where she was going for the tears that half-blinded her, hoping she was keeping to the path and willing herself not to turn around, in case she were unable to resist running back into his arms. Shocked to the core by William's passionate confession, she had been at great pains to avoid seeing him ever since, knowing that it would be all she could do not to say something in an unguarded moment. Despite telling herself repeatedly that he was a married man and she had no right to feel the way she did, her feelings for him had never changed in the two years since she had left the farm. She doubted they ever would, but it would be madness to pursue them. Best to concentrate on her job with the Duchess Eleanor and perform her duties to the best of her ability. It was certainly what Alice would have done.

***

There were still a few people left in the throne room when the Duke and Duchess of Gloucester arrived for an audience with the King. A scattering of foreign dignitaries had contrived to get themselves invited to attend him and this was their opportunity to make a case for grants, offices and cash from the royal purse. The King was rarely known to refuse such requests, indeed granting them seemed to give him great pleasure and he was fast gaining a reputation for generosity in some quarters though his munificence was viewed by others as rash and ill-considered.

He was looking almost animated as he rose and descended the steps from the throne to greet his aunt and uncle.

'You are both most welcome,' he said, as the Duchess curtseyed deeply. 'I'm so glad you were able to attend me today. Come, let us sit for a moment because I am anxious, Uncle, to hear all about Oxford. I understand you paid a visit to the University as well as to your manor houses in the area.'

'I did both, Your Highness,' said Gloucester, taking a seat next to his wife, 'and I was delighted to have the opportunity of doing so. I managed to visit both Stonesfield and Woodstock on this occasion and both appear to be running smoothly. The farms are being excellently managed and are most productive.'

'Yes, yes, I'm pleased to hear it,' the King said dismissively. 'But what about the university?'

'The university does well, too. There are plans to build a new library, though that will be expensive.'

'Is it not possible to extend the existing library?'

'It's really too small. It was built more than a century ago…'

'By one of my ancestors,' Eleanor interrupted, never one to miss an opportunity to boast. 'He was Thomas de Cobham, the Bishop of Worcester.'

Her husband smiled at her indulgently. 'He was the only

bishop the family ever had and they've never stopped bragging about him.'

'But that is only right and proper,' said the King. 'Any family should be proud to boast of a bishop in their midst.' The Duchess gave him a grateful smile.

'Yes, of course,' Humphrey agreed, 'but Thomas de Cobham's library is woefully inadequate. It must be replaced.'

'And will you be helping in that, Uncle?'

'Indeed, yes, with the gift of some of my books. And that pleases Eleanor greatly, doesn't it, my dear?'

'Naturally,' said the Duchess. 'I am most anxious to pay tribute to the memory of my … er, my great-uncle.' She paused, uncertainly. 'At least, I believe that's who he was.'

'An honoured ancestor, anyway,' said her husband. 'Which is why it seems only right and proper for the library to benefit from the gift of some of my books.'

The King nodded in agreement. 'So important …' he said, half to himself, then raised his voice and went on: 'It is so important that students have the opportunity to read the Bible, to better acquaint themselves with the scriptures, with the word of God. It is all that will save the world from perdition. If only books were not so very expensive.'

'Ah, but from what I've heard, that is something which may well change in future, Your Highness,' Humphrey said and his nephew raised questioning eyebrows. 'Yes, there is some very exciting news from the Rhineland in Germany. It seems that some enterprising inventor is working on a system for a mechanical process of transferring words to paper. I have only recently heard of it but, if the system can be made to work, it could be a very exciting development.'

'But surely, Uncle, there can be no substitute for quill pen and parchment?'

'Apparently there could be. The development is in its early stages, of course, but from my understanding, the device is some sort of press, not unlike the type used in pressing grapes for the wine harvest.'

The King bestowed one of his rare smiles on his uncle. 'That would hold an appeal for you, then, my Lord Uncle!'

Humphrey had the good grace to smile in return. 'Wine is one of God's greatest gifts to mankind,' he said.

'God makes us all gifts in abundance, Uncle: wine is merely one of them. And there are some who will abuse that gift.' He seemed on the point of saying something else before changing his mind. 'But tell me more about this new idea for making books.'

Humphrey was only too pleased to oblige. His pious nephew was known to disapprove of the immoderate consumption of wine.

'As I understand it,' Humphrey explained, 'the press is loaded with letters of the alphabet, made of metal, which are coated with ink, formed into words and pressed into paper. Then, when the ink dries, the page bears a permanent record of what was imprinted upon it. The possibilities are endless.'

The King was quiet for a long moment, trying to imagine what his uncle had described. 'Could more than one book be made in this way?' he asked.

'Possibly several could be made,' said Humphrey. 'Perhaps even several hundred, which would make the process very cost effective. If it fulfils its promise, this invention is a work of great genius. It could change the world as we know it.'

'Then every student would be able to study the Bible, even the very poorest boys!' Beginning to see the great possibilities of the new book-making device, the King was becoming excited. 'By Heaven, Uncle, if what you say is true, then this new invention will be of the greatest benefit to me in my plans for my new school!'

'Your new school?'

'Yes, I have a plan to establish a new school for poor scholars. I wanted to ask your opinion about the idea. I think it so important that I should nurture and care about the education of my subjects. All my subjects,' he emphasised, 'even the poorest boys. Now I'm of age, I would like my reign to reflect the comfort and strength I myself derive from my readings of the chronicles, the scriptures and all manner of other writings.'

'Most laudable,' Humphrey muttered.

'I truly believe education and literacy are of vital

importance. I have talked to Archbishop Chichele at length about this and he is in total agreement with me.'

'And I am in agreement with you both,' said Humphrey.

'Where would you establish this school of yours,' asked the Duchess Eleanor, 'here in Westminster?'

'No, my Lady,' said the King. 'The only suitable place in the Palace of Westminster would be the chapel of St Stephen's and I would prefer to keep that as it is.'

'That will certainly please Canon Southwell,' said Eleanor. 'He is very proud to be of service to you at St Stephen's.'

'So he takes every opportunity to tell me,' said the King, his expression impassive.

'I'm sure it's no more than the respect he should accord you, Your Highness,' said the Duchess.

'Be that as it may. But no, St Stephen's is not suitable. However there is a chapel within a stone's throw of Windsor which would suit my purpose very well. It's the chapel of Our Lady of Eton, just across the river from the castle and, of course, I am quite often there so I could keep an eye on it. It could be easily converted into a collegiate foundation for, say, seventy poor scholars. It would give them the opportunity of a lifetime. I would derive great satisfaction from thinking I had helped them in this way.'

'An excellent idea,' Humphrey agreed, 'and most generous of you.'

He was pleased that his nephew shared his own enthusiasm for books and for learning, but he did wish the King would show more interest in other aspects of kingship: in politics, for example, or in bringing France more effectively to heel. Things had been going rapidly downhill in France, ever since that damned woman they called Joan of Arc had been burned at the stake for her nonsensical beliefs. She was clearly a witch, but, from what he'd heard, the French were still talking about her as though she had been martyred in the service of her country. But they should be made to see that their country was ruled by an English king ... ruled, in fact, by this pallid young man who always had his nose in a book.

Humphrey was worried.

***

It didn't seem like a whole year since the last time Kitty had sorted the stones for the catapults. She didn't really mind being the one who'd been given the task of finding stones: after all, the others had to be armed with missiles in the eternal fight between men and birds when it came to planting seed corn. Kitty's special friend Jack, who was learning to be a shepherd, had made her feel better about it because he said she was just like a proper armourer at the battle of Agincourt where the old king had won a famous victory. The armourer always had a really important job to do, Jack said, because he had to make sure the knights and the men-at-arms had the proper bows and arrows and hatchets and spears they needed to fight the enemy and win the battle. What Kitty was doing was the same thing except that for Jack and the other boys, the battle was to keep the birds off the newly ploughed furrows in the five-acre field, so that Master Jourdemayne and the other men could get on with the job of planting the seed corn before the birds could eat it.

But Kitty also knew she'd been given the job of collecting stones because her aim wasn't very good and she'd managed to kill one of the Abbot's white doves while she was supposed to be stoning the crows. Jack had covered up for her and said a fox had probably eaten it, because she could have got into real trouble for killing one of Abbot Harweden's doves, even though the wretched birds were as keen to get at the seed corn as any of the crows.

She liked Jack. Perhaps he was the one she would marry.

Though she was growing up rapidly, Kitty was still perplexed by the whole business about who should marry whom and how these things should be decided. She had been watching Master Jourdemayne covertly as she worked, glancing sideways at him from time to time as she sorted through the stones she had gathered in her apron.

On the day, two years ago, when Jenna left the farm for good, Kitty, rigid with the fear of being caught, and as quiet as a mouse in her hiding place behind the hawthorn bush, had been

185

deeply shocked to see the Master leaning helplessly against the trunk of the big oak tree with tears streaming down his face. The sight had affected her deeply. She had never seen a man cry before but she knew enough about the relationship between a man and a woman to realise that Master Jourdemayne wished he wasn't married to Old Mother Madge any more and could be married to Jenna instead. Kitty wished that, too, but she also knew this couldn't happen and it was the reason why she was still worried about him.

He had the look of a real crosspatch these days, like a man whose shoes were pinching. Perhaps they were, but it seemed unlikely to Kitty, who had noticed that the Master always wore the same pair of stout leather boots every single day on the farm, summer or winter, whatever job he was doing. He was wearing them now as he manoeuvred the heavy iron plough in the wake of eight yoked oxen. A couple of young lads were goading the animals with hazel sticks to keep them moving. Bringing up the rear of this rustic procession were four other men with mallets breaking up any heavy lumps of Westminster clay which the ploughshare had failed to convert into usable topsoil. Everyone had a job to do when it came to ploughing, Kitty reflected, even the girl who collected the stones for the catapults.

It was quite a lonely job though, because she had no one to talk to. It wasn't like the old days of working in the dairy a long time ago when Jenna was there, when the dairymaids chattered and gossiped and giggled the live-long day. It had all been such fun. Kitty still worked in the dairy most of the time, but she didn't enjoy it as much. It wasn't the same without Jenna. Nothing was the same without Jenna. Kitty didn't see her at all except when she came back to Eybury farm to see Mistress Jourdemayne, to collect something for the Duchess. Then the two of them would have their heads together, talking about Heaven knows what – but whatever it was, it didn't include Kitty. Jenna would give her a hug, of course, whenever she saw her, and tweak her nose and call her Kittymouse like she always did, but it wasn't the same as having her there all the time.

Kitty still missed her, but she was delighted on those few

occasions when Jenna did come to the farm. She looked so pretty these days, dressed in her elegant clothes just like a great lady. Of course, as the Duchess's personal maid she would have to dress like that all the time – but in Kitty's opinion Jenna would look lovely in anything. The last time she came on an errand for the Duchess, her dark hair had been caught up in a charming crispinette with a short veil falling to her shoulders at the back, the gift of her royal mistress, she said. Nobody had been expecting her and no one recognised her because she looked so grand – and everybody laughed when they realised who she was, even Sarah, who had been the Duchess's maid until she'd hurt her ankle so badly. Then, when the Duchess had said she wanted Jenna to work for her all the time, Sarah had been quite upset about it until she took up with Piers. And now she was going to marry Piers so that was all right in the end. Poor Sarah still had a terrible limp but Piers didn't seem to mind.

Jenna had arrived at midday, just as the last of the dinner was being cleared away and Mistress Jourdemayne had fetched a bowl and given Jenna some of the left-over broth. Master Jourdemayne muttered something about getting back to work and went out, slamming the kitchen door and Mistress Jourdemayne made a face behind his back, thinking no one could see her. But Kitty saw her and she remembered that Jenna had blushed.

***

At this time of an afternoon it was usually fairly quiet in the farmhouse kitchen and Jenna expected to find Mistress Jourdemayne at work in her own room, making up her clients' orders. Her heart always quickened as she opened the door but it was only very rarely that she had encountered William and on those few occasions when their meeting was unavoidable, he greeted her briefly and asked after her health, then made a hurried exit as soon as he decently could. Neither of them dared take the conversation any further.

'Is that you, Jenna?' Margery called, in response to Jenna's tentative knock.

'Yes, mistress. I have an order from the Duchess.'

'Then come in, come in. I saw you through the window, coming up the Willow Walk. How is Her Grace?'

'She's well, but in need of some almond and violet oil and another pot of the marigold face cream.'

'Still using it, then, is she?'

'Oh, yes. She still swears by it.'

Margery had been so convinced that her idea of sending Jenna to work for the Duchess of Gloucester would be to her own immediate benefit that it had not occurred to her that things might not work out exactly as she wanted them to. She didn't like it when her best-laid plans went awry. The Duchess, far from relying absolutely on Margery's advice as she had always done hitherto, was now confiding more and more in Jenna. Margery was being consulted less and less. In fact, she had not been summoned to the palace since well before Christmas.

Moreover, since she was spending more of her time at home, William had actually suggested she should return to work in the dairy. She had given him short shrift in reply to that suggestion but wasn't in the slightest bit upset by the argument which had ensued.

William had often challenged her about the wisdom of sending Jenna up to the palace and had made his scorn for the idea quite plain. Margery perfectly understood why, of course, though she had stopped short of accusing him of being in love with Jenna. There was no purpose to be served by that: the most efficient way of dealing with the problem had been to remove the temptation that Jenna represented and she had no regrets about having done so.

Men – they were so easy to manage.

But it still irked her that she was less of an influence on the Duchess of Gloucester than she had once been. It had been a prestigious relationship and she needed to find a way of re-establishing it. Taking Jenna into her confidence was a good way to start.

'So how is Her Grace these days?

'She's well. Demanding as ever, of course.'

'Tell me', Margery said, 'has she given up the idea of trying to conceive a child since that tincture of Old Mother What's-her-name's was such a disaster? Or has she had any success with anything else?'

'Not if her nether clouts are anything to go by,' Jenna rolled her eyes. 'And I don't enjoy having to wash them for her.'

'Ugh,' Margery made a face. 'I don't think anyone would. But Jenna, don't rush to go back. Sit down for a moment and drink a cup of small beer with me. Or some buttermilk, if you'd prefer it.'

'Neither, thank you. Her Grace doesn't like being kept waiting.'

'That's what Sarah always said.'

'Yes, so she did. How is Sarah?'

'Much the same,' said Margery. 'She'll never walk easily again. Still, it doesn't seem to bother young Piers. He's keen to marry her.'

'Then I'm pleased for them both,' said Jenna, picking up the Duchess's order. 'I'll ask Her Grace if I can have a few hours free to attend the wedding. But now, I really must go. I'll just call in to the dairy on the way and see how Kitty's getting on.'

'She's doing well,' said Margery. 'William says she's very good at that Devon sheep's cheese you taught her to make. Abbot Harweden likes it too.'

Jenna smiled. 'I'm glad,' she said. 'I'm very proud of her.'

After Jenna had left, Margery poured herself a cup of buttermilk and sat down. She needed to think. She had one last trick up her sleeve that might help the Duchess conceive a child, but this plan was not without its dangers. If things went wrong she could be in deep trouble. Mindful that she had already been given one stern warning, she knew that if she fell foul of the church authorities a second time, the consequences didn't bear thinking about.

Margery had learned the wisdom of keeping her own counsel. That wisdom had been learned the hard way. Her incarceration in the grim dungeons of Windsor Castle nine years ago had made her realise that her gravest mistake had been to believe the flattering words of the men who had wheedled knowledge out of her by making her feel she was their intellectual equal. Eagerly seeking out the company of that clerk, John Virley, and Friar John Ashwell, Margery had assisted them in their experiments with various different medicines, sharing with them her extensive knowledge of plants and herbs. Socially, she was pleased to be able to boast about her scholarly friends to William's brother, Robert, and his supercilious wife.

But an accusation of sorcery had turned everything sour for Margery and she bitterly resented every moment she had spent in prison. Had John Virley not also been sentenced, she would have suspected him of informing on her. The man had the look of a sneak about him and after all, she had spurned his sexual advances often enough. Though she still glimpsed him occasionally on the streets of Westminster as he went about his business, he had never spoken to her since.

On her eventual release, Margery had been made to give her word, on pain of death, that she would never again have anything to do with sorcery and the black arts. She was only too glad to give that assurance. She was also grateful to William who had readily believed her version of the story, collecting together enough money for her ransom and opening his arms to welcome her back home to Eye.

But she was powerless to stop the malicious, ill-informed gossip, which credited her with being able to raise corpses from the dead and whispered that fiends and fairies were her familiars. Absolute nonsense, of course, but she had been forced to work very hard to restore her own good reputation as a wise woman. Nowadays there were few who had the temerity to call her the Witch of Eye – not to her face, anyway.

Her reputation was still a fragile thing and she couldn't run the risk of anything like that ever happening again. This plan was her last resort because it involved the making of waxen images and, it if went wrong, she might be risking more than her reputation. She could be risking her life.

Margery had learned the craft of working with wax from a gipsy woman whom she had originally consulted about the Romani techniques of fortune-telling. But she had also been surprisingly adept at shaping softened wax into life-like flowers. Surely, it would do no harm to try to fashion a little poppet in the shape of a baby, its small body of fine linen plumped out with warm wax into which she had mixed all the herbs, spices and minerals which were known to aid conception.

She would strengthen its power by mixing into it some snippets from strands of the Duchess Eleanor's own hair which she had managed to steal from a comb on Her Grace's dressing table. And with Jenna working for the Duchess as her personal maid, it might be possible to obtain the most powerful ingredient of all – some of Her Grace's menstrual blood on a scrap of linen: that was almost a guarantee of success. It wouldn't be easy but, somehow, she would have to trick Jenna into providing her with that.

Then, having created the little poppet, she would swaddle it in a tiny blanket of the softest lamb's wool, place it in one of her small wicker baskets and cover it with a scrap of satin, just like a cradle.

No one need know.

CHAPTER FOURTEEN

Early autumn 1439

Magister Roger Bolingbroke and Canon Thomas Southwell were sitting next to each other on a bench outside the library at the Palace of Westminster. Between them, carefully wrapped in a padded, soft leather bag for protection was the precious astrolabe.

'Her Grace has surely not forgotten us,' said Southwell, drumming his fingers on the scrip balanced on his plump knees. 'How long do you estimate we have been waiting?'

Bolingbroke looked at him over his spectacles. 'Mmm? I'm sorry, Canon, what did you say?'

'I said we seem to have been waiting for … ah, here's Hume.'

Walking briskly towards them was the Duke and Duchess's secretary, Canon John Hume, a tall, taciturn man who wore a belligerent expression.

'Her Grace has sent for you,' he said. 'Today, she would like you to attend her in her private withdrawing room. Follow me.'

Southwell turned to Bolingbroke, his eyebrows raised in an enquiring arc as they got up from the bench and prepared to follow Canon Hume. With purposeful strides, Hume led the way, towering head and shoulders above the rotund Canon Southwell who scuttled behind him, anxious to keep pace. Bringing up the rear, the stooped figure of Magister Bolingbroke was bent protectively over the astrolabe he carried.

Hume said nothing and offered no explanation for the change of plan. The two clerics followed him away from the public areas of the palace where these meetings usually took place, and towards the rooms where the royal family had their private accommodation.

'Your advisers are here, Your Grace,' said Hume as he opened a door and showed them into the presence of Her Grace, the Duchess of Gloucester.

'Gentlemen,' she greeted them, 'I'm pleased to see you.' She turned and gestured imperiously to her maid. 'That will be all, Jenna. You may leave me.'

'Thank you, Your Grace.' Jenna curtsied then, picking up a cup, a dirty plate and a basket of embroidery threads, she left the room, closing the door quietly behind her.

The Duchess rose from her chair and took a seat at the head of the table, gesturing to Southwell and Bolingbroke to be seated on either side of her.

'Now,' she said, 'I expect you are wondering why I have decided to receive you here rather than in the library where we usually meet.'

'It is a pleasure to meet you anywhere, Your Grace,' said Southwell, 'and we are very privileged to be invited to attend you in your private withdrawing room. Are we not, Bolingbroke?'

'Quite so, quite so,' said Roger Bolingbroke, staring about him at the rich colours of the tapestries, which hung on every wall. He was seldom privy to such obvious wealth.

'Magister Bolingbroke, I trust you've brought the astrolabe with you?'

'Of course, Your Grace.' He began unpacking the precious scientific instrument. 'In fact, I particularly hoped you might want us to use the astrolabe for you today, since I have spent a great deal of time working with the instrument of late, perfecting my techniques, and I feel entirely at ease with it. I seem to have mastered the art of using it for divination.'

'That is excellent news,' said the Duchess. 'Divination is precisely what I have in mind.'

Canon Southwell produced several sheets of parchment from his scrip. 'I have taken the liberty, Your Grace,' he said, 'of preparing a new astral chart, based on the information you have given us about the time and place of your birth. It is unfortunate, however, that you cannot be more precise about the exact time of day you were born.'

'Is it really that important?' she asked.

'The more detail we can put into the chart, the better,' Southwell replied.

'But we can obtain a very reasonable reading from the information we already have,' said Bolingbroke, anxious to allay Her Grace's fears. Producing the astrolabe from its padded bag with the air of a conjuror in a jongleur's entertainment, he placed it in the centre of the table. 'There! Now Your Grace, we can begin whenever you wish.'

Eleanor rested her elbow on the table and cradled her chin in her hand. She was looking intently at Roger Bolingbroke.

'Just before we do, Magister ...' she said, hesitating, then with a sharp intake of breath she went on, 'tell me ... how difficult is it to cast a horoscope for someone else?'

'For someone else? Well, given that the basic information is available, Your Grace, it is just as easy to cast a horoscope for one person as it is for another. Did you, perhaps, wish us to cast a horoscope for His Grace the Duke, my Lady?'

'Your Grace.'

'Mmm?' Bolingbroke realised his error and blushed. 'Oh, yes, of course. I'm so sorry ... Your Grace.'

Canon Southwell came to the Magister's rescue. 'It is possible to produce an accurate horoscope for anyone,' he said. 'Indeed, I myself produced one for His Grace the Duke before he left for Calais two years ago, predicting his great success in that campaign.'

'Yes, of course, so you did. I remember now.'

'Do you wish us to produce another one for him, Your Grace?'

'No,' said Eleanor. 'No, not for my husband. But I do want you to use your skills in casting a horoscope for someone else and this is the reason why I wanted this meeting between us to be in private today.'

She paused for a moment, looking at the two faces fixed expectantly on her own. 'I must tell you, gentlemen, that I have become more and more concerned recently about the health of my noble husband's nephew, the King.'

'The King!' Southwell's eyes widened. 'Surely you do not

wish us to cast a horoscope for the King, Your Grace? That might be construed as …' he paused, hesitating to add the word 'treason' to the end of his sentence.

'I think merely that it might be a way of finding out exactly what ails His Highness,' said Eleanor firmly, 'thereby enabling his uncle, my husband, to help him back to the best of health. The King is prone to melancholia and he is more pale and listless than usual these days. I am very concerned about him.'

'But what of his learned physician?' asked Bolingbroke. 'John Somerset is a doctor of great distinction and he has looked after the King devotedly since he was a small child. Surely Somerset will know what is best for him.'

'And I'm sure His Highness is very appreciative of that,' added Southwell.

'I'm sure he is,' said the Duchess, treading carefully, 'he must be. But we have to remember that the King is at an age where his thoughts must surely be turning to young women, to romance and chivalry. A lot of young men are very shy about it. It could be causing an excess of black bile in His Highness and perhaps he does not wish to discuss it with his physician. We must bear in mind that there will soon be the question of a suitable royal marriage for him so, in order to do what's best for him, we need to know how he feels about things of this nature. Without upsetting him, of course. That's where I believe the astrolabe might help us.'

Eleanor was watching the way in which her advisers were responding to her suggestion. She was well aware that any attempt to foretell what would happen in the King's life would be frowned upon by every court in the land, civil or ecclesiastical. It could, in fact, be regarded as a crime, a treasonous act, and would bring down the harshest punishment on the head of the perpetrator. That was why she must be so very, very careful in making sure that neither Southwell nor Bolingbroke would betray her.

But she had reached the point of desperation. King Henry was such a dismal young man, so negative and lacklustre. Now, at the age of eighteen, he should be delighted with life, ambitious for himself and for his country, savouring carnal pleasures, jousting, hunting, wenching and doing all the other things that healthy young men of great wealth would normally want to do. Instead, he immersed himself in his books and spent an inordinate amount of time on his knees in St Stephen's Chapel or in visiting the Westminster monastery to engage in theological debate.

Irritated and infuriated by the King's attitude and lack of motivation, Eleanor could not imagine him leading the country into anything but oblivion. He seemed to care not one jot about France, the country his own father and uncles had fought so hard to conquer.

At the core of her frustration was the need to know whether he would survive his troubled teenage years and marry, then go on to become a successful king. She doubted it. Her husband would do the job so much more effectively – with herself at his side as Queen.

That was the future she hoped to see.

***

Margery had spent several days in preparing carefully for the interview she had requested with the Duchess and now, as she waited in the ante-room outside Her Grace's private withdrawing room, her heart was racing with anxiety. Once she had revealed her plan, she knew her fate would hang in the balance. She'd never be able to retract her words and if she should deny that she'd ever made any such suggestion, the Duchess' word would count for considerably more than hers. The wife of a stockman would hardly be believed. Either Eleanor would accept her proposal with enthusiasm or she would banish her from court and ruin her. The risk was enormous, but all her dreams for the future were at stake. She must tread carefully.

Startled by the sound of the door opening, she rose from her seat as calmly as she could, smiling as Eleanor beckoned her in. The Duchess was entirely alone, there was no sign of any of her ladies.

'Come in, Margery,' the Duchess greeted her, closing the

door behind her. 'I'm glad I wasn't too busy to see you. That coffer looks very heavy. Put it down over there.' She indicated a table near the window. 'So, tell me, what brings you here today? You mentioned some experiments with new combinations of flower fragrances. Were you successful?'

'Up to a point, Your Grace. I have been looking at the possibilities of angelica. We know it as a culinary plant but the root combines well with lavender. I am still working on its possibilities. I'm not sure yet.'

'Then what...'

Margery took a deep breath: the moment had come. 'By your leave, Your Grace, please tell me if you think I'm speaking out of turn but, as you know, I do have your best interests at heart...'

'And?'

'And ... well, I wondered ... since you had no success with my recommendations for ... for your attempts to conceive, whether you had ever tried anything else, some St John's Wort perhaps, though it is difficult to collect in the prescribed manner. I have no great faith in its ability to help you, but...'

Eleanor's face looked utterly forlorn. 'No, Margery, I have tried nothing else, though I haven't quite given up hope. But last week ... my menses, just like every other month.'

Margery already knew this. There were definite advantages in having a spy in the royal camp. Jenna had mentioned a few days ago that she was having to soak the Duchess's intimate linens in urine overnight to bleach out the blood stains. Wrinkling her nose in distaste, she'd said she felt quite nauseated by the task. Margery, far less squeamish than Jenna, bided her time and managed to purloin a small item of the Duchess's soiled linen while Jenna's back was turned. It had been quite easy, really.

'I'm sorry to hear that, Your Grace,' said Margery. 'And His Grace the Duke, if I might be permitted to ask ... is he as...'

'You know, Margery,' Eleanor cut across her, 'I would not tolerate these questions from anyone else and my patience is wearing thin, even with you. My private life with my husband is my own affair. But –' She broke off, biting her lip before she went on. 'Margery ... you know how much I still want a child and how I'll do anything ...' Tears were welling in her eyes now, and she looked upwards, trying to stem their flow by blinking hard. 'I'm sorry. Please forgive me.'

'Yes, yes, of course, Your Grace. I do know how much it means to you.'

Eleanor took a deep breath, shuddered and then looked anxiously into Margery's face, her hand once again on Margery's arm. 'Is there something new? Something ... something else you know of?'

'Well, perhaps, Your Grace. I'm not sure yet.'

'Because you know, Margery, don't you, that if there was a way ... any way to ... oh, dear God!' She turned away again and covered her face with her hands for a moment before going on, her voice steadily rising in pitch. 'What have I done, Margery? Have I offended the Almighty in some way that He denies me what I want most in the world? Something every other woman seems to be able to achieve with ease, even the commonest peasant, while I remain barren as a stone. Me, the Duchess of Gloucester, wife of the most powerful man in the land.'

'Indeed, Your Grace, your husband is second only to the King.'

'Yes, second only to the King. And if the King should ... no, I must not think like that. But we must consider the possibility that something might happen to His Highness. He doesn't always enjoy the best of health. And if my husband should become King then I must be able to give him an heir, a legitimate heir who could inherit the throne after his day and secure the succession of the House of Lancaster. So why can I not give him an heir? Eh? Tell me that, Margery, tell me that!' She was verging on hysteria now, her voice surely audible in the vestibule outside the door. Margery must quieten her.

'Your Grace ... please, calm yourself. I might be able to help you. But it depends on how much you trust me and how you view certain skills and crafts I have, skills which have been practised for centuries by wise women and cunning men, especially in country districts.'

'Wise women? Cunning men? Margery, are you telling me that –'

'Your Grace, please, hear me out. My mother was a wise woman, well respected in the village of Westminster, and from her I learned many, many skills, not only in the use of herbs and flowers.'

'Yes, tell me, Margery! Please.'

'There is much knowledge which is beyond the sphere of physicians and doctors. Sometimes women know much more than men give them credit for.'

Eleanor nodded slowly. 'Yes, yes, I have often thought so myself. But we're only women.'

'That shouldn't stop us taking things into our own hands occasionally, Your Grace.'

Eleanor was listening intently, her eyes riveted on Margery's face. 'So what are you saying, Margery?'

'Well, Your Grace, I am beginning to think that any potion or decoction you might take to help you conceive might be more effective if it is used in conjunction with something else.'

The Duchess Eleanor's face was a study in doubt. 'No, Margery, there can be nothing else. I have tried everything…'

'Please, Your Grace, let me explain. Not many people know this, but I am conversant with a rare technique, one which was taught me by a wise woman, a woman from another country and even more skilled than my own mother. You might not like it, but it could well increase two-fold your chances of child-bearing.'

Eleanor hesitated, but curiosity got the better of her. 'Then, for God's sake, Margery,' she whispered, 'tell me! Tell me what it is!'

'It's this, Your Grace.'

The Duchess watched spellbound as Margery, trying desperately to stop her hands shaking, opened the coffer she had brought with her and took out a small cloth-wrapped bundle, perhaps a foot long and a hand-span wide. She began to unwrap it, then paused.

'We will not be interrupted, will we, Your Grace?'

'No, no. No one comes into this room other than by

my invitation. No one.'

'Not even Jenna?'

'No, certainly not, not unless I've asked her to do something for me.'

'Then may we be seated, Your Grace?'

'Yes. Whatever you want. Just tell me. Tell me what it is.'

Pushing the coffer to one side, Margery made room for the Duchess to sit beside her.

'It is something very special, Your Grace.'

Margery finished unwrapping the bundle and placed a miniature cradle on the table where it was lit by a shaft of sunlight from a nearby window. In a voice barely more than a whisper, she said, 'It is a small baby.'

'A baby? How can that be? It is so still.'

'The baby has yet to live and breathe, my Lady,' said Margery, 'but it is a baby in all but life.'

'Is it of wax?'

That was the question on which the rest of Margery's life depended. She answered slowly, choosing her words with care.

'Your Grace, the babe is fashioned with beneficial herbs, precious stones and spices, all combined with strands of your own hair in a special blend of bees' waxes from carefully selected flowers. All these elements are imbued with a natural power of divinity. The only thing the child does not yet have is a soul. And with the right hymns and praises and sweet sounds it will have a soul in time. And you will have a child of your own.'

Eleanor's face was pale, entirely drained of colour, as she bent over the small wicker cradle and the skilfully crafted poppet which lay within it.

'It looks very like a baby,' she said.

With her heart thudding slowly, anxiously, in her chest, Margery watched her. She could read nothing in the other woman's impassive expression and the moment seemed to last for an eternity. If the Duchess was repulsed by the poppet and rejected it, then Margery was in dreadful trouble.

Slowly, very slowly, Eleanor reached out a tentative finger and stroked the satin coverlet of the small cradle, then pulled it back almost tenderly to reveal the little blanket of lamb's wool beneath it, swaddling the waxen likeness of a baby.

'Soft,' she whispered. 'So soft. It's beautiful, Margery. I had no idea you had such skills. It's quite, quite beautiful. Is it a boy?'

'Why, yes, Your Grace. It's what you want, isn't it?'

'Oh, yes,' breathed the Duchess. 'That's what I want more than anything else in the whole world. A boy. A son for Humphrey.' She turned to look at Margery. 'Is it ... you know ... if we keep it secret – is it all right to do this?'

'I have faith that it is, Your Grace. And so should you.'

'Yes, yes I will.' Eleanor paused. 'But I should ask Canon Southwell, just to be sure. Just to be on the safe side. He will know. We must not ... must not offend God, the Almighty Father.'

So Margery wasn't yet in the clear. She would rather the Duchess had not suggested seeking Canon Southwell's approval of her suggestion, but she knew full well that the attitude of the Church was ambivalent when it came to drawing divine powers into images, so luck might be on her side. The Duchess was desperate to have a child and she was, after all, the wife of the most powerful man in the country – next to the King – so few people would dare to argue with her or deny her what she wanted. Margery also knew that if Eleanor wanted anything badly enough, then Canon Southwell would be the first to condone it.

***

Of the two chapels dedicated to St Stephen at which Thomas Southwell served as curate, his preference was always for the Royal Chapel of St Stephen within the Palace of Westminster, particularly now that the King was expected to return after his most recent royal progress. The whole palace had an air of excitement about it, something which had been noticeably lacking while His Highness was visiting the midlands and the West Country during the summer. Servants went purposefully about their business, cleaning tapestries, polishing silverware and pewter, opening windows, stocking the larders and generally preparing for the King and his entourage to return. He and the other members of the royal party would be taking up residence in Westminster again after a meeting of the Great Council which had been held at Sheen.

The first thing the King would want to do would be to give thanks for his own safe return and it was Canon Thomas Southwell's responsibility to make sure the two-storey Royal Chapel was ready for use. While the King had been away, the members of the household and courtiers who had remained at Westminster had been using the Lower Chapel. The Upper Chapel had been locked up because it was exclusively for the use of the Sovereign with close members of the royal family and members of the clergy, which was why Canon Southwell was anxious to ensure it had been properly prepared.

He had asked Roger Bolingbroke to meet him since there was something he wanted to discuss and, until the King returned, it was as private a place as any in which to do so. This would be a conversation which Southwell did not want overheard. He found that Bolingbroke had arrived before him and was waiting for him near the stairs to the Upper Chapel.

'Magister Bolingbroke,' he greeted him. 'Well met.' He produced a huge key and inserted it into the door lock, beckoning Bolingbroke to enter. 'I trust I find you in good health?' he asked as he locked the door again, this time from the inside. He began to climb the stairs.

'Indeed,' said Bolingbroke, following close behind him. 'And you, Canon Southwell?'

'Yes, well enough, thank you, and anxious to get St Stephen's prepared for the King's arrival.'

'Confusing,' observed Bolingbroke, 'that both chapels in which you serve are dedicated to the same saint.'

'Oh, not really,' Southwell replied. 'There's not much to be done at St Stephen Walbrook until such time as the new building work is completed. It makes few demands of me. To be truthful, I'm hardly ever there. I spend a great deal more time here at St Stephen's Royal Chapel.'

'His Highness seems to have been away for some considerable time,' said Bolingbroke, making conversation while Southwell began busying himself with the silver altar pieces, re-grouping them around the heavy silver cross in the centre, making sure they were neatly aligned.

'It was quite a lengthy progress from what I understand, and the Council meeting at Sheen was of crucial importance now that he is getting older and taking on more and more responsibilities.'

'He'll be tired,' said Bolingbroke. 'He's growing towards adulthood, of course, but he is really still a boy, too young for all the arduous duties of kingship. Young men of his age seem to outgrow their strength very easily.'

'He's growing up to be a very dignified and well-mannered young man,' said Southwell, 'and a credit to his uncle, the Duke of Gloucester, who has been a great influence on him. The King will be eighteen years old come December. Old enough to start making his own decisions, to start taking over the reins of government from his uncle of Gloucester.'

'And from his great-uncle, Cardinal Beaufort,' said Bolingbroke. 'But it's just as well he has older and wiser men to advise him because I imagine he will still need to turn to them from time to time. I don't think I could have made major decisions when I was his age. Still, I wasn't a king, so it didn't matter.'

Southwell was only half-listening to Bolingbroke. He was behaving like a fussy spinster, moving a chalice here, flicking at a speck of dust there. He was trying to broach a tricky subject and wasn't quite sure where to begin. Perhaps it was as well to get straight to the point.

'The Duchess Eleanor has asked me rather a difficult question, Magister,' he said, 'and I have promised to think about it before giving her an answer. I really need to discuss it with another theologian, one whose opinion I respect.'

'And am I that theologian?'

'You are.'

'Then I will do my best to give you an honest answer.'

Southwell took some time to compose himself and Bolingbroke watched the canon's face as he framed the question.

'What is your opinion on the use of imagery in the act of worship?'

'Imagery? What sort of imagery? Do you mean paintings, statues and so on?'

'Er, in a manner of speaking, yes.'

For Bolingbroke, the question hardly merited consideration. He glanced around him at the exquisitely decorated Royal Chapel of St Stephen's. There was hardly a square inch of the walls which had not been used to illustrate stories from the Bible by means of the most beautiful artwork.

'Well, look around you, Canon,' he said, 'and you will see imagery everywhere. That superb silver cross, the delightful portrayal of the Virgin Mother with the infant Christ in that wall painting. The depiction of Job's children at their banquet is particularly fine. Surely, imagery such as this serves to remind us of whom we worship. There is nothing wrong with imagery if it exists for the greater glory of God.'

'Yes, but…'

Bolingbroke was warming to his subject. 'Moreover, few people can read and not everyone has access to the written holy word. Bibles, psalters, missals, prayer books … these things are beyond the reach of most people. Images of Christ and the Holy Family concentrate the mind of man, the minds of all men, rich and poor, on what is important in the scriptures.'

'And do you believe that these images can take on the … the *essence* of what they represent?'

This time, Bolingbroke did hesitate before replying, weighing the arguments in the balance, his expression difficult to read behind the lenses of his spectacles. Southwell was watching him intently. At length, the magister spoke, but only to pose a question of his own.

'Tell me, Canon, do you believe in the doctrine of transubstantiation?'

'Why, of course!'

'You genuinely believe that when you take Holy Communion, the elements of the Eucharist, the bread and the wine, become the flesh and blood of Our Saviour Jesus Christ at the moment of consecration?'

'Without question, Magister!'

'Then there you have your answer, Canon. If you believe that bread and wine can become *Corpus Christi*, then yes, you must also believe that with prayer and diligence on the part of the believer, an inanimate object can take on the essence of life. More than one miracle has been recorded in which bread left upon an altar has become as red as blood without the intervention of any mortal. So there can be no doubt. St Thomas Aquinas is quite clear on the subject and he is, after all, our most venerated theologian and philosopher. There, has that answered your question?'

'I truly believe it has, Magister. Thank you.'

In turning towards the altar, Southwell suddenly found himself face to face with a powerful image of the Lord Jesus Christ. Under the unwavering gaze of the painted eyes, it seemed to him that Christ looked into his very soul and approved of what he was doing. He crossed himself and offered a prayer of thanks for the divine guidance that had come by way of Magister Bolingbroke's stated belief and the miraculous gaze of the wall painting. Now he could advise the Duchess Eleanor that her little waxen poppet would cause the Almighty no offence.

CHAPTER FIFTEEN

Autumn 1439

With the onset of a chilly autumn, it was far too cold to enjoy the delights of the garden at La Pleasaunce. So, having dined in the sumptuously furnished great hall, the Duke and Duchess of Gloucester were entertaining their house guests in their private solar. Fragrant apple logs burned in the huge grate as some twenty of Humphrey and Eleanor's friends were relaxing, some talking amongst themselves while others were listening to John Dunstable playing skilfully on his lute in the corner of the room as he tried out another of his compositions on his distinguished audience.

The music was entirely to Eleanor's taste but, though he liked music well enough, Humphrey's preference on these occasions was a spirited debate with like-minded friends about astronomy, astrology, physics and mathematics. He admired the great Italian philosophers and had several Italian friends whom he would often invite to join these small, exclusive gatherings.

'La Pleasaunce is a haven for all the senses,' Roger Bolingbroke remarked, leaning back in his chair after a particularly fine meal. His spare, slightly bent frame was beginning to fill out with the generous quantities of food he consumed at the Duke's table. Tonight, he had worked his way through an excellent pike stuffed with oysters, followed by a dish of spiced quinces with cream.

'I'm glad you feel so happy here, Magister,' Eleanor replied. 'It is certainly an advantage for His Grace to be able to call upon your superior knowledge should the need arise to settle a debate.'

Smiling at the compliment, Bolingbroke closed his eyes and

gave himself up to the twin sensual delights of a warm fire and a particularly charming *rondo* being played on the lute. Watching him, Eleanor thought it would be rather easier to talk to the astronomer if he always kept his eyes closed since his left eye sometimes led a life quite independent of its companion on the right, especially when Bolingbroke was tired.

A small, black louse began its leisurely progress between the sparse hairs on the Magister's head and he suddenly sat up, ramrod straight in his chair, having felt himself begin to drift impolitely off to sleep before feeling the compelling need to scratch. It would never do to fall asleep in the presence of his patron and his wife.

'Forgive me, Your Grace! It is so pleasant in this room and the warmth from the fire is most conducive to sleep. Please, forgive me.'

'Are you feeling quite well, Magister Bolingbroke?' asked Eleanor solicitously. 'You are not sickening for anything, I trust?'

'No, no, not at all Your Grace,' said Bolingbroke, 'and thank you for your concern. It is merely that my studies kept me from my bed until the small hours last night. I should learn more discipline. I plan to retire early tonight.'

'Very wise,' said Humphrey, draining his glass of Burgundy wine before beckoning a footman to come and refill it. 'And what were you studying that proved so fascinating as to deprive you of your sleep?'

'Your Grace, I was re-reading Poggio Bracciolini's treatise on greed.'

'What, in the Italian?'

'It was not easy, Sire, but I did my best. I understand the treatise is in the process of being translated.'

'That will keep someone busy for a very long time,' said Humphrey, 'and then we shall have to wait for it to be copied. Unless that enterprising Gutenberg fellow in the Rhineland can make a copy of it on his new printing press machine. Either way, it will be several years before we see a translation of *De Avaritia* here in Greenwich. Mind you,' he added, 'we saw the author in London several years ago when he was in the service of our esteemed Cardinal Beaufort.' He rolled his eyes as he spat out the name.

There was an embarrassed silence in the room though the Duke, concentrating on having his glass refilled, seemed unaware of it. Dunstable's fingers hovered above the strings of his lute and he looked around expectantly. Several people exchanged furtive glances: no one was anxious for Humphrey of Gloucester to pursue the subject of Cardinal Beaufort. That way lay bitter back-biting. Anxious to lighten the atmosphere, Roger Bolingbroke felt he had to say something.

'I understand that Signor Bracciolini is a very well-travelled man, Your Grace.'

'Well,' said Humphrey with a short laugh, 'he'll never travel in this direction again – the churlish Beaufort had no idea how to treat a man of his prodigious intellect! Poor old Poggio was bored to tears for most of the time he was here and hared off back to Italy after a few years.'

Amid the relieved guffaws of the other guests, Eleanor's tinkling laugh rang crystal clear, an appreciative audience for her husband's remark.

'Your Grace,' said Bolingbroke, turning towards her, eager to change the subject, 'could you, perhaps, be persuaded to sing? After all, it's not every evening that Master Dunstable can be here with us, so we should take advantage of his presence and I'm sure we would all dearly love to hear you both perform for us.'

Graciously, amid a scattering of polite applause at the suggestion, Eleanor inclined her head in acknowledgement of the compliment and rose to her feet. She possessed a very pleasant singing voice and was rarely averse to showing off her musical talents. Seated behind his lute, John Dunstable looked up at her.

'You do wish me to play for you, do you, Your Grace?'

'Of course,' replied Eleanor. 'Singing unaccompanied is no great pleasure, Master Dunstable. Shall we try "O Rosa Bella"? It is one of my favourites.'

'A favourite of mine too, Your Grace,' replied Dunstable, positioning the lute comfortably in his lap and checking the tuning. Then, at a nod from Eleanor, he began to play the introduction to the song and everyone turned expectantly towards them.

As his wife began to sing there was a look of genuine contentment on Humphrey's face; he always enjoyed listening to her and she was a skilled performer. All he needed to complete his pleasure was the deep, inviting red glow of another goblet of Burgundy wine. He beckoned the footman to bring the decanter yet again.

***

'To be honest with you, gentlemen, I might just as well have stayed at home,' said Henry Beaufort with a shrug, 'and not bothered to make the journey to France at all, much less stay there for so many months at Gravelines for that interminable, never-ending conference.'

The Cardinal-bishop shuffled some notes on the table in front of him. In awaiting the arrival of the King at this important Council meeting in Westminster, he had taken advantage of a lull in the conversation to express his opinion about the increasingly worrying situation in France.

'Be upstanding for His Highness, the King,' boomed a deep voice at the door and the council members scrambled to their feet as the King entered and took the vacant seat at the head of the long table.

'Good afternoon, my Lords,' he greeted them as he sat and, in chorus, the Council members wished him a good afternoon in return. The King glanced at them.

'Is my uncle of Gloucester not to be present at our meeting?' he asked.

'His Grace does not attend our meetings as regularly as he once did, Your Highness,' Humphrey Beaufort explained. 'If he should happen to be staying at his manor house in Greenwich, then maybe he finds it quite a long way to travel.'

'From Greenwich? It's not that far, surely! It wouldn't take him upwards of an hour or so by river barge.'

'But perhaps, Your Highness, he has not yet returned from St Albans.'

'Ah yes, very possibly,' said the King. 'And the renewal of the charter must be done properly, of course. Yes. Very well.'

'And now that you are more of an age to guide us yourself, Your Highness, and taking more responsibility, no doubt the Duke of Gloucester feels less compelled to attend our meetings.'

'Perhaps so,' said the King, 'perhaps so.' He remained silent for a moment, looking around the table to see who had put in an appearance and they were almost all senior members of the clergy. As well as his great-uncle, there was Archbishop Chichele, Bishops Stafford, Lowe and Ayscough, the Earl of Suffolk, the royal physician John Somerset, Adam Moleyns and, on Beaufort's right, Archbishop John Kemp of York. Ah yes, the King thought, there was something he must remember to say.

'Before we get down to business then, my Lords, let me start by offering my sincere congratulations to Archbishop Kemp on becoming a Cardinal. And I would like it to be recorded that all members of the Council wished to congratulate you, Archbishop Kemp.'

Two clerks scribbled furiously, trying to take down every word the King said, while the new Cardinal, a broad smile on his face, inclined his head towards the King.

'Thank you, your Highness, you are most kind. I was of course delighted when His Holiness the Pope agreed to elevate me to the cardinalate. It is a great honour.'

'And I'm sure the cardinal's hat will always sit becomingly on your head, John!' said Beaufort, clapping his friend gently on the back before joining in a restrained round of applause. 'But we must get on with the business in hand. We need to present our report from the conference at Gravelines.'

'Was it a complete failure,' asked the King, 'as I have been led to believe?'

'Not entirely, Your Highness,' replied Beaufort, 'but it was very hard work to try to persuade the Burgundy delegates to see our point of view. The Duke wants the Duke of Orléans to be returned to France – and that's the crux of it. Archbishop Kemp ... I'm so sorry, *Cardinal* Kemp and I never succeeded in persuading them otherwise.'

'What has made Burgundy change his mind?' the Earl of Suffolk wanted to know. 'It's taken him twenty-five years to do it. Charles of Orléans has been imprisoned here in England ever since Agincourt and the Duke of Burgundy hasn't been remotely interested in him until now. So what's brought this on?'

'I understand he wants to create a Council of Princes,' said Beaufort, 'some sort of triumvirate at the head of the French nation. No doubt to strengthen the bonds, as it were. Charles de Valois is fairly firmly established as the man at the top, calling himself King.'

'But he will never really be King of France, so why are we even considering this?' Suffolk objected. 'It doesn't sound like good news for England.'

The King held up his hand. 'Please, gentlemen, I would be grateful if we could discuss this without a heated argument. I must remind you that Charles de Valois is my uncle, my mother's brother, and I really have no wish to antagonise him unduly, even though he disputes my right to the French throne. After all, there is a lot to be said for peace, so perhaps the Duke of Orléans should be released.'

'But not at any price, Your Highness,' Suffolk insisted, 'not if it means surrendering anything to France.'

'Of course,' Beaufort observed, 'there is the little matter of money involved. If we agree to French demands for the Duke's release from his imprisonment, they would have to pay the ransom we have demanded. And, believe me, one hundred thousand marks would greatly ease the financial burden of maintaining a presence in France. I can produce the exact figures for you if you wish but, take my word for it, it is a considerable amount.'

Beaufort was well qualified to comment on this. He had personally lent the Crown significant amounts of money in the past and though he could well afford to do so, he still wanted to have every last penny returned to him, with interest. He was a man who enjoyed his wealth.

Archbishop Chichele knew that the Duke of Gloucester

would be certain to object to the proposal and, since Humphrey was not here to speak for himself, the Archbishop felt that perhaps he should mediate on his behalf. Besides, there was always wisdom in putting the other point of view.

'We do have to remember, my Lords,' he said, 'that our esteemed King Henry – your late father, Your Highness – felt very strongly that we should keep a tight rein on France. He certainly would not have agreed to release the Duke of Orléans, not under any circumstances, until the whole of France had been brought under English rule.'

'I have not got my late father's taste for warfare,' said the King, 'nor yet his skills in battle. I would far rather that the people of France would accept me as their King without objection. After all, I wish them no ill.'

'How old is Charles of Orléans now?' asked John Somerset suddenly. 'Must be around fifty, surely? He can't pose much of a threat to us, not at that age.'

'He's hardly in his dotage!' Henry Beaufort objected and a low rumble of laughter ran around the table. Every man present knew that Beaufort was well past his sixtieth birthday.

Archbishop Chichele's expression of amusement creased his already wrinkled face. He *was* burdened by age, being older than anyone else present by at least a decade. 'The release of the Duke of Orléans is merely a bargaining token at this stage, of course,' he said, 'and we do not have to make a decision on the subject in the short term. Let us decide to meet again a month hence and, in the meantime, give the problem our deepest consideration. Are we all agreed, gentlemen?'

The suggestion met with grunts of assent. 'Agreed,' everyone muttered as the King rose from his seat, bringing the meeting to a close.

***

'Humphrey, that is your fourth glass of Burgundy wine since dinner.'

The Duke and Duchess of Gloucester were sitting in her boudoir, Eleanor in the window seat and Humphrey hunched up in an expensively upholstered chair by the log fire, staring into the flames. As usual, Eleanor had ordered a decanter of wine and two goblets to be placed on a tray, in case Humphrey should call on her in the afternoon. She would have to order another decanter in a few minutes if he was going to go on drinking at this rate.

He rounded on her, a thunderous expression on his face.

'Don't criticise me, woman, I know what I'm doing.'

'Please, Humphrey, don't be angry with me. There's no need to shout. I have only your best interests at heart. Why are you so upset? You haven't told me. I wish you would.'

'All right. I'll tell you exactly why I'm upset. And I'm not just upset. I'm furious, absolutely furious. Did you know that a meeting of the King's Council was held last week?'

Eleanor hesitated. She had no way of knowing the answer to that question and she had a feeling that any kind of guess would be the wrong one. She compromised by looking questioningly at her husband, shaking her head and saying nothing.

'Well, no, of course you didn't. How could you know if no one told you? No one told me, either, so it has come like a bolt from the blue. But it seems that His Highness the King was present at a meeting of Council members held at the Palace of Westminster. It was, apparently, well attended.'

'And you didn't know?'

'No, I did not know. Nobody told me. My invitation to the meeting must have been "lost" somehow.' Humphrey snarled with irony. 'Now, isn't that strange?'

'But are they allowed to hold a meeting without you? Wouldn't the King forbid it?'

'That is not the point, Eleanor. Of course, not every Council member is able to attend every meeting. But they never even invited me to this one, and I dare say it's not for the first time, though it's the first time I've found out about it. And they have also been holding meetings in the homes of individual Council members. No doubt my dear uncle, the Rich Cardinal, will come up with a perfectly plausible reason why the Council members should meet in his London residence from time to time.'

Eleanor watched her husband's handsome face twisting with

fury. She reached forward and put her hand on his arm. 'Promise me you'll be careful, Humphrey. It would be dangerous to antagonise Henry Beaufort.'

He shook his arm free of her hand. 'Eleanor, when I want your advice, I will ask for it. Let me think. I must see the King. Yes, that's what I'll do. I must see him. I'll request an audience with my nephew and tell him exactly what a snake his great-uncle Henry Beaufort really is. He needs to know.'

'But you won't lose your temper, will you, Humphrey? You know how you can get upset about things like this.'

'Stop nagging me, woman! I am already upset. I have every right to be upset. The King must be made aware of this. After all, his own father, my brother, gave his life for this cause. My brother Thomas died at the battle of Baujé for the same reason and my brother John always said we should keep hold of France. Damn it all, he even married a French woman!'

'But John loved Anne of Burgundy, didn't he?'

'He'd have married her anyway, even if she looked like a bull's backside, if it strengthened the English claim to the French throne. And now that arrogant, interfering uncle of mine, Cardinal bloody Beaufort, is again talking about releasing Charles of Orléans! And this time he's serious.'

Humphrey always pronounced his uncle's name in the same way, with the emphasis on the initial 'b' of the surname, a percussive puff of venom, the soft thud of an arrow hitting a distant target.

Eleanor was only too aware of her husband's hatred of his uncle. She was also perfectly aware of the argument which raged intermittently about the release of the Duke of Orléans from captivity.

She had once met the Duke, since his custodian was none other than her own father, and she had been curiously unnerved by the Frenchman. Even in middle age, Charles of Orléans was still handsome and charismatic. When they were introduced, he had raised Eleanor's hand to his lips and kissed it with great reverence, as though he'd been entrusted with a thing of rare beauty.

'*Dieu!*' he exclaimed, raising his head to meet her eyes with a look of quiet intensity, *'qu'il la fait bon regarder, la gracieuse bonne et belle!'*

Her heart tumbled in her chest at the sensation of his lips on her skin. There was none of Humphrey's arrogant pushing of his tongue between her fingers, simply a kiss which felt as though an exquisite butterfly had alighted on the back of her hand.

A gifted poet, Charles of Orléans could have been a friend of Humphrey's had things been different: they were both men of letters who delighted in all manner of artistic endeavours. As it was, the Frenchman had been captured at the Battle of Agincourt, uninjured but lying half-buried in the mud of the battlefield under the weight of his own armour and the bloodied corpses of his compatriots. Brought back to England as a prisoner of war, he had languished in luxury ever since, allowed everything but his freedom, under the watchful eye of minor noblemen like Eleanor's father. During the course of a quarter of a century of imprisonment, he continued to write his exquisite poetry, but the language of his verse underwent a gradual change from French to English which, nowadays, he spoke rather better than he did his mother tongue. Though he had never ceased to demand his return to his native France, he knew he would only be given his freedom if it was in the political interests of the English to release him.

In recent years, several members of the King's Council of advisers had begun to advocate peace with France and the tide now seemed to be turning in favour of releasing the Duke of Orléans. From the English point of view, one advantage of this suggestion was that the payment of a hefty ransom would go a long way towards cancelling the huge debts owed by the English crown. For his part, the Duke of Orléans was keen to be an intermediary in the drawing up of an amicable truce between the two old enemies. But Humphrey of Gloucester was deeply, adamantly, opposed to the suggestion.

'If Orléans is released and sent back to France, it will only strengthen Burgundy's position. My poor brother knew how much that rat wanted power in France. That's why Henry insisted, on his death bed, that Orléans must be kept prisoner in

England until the whole of France was finally under English rule.' Humphrey was becoming more agitated, his voice more harsh. 'And now this subversive faction on the Council, Beaufort and Kemp and all their fine friends, are trying to change everything. Have they no respect for my brother's memory?'

'Perhaps you would do well to write to His Highness,' Eleanor suggested.

'Why should I? Why on earth should I go to all that trouble? I'll talk to him. I have only to request an audience. I am his uncle, his father's brother. I am heir to the throne. The King would never refuse to see me.'

'But think, Humphrey, just calm down and think for a moment. If you had an audience with the King, you might easily become emotional about your brother, all your brothers and how they died. You could lose control, forget what you were going to say...'

'Never! No matter how upset I feel, I'd never lose...'

Eleanor cut across him. 'But if you wrote to the King, you would be able to enumerate your grievances very clearly, you could express yourself better, you could put your point of view much more succinctly. And if he has a letter to refer to, he can read over the points you make as often as he likes; perhaps even commit them to memory. And he will have a written list to hand if he wants to discuss those points with other people, other members of the Council, perhaps. He is still a young man. He needs guidance.'

Eleanor stopped abruptly, catching Humphrey's eye. He was looking intently at her with appreciative eyes.

'You know, Nell,' he said, 'I sometimes think I only want you as a bedfellow, because you always please me so much in that regard. But then I realise that you have an astonishingly good brain behind that pretty face of yours. There's wisdom in those lovely grey eyes. If you were a man, you'd be invincible!'

Eleanor preened herself, pleased by what she was hearing, relieved that she had succeeded in calming him down.

'I'm very glad I'm not a man,' she said, lowering her eyes becomingly, 'otherwise I would have no place in your bed. And

I always want to please you, Humphrey, there and elsewhere. You know that.'

'I do, my sweet Nell, I do. I thank God for a woman like you.'

He rose from his chair and put down his goblet on the table. Then he took her face in both his hands and kissed her fulsomely on the lips, his probing tongue promising later delights. Eleanor tried hard not to recoil from the stink of wine on his breath.

'That should keep you going until tonight,' he said, releasing her, 'because now, my love, I must take my leave of you. I have to find John Hume. I want to dictate a letter and it's likely to be a long one. I am going to write a complaint to the King, a very serious complaint about my esteemed Uncle Beaufort.'

He spat out the name: he always did.

CHAPTER SIXTEEN

March 1440

Nowadays, John Virley took pleasure in the way he made his living because it allowed him the flexibility so essential to a red-blooded man who enjoyed the company of women. His work took him to all corners of the city and he was not averse to crossing the Thames from time to time to seek out the company of a pretty little Winchester goose in Southwark, where many properties owned by the church were rented out as brothels. It was yet another source of income for the rich clergy.

After his brush with authority and his long imprisonment, Virley had emerged from the dungeons under Windsor Castle a chastened man and spent some time considering the options which were open to him. He was hardly likely to be welcomed back into the clerical life with open arms; he couldn't imagine Abbot Harweden hailing him with a friendly greeting on his return to the monastery at Westminster, as though nothing had happened. Besides, there came a time in every man's life when he had to make a decision about what lay ahead and Virley was disinclined to return to the monastery, where the working day in the scriptorium could be indescribably dull and monotonous. Even the cheerful sound of birdsong outside the dusty windows was invariably drowned out by the continuous droning voice of the monk who read aloud from the works of St Benedict. There must surely be something more agreeable elsewhere.

In weighing up the advantages and disadvantages of attempting to return to his old life, or something resembling it, Virley had acknowledged that he valued his freedom above all else. But he had also realised that he could turn his experience, and his contacts within the monastic life, to his advantage.

Balancing this against his natural desire for self-determination and his instinct to become an independent spirit, he knew he could possibly make a satisfying career for himself in supplying the many monasteries, priories, friaries and convents in London with the materials they needed for producing manuscripts. The more people who were learning to read, the more demand there was for books. Therefore, the more need there was for a reliable service to provide quill pens, vellum, parchment and inks for the clerks and scribes, gold leaf and colour pigments for the limners. He could work up a nice little business for himself by provisioning these religious establishments in this way. All he had to do was work out a fair profit, not too much and certainly not too little, and he had a steady job for the rest of his life. Moreover, he had his cherished freedom and that was crucially important to him. He would become a peripatetic stationer.

His plan paid off and he had soon built a solid reputation as a reliable supplier, work which often took him to St Paul's Cathedral within the city walls of London where he sourced many of his supplies. The townsfolk made the nave of the huge cathedral their own and the atmosphere was noisy and colourful. More often than not, Virley would see someone he knew among the people who used the north and south transepts as a short cut between Paternoster Row to the north of the building and Carter Lane to the south, particularly when the weather was bad. They would call out greetings to each other and congregate in groups, chatting and gossiping, or they would amble around the walls to browse among the books. Those booksellers and stationers whose main premises were in Paternoster Row would often set up temporary stalls inside the cathedral where they did a roaring trade selling some of their wares at second hand.

In the churchyard outside, under St Paul's Cross, public announcements were made and sermons were preached to save the souls of the ungodly while urchins played hide-and-seek and leapfrog around the handcarts of the street traders, risking a clip around the ear if they got in the way.

Today, the cool spring air was full of sounds, shouts, street cries and laughter. John Virley loved the hustle and bustle around St Paul's: it was where he felt most at home. Born and bred a Londoner, he revelled in the opportunity to catch up with friends or to visit one of several welcoming women he knew who lived within the city walls. His narrow eyes shone with pleasure at being a part of all the colour and movement which surrounded him.

He made his way down to St Faith's Chapel in the undercroft of the cathedral, where he bought two bags of iron gall ink powder. He always mixed his own ink, using wine rather than water for the purpose. In Virley's opinion, wine gave the finished ink a far greater intensity. He usually bought his vellum in bulk from another trader and was waiting impatiently while the man took his time in counting out the sheets and calculating the bill of sale.

'I'm sorry to keep you waiting, Master Virley, but we have been very busy this morning,' the trader grumbled apologetically. 'Trouble is, there are too many people learning to read these days.'

'And we have to supply the books for them,' snapped Virley, 'so I'd appreciate it if you –' He broke off at the sudden sound of raised voices from the other side of the chapel.

'Run out! What do you mean, you've run out? You can't possibly run out of ink powder, man! So what do you expect me to do, eh? Tell me, what do you expect me to do? Tell my master he'll have to write a letter for the Duke in his own blood?'

Virley knew those stentorian tones, he'd know them anywhere. The pugnacious William Woodham had a famously short temper: he'd always been the same, even when he and Virley were youngsters growing up in Aldgate Street to the east of the city.

'I'm sorry, sir.' The trader had taken fright: his back was against the wall and he was cowering away from the onslaught. 'You see, sir, that gentlemen over there bought the last of my ink powder not a minute since … and I haven't had the chance…'

Woodham turned and spotted Virley. 'Virley,' he roared, 'you old dog. You've bought the last of this man's ink, drat and damn you!'

'Have I? I wasn't aware that I had. And I certainly didn't do it on purpose. So calm down, William. You'll do yourself harm, carrying on like that. There are other traders who sell ink.'

'Yes, I suppose there are,' Woodham said grudgingly, his anger subsiding. 'Well, it's good to see you anyway, Virley, even though you might have got me into trouble. You know me, I've a temper like a tinderbox if I can't have what I want when I want it. And Canon Hume will be furious if I go back to the palace empty-handed.'

'Why does he need ink so urgently?'

'Why does anyone need ink, Virley? That's a stupid question. My master needs ink because he serves as secretary to their Graces the Duke and Duchess of Gloucester.'

'And one of them wants to write a letter?'

'The Duke does. Well, dammit, Virley, Canon Hume can't do his job without the right tools, can he?'

'Language, language, Woodham! This is a church, remember, for all that we're in the crypt.'

'I don't care. Well, yes, I do care, of course I do. And it's my fault anyway, for forgetting to order it. Forgive me, Lord,' he crossed himself quickly, bending his head. No good would come of offending the Almighty. 'Anyway, Hume has run out of ink so I've had to come all the way up from Westminster to get him some. I don't suppose you could let me have half of what you've just bought, could you? It would save me having to go hunting for it. I'm dying of thirst and I can't drink ink so I don't want to waste more time on it. I'd rather be in The Bush. So, will you, Virley?'

Virley appeared to hesitate while he considered the proposal.

'If the price is right,' he said.

'Oh, come on man, for old times' sake. Split it with me and I'll give you a ha'penny more for half of it than you paid. I'll just tell Hume it's gone up in price. He'll never know.'

'Done!' said Virley, never a man to pass up a bargain.

Not having seen each other for some months, Virley and Woodham decided to walk to Westminster together, Virley heading for the monastery to deliver parchment to the monks and Woodham to take the ink to Canon Hume at the palace. After crossing the Fleet Bridge, just outside the city walls, Woodham stopped on the corner at the entrance to Cock and Key Alley in front of a large, square building, a branch of hawthorn nailed above the door.

'Ah, The Bush,' said Virley. 'Probably the best ale house in London!'

'No question of that,' said Woodham. 'The alewife isn't bad either! Used to be a Winchester goose when she was younger, one of the prettier ones. I knew her well. Mind you, she's no gosling nowadays. Must be thirty years old if she's a day, but she's still got most of her teeth so she's not too bad-looking.'

As they entered the low-ceilinged room, Woodham was greeted with shrieks of pleasure by a plump woman with greying fair hair and a greasy apron tied around her ample waist. A table laden with jugs of ale stood at one end of the room and a pall of smoke from a peat fire hung over the dozen or so men who sat talking and laughing loudly, mugs cradled in their hands.

'William Woodham!' she shouted above the din. 'Where've you been? We haven't seen you for … oh, I don't know … I was only saying to the girls last week … it must be nigh on a month.'

'Quiet, woman, and give us each a measure of your best ale.' Woodham seemed not to be a man for polite conversation. He turned to Virley. 'It's as well the ale is good. Otherwise I couldn't abide the noise in here.' Then he grinned and gave the woman a great thwack on the backside. She cackled with laughter.

'How have you been keeping, you old jade?'

'Oh, all right, you know,' she laughed again. 'Better for seeing you, though. Where've you been? Still working for Good Duke Humphrey, are you?'

'Why not? It's as good as anywhere else.'

'Better than most, I'd say. He's a good man, that Duke Humphrey. Everybody says so. You should count yourself lucky to be working in his household.'

'And he doesn't know how lucky he is to have me!' said

Woodham, pushing away Virley's half-hearted attempt to pay for the ale. 'You can get the next ones,' he said. They were clearly going to be there for some time, which was just as well since they had a lot of catching up to do.

The two had grown up together in a rundown area just to the east of the city walls, the closest of friends. Woodham's father was the landlord of the Crown Inn in Aldgate Street, just next door to the church of St Botolph-without-Aldgate in which Virley, the possessor of a fine treble voice, had been a choirboy. With his face framed in a collar of pleated white linen, Virley always looked the very picture of innocence and purity as he sang, though under the red cassock and white surplice his knees were as grubby as any other boy's and he was quite likely to have a few worms in his pocket for an afternoon's fishing with his friend William.

This early career as a choirboy meant that, of the two, Virley was by far the better educated, having been taught to read and write by a minor canon of St Botolph's who had taken an unhealthy interest in him. Woodham, on the other hand, was the son of a brutish bully who normally got his way simply because none of his neighbours wanted to antagonise him. Whereas he could see the sense of reckoning up the number of tankards of ale he'd sold and the profit he'd made, there didn't seem to him much sense in spending that profit in educating his son. Woodham's education came much later, when he'd gone into service and realised that the ability to read was a very valuable skill for someone with ambition. The friendship between the two boys had been an unlikely one and yet it lasted throughout their childhood until they eventually went their separate ways in search of employment.

'So, what's it like working for the Duke of Gloucester, then?' Virley asked as they sat on a bench near the fire. 'It can't be bad. He certainly seems very popular around here.'

'Oh, aye, he is. Londoners love him,' said Woodham. 'Mind you, they aren't so keen on his wife.'

'No, so I've heard.'

'An arrogant bitch,' said Woodham, never one to mince his words. 'She loves showing off, riding around town in her carriage so everyone can see how elegant she is, how rich her clothes are. It's no wonder people think she's too big for her boots.'

'Boots? Surely not!'

'No, of course she doesn't wear boots, blockhead! Only the finest leather shoes from the best cordwainer in London will do for Her High and Mighty Grace! But you know what I mean. Everyone thinks she's just a little upstart who married well.'

'Came from Kent, didn't she?'

'Yeah. A place called Sterborough. Her father's Sir Reginald Cobham. He's fairly low down the pecking order as these things go. Mind you, he has the care of the Duke of Orléans at the moment. He's his custodian, so someone must think something of him.'

'I thought the Duke of Orléans was being sent back to France. That's what I heard, anyway.'

'Not if Duke Humphrey has anything to do with it. He's dead against it. I overheard him talking to Canon Hume about it the other day, when he was dictating a letter. To the King I think it was. Anyway, he was damned furious when Hume ran out of ink, I can tell you!'

'Then shouldn't you be getting back to the palace with it?'

'All in good time.' Woodham leaned his back against the wall, stretching his legs out comfortably towards the fire. 'I'll have another mug of this excellent ale first. For my trouble. You can get this one, Virley. And don't take all day buying it!'

He wiped his mouth on the back of his wrist and burped loudly.

***

'Uncle, tell me for pity's sake. What have I done to deserve this?'

King Henry paced up and down on the luxurious Persian carpet in the private royal solar at the Palace of Westminster, a roll of parchment in his hand. Every now and then he would stop his pacing to shake the letter aloft, in the direction of his great-uncle Cardinal Beaufort, who stood impassive, watching him.

'I mean,' the King went on, 'why does my uncle of Gloucester see fit to sign his name and include all his titles? Look at it. He styles himself *Duke of Gloucester, Holland, Zeeland and Brabant, Earl of Pembroke, Hainault and Flanders...*'

'To be fair to him, you must allow that he has been all these things in his time. That is to say he was all these things while he was married to the Duchess Jacqueline, but since he divorced the poor woman, I doubt he has a right to use those titles any longer. Perhaps he's included them because the document is to be read out in Parliament, just to remind everyone exactly how important he is.'

The King turned down his lower lip in a pout and shrugged his shoulders. 'Be that as it may,' he said. 'But, my Lord Uncle, he says some dreadful things about you.'

'That's nothing new,' Beaufort responded with a hollow laugh.

The King began his pacing again, looking down at the roll of parchment in his left hand, flicking at it with the back of his right hand as he enumerated each of the many points Humphrey of Gloucester had noted in his complaint.

'He says you shouldn't have been allowed to become a cardinal, that my late father forbade it. Then he says that you and Cardinal Kemp are taking over the council and thereby the running of the country instead of me ... *in derogation of your noble estate*, he says. And he's at pains to denounce the whole Congress of Arras as a complete waste of money. He states quite plainly that you are stripping the English crown of its assets and manoeuvring to get the Crown Jewels into your possession. He demands to know how you have come by your wealth!'

He looked up from the letter and was surprised to see his great-uncle appear quite calm, a slightly sardonic smile on his lips.

'Is that all he says?' asked Beaufort mildly. 'Can't he think of anything else? Hasn't he got any bigger sticks to beat me with?'

'Oh yes, plenty.' The King continued reading from the

226

lengthy document. 'He professes himself profoundly surprised that you procured the release of James of Scotland from English captivity without the consent of Parliament and turned this to your advantage by marrying your niece to him.'

'I can't see how that benefits me personally,' said Beaufort, brushing an unseen speck of dust off his sleeve, 'though it's true, Joan did become Queen of Scotland.'

'Then he goes on to accuse you of selling benefits and offices in England and France which were not yours to sell and says that by these ill-gotten gains, you have assumed the pomp and magnificence of royalty.'

'I was conceived on the wrong side of the blanket for that,' said Beaufort, drily.

'You can't be blamed for that, Uncle. At least you were legitimised when your parents were finally able to marry.' The King turned his attention back to the letter in his hand. 'But listen to this: my uncle of Gloucester goes on to say that you and Cardinal Kemp have estranged me from the Duke of York, the Earl of Huntingdon and the Archbishop of Canterbury, who should be counted among my chief advisers. I would disagree most strongly with that! I rely heavily on their advice, but I also rely on yours.'

Beaufort sighed deeply before replying. 'It's a nasty, malicious little missive, is it not?' he said.

'Indeed it is,' agreed the King. 'And I wonder what my uncle of Gloucester hoped to achieve by writing it.'

Henry Beaufort had another question to ask. 'Does he make any mention of Charles, Duke of Orléans?'

'No, he doesn't. Would you expect him to?'

'Oh yes. Your uncle is fervently opposed to the release of the Duke of Orléans, on the grounds that it would strengthen the position of the Duke of Burgundy in his claim that Charles de Valois is the rightful King of France. That is the fundamental disagreement between us.'

'That is nonsensical,' said King Henry. 'I am King of both England and France and everyone should acknowledge the fact. But I wish there was not so much enmity between us.'

'Of course, if you renounced your claim to the French

227

throne, life would be a great deal more peaceful.'

The King hesitated for a moment before replying. 'Peace is what I aspire to,' he said quietly. 'It is what I crave more than anything.'

'Even to the extent of renouncing the throne of France, Your Highness?'

'No, of course not. And, with God's grace, it will not come to that. But for the present, I can see nothing to be gained by holding the Duke of Orléans in captivity against his will.'

'Even though your late father decreed that he should be held at all costs?'

'Uncle, the Duke of Orléans was taken prisoner at the Battle of Agincourt. That was many years before I was even born. You know better than anyone how greatly I revere the memory of my late father, but I am King now. I am old enough to make my own decisions and I would dearly love to see peace between France and England. Surely it would be wise to pursue a peaceful foreign policy?'

'Certainly the ransom, which France will have to pay for the Duke's release, will ease the debt which burdens us.' Money was invariably a major consideration for Beaufort. If the full ransom was paid, then he himself might stand a reasonable chance of being repaid the money he had lent the crown. Perhaps even with a decent rate of interest.

'Then he must be released. And I will issue a manifesto to assure my people that the release of such an important prisoner from captivity is entirely my decision and my responsibility,' said the King decisively. 'Everyone must understand quite clearly that I am doing this on my own initiative for the sole purpose of bringing to an end the war in France.'

'There is both wisdom and bravery in that decision, Your Highness.'

'The war has gone on too long, it has killed too many Englishmen and has been too great a drain on the resources of the English crown. If the best way to secure peace is to release the Duke of Orléans, then so be it. After all, he is not privy to any of our state secrets so he can do no harm. Besides,' added the King with typical piousness, 'it is immoral to keep a prisoner of war in perpetual confinement.'

'Quite so,' agreed Beaufort. 'Quite so.'

There was no more to be said, particularly since he seemed easily to have won the King around to his way of thinking. That made him the victor in this, the latest skirmish in the ongoing battle between himself and his nephew of Gloucester.

***

From where she sat at her dressing table, the Duchess of Gloucester could see a perfect mirror image of Jenna's face. It was a study in concentration as she stood behind her mistress, pinning up her hair to make certain it would stay in place under the elaborate hennin that perched like an exotic bird on a wooden block on the dressing table, ready to be placed in position on Eleanor's head.

'You know, Jenna, no one would ever know that you had no experience of hairdressing at all when you started working for me.'

'I'm glad you're pleased with my work, Your Grace.'

'Very pleased. You've always been adaptable and you're prepared to work hard.' The Duchess watched her again, for a long minute. Grudgingly at first, she'd come to admire Jenna more and more as time went by, appreciating the way she applied herself to the job in hand, whatever it happened to be.

'But I do wish my skin was as good as yours,' Eleanor went on. 'Margery Jourdemayne insisted it was all due to her marigold face cream, but I've been using it for nearly three years now and my skin still can't compare with yours.'

'I think I'm just lucky, Your Grace.' Jenna smiled: she couldn't be disloyal to Margery, even now. The woman was a liar but, apart from anything else, she was William's wife, though the fact still stuck in Jenna's craw and, in her most despairing moments, it threatened to choke her.

William still trod the byways of her mind. The memory of the agonised expression on his face the day she had left the farm and walked out of his life was often the stuff of her bad dreams. She had seen him since, of course, but they'd both been stiffly formal with each other, neither wanting to meet the other's gaze, neither wanting to open up old wounds.

Almost as though she was reading her maid's thoughts, Eleanor said suddenly: 'I'm surprised you've never married, Jenna. You're pretty enough and with your skills, you would surely make some man a good wife. You do like men, do you?'

'I … well, I …' Jenna met the straightforward question with an embarrassed laugh.

'I understand there are some women who prefer the company of other women for, well, you know, that sort of companionship. Though I've never understood it myself.'

'No, Your Grace, I like men well enough. Women too, of course, but only as friends. I was very fond of my childhood friend Alice when I lived in Devon.'

'And what happened to Alice? Did she stay in Devon?'

Jenna looked away for a moment. 'She died, Your Grace.'

'Oh. Oh, I see, yes. I expect you missed her, did you?'

'Very much, Your Grace. I still do. She was a good friend.'

A good friend. Eleanor had never had a good friend. While she was younger she had concentrated all her energies on finding herself a rich, titled husband rather than a friend. And once she had ensnared the Duke of Gloucester, she regarded any other woman who came within two yards of him as a potential rival. She took nothing about Humphrey for granted. After all, he had been eager enough to desert his first wife's bed in favour of hers and she dared not run the risk that he might repeat that performance. So she had never let down her guard: she kept every other woman at arm's length and the greatest triumph she had ever known was when she walked out of church on her new husband's arm, secure in the knowledge that she was now the wife of one of the most important men in the land. By implication, therefore, she herself had become one of the most important women in the land. She revelled in the realisation.

Now, having devoted the best part of her life to him, she was beginning to wonder whether she had become too blinkered in her attitude, seeing neither to the left nor the right, with nothing on her horizon except Humphrey.

It wasn't as if Humphrey could be the kind of good friend

she sometimes needed, certainly not these days, and that was plain. He wasn't rude or unpleasant towards her – on the contrary, he always appeared to be charm itself. But he seemed preoccupied and distant. He didn't come to her boudoir of an afternoon as he had always done in the past; she would have to go in search of him. More often than not she found him at the writing desk in his study, behind a pile of heavy books on weighty subjects like mathematics, astronomy and the Greek philosophers, almost as though he had built himself a literary fortification against the rest of the world.

The truth was that her urbane, debonair husband was becoming something of a recluse, and when he did spend time with her, the talk soon turned not to the light-hearted topics she enjoyed but to subjects she found tedious and tiresome: the situation in France and how best that country should be ruled, how much he hated his uncle Henry Beaufort and, more than anything, how everyone was forgetting the good old days of England's glory, when his brother was King.

As he aged, so Humphrey had become embittered, and he now found his refuge not only between the covers of books but increasingly within decanters of wine: any wine – he no longer insisted on drinking nothing but the finest Burgundy. By mid-afternoon, his speech was often slurred and his hands shook.

Eleanor was worried about him. If he was to become King, this was no way to behave. His brother Henry had been a paragon of kingship and though he'd been dead nearly twenty years, the people still spoke his name with pride and reverence. If anything should happen to Humphrey's insipid nephew, and Humphrey himself was to inherit the throne, then he must at least try to live up to his late brother's glowing reputation. Becoming a drunkard was not the way to do that.

If only she could foresee the future…

'There, Your Grace,' Jenna said, placing the hennin on Eleanor's head and adjusting it to fit comfortably. 'Are you happy with that?'

'Let me see.' Roused from her reverie, Eleanor leaned forward to take the long-handled mirror out of its holder, and held it up so that she could inspect her reflection more closely in the light from the window. 'Mmm. Yes, that's not bad. What do you think of the colour?'

'I think that shade of blue suits you very well, Your Grace. It complements the grey of your eyes.'

'Good. Then help me into my houppelande. I must leave very soon. Canon Southwell and Magister Bolingbroke will be expecting me.'

'Are they not meeting you here, Your Grace?'

'No, our meeting will take place away from the palace today and it will be in private. Now, make haste with that houppelande, Jenna. I don't have time to waste.'

***

'Quick, Jane, quick! You'll never guess who's coming!'

Jane had been rhythmically sweeping the floor, with a long-handled cane besom, towards the stream that ran through the centre of the dairy. Now she stopped and looked up, alarmed.

'Who is it? What's the matter?'

Kitty was standing on tiptoe to look through a gap between the door frame and the wall which afforded her a good view of the Willow Walk. A hooded figure in a dark cloak was approaching the dairy at a determined pace.

'It's Mistress Jourdemayne!' she whispered dramatically.

'Old Mother Madge!' Jane's voice was hoarse. 'What on earth does she want? We haven't seen her here in the dairy for months. It's a wonder she remembers where it is!'

'She's probably up to no good,' said Hawys.

All three of them hurriedly took up positions of concentrated application to their work and when the door opened abruptly, they looked up, feigning surprise.

'Oh, Mistress Jourdemayne,' said Hawys from her pose behind a butter churn. In fact, she churned very little these days, being in an advanced stage of pregnancy. No sooner had she and Seth settled into one of the tiny workers' cottages on the Eye estate than she had become pregnant, and work in the dairy was getting more and more punishing for her. So, now that Kitty had grown much taller, she had taken on a great deal more of the churning for the sake of Hawys's aching back. If this was what knowing men and having babies did for a woman, Kitty thought, she really couldn't see why women were so keen on the whole idea. It was not something she was eager to do.

Margery Jourdemayne looked at the three faces turned expectantly towards her. Ah, yes, there she was, the youngest one. Kitty. The virgin. She had a job for Kitty to do, a very specific job, but she would have to be careful how she asked her to do it.

'Well, girls,' she said, addressing them all, 'I thought it was high time I paid you a visit. I have deserted you all for too long and I wondered how you all were. Is everything all right?'

'Yes, thank you, Mistress Jourdemayne,' they chorused obediently.

'And you, young Kitty,' Margery said, turning towards her with a winning smile. 'How are you getting along?'

'Very well, thank you, mistress.'

Kitty was no longer the shy little girl she had been a year or two ago – indeed, it would have been difficult to remain entirely naive while she worked every day with a gaggle of dairymaids who weren't above making lewd comments from time to time and cackling raucously at each other's bawdy jokes.

'I expect you're all looking forward to May Day, are you?'

'Yes, Mistress,' they chorused again, each one wondering what trick the Master's wife had up her sleeve. They were all aware of her reputation for duplicity.

'Well now, I wonder which one of you will be Queen of the Pea! Would you like to be, Kitty?'

Kitty was quite taken aback. 'Queen of the Pea, mistress? That's on Twelfth Night.'

Margery's hand flew to cover her mouth in an exaggerated gesture. 'Oh, yes! A slip of the tongue, of course. I meant Queen of the May.'

'Well, mistress … I … I don't think…'

'Do you remember when Jenna was Queen of the Pea?'

Kitty rewarded her with a huge smile. 'Oh, yes, mistress. She was lovely.'

'Yes, wasn't she? It's a pity she doesn't work here any more, isn't it? I expect you miss her, do you?'

'Oh, yes, mistress. I miss her all the time.'

Good, thought Margery Jourdemayne, she had hooked her fish. She smiled, encouragingly.

'Jenna was very good at counting. Have you learned to count, Kitty?'

'Yes, mistress. I can read a few words, too.' Kitty nodded, rightly proud of her own improving skills.

'That's very clever, Kitty. Would you like to come up to the farmhouse and help me, just like Jenna used to? If you'd like to, then you might see Jenna from time to time, when she calls to see me.'

Kitty hesitated. She had a bad feeling about Mistress Jourdemayne … and yet … and yet she knew she was far more likely to see Jenna in the room off the farmhouse kitchen than she ever did in the dairy. She played for time. 'What would the Master say?' she asked uncertainly. 'Wouldn't he be angry?

'Oh, I shouldn't think so, Kitty. But leave that to me. I'll explain it to the Master and I'm sure he won't mind a bit.'

'But what about the milk tallies, mistress? I've been learning how to do them and I do them quite often now. Master Jourdemayne –'

'Never you mind about Master Jourdemayne, I'll tell him.' Margery was becoming a little exasperated. 'And it doesn't matter about the milk tallies, either. Hawys can carry on with those. Now, come, child. Come with me.'

With her hand firmly clamped on Kitty's shoulder, she turned on her heel, pushing the girl towards the dairy door. Opening it, she thrust Kitty through in front of her.

Hawys and Jane stood stock still, staring at the back of the door as it closed.

'Dear God,' whispered Jane, 'what on earth does that old witch want with Kitty?'

'And how can I possibly go back to doing the tallies?' wailed Hawys. 'You know how much I hate doing them, Jane! You know, don't you? And in my state! I won't be able to get near an abacus, not with this big belly in the way!'

'Oh, get on with you,' said Jane with a nudge. 'I'll help you with the milk tallies. We'll manage them between us somehow and Nature will take her course with your belly. I'm far more concerned about what's going to happen to Kitty. I've got a very bad feeling about all this.'

Part Three

Accomplice

And moreover I saw under the sun the place of judgement, that wickedness was there; and the place of righteousness, that iniquity was there.

Ecclesiastes 3:16

CHAPTER SEVENTEEN

April 1441

Jenna's spirits always seemed to lift around the time of St George's Day. With winter well and truly departed, it was time to prepare the Duchess Eleanor's summer wardrobe and, for the past week, the rosemary bushes in a secluded part of the kitchen garden at La Pleasaunce had been festooned with Her Grace's light linen shifts drying in the spring sunshine. The laundresses had made up a mild solution of cuckoo-pint root for Jenna so that she could lightly starch the pristine white undergarments. Now they were thoroughly dry, she could fold them and store them neatly in the linen press. Then she'd be able to find exactly what the Duchess wanted whenever she demanded it.

Her Grace did seem to be particularly demanding at the moment. She had been restless and irritable for several weeks and there had been occasions when Jenna had been hard put to hold her tongue. She did her best to remember that she was dealing with a frustrated woman who was hopelessly irritated by the fact that her husband seemed to be taking less and less interest in her. No doubt the Duchess was also worried about the Duke's excessive drinking, Jenna thought, and though she understood it well enough, it was not her place to say anything until she was asked. The question, when it came, took her entirely by surprise.

'Do you think my husband looks ill, Jenna?'

She wasn't sure how to reply. If she expressed her honest opinion that the Duke looked whey-faced and sick, she could expect to be slapped down for having made an insulting remark. If, on the other hand, she said she thought the Duke looked well, she could be accused of lying. The judicious answer lay somewhere in between.

'I think perhaps he is working too hard, Your Grace,' she ventured hesitantly. 'He seems to spend a great deal of time in studying his books.'

'And in drinking his wine!'

The comment was like the crack of a whip and it was difficult to think of anything sensible to say in reply. The Duchess slumped down onto the stool at her dressing table, cradling her head in her hands.

'He'll kill himself. I'm almost beside myself with worry about him.'

'Oh, please, Your Grace, try not to distress yourself. I'm sure your husband can be persuaded to drink less. Perhaps he needs to talk to someone ... I don't know, a physician perhaps. Someone whose opinion he respects.' Not knowing what to do, Jenna found herself stroking the back of Eleanor's head in a helpless gesture of comfort.

'Oh, what can you possibly know about it!' The Duchess shook off Jenna's hand with an impatient toss of her head. 'You have no experience of anything like this.'

Jenna didn't reply immediately. Her mistress had dropped her guard and given in to her concerns: she might have been any woman in desperate need of understanding and friendship. It was time to share a secret, time to acknowledge a common problem and make a gesture of reassurance and support.

'In fact, Your Grace,' Jenna said hesitantly, 'I do have experience of it. Quite a lot of experience as it happens.'

'What? What do you mean?' Slowly, Eleanor turned to face Jenna. 'What sort of experience?'

'I ... well, you see, I ... I have been married myself, Your Grace. And I was married to a man who was unable to control his drinking. Jake couldn't control his temper either, and he was twice as bad when he was drunk.'

'But you've never said a word about this!' Eleanor's grey eyes were wide with surprise.

'The subject never arose, Your Grace. You never asked and I've never really wanted to discuss it with anyone.'

'Then why are you telling me this now?'

'Just ... oh, I don't know ... just so that you know you're not alone. You're not the only woman who has had to face the problem.'

'I knew nothing of this. Why did you not tell me you had been married?'

'It never seemed relevant, Your Grace. I didn't see any reason to burden you with the information. Besides, I wanted you to judge my work on its merits. I didn't want you to feel sorry for me.'

'Why should I have felt sorry for you?'

Now that she had started talking about her past, Jenna knew there was no way out. She had to be honest.

'Drinking ale made my Jake very violent, Your Grace. He ... he often used to hit me. More than once I went to church with a black eye. And I have Jake to thank for this puffball ear.' She lifted the corner of her linen coif to show her mistress the distorted ear she still hid from view and always would; Eleanor winced at the sight of it. 'I'm still slightly deaf from his blows. He beat me much more than is reasonable for a man to chastise his wife. My mother always said so. He never took a stick to me, but he used to lash out, punch me, slap me, kick me ...' Her voice faded.

'So ... what happened? Were you ... did you...'

'I ran away, Your Grace. I couldn't take any more. I was afraid he'd kill me one day. I was in constant fear for my life. My mother used to say that if I gave Jake a son, he'd change his ways, but I didn't want to have a child, not if the poor little thing was going to be beaten black and blue by his father. I couldn't bear that. I couldn't possibly bear that. I never wanted his baby.'

A bitter expression distorted Eleanor's mouth. 'And I've done everything possible to give my husband a child, but much good it's done me. Lately I've been trying to arouse him at the time of the month when Margery Jourdemayne says I'm most likely to conceive, exactly according to her instructions. Sometimes I've behaved like a Winchester goose, but it's no use; he's usually too drunk to do anything but snore.'

'I know the sound of snoring, Your Grace!' Jenna

241

ventured a conspiratorial smile.

'Jenna, sit down.'

'No, really, Your Grace, it's not my place…'

'Jenna, I'm telling you to sit. No … I'm asking you. Please. I need to talk to someone, someone who understands. So, please sit down. I'd be grateful. Please sit and listen to me … I think you could help me answer some questions. I don't know who else to turn to and I'm desperate.'

Jenna lowered herself tentatively onto the edge of a chair alongside her mistress. This felt very wrong to her. She had never sat down in the presence of the Duchess.

'Tell me, Jenna, when did you become aware that your husband was drinking too much?'

'Soon after we were married, Your Grace.'

'Did you never suspect it before that?'

'No. At least, I don't think so. He always seemed such good company, so popular. And very handsome. My friend Alice … well, no, not just Alice, all the girls in Kingskerswell had an eye for him, wanted him for a husband. I was so proud when he chose me. I suppose, looking back, he had been trying to impress me in the days before we were married and I thought he would always be the same. Then when I became his wife, I saw the other side of him, the darker side I hadn't seen before.'

'How did that happen?'

'Well, I had seen him after too much ale several times and at first it didn't seem to matter. Most men of his age got cidered-up – skimmished – from time to time, on Twelfth Night, May Day, Harvest Home, that sort of thing. Then I realised how much money Jake was spending in the ale house when I needed it to buy food. So I asked him to stop.'

'And?'

'He hit me. That was the first time. He told me to stop being such a stupid, interfering bitch … Oh, I beg your pardon, mistress! I had no wish to give offence!'

'Don't worry. I won't punish you for that. This is just between the two of us. Mercifully my husband has never hit me, but I sometimes find his behaviour very difficult to understand. So, perhaps you can help me come to terms with it. It could be that we have much in common.'

The floodgates, once opened, released a torrent in both of them. Importantly for Eleanor, she felt she was unburdening herself to a friend.

***

'Is the man mad! What can he possibly be thinking of?'

'I don't think my hot-headed nephew is any more mad now than he was six months ago,' Henry Beaufort said matter-of-factly. 'He has always been stubborn and he is adamant that Charles of Orléans must not, under any circumstances, be released from English custody.'

The two men were sitting in a pool of candlelight at a table in the sumptuous library at Winchester Palace in Southwark, where a small pile of logs lay ready to be burned in the inglenook fire basket as daylight faded. The table was bare save for a decanter of wine, two goblets and a small plate of sweetmeats placed between the two. They were deep in conversation.

'Then he must be persuaded to see our point of view,' said John Kemp, 'it is imperative. Otherwise England will be bankrupt. Just because the Duke of Gloucester can't bear to let go of France.'

'The trouble,' said Beaufort, 'is not simply that he can't bear to let go of France, but that he will not let go of an old concept. Humphrey cannot accept that things are not as they used to be. His brother is dead. For Heaven's sake, King Henry V has been dead these twenty years. Humphrey can't hold on to the past. It's gone. He has to let it go.'

'And you're quite certain, are you, Beaufort, that His Highness the King thinks Charles of Orléans should be returned to France?'

'Certain. Absolutely certain of it. He said so only a week or so ago when he had received that malicious complaint in which Gloucester attacked me – and indeed you, Kemp – implying that we were trying to take over the whole country. That astounded the King.'

'He didn't believe it though, did he?'

'No, of course he didn't believe it. He dismissed it. The mere suggestion is preposterous and the King has refuted the accusation entirely. He has already issued a manifesto which says that the decision to release Charles of Orléans is his own, influenced by God and reason alone.'

There was a long silence between the two of them. As the April evening set in, so the air took on a distinct chill and Henry Beaufort stood up to close the window himself, rather than summoning a footman to do it for him. He didn't want any member of his staff to overhear the conversation he was having with Kemp.

'What do you imagine goes on at those entertainments Humphrey and his hussy of a wife hold in their house at Greenwich?' he asked, as he returned to his seat.

'I dread to think.'

'Well, I'm told that my nephew has always been keen on discussing philosophy, astronomy, astrology, that sort of thing. And I have that information on very good authority.'

'Really?'

'Yes. Many years ago, I invited the Italian Poggio Bracciolini here to London. A charming, intelligent man. Oh, it must be at least twenty years ago, long before Humphrey started renovating his house at Greenwich. But Bracciolini would sometimes meet Humphrey and his friends of an evening and he always said that the talk was of little but books, astrological texts, history, moral philosophy and so on.'

'In what context?'

'I'm not really sure, to be honest.' Beaufort seemed to hesitate before continuing. 'You know, I've never expressed this opinion before and I'd be grateful if you would keep it to yourself and say nothing to anyone else, but … well…'

'But what, Henry? You can tell me. It won't go any further than this room.'

'Well, just think for a moment, John. I wonder whether the subjects which interest Humphrey of Gloucester most of all sometimes border on humanism.'

'Humanism!' Kemp was aghast. 'Surely not! Humanism runs contrary to all the teachings of the Holy Mother Church. It questions the authority of the Divine. It's only a very small step from humanism to Lollardy.'

'Careful! Careful, Kemp. You can't accuse Gloucester of Lollardy. That is a very serious accusation. Inflammatory!'

'But Gloucester clearly doesn't give a tinker's cuss what he says about you, Beaufort. Just look at the complaint he sent the King.'

'The King has repudiated it. He does not accept any of the accusations Gloucester made.'

'That's a great mercy and let us be grateful for it. But do go on, Henry. What else did Signor Bracciolini tell you about the entertainments your nephew enjoys?'

'Music plays a part in them, certainly. And since that lutenist fellow, whatever his name is, has become a member of the Gloucester household, it wouldn't surprise me to hear that he treats the assembled company to some of his compositions.'

'Oh, you mean Barnstable? Yes, he's a fine composer. His motets and so on are excellent.'

'I don't imagine for a moment that he performs his sacred music at La Pleasaunce.'

'Well, it's hardly a church!'

'Quite. But I'm told he composes some rather fine songs, too, which would make him popular with my nephew's flibbertigibbet of a wife. A little bird told me that she will get up and sing at the drop of a hat!'

'But not a cardinal's hat!'

'No, never that! A cardinal would have more sense than to drop his hat anywhere in the vicinity of that dreadful woman.'

They laughed. Neither man was impressed by the Duchess of Gloucester.

Kemp looked thoughtful for a moment as he took a sip from his wine goblet. 'Would it be possible to discredit her in any way?' he asked.

'To what end?'

'To embarrass Gloucester. It's no more than he deserves after sending that complaint to the King.'

Beaufort paused while he considered Kemp's question. 'It could be a means to an end, I suppose. But it might not be an easy thing to achieve. If she were to fall from grace in any way, he would immediately leap to her defence.'

'Not if he wasn't here.' Kemp leaned forward, his elbows on the table. 'I've been thinking, Henry, so hear me out. Now, as it happens, the matter of charter renewal for the Abbey at St Albans has not been entirely resolved. So, perhaps His Grace the Duke could be persuaded to visit his old friend Abbot Wheathampstead once again.'

'Ah, I see what you mean,' Beaufort said. 'And, of course, in his absence, we would be forced to hold Council meetings without him.'

'Exactly.'

'So he would be unable to obstruct the decision-making process.'

'Precisely.'

'But it would suit our purpose even better if he could, perhaps, go further afield and visit another part of the country, to keep him out of the way for a few months. That would give us all a welcome breathing space.'

'Indeed,' said Kemp, 'and am I not right in thinking that he has recently been made Chief Justice of South Wales?'

'He has. That was agreed by the Council back in February.'

'Well,' Kemp went on, 'I understand that there are Assizes to be held in Cardigan and Carmarthen later in the year. So might he, do you think, be persuaded to oversee the administration of justice there during the coming summer? After all, his ability to suppress disturbances is well known. He's quite famous for it.'

Beaufort was regarding his companion with an exaggeratedly quizzical expression on his face. 'So, are you implying that he could bring his skills to bear on the unruly Welsh?'

'I'm sure he could. Particularly if a small grant could be made available to help him,' suggested John Kemp, a smile tweaking his thin lips.

'That should not present a problem,' said Beaufort. 'No doubt the Council could put aside a sum of, say, around two hundred pounds for that purpose. It shouldn't be difficult.'

'Then,' said Kemp, 'in Gloucester's absence, the Council would be able to arrange the repatriation of Charles of Orléans without interference. Perfect!' he concluded delightedly and both men laughed.

'And you know,' Beaufort said after a pause to replenish their goblets, 'while the field is clear, we might take a closer look at the Duchess's activities. A few discreet inquiries could yield interesting results.'

Kemp looked doubtful. 'Wouldn't she be travelling with her husband?'

'To the far west of Wales? No, not if I have the measure of the woman. It would be far too uncomfortable for her! And if he should happen to be unexpectedly delayed in Wales for some time while she remains in Westminster, we will have ample opportunity to find out quite a lot about her.'

'That could be most entertaining!' said Kemp, and they both laughed again.

***

For the last week or so, Jenna had felt, oddly, as though a weight had been lifted from her mind. Her relationship with her mistress had taken on an entirely different dimension; there was a new honesty between them and Eleanor had begun to treat her maid as though she was a person of some worth, but Jenna doubted that she would ever treat her with respect. Not that she needed that. At least the secret of her unhappy marriage was now out in the open, she had shared it with someone, even though the wife of a Duke was the last person on earth she would have expected to share it with.

The Duchess was keeping another of her assignations that afternoon and was not expected back at the Palace of Westminster for two or three hours. For all that she had begun to confide in Jenna, Eleanor had never shared the information about where she went on these occasions. All she would say was that she had business to attend to away from the palace and would be gone for some time. She never took any of her ladies nor her maids with her, she was accompanied only by Canon Hume, the secretary whose services she shared with her husband, and two guards to provide protection for them both. She dressed circumspectly, too, which was certainly unlike her. Though Jenna's interest was aroused, she was not inquisitive enough to try and find out where her mistress went on these occasions; it was not her business to know.

With a few precious hours to call her own, she took advantage of the opportunity to visit Eybury farmhouse. It was several weeks since she'd been able to snatch even a few minutes with Kitty.

If she had a little time to spare, Jenna always preferred to take the riverbank route to the farmhouse because it gave her time to think, free and unencumbered by the regulations and expectations of others, almost as though she was totally in charge of her own life. In these rare private moments, it delighted her to catch the occasional glimpse of a shy, blunt-nosed water vole or watch a dabbling mallard upended in the water, industriously fishing, her tail in the air and her busy bill below the surface. It always amused Jenna that the female was a drably brown little duck while her mate boasted beautiful multi-coloured feathers with a proud head of iridescent green. Just like a man, she thought, he'd wait until the dowdy little female was committed to her nest, brooding her young, then he'd abandon her and go off somewhere else with a group of like-minded drakes.

Of course, it wasn't always the case that men went away and left women to fend for themselves. She herself had made the choice to leave her man and she had never regretted her decision for an instant. Now her life had taken on a rhythm, a routine; she knew where she was and what her duties were and the Duchess seemed to appreciate her work. She wouldn't allow herself to think about William Jourdemayne.

It didn't seem to worry the Duchess that her own husband was preparing to go away very soon. It would not be for long, she assured Jenna, so she didn't think she needed to accompany him. Besides, he was going to the far west of Wales where he was Chief Justice and, surely, nobody went to any part of Wales unless they had to. The place bordered on the barbaric from what she had heard. No, she would not accompany him; she would be content to stay at home. Of course, she would concentrate on making her husband feel very welcome on his return – and she well knew how to do that!

Not only was the Duchess calm in her acceptance of the Duke's imminent absence, Jenna thought, it was almost as though she appreciated the respite this would afford her. She said she planned to spend a considerable amount of time in reading. Her Grace had an eclectic taste in books. Jenna often looked at their titles as she tidied them away in the library after her mistress had finished with them. Here were the chivalric romances she was so fond of, Geoffrey Chaucer's *Canterbury Tales* and *The Parliament of Fowls* as well as a beautifully bound copy of the same author's treatise on the astrolabe. Jenna had seen the astrolabe, but had no real idea what use was made of it. That was for men of learning, men like Canon Southwell and Magister Bolingbroke. They spent a considerable time with her mistress and Her Grace appeared to have great respect for their scholarship. The Duchess herself didn't usually give the impression of being learned, but then a woman had very little to gain by appearing too clever.

Rounding a bend in the path on the way to Eybury farmhouse, Jenna's heart skipped a beat as it always did at the sight of it. She rarely saw William these days, but he was never far from her thoughts and being anywhere on the Eye estate meant she ran the risk of bumping into him which always made her feel apprehensive. Pushing open the big door of the farmhouse kitchen, she stopped on the threshold for a moment to listen but there was no sound.

'Hello,' she called. 'Is there anybody here? Hello!'

There was no answering call so she crossed the kitchen floor and knocked, cautiously, at the closed door of Margery's room. Again, there was no reply; Mistress Jourdemayne was clearly not at home. She might be up at the palace, of course, because she still supplied several of the ladies of the court with their essential cosmetic requirements, but the Duchess Eleanor only rarely made use of her services nowadays. Jenna moved to the kitchen window and looked out but, apart from meeting the malevolent stare of a small black cat which had leapt onto the windowsill outside, she could see no clue to Mistress Jourdemayne's whereabouts.

'Where's your mistress, Gib?'

The cat lost interest in Jenna, licked its paw and began washing its face. There was nothing to be gained by remaining in the farmhouse so she might as well go and see her friends in the dairy. Besides, she could hardly wait to see her Kittymouse again.

Having run the length of Willow Walk, she was panting slightly as she pushed open the door to the dairy without ceremony and every head turned towards her.

'Jenna!'

'Good Heavens, Jenna! Where have you been all this time?'

There were only three people in the big room, though Hawys looked as though she was about to give birth to another one at any moment. Jane and another girl, a complete stranger to Jenna, abandoned their butter churns, wiping their hands on their aprons as they came to join Hawys, forming an excited, chattering circle surrounding the newcomer. Kitty was nowhere to be seen.

'Where's Kitty?'

Churns, butter paddles and skimming dishes lay idle and everyone was talking at once.

'Where's Kitty?' Jenna demanded to know a second time.

'Oh, Jenna,' wailed Hawys, 'we're all so worried. We didn't know what to do for the best...'

'Let me tell her,' said Jane, elbowing poor Hawys to one side, 'I know exactly what happened –'

'So do I!' said Hawys, indignant.

'No you don't, Hawys, you don't know what Kitty tells me in the dormitory. You sleep in your cottage with Seth so you don't hear secrets.'

'Secrets? What secrets? Where is Kitty? What's happening?' Jenna was scanning the excited faces in front of her, anxious to know what had happened.

'Kitty's working with Mistress Jourdemayne,' said Hawys, 'and we don't know what she's doing. She won't tell us.'

'What do you mean?'

'Mistress Jourdemayne came here to the dairy about a fortnight ago,' Jane said, 'and she took Kitty away with her. We haven't seen very much of her since then.'

'She's working with Mistress Jourdemayne?' Jenna was dumbfounded. 'Is she doing what I used to do? Labelling containers, packing the orders? Is that what she's doing?'

'Oh, yes, of course,' said Jane, folding her arms and nodding her head, 'she's doing that, all right. She's a bright child, she can read more words than I ever could and she's very good at reckoning.'

'But we think she's doing something else as well,' Hawys interrupted, 'except she won't tell us what it is.'

'Something like what? Tell me! For God's sake, tell me!' Jenna turned to Jane who seemed to be the one who knew most and grabbed her by the arm. 'Jane, what did Kitty tell you in the dormitory?'

Jane shook her arm free then looked down, seeming unwilling to meet Jenna's questioning eyes. She thrust her hands deep into her apron pockets and shook her head.

'She won't say. She wouldn't tell me anything except that she's helping Mistress Jourdemayne and two clerical gentlemen with some experiments.' She looked up again, this time directly at Jenna. 'And I'm worried about her, Jenna, she's unhappy. But she won't tell me why, or exactly what she's doing. I've got a very bad feeling about it.'

Jenna was quiet while the other women watched her face, anxious, waiting for her to react. What they saw there was an expression of white fury. Jenna's lips were compressed into a hard line and her eyes glinted like tempered steel under the thunderous furrowed arc of her brow. At length she spoke.

'If that damned witch harms a hair of Kitty's head, I swear I'll kill her,' she snarled. 'By the blood of Christ, she'd better have a good reason for this.'

Turning on her heel, she slammed the dairy door behind her.

CHAPTER EIGHTEEN

June 1441

John Virley was looking forward to the reward of a well-earned tankard of ale on his way home. He had already done the best part of a day's work and the cobbled city streets of London could be hard on a fellow's feet, especially when he was carrying a heavy bag full of parchment. To be fair, the bag got lighter and lighter as he delivered his orders to different places along his route and, in truth, he didn't really mind working on a fine spring day like this.

He had already delivered three reams of parchment to St Bartholomew's Priory, just to the north-west of the city wall, then a dozen quill pens to St Botolph-without-Aldgate, the church he'd attended as a child. Back inside the city walls again, a pleasant stroll down St Martin's Lane brought him to the collegiate church of St Martin-le-Grand where the canons had ordered only four quires of parchment.

By the time he had delivered an order to the Franciscan Grey Friars, it was an easy matter for a man who knew the area so well to cut through the maze of narrow backstreets to his final destination. Once through Newgate, the churchyard of St Sepulchre-without-Newgate was directly in front of him. The vicar at St Sepulchre's hadn't placed a very big order this time, he only needed ink and that hardly weighed anything at all, so Virley's step was light as he crossed the road between Newgate Jail and the church. It was his last call of the morning and he was glad to get inside the building and take shelter from a sudden, heavy shower of rain.

'A very good day to you, Vicar!' he greeted John Stone as he walked up the nave towards the rood screen in front of the chancel. Stone was busying himself re-arranging the chalice, the paten and the other silverware on the altar.

'Ah, yes, good morning, Master Virley. It's a lovely day! We must thank the Good Lord for that.'

'Well, it *was* a lovely day, Vicar, but it's just started raining. Still, it's only a passing shower. Shouldn't last long. I've brought the ink you ordered. Shall I take it through to the vestry for you? And leave it on the table?'

'Ah, yes. Yes, of course. I'm grateful. Thank you. I've nearly finished here.'

Emerging from the vestry after delivering the ink, Virley looked hard at the older man. He seemed unusually edgy, pulling at his earlobe and directing snatched, anxious glances down the nave towards the door. He appeared to be clearing a space at the centre of the altar.

'Well, goodbye for now, Vicar. Expecting visitors, did you say?'

'Er, no, I didn't, did I? No. Well, yes, in a way. Not just yet. A little later.'

'Anyone I know?' Virley wasn't usually so inquisitive. Perhaps it was just that the vicar seemed oddly nervous.

'Oh, er, no. No, just some colleagues. Canon Hume and Canon Southwell of Westminster and Magister Bolingbroke, late of Oxford. They have been here before.'

'Ah, Canon Southwell. Yes, I know him from my own days at Westminster. They'll be saying mass, then?'

'Er … yes, yes. Saying mass. Yes.'

Virley looked around him. There wasn't another soul in sight. The place was deserted. That struck him as strange. Surely members of the congregation should have started arriving by now. The sound of the door being opened distracted him and he looked round. Yes, there was Southwell, brushing raindrops from his dark woollen cloak before strutting, pompous as ever, towards the altar. He'd recognise him anywhere. With him was a tall, stooping man with thinning hair who was removing his spectacles in order to wipe the wet lenses on his sleeve. That must be the Magister, thought Virley.

'I'll be on my way, then,' he said quietly to Vicar Stone.

'Best get a move on if I'm to be in time for my dinner.' He didn't particularly want to stay if Southwell was going to be involved in the mass.

'Yes, yes. Well, goodbye then. God be with you.' Distractedly, the vicar made the sign of the cross in Virley's direction and turned to greet his visitors. Virley moved out of sight behind a stone pillar near the door without being noticed.

Having slipped quietly out of the church, he stopped for a moment in the churchyard and looked back towards St Sepulchre's. He couldn't rid himself of a feeling that something was wrong, but he had no idea what. There were three men of God inside the church and there was nothing unusual about that. They were just going about their business, saying mass. He shrugged as he turned towards the path.

Then he saw Margery Jourdemayne and froze.

She was sheltering under the lychgate, peering out to see if the rain had stopped, her cupped hand stretched out in front of her. Margery Jourdemayne, the instigator of his downfall a decade ago, the reason why he had spent those long, dreary months incarcerated in the damp stinking dungeons of Windsor Castle. And here she was again, under the thatched roof of the lychgate. That was the best place for her, thought Virley, a place of corpses and death.

But what, in God's name, was the damned woman doing here? Wanting to avoid her at all costs, he was grateful that the trunk of the churchyard yew was wide enough for him to duck down behind it, out of sight. Virley's memories of Margery were still vivid and, to his mind, she was something a great deal more sinister than the wise woman she had claimed to be. She was a witch.

The witch had a child with her, a girl. From this distance, it was difficult to tell how old the girl was, she looked as though she might be ten or eleven but small breasts were evident under her working smock so Virley, with his experience of the female form, judged her to be about thirteen or fourteen years old, but small for her age.

The shower was passing as quickly as it had arrived and Virley watched as the two of them cautiously emerged from the

255

lychgate then hurried up the path towards the church porch. Whatever the reason they were here, the child was clearly reluctant about it because the witch, with a firm hold of the girl's arm, was having to drag her along the path.

Virley waited until the heavy church door opened from within to admit them. As it closed, he was about to make a dash for freedom when, to his astonishment, the door was opened again. The vicar emerged and walked quickly away down the path. He was clearly not going to be taking part in any mass that was going on inside: if it was a mass.

As soon as John Stone had pulled the lychgate closed behind him, Virley emerged from his hiding place behind the great yew tree and prepared to follow him. He must get to the bottom of this, whatever it was. It looked as though the witch was up to her old tricks again and she was clearly associating with Southwell and Bolingbroke as she had once done with Friar Ashwell and himself.

But, if that's all it was, what was the child doing there?

***

The Duchess Eleanor's dressing room was where Jenna seemed to spend her whole life. It was almost like home. She knew every inch of it, the contents of every drawer and cupboard, the linen press and the laundry basket. The Duchess had been impressed by Jenna's ability to write and was delighted at the suggestion that she should keep a daily record of which gown and shoes her mistress had worn on what occasion, and which jewellery she had worn to complement the ensemble. Whatever the Duchess wanted, Jenna was expected to know exactly where it was; and she always did. By now, Her Grace would not tolerate anything less.

In the few short years she had been working at the palace, Jenna's appearance had changed considerably and her clothes were modestly fashionable for a woman in her position. Her hands, always roughened by farm work in years gone by, were softer and smoother, and her trimmed fingernails would never snag the delicate fabric of her mistress's finest veils. Under her linen wimple, the sun-tanned face of yesteryear had become fashionably pale since she worked almost entirely indoors. But she still harboured a secret longing for the satisfaction of a good day's toil. Indulging the every whim of a spoilt mistress never seemed like real work to Jenna.

She would have gone back to the farm in a heartbeat, but she knew she couldn't. Of course, she was very concerned about Kitty, but it wasn't just that. Now she was no longer honestly exhausted when she went to her bed, she had begun to sleep badly and was often plagued by dreams in which William was angry with her and she didn't know why. These dreams left her feeling distressed and saddened. Obeying some nameless instinct, she ran her hands over the soft skin of her body, the outline of her thighs, the curve of her breasts, yearning for the touch of a man – but not any man. She ached for the sheer, raw presence of William Jourdemayne, longing to be as one with him. Jenna had never known a desire as strong as this and it didn't diminish with time. Equally, she knew that her yearning was hopelessly misplaced: she was in love with another woman's husband. It was a forbidden love, a dangerous love. *Thou shalt not covet thy neighbour's wife*, said Moses. No, nor thy neighbour's husband, either, thought Jenna. However deep it was, hers was a love forbidden by God.

And now her anxieties were heightened by her worry about Kitty. She longed to get back to the farm to find out what was going on. She needed to know exactly what Kitty was doing for Mistress Jourdemayne and whether the other dairymaids' fears were well founded. Between them, William and Kitty, the two most important people in her life, were causing her deep concern.

'When did I last wear this gown?' the Duchess demanded, interrupting Jenna's thoughts. Mistress and maid had been going through the richly gilded armoire in the dressing room where Her Grace's best gowns were kept. Both doors of the big cupboard were open and some twenty or so sumptuous garments hung in a serried rank within it. The Duchess was pulling at various hems, inspecting the colours and the fabrics, prompting her memory of individual dresses, trying to make a decision. Jenna had been standing behind her, waiting for Her

257

Grace to choose what she wanted to wear when she went out.

'Is that the dark blue samite, Your Grace? I'm almost certain you wore it at the reception which His Highness the King gave for the Spanish Ambassador, but I'd better look it up.' Jenna opened the small leather-bound volume in which she made a note of the Duchess's social engagements and what she had worn for each.

'I must have had that one made for me at least five years ago,' said the Duchess, 'but it's still one of my favourites.' As Jenna consulted her notes, Eleanor draped the fabric of the gown over her left hand, smoothing it with her right, looking at it this way and that. She loved the way the rich blue silk was interwoven with threads of pure gold. Gold: the pinnacle of the alchemist's achievement, the fabulous metal that would never change its lustre, no matter what man did to it, whether it was used to make a wedding ring or beaten as thin as a leaf, thin enough for a limner to use in illuminating a manuscript.

'The blue suits you very well, Your Grace, it brings out the colour of your eyes.'

'Do you really think so, Jenna?'

'Indeed, Your Grace. And I was right,' she added, nodding her head as she checked an entry in her note book, 'you last wore the blue samite at the King's reception for the Spanish Ambassador and you haven't worn it since. On that occasion you also wore the diamond and sapphire necklace which was a birthday gift from His Grace the Duke.'

'Ah, sapphire, the stone of destiny, and as you say, that lovely dark blue does enhance the grey of my eyes.'

'While I have my notebook to hand, Your Grace, I'm anxious to bring it up to date,' Jenna said. 'Have you any engagements I don't know about?'

'No, nothing while my husband is away in Wales, except for dinner at the King's Head in Cheapside later in the month.'

'Yes, Your Grace. June the twenty-eighth. I have a note of it.'

'These days,' the Duchess said, 'I tell you what has been arranged before I tell anyone. I rely on your little notebook rather more than I rely on Canon Hume. It's very clever of you to be able to write. I value that ability in a member of my staff.'

'I'm always grateful I was taught the skill, Your Grace.'

'Do you read much, Jenna?'

'Not really, Your Grace. I don't have much opportunity, nor have I any money to buy books.'

'No, quite. Books are expensive. But perhaps, one day, I'll let you read one or two of mine.'

'That is most generous of you, Your Grace. I would be very grateful.'

'Yes, I'm sure you'd enjoy them. The simpler ones, of course.'

Jenna hid a smile. 'Of course, Your Grace. The simpler ones would be best.'

***

Virley followed Vicar Stone at a discreet distance, anxious in case his quarry should happen to glance around suddenly and spot him. Stone walked at a smart pace but Virley, a decade younger, was easily able to keep up with him. By now he was burning with curiosity to know what was going on, even happy to sacrifice his reward in the ale house if only he could find out.

From Newgate, John Stone turned right into Warwyke Lane then kept up his brisk walk until he turned left into Paternoster Row. Virley slowed his pace. Clearly the man had business in St Paul's and since the cathedral was such a public meeting place, that business was unlikely to be of a private nature. So there would be nothing to be deduced from that. He might as well find an ale house after all.

'Virley! You old dog!'

He knew that voice. Odd, he thought, that he'd hardly seen the man since they were youngsters, but now he seemed to bump into William Woodham every few weeks. And always in the vicinity of St Paul's. He turned to see Woodham riding up behind him, leading another horse by the bridle.

'Collecting some more stationery, Virley?' bellowed Woodham, slithering down from his mount.

'No. I've just been delivering some. And you? What are you doing round these parts?'

'Oh, this and that, you know. I'm footloose and fancy-free as it happens, for an hour or so anyway. Time to squeeze in a mug or two of ale. Care to join me? I've just accompanied Canon Hume to St Sepulchre's and he didn't want me to wait...'

'St. Sepulchre's!' Virley exclaimed, taken aback. 'But I've just come from there. I didn't see you.'

'Ah, you wouldn't have. I didn't stay outside more than a minute. Just enough time for him to dismount and go inside. He never wants me to wait. This is his horse.'

'Then you dare not tie up these animals outside an ale house, Woodham. They're valuable, surely.'

'I'll find a boy to look after them. That'll be worth a farthing to any street urchin. 'Ere, boy!' he shouted and was instantly surrounded by a cluster of youngsters, vying for his attention. 'Who wants to earn a farthing for an hour's work?'

There was no shortage of willing volunteers and from the small window of the ale house which looked out on to Paternoster Row, William Woodham was easily able to keep an eye on the two horses and the adolescent boy who had firm hold on their bridles. From the look of pride on his grubby face, he might have been given responsibility for the crown jewels.

'That'll be something to go home and tell his mother,' Woodham said with a smile, turning back from the window. 'If he's got a mother, that is.'

'Who knows?' said Virley. 'Probably never had the benefit of a father, though!'

'Poor bastard. That was you and me twenty years ago, Virley.'

'Well, at least we both had fathers,' Virley objected, 'so you can't call us bastards.'

'I wasn't going to. We were the lucky ones.'

Despite the noise in the small room, they drank in companionable silence for a moment. There was a question Virley wanted to ask and now was the time to ask it.

'What's going on in St Sepulchre's?'

'How do you mean, "going on"?'

'Well, I've just delivered some ink to the Vicar and he was behaving very strangely. Then that tub of lard Thomas

Southwell turned up with a tall, thin fellow wearing spectacles.'

'That'll be Roger Bolingbroke. They're both advisers to the Duchess of Gloucester.'

'That's what the vicar said, though he didn't mention the Duchess of Gloucester. He said they've met there before this.'

'Yes, they do meet quite often, with or without Her High and Mighty Grace. Not always in St Sepulchre's. Sometimes it's St Martin-in-the-Vintry ... St Benet Hithe ... could be anywhere, really.'

'And is the Duchess the only woman involved in these meetings?'

'As far as I know she is. I've never seen any others.'

'Interesting,' said Virley thoughtfully. 'They meet to say Mass, do they?'

'Yeah. As far as I know. I'm never invited to stay.'

'Aren't you ever curious, William?'

'It doesn't pay to be. Me? I keep my mouth shut and mind my own business. It's easier that way.'

Virley changed the subject. He clearly wasn't going to get any more information from Woodham so it was pointless asking him if he knew why Margery Jourdemayne and the girl might be involved. He'd have to carry out his own investigation.

'Let me get you another one of those,' he said, getting to his feet and draining his tankard to the dregs. 'And then I'd better get going. I've promised to meet a very promising companion and she's cooking dinner for me.'

'Hey, hey!' Woodham leered. 'Don't let me stop you if you've got *that* sort of dinner in prospect!'

'I won't.'

***

Kitty's arm felt very sore where Mistress Jourdemayne had dragged her up the path towards the church. Terrified, she wanted to run as fast as her legs would carry her, away from what might happen behind the church door, away from the unknown.

But where would she run to? If the church had been in Westminster, she'd have known the good hiding places and she

261

could have stayed out of sight until there'd been a way of finding her friend Jack or one of the other boys, or perhaps Master Jourdemayne. She might even have run to the monastery and asked the monks if she could stay there. But this wasn't Westminster: this was London. She stood in her damp clothes, shivering in abject misery, dreading whatever was going to happen.

In the church porch her mistress, still holding Kitty's arm in an iron grip, pulled her round to face her.

'Now, you're sure, aren't you, Kitty, that what you told me was the truth?'

'What ... about what, mistress?'

'That no boy has ever interfered with you ... put his hands on your ... down there?'

'No, mistress,' Kitty snivelled unhappily. 'No, never.' She couldn't imagine why Mistress Jourdemayne wanted to know such a strange thing.

'You'd better not be lying to me, Kitty!' The Mistress knocked at the door and, almost immediately, there was the sound of a key turning in the lock. The door was opened by a tall, thin man who nodded distractedly and mumbled a greeting. Then he bent down to look at Kitty as though inspecting her, adjusting his spectacles to get a better view.

'Oh, a girl!' he said, sounding disappointed. He made to close the door then had to hold it open again for another man to leave, a man who had a kind-looking face. If he really was kind, Kitty thought, she could have tried to slink away behind him and asked him to help her, but the mistress still had hold of her arm.

The thin man closed the door and glanced down again at Kitty. 'Couldn't you find a boy, Mistress Jourdemayne? A boy would have been better for what we hope to achieve.'

'I'm sorry, Magister,' said the Mistress, 'there was no guarantee that the boy I had in mind would be entirely pure. You can't always predict these things with farm boys. They behave like the animals they live with.'

'Ah, well,' said the thin man, 'we'll have to do our best.' He turned the key to lock the door again and tried the handle to make sure, then he beckoned them forward.

'The most important thing,' he went on, 'is that the child is a virgin. 'You are quite certain of that, Mistress Jourdemayne?'

'Yes, absolutely certain.'

'That's good. Because in fact, it's the only thing about which the First Mirror of Lilith is absolutely specific. So maybe it's not important that we have a girl rather than a boy. Perhaps we'll be still be able to achieve a successful result. Come along, little girl,' he said, leading the way up the nave as Mistress Jourdemayne prodded Kitty in the back, 'don't be frightened, we just want to carry out a small experiment and we want you to help us.'

Kitty's heart was thudding as she took in her surroundings. The church looked like any other church so, surely, it was nothing to be frightened of. It all looked comfortingly familiar. This was the nave, there was the rood screen with the altar beyond it and the cross...

No! There was no cross. It was only as Kitty was pushed towards the altar she realised that a large circular object lay flat at the centre of it. It looked a bit like a shield, or perhaps it was a mirror, but it wasn't easy to tell since the surface had been smeared with some sort of oil. And behind that stood, of all things, a doll's wicker cradle with a doll in it. There were candles, too, a bit too near the dolls' cradle, Kitty thought. It could catch fire. And the smell! What was that smell? Hyssop? Vervain? What was it?

A shorter, plumper man stood behind the altar, watching as Kitty approached with Mistress Jourdemayne behind her. At first he smiled encouragingly then he looked more closely at her.

'Is this a girl?' he asked. Kitty felt indignant. Did she look like a boy? No, on second thoughts, she didn't like his smile very much at all. He didn't look as if he really meant to smile.

'A boy would have been more appropriate,' he said. 'Couldn't a boy be found?'

'I'm not sure it's really that important,' said the tall man. 'The child's innocence and virginity are the most important things.'

'Very well then,' said the other man with a sigh. 'We'll have to do what we can with what we've got.' Reaching forward, he tilted the big shield-like object in Kitty's direction.

'Now, Kitty,' whispered Mistress Jourdemayne, 'all you have to do is to look into the mirror and tell us what you see. That's all. Don't worry, it's only an experiment, but you must be sure to describe exactly what you see.'

With that, the short man looked upwards, closed his eyes and began intoning some words in a language that Kitty had never heard before.

***

'I deserve that!' said William as Robin Fairweather placed two pewter tankards of ale on the table.

'No more than I do,' said Robin. 'It was a tough drove this time. Thirty more bullocks than usual and it's amazing what a difference they make. Still, I always enjoy the midsummer drove. Can't complain.'

William pulled a tankard across the table towards him and raised it to Robin's health as they settled themselves comfortably in the village ale house. The low light of the setting sun was streaming through a small window as they both relished their reward for a long day's labour.

'More animals, more responsibility,' said William, 'it stands to reason. But, believe me, it's no more tough, in its way, than construing the accounts for the new abbot!'

'You're right. Reckoning is hard work,' Robin agreed. 'I'm always pleased when I get back home to Devon and hand over exactly the right amount of money to the cattle traders. Doesn't Margery help you with the figures?'

'No,' said William abruptly. 'She used to, but she hasn't done that for a long time. Mind you, believe it or not, young Kitty had started to help me and she was shaping up very well. Had a natural knack for it.' William frowned.

'Isn't she doing it any more?'

'No, she isn't. Margery grabbed her as soon as she realised the girl was getting good at writing and reckoning. She's done that before.'

He had to change the subject. He was so angry with Margery and her selfish behaviour that he could hardly bring himself to speak about it and any more talk on the subject would surely bring the conversation round to Jenna. He certainly didn't want to talk about Jenna.

'How's everything in your neck of the woods then, Robin?' he asked. 'Is your new wife still putting up with you?'

'She does her best. Poor Rosamond, being married to a drover is no life for a woman. Her old man is away from home too often. Can't rely on him not to have a mistress in every parish on the road!'

'And have you?'

Robin glanced at William from under his eyebrows and tapped the side of his nose. 'That's for me to know and you to wonder about,' he said. 'And talking of secret passions, how is yours?'

'I don't know what you're talking about.'

'Oh yes you do. I'm talking about Jenna Harding. The last time her name came up in conversation in this self-same ale house, you admitted you were in love with her.'

There was a long silence before William said quietly, 'Yes, I did, didn't I?'

'And?'

William took a morose draught of ale. 'And yes, nothing has changed,' he said and sighed as he replaced his tankard on the table, 'for all the good it does me. I never see her. She's working for the Duchess of Gloucester now: she hardly ever comes back to the farm except to collect face creams and so on from Margery. And that's not very often these days.'

'So it's just as well, then, in a way. After all, Margery is still your wife –'

'And a damned bad-tempered one at the moment.'

'So Jenna's husband is irrelevant.'

William, trying to control his ire, didn't really take in Robin's words at first. Then, in the act of raising his tankard to his lips once again, he slammed it back down in astonishment, spilling ale on the table.

'A husband! How do you know?'

'I made it my business to find out.' Robin was enjoying this. He leaned closer to William, with his elbow on the table, talking quietly.

'I happened to be working for a trader in the Newton Abbot area who's new to the game and he didn't have the animals ready in time. So I had to wait for a couple of days, kicking my heels in Kingskerswell until he had them all assembled in one place.'

'Kingskerswell? Isn't that where…'

'Where Jenna comes from, yes. Yes, it is. She told me quite a bit about the village while she was on that drove with me a few years ago, but she never said anything much about her own background, her family and so on. So I made it my business to ask a few questions. Thought you might be interested.'

'And was there … is there … a man?'

'What do you think? Where there's an attractive woman, there's always a man. And she's an attractive woman. I took quite a liking to her myself at one time. I even hoped I might get somewhere with her. But that was before she set her pretty brown eyes on you.'

'And? What about the man? Come on, Robin, tell me.'

Robin nodded. 'A hopeless drunkard. Well known for it, apparently. I got talking to the Parson after mass the Sunday I was there. Nice fellow. Name of Middleton. I didn't say who I was, of course. Pretended I'd met Jenna a long time ago and I was just making casual enquiries.'

'You lied to a parson?'

'Not really. I just … well, gave him to understand. You know. I don't think I'll rot in Hell for that.'

'And what did he tell you?'

'He said he remembered her very well, and it was a pity things turned out the way they did. But everyone knew her husband was a drunkard and that he hit her. They were quite used to seeing her turning up in church with a black eye or a cut lip.'

'Bastard!' William's hand clenched into an involuntary fist under the table. How could any man hurt Jenna? If he ever met the bastard, he'd … well, he'd…

Robin laid a hand on his friend's arm. 'Don't, William,' he said. 'It won't get you anywhere. It won't solve anything.'

'Just don't tell me his name,' muttered William. 'I might go looking for him.'

'What, all the way to Devon? Don't be stupid. Wouldn't do you any good anyway, so I might as well tell you. His name was Jake. But he's dead.'

'Dead?'

'Apparently he drank himself stupid most days. Everyone knew that. But last summer, come harvest time, he was drunk in charge of a scythe, newly sharpened, and all but harvested his own leg. They say he bled like a stuck pig. Didn't stand a chance after that.'

Of all ways to go, that was a bad one. William was silent for a long, long moment, his mind reeling. His instinctive revulsion at the thought of any farm worker dying from a stupid, careless accident like that was fighting a losing battle against his initial desire to avenge Jenna's hurt. But above all, he was trying to control his feeling of pure exultation at the knowledge that she was not tied by her vows to any other man. She was free but he wasn't, so there was no hope that she could be his. His mind was in turmoil. He didn't know what to think.

Robin had the sense to stay silent with his friend, to let him take in all he'd been told.

CHAPTER NINETEEN

June 1441

It was quiet now that the Duchess had finally left for the King's Head. She had been especially pernickety this morning, deciding first on one gown then another, changing her mind at least three times about which shoes to wear. And when it came to choosing her jewellery, Jenna had almost despaired. No sooner had she written *garnet necklace* in her notebook than she had to cross it out again and amend it to *ruby necklace and earrings*. It had taken more than an hour before the Duchess Eleanor was satisfied that she was looking her best.

Jenna couldn't imagine why she was being so fussy. After all, the Duke was away so she didn't need to please her husband and she wasn't going off on one of her secret expeditions with Canon Hume: besides, she always dressed circumspectly for those. This time, she had simply arranged to dine with several of her ladies and some of the more entertaining gentlemen in her social circle. They had all left the palace in a noisy, colourful procession of carriages and a blessed silence descended on Jenna's domain. She only needed to tidy up the dressing room before removing her apron and going out.

With some precious time to herself, she knew exactly where she was going because she still hadn't managed to see Kitty since she'd found out she was working for Margery Jourdemayne. The new arrangement could be perfectly innocent, of course, indeed it could be to Kitty's benefit if she was learning to read and write and reckon. In fact, there had been moments when Jenna had felt rather embarrassed at the memory of her outburst in the dairy in front of Hawys and the other dairymaids; but there was still a worm of worry gnawing at her heart.

Rather than take her favourite leisurely route along the banks of the Thames, she took the shortcut through the fields, keeping a sharp eye open. While on the one hand she ached to see William, on the other hand she dreaded seeing him. Nothing had changed and though she still felt exactly the same about him, he was still the husband of another woman and she could never trust herself not to blurt out something she might regret.

In the hour before the midday dinner, the kitchen was a hotbed of clattering activity. Pottage simmered in a cauldron over the open fire and one young woman was cleaning and chopping vegetables while another removed a batch of loaves from the bread oven. At the big table in the centre of the room, two kitchen maids were filling jugs with small beer and assembling trays of bread and cheese to be taken out to the workers in the fields. They barely looked up as Jenna entered the room. There was no sign of Kitty.

'Has anyone seen Kitty?' Jenna shouted above the din. 'Is she down in the dairy?' She was answered with blank looks and shrugs. No one seemed to have seen her.

'She might be in there,' one of the women said casually, nodding towards Mistress Jourdemayne's room. 'She works in there quite a lot these days.'

'Thank you, Janet.'

Jenna approached the door and knocked cautiously, quietly, using only the knuckle of her index finger, her ear almost against the door. Having no reply, she knocked again, louder this time.

She didn't quite know what she'd been expecting but the door opened a crack and Kitty's face, pale and drawn, peered round it.

'Kitty!'

'Oh, hello, Jenna.'

Kitty opened the door as far as she needed to in order to admit Jenna then closed it immediately. She was entirely alone. Jenna, used to having Kitty throw herself at her and hug her in great excitement, felt uneasy.

'What's wrong, Kitty? What's the matter?'

270

Kitty shook her head and avoided Jenna's gaze.

'Nothing's the matter,' she said in a small voice.

'Yes there is, Kitty, I know it! Tell me. Tell me why you're not in the dairy any more. Are you helping Mistress Jourdemayne? What are you doing? Tell me, Kitty, please, for God's sake tell me!'

Jenna's voice was rising and anxiety threatened to get the better of her when Kitty gave a gulping sob. Immediately, she wrapped her arms about the girl.

'Hush, hush, my dove. It's all right. It's all right, sweetheart.' She rocked the little bundle of misery that was Kitty from side to side, crooning comforting words, stroking her head. 'It's all right, my dove. Come on, just tell me what's the matter. I'm here now. You mustn't worry about it, whatever it is. I'm here now, I'll look after you.'

Kitty raised a tear-stained face to look at Jenna. 'M ... Mistress Jourdemayne has been ... doing ... making ... making me do ... ex ... exmeripents.'

'Exmeri ... do you mean experiments, Kitty?'

'Yes,' Kitty sniffed. 'Exmeripents. She said it was a big secret. I mustn't tell anyone.'

'What sort of experiments? No, wait. Dry your eyes. Tell me first of all – where is Mistress Jourdemayne?'

'She's just gone out to the physic garden. She doesn't trust me to cut herbs. She says I bring the wrong ones.'

'All right. Is that water in the bowl over there?' Kitty nodded, sniffing. 'Right, then, go and bathe your eyes and blow your nose.'

Kitty drew back. 'No, Jenna, I'll ... I'll just blow my nose.'

'All right, Kitty, but try to stop crying, my dove. We may not have much time before the mistress comes back and we mustn't let her know that I know anything at all. So if she sees me, we'll have to pretend I've called to collect something for the Duchess. I'll try and think of something she needs.'

Inwardly, Jenna was seething, but she must be very wary about not upsetting Kitty any more. She would have to be very gentle if she was to get at the truth of what had been happening without causing her more distress than she was clearly feeling already. She didn't even chide the child for wiping her nose on the back of her hand.

'Come and sit down, Kitty,' Jenna said, patting a place on the bench beside her. 'And tell me as calmly as you can what Mistress Jourdemayne has been asking you to do.'

Kitty took a deep, juddering breath before speaking. 'I don't rightly know where to start.'

'Try starting at the beginning,' Jenna suggested gently.

'Well, she came and got me from the dairy,' Kitty began and, as she told her story, Jenna heard a repetition of exactly what her own duties had been, helping around the work room, washing up, labelling bottles, packing orders. But what followed astounded her.

'She asked me if I was a virgin,' said Kitty.

'Why on earth did she want to know that?'

'Because she said it was important for her exmeripents. I had to be a virgin before I could do the exmeripents in the church. With the looking-glass,' she added, 'and the water.'

As Kitty warmed to her tale, Jenna gradually built up a picture of a nervous, reluctant child being dragged to several of London's churches to take part in curious ceremonies which involved her having to stare into various reflective surfaces, mirrors or, occasionally, bowls of water, until she was able to see images.

'What sort of images, Kitty?'

'I don't rightly know,' said Kitty. 'I think they wanted me to see the face of the King, or at least, to see a picture of a throne and see who was sitting on it.'

'And did you ever see anything, Kitty?'

'No, never,' said Kitty bleakly. 'I could only see myself in the looking glass and I couldn't see anything in the water except the bottom of the bowl, even though I really wanted to see something, so I could say I had.'

No wonder Kitty had been reluctant to bathe her eyes, thought Jenna. She'd probably be terrified of seeing images in the bowl of water.

'And who was there in the church with you and Mistress Jourdemayne?'

'Oh, some gentlemen. I never knew their names. One was short and fat and another was very tall but he was bent.'

Immediately Jenna's suspicions were aroused.

'Did you notice anything unusual about the tall one, Kitty? Because I think I know who it might be.'

'No, not really. He seemed quite nice, though. Oh, but wait ... yes, he had those things people put on their noses to look at things.'

'Spectacles, d'you mean?'

'Yes, those. Not many people have those.'

'No indeed, not many can afford to buy them.'

Roger Bolingbroke couldn't have afforded to buy them either, not unless he'd been employed by the Duke and Duchess of Gloucester. Jenna had no need of mirrors or spectacles. She was beginning to see exactly what had been happening.

Mirror magic. She'd heard of it and knew that it was frowned on by the church. Apart from that she knew little except that it was a method of divination, a ritual in which a virgin was required to look deeply into a reflective surface until an image appeared, foretelling the future.

So, that was it. But she needed to know more before deciding what to do. For now, the most important thing was to reassure this bewildered girl.

She put her finger on Kitty's lips. 'I must go now, Kitty, and I don't want you to tell Mistress Jourdemayne I've been here and that you've talked to me. D'you hear? I think I know who those two gentlemen are, but I don't know what to do about it. Not yet, anyway. I need to think.'

Kitty put her arms around Jenna's neck. 'Don't leave me, Jenna. Please. I'm frightened.'

'Kittymouse, you're going to have to be very brave. Listen carefully. You must forget I've been here, but always – always – remember I'll be doing everything I can to help you. I just have to work out what's best. But whatever happens, you mustn't be frightened. I promise I'll look after you. And you can always talk to Master Jourdemayne if I'm not here. He'll look after you, too. Now, give me a kiss and let me go.'

Kitty loosened the grip of her arms around Jenna's neck and

offered up her cheek to be kissed.

'Be brave, my Kittymouse,' Jenna said, 'and remember I love you.'

***

Magister Bolingbroke, in his role as secretary to the Duchess Eleanor, was housed in a small office in a corridor behind the palace kitchens. Here, working at an ink-stained table, he made fair copies of the letters she dictated. It was an extraordinarily untidy little room. Crumpled-up scraps of parchment littered the floor and generations of candles had been allowed to drip their melted wax unchecked, to build up into small greasy hillocks around the dirty candlesticks. By contrast, the Magister's books were neatly stacked on a shelf.

William Woodham had spent most of the morning in running an errand to Paternoster Row for Canon Hume. Now he stood in Bolingbroke's room, arms akimbo, surveying the scene and trying to decide how best to create order out of chaos. There was no sign of Roger Bolingbroke himself except for a quilted jerkin on the floor, a powdering of dandruff still on the shoulders. It appeared to have fallen off the overturned chair.

Really, it was the job of the housemaids to clean up in here but Canon Hume had decreed that Woodham must be the one to do it, whenever the room was empty. Bolingbroke was given no choice in the matter. The reason was simply that William could read well enough to be able to decide whether any abandoned or mislaid pieces of parchment might be of interest to Canon Hume or were important enough to merit retention for any other reason. Shaking out a blue and white dusting cloth with bad grace, William set to work.

The task was easier than it had first appeared. Within the hour, he had a small but satisfying stack of half-written letters, notes and out-of-date bills of sale. William decided to consign them to the fire under the bread oven in the palace kitchen when he had finished clearing up. He pushed them down into an empty log basket and, wrinkling his nose, dropped in two rotting, half-eaten apples on top of them.

Dusting off a discarded ledger, he tried to place it on the

shelf with the Magister's books, but realised he'd have to re-arrange them slightly to create enough space. He pulled out Roger Bacon's weighty encyclopaedia of all knowledge, the *Opus Maius*. Of course, Bolingbroke would have a copy of that one, wouldn't he, being an Oxford man. No doubt he followed the teachings of the unconventional old Oxford scholar they called Doctor Mirabilis, though some refuted the claims he made about alchemy and magic. Interesting, Woodham thought, but way beyond most people's understanding or knowledge. Putting the big book to one side, he noticed a small wicker basket which had been pushed in behind it. Inquisitive by nature, he reached in and took it down from the shelf.

At first, he failed to understand why Magister Bolingbroke should want to keep a lump of candle wax and some scraps of lamb's wool. Then he realised that whatever it was had been moulded from the finest beeswax and, though it had melted slightly, he could see it had once represented a figure. And the wax had been mixed with other things, small crystals and herbs, some hairs and tiny pieces of dirty-looking fabric before being made into an image. Could it be the image of a child, perhaps? Possibly. And it seemed likely that it was, particularly since the basket which contained it was shaped very like a cradle.

Suddenly, the small room seemed eerily quiet. Image magic! Woodham knew it for what it was, but he also knew that it was against the teachings of the church. He shook his head. His discovery didn't really surprise him because it was well known among the gossips on the palace staff that the Duchess Eleanor was a woman who desperately wanted to give her husband a child to reinforce the Lancastrian line of succession to the throne. But she had never managed to, poor woman. Now it looked as though Magister Bolingbroke had been attempting some image magic to help her.

Replacing the little basket in its hiding place on the shelf, he slid the *Opus Maius* in behind it. He needed time to think about his accidental discovery. Woodham's bluff exterior and quick temper both hid an unexpectedly sympathetic heart and he couldn't help but feel a little sorry for the Duchess. So, for the moment, he resolved to say nothing to anyone though it might be wise to mention it to Canon Hume. He would know what to do.

For now, the job in hand was done, exactly as Canon Hume had wanted, and it was time for dinner. He picked up the log basket containing the papers to be burned, then left Magister Bolingbroke's room, closing the door behind him.

'William!'

In the long corridor outside the kitchen, the woman's voice that screamed his name held a note of hysterical urgency. He spun round to see Tilda, one of the maids, running towards him.

'William! Thank God!' She crossed herself. 'Where have you been? I've been looking everywhere for you.'

'Whoa, Tilda! You're not usually in such a hurry to see me!' Though Tilda had repeatedly repelled William's amorous advances in the past, she now clung to his arm as though he was all that stood between her and the gates of hell itself.

'It's Canon Hume,' she panted.

'Tilda! Tilda, calm down. What on earth is wrong with you, woman?'

'But they've taken him!'

'Taken him? What do you mean? Who has taken him?'

'Some men … oh, I don't know. Magister Bolingbroke, too. He's gone. I didn't know what to do. None of us knew!'

Tilda couldn't seem to stop jabbering. She'd start a sentence then stop as she remembered something else, tumbling over her words, wringing her hands, plucking at her apron. She had clearly been very frightened. Woodham put an arm around her shoulders.

'Now, calm down, Tilda and tell me what has happened. From the beginning. Tell me slowly.'

Between sobs and juddering breaths, Tilda eventually managed to tell him how she and several of the other house maids had been going about their work in the palace, dusting, sweeping and washing down walls when, without warning, there had been a sudden great commotion. Loud voices barked commands and at least half a dozen guards in royal livery had grouped themselves outside Canon Hume's room.

Alarmed, the women had taken cover, hiding themselves

behind wall hangings and bulky furniture, staying well out of sight. What they heard and managed to see terrified them. Canon Hume's door was kicked open and the man himself was dragged out. In the corridor behind the kitchen, the same was happening to Magister Bolingbroke. Then the two men were frog-marched away, their arms pinioned roughly behind their backs. Hume was shouting at his captors at the top of his voice. Bolingbroke said nothing and appeared totally bewildered.

Woodham listened to her disjointed account with mounting concern, thinking back to the state of Bolingbroke's office. The abandoned jerkin and the overturned chair did seem to indicate that he had left in a hurry, or been forced to leave. What Tilda was telling him had all the makings of a major crisis. The Duke of Gloucester was far away from home and William knew that the Duchess had gone up to the city with her friends. She would have to be told what had happened, but Canon Hume, normally the one to tell her such things, had been taken away.

There was nobody in charge and there was nothing for it but that he, William, would have to find out exactly where the Duchess was and get a message to her.

***

A small crowd had gathered outside the King's Head tavern on Cheapside. Few Londoners could resist the temptation to loiter and gawp at the Duchess of Gloucester, resplendent in a magnificent gown of deep red silk with rubies at her throat and in her ears. She was smiling and waving graciously as she was helped down from her carriage.

''T'ain't right,' muttered one old man on the periphery of the crowd. ''T'ain't right to be cavorting around like that on a day like this.'

'Why not, you old curmudgeon?' His wife, fat and toothless, was craning her neck to get a better view. She turned to her husband and nudged him in the ribs. 'She's got it, so she might as well flaunt it.' The woman followed her observation with a cackle of raucous laughter.

'Yes, but how did she get it? That's what you should be asking yourself. How did she get it? On her back, that's how.'

'Oh, get on with you. She's not the first woman to do that and she won't be the last.'

''T'ain't right. Tomorrow's one of the holiest days in the calendar, the feast of St Peter and St Paul. She should be keeping a vigil, not cavorting around like a performing bear. There'll be trouble. You mark my words, there'll be trouble before the night's out.'

The small voice of dissent was drowned out by the excited applause and cheering that continued as the Duchess and a dozen or so of her aristocratic companions, alighting from carriages and dismounting from horses, made their way towards the tavern. Waving elegantly once more, Eleanor led the way inside.

The scene that greeted her was warmly welcoming. The King's Head had justly gained its reputation as a playground for the aristocracy. The huge building provided a comfortable vantage point from which the Royal Family and their noble guests could view the city's great pageants and festivities while enjoying lavish entertainments and every comfort. It was one of Eleanor's favourite places; she loved to dine at the King's Head.

The big dining room at the front of the building which afforded a splendid view of Cheapside, also presented a scene of extravagant hospitality. Four long trestle tables were laden with trays and serving dishes while side tables against the walls at either end of the room were piled high with chafing dishes and bowls and platters full of food, interspersed with decanters of wine. Standing smartly to attention while the guests seated themselves, a small army of ewerers and cup-bearers awaited their instructions from the butler.

Eleanor took her seat on the dais and looked about her with a self-satisfied smile. Sometimes, it was good to be abroad on a sunny day with companions other than Humphrey. With him, she would have been there merely as his wife and he would have taken precedence in all things. Without him, she was the most important person in the room. No, wait a moment, with Humphrey away in the wilds of Wales, she was the most important person in the whole of London except the King. And, as it happened, even the King was away, staying for some days at the palace in Sheen. It gave her a good, warm feeling. She smiled for the sheer joy of being alive and, amused by a remark made by one of her companions, she laughed her unmistakable silvery laugh.

The Duchess of Gloucester was on top of the world.

***

The little physic garden was quiet save for the sound of a hoe busily loosening the soil around the very few weeds which dared to appear there. Margery always went to the garden when she was annoyed about something, venting her spleen by attacking the weeds which threatened her precious medicinal plants. Poison darnel was one of the more persistent, no doubt as a result of the garden's close proximity to fields of grain, but it was no match for Margery when she was in a bad mood. Careful not to spread their pernicious seeds, she would throw the weeds into a heap at the far end of the garden, to be burned when they had dried out.

Her hoe struck a stone and, bending, she picked it up then turned and threw it, hard, giving vent to her anger in the throwing. These were bad times and Margery felt uneasy. There'd been a blood moon only last week and it was always a reliable sign that things were not as they should be.

In her heart, she knew it was unreasonable to be angry with Kitty. After all, she had used the child to achieve her own ends. For all the use that had been, she needn't have bothered. If only she could have found a virgin boy innocent enough to do what Kitty had failed so miserably to do, then there might have been some tangible results. Perhaps a boy would have looked into the mirror and been able to see exactly who sat on the throne. And, if the mirror had shown an image of the Duke of Gloucester, the Duchess Eleanor would have heaped praise and prizes upon all her advisers, including Margery herself. The future would have been assured.

Kitty's anxious, apologetic little face did prick Margery's conscience from time to time and when she chastised the girl for her awkwardness or lack of knowledge, it did feel a bit like kicking a small, defenceless dog. She resolved to be kinder to Kitty in future and try not to frighten her too much. Perhaps she would send her back to work in the dairy because, in any case, she would never be as good an assistant as Jenna had been.

She looked up at the sound of approaching horses. Not two riders, but five … six … guards in livery and a tumbrel bringing up the rear of the procession. Dear God, what was this…?

'Mistress Margery Jourdemayne?'

'Who wishes to know?' Margery was wary and suddenly felt genuine terror. All six men were dismounting and beginning to surround her.

'You're to come with us. Sheriff's orders.'

'Sheriff … but why? I haven't done anything.'

'That's not what we've heard. You're in big trouble, Mistress. You're to come with us.'

Two of the liveried guards grabbed her arms and yanked them painfully behind her back, tying them there. Margery began to scream.

'William! For God's sake, William! Let me speak to my husband, you great brute! You're not taking me anywhere. I want to speak to my husband. You must let me. You must!'

'He can come and visit you if you want him to. Then you can speak to him.'

'Visit me? What are you talking about? Where are you taking me?'

'The Tower,' said the biggest and ugliest of the guards as the two who had tied her arms now manhandled her, screaming and kicking, into the tumbrel.

'Put a gag on her,' said another of them, 'could be dangerous if she bites you. She's a witch!'

'I'm not a w …' Margery's head was pulled forcibly back by her hair while a strip of linen was tied firmly across her open mouth.

'That'll keep you quiet 'til we get to the Tower,' said the biggest guard as Margery squirmed and struggled. 'They've got a nice little cell for you there. It's got your name on the door. It says *RESERVED FOR THE WITCH OF EYE* on it. Leastways, that's what we've heard. So your husband can visit you in the

Tower, if he wants to. By appointment, of course!'

He guffawed with laughter and the other guards laughed with him.

***

Eleanor leaned back in her chair, replete and contented. Her noble companions had feasted on roast beef and on boiled chicken stuffed with seasonal green grapes. Now the tables had been cleared and it was time for wafers with whole spices, accompanied by sweet wine. The minstrels who had played while the diners ate their meal were being replaced by jongleurs and jugglers for their entertainment. Her Grace was entranced at the prospect.

The cup-bearer approached the dais and the butler, standing behind Eleanor, snapped his fingers for the decanter. As he bent to fill her glass, he said something to her very quietly.

'Speak up, man,' said Eleanor. 'I can't hear you.'

He bent again. 'I'm sorry, Your Grace, I don't want to speak too loudly, but a gentleman is here to see you. He says it's very urgent. He says he has to see you personally on a matter of the utmost importance.'

Eleanor was immediately wary. 'Did he give you his name?' she demanded.

'Yes, Your Grace. His name is William Woodham. He said he was a member of Your Grace's household staff.'

Woodham. Woodham … Eleanor racked her brains. She couldn't think of anyone by that name.

'Did he give you any indication of why he wanted to see me? I can't see just anyone, you know.'

'No, of course not, Your Grace. I'm quite aware of that. And so is the man who wants to see you. But he asked me to be sure to tell you it was an urgent message about his master, Canon Hume, and another gentlemen of your acquaintance, a Magister … er … Magister…'

'Bolingbroke?' snapped Eleanor, turning towards him. 'Hume and Bolingbroke? What did he tell you about them?'

'I'm sorry, Your Grace, but perhaps I am the bearer of bad news. I do hope not, but it seems that the gentlemen have been

281

arrested. Master Woodham thought you should know.'

'Arrested!' Eleanor's heart seemed to stop in that moment and the blood drained from her face. 'Arrested?'

She looked towards the door where William Woodham hovered anxiously on the periphery of the dining room. Yes, of course, she recognised him now. He was the one she'd seen trailing around the palace in the wake of Canon Hume; she'd seen him several times though she'd never had much to do with the man.

'You had better find a room where I can speak privately to him,' she said quietly to the butler, rising from the table while her companions looked questioningly up at her. 'And make sure no one disturbs us.'

'Please carry on, everyone,' she said with a reassuring smile and a half-wave of her hand. 'Someone wishes to see me, but it shouldn't take long. I'll be back very soon.'

Her companions turned their attention back to their wine and wafers and the jongleurs began their entertainment. It would be some time before Eleanor rejoined them.

In a private room to the rear of the King's Head, with the butler standing guard outside the door at her request, she and William Woodham faced each other across a small table. As he whispered to her in a low, urgent voice, telling her exactly what had happened, it didn't take Eleanor long to realise that she stood on the brink of a potential catastrophe. And, until her husband returned home, she would have to think for herself and think fast. There was no one else to turn to.

CHAPTER TWENTY

July 1441

'How are you, Henry?'

William de la Pole, the Earl of Suffolk, was always pleased to welcome his old friend Henry Beaufort to the palace. As Steward of the Royal Household, it was his duty to show important guests into the presence of the King.

'Well enough, William, thank you,' Beaufort said, 'considering the weather we're having. But my right foot is a little damp. I suspect I have a leak in my boot.'

'Do you need to change your boots before you see the King?'

'No, please don't worry. There are far more important things than wet feet to worry about and I don't want to keep His Highness waiting. '

'Very well. He asked me to show you into the solar. Come this way.'

Feeling more than a little concerned, Henry Beaufort followed de la Pole towards the private royal solar. He prepared himself mentally for some awkward questions: the King had never before summoned him to Westminster with this degree of urgency.

'Do you know what this is about, William?'

'He has recently returned from Sheen and I'm afraid he's heard the rumours,' William de la Pole answered briefly.

The city of London was ablaze with rumours. As soon as news of Canon Hume's arrest got out, tongues started wagging. Magister Bolingbroke's name was not so well known but it didn't take long for the gossip-mongers to associate him with the Duchess of Gloucester and when news broke that a Canon of St Stephen's, Westminster, had also been arrested, gossip reached fever pitch.

And then the rains came. Shortly after midsummer, as the whole of England basked in innocent sunshine and crops stood ripening in the fields, black thunderclouds began to gather in the west. The occasional summer storm wouldn't normally be a cause for much concern, but this one moved in swiftly, only to be followed by another and, a few days later, yet another. Torrential downpours flattened the wheat crop and barley fared little better. Storms raged and battered the entire country for more than two weeks, rivers overflowed their banks and flooded low-lying buildings. People could do little but huddle together in their homes to take shelter from the incessant rain.

There must, they reasoned, be an explanation for storms of such biblical proportions. Not within living memory had there been such winds, such thunder and lightning. The people of England had offended God in some way and this was how He wreaked divine vengeance upon them. It had never happened before, so it could only be because of recent events.

The King, looking concerned, rose to greet his great-uncle as he was announced.

'My Lord, I trust you are not too wet?' he asked. 'This storm is quite unprecedented. And in the middle of July! It seems well nigh impossible.'

Beaufort bent to kiss the ring on the King's outstretched hand. 'Oh, please, Your Highness, don't concern yourself about me. I couldn't let a few drops of rain put me off responding to your urgent request to see me. After all, Southwark isn't so very far away and I did have the advantage of a covered carriage.'

'Come then, and warm yourself anyway,' said the King, leading the way towards the huge fireplace where a pile of logs burned. 'It is unreasonably cold for the time of year.' He took a seat in the inglenook and gestured to the Cardinal to join him.

'Now tell me, my Lord Uncle, what is going on. The Earl of Suffolk says every servant in the palace is living in fear and trembling that these storms are visited upon us by the wrath of God. I need the assurances of a man of the Church before I make any of the pronouncements I feel I should make. Why is there so much panic, do you think?'

Beaufort smiled. 'Panic is easily transmitted from one person to another, Your Highness,' he said, 'and once someone makes a claim like that, it adds fuel to the fire. It is a kind of mass hysteria, I suppose, though none the less real for that. And I'm afraid this dreadful, unseasonal weather is not helping things.'

'I'm told,' the King said, 'that people in the city are saying it's a sign of God's displeasure at the activities of certain clerks and women they're calling witches. No word of this had reached me while I was staying at Sheen so it has all come as quite a surprise. I do hope you can explain it.'

Pleased to have the ear of the King, Beaufort took the opportunity to tell him how it had come to the attention of the Council that certain members of the Duke of Gloucester's household, who were hitherto respected members of the clergy, had been indulging in practices which smacked of heresy and witchcraft. Somehow, word had spread.

'What kind of practices?' the King demanded.

'Casting horoscopes, Your Highness, and the rumour is that they were doing this at the behest of the Duchess.'

'Really? But all the ladies of the court enjoy that kind of thing, don't they? Horoscopes and so on. There's no great harm in that, surely?'

'Not normally, Your Highness. It is usually a perfectly innocent pastime, but not in this case.'

'Why not?'

'Because these horoscopes were chiefly related to...' Beaufort hesitated. Ideally, what he had to say should be delicately put but there was no way around it.

'Yes, yes?' the King urged him, 'related to what?'

'To your death, Your Highness.'

The King's jaw dropped. 'My death?'

'I'm afraid so, Your Highness.'

'But that's dreadful! I can hardly bring myself to believe you, except that I cannot doubt your word as a man of the Church. But surely, this can't be true!'

'I'm afraid it is. I understand they regularly employed techniques of divination, including an astrolabe, which is not unreasonable, I suppose, but apparently they ventured a step too far. They had begun conducting heretical masses within consecrated buildings.'

'Consecrated buildings?' King Henry's normally dull brown eyes were wide with disbelief, his face drained of colour. 'Churches, you mean? Monasteries? Priories?'

'Churches, in the main, Your Highness. It seems that these masses involved removing the crucifix, the holy chalices and so on from the altar and replacing them with heretical paraphernalia.'

'What kind of things?'

'Mirrors, water bowls, anything which might produce an image they wished to see. Mirror magic is much favoured by sorcerers, Your Highness. As is all image magic.'

'Magic of any kind is to be vehemently discouraged,' said King Henry. 'Especially where it violates the House of God.'

'Exactly,' agreed Beaufort. 'Lollardy is bad enough, but outright devil worship…'

The King was horrified. 'You don't think it was devil worship, surely? I can hardly bring myself to believe that any uncle of mine would…'

'It may well be, Your Highness, that your uncle knew nothing about it.'

Beaufort was quick to interrupt because he knew he should appear to defend Gloucester in all this. After all, the Duke was the young King's uncle and he could well have an affection for him. But Beaufort really did want to make Gloucester pay for sending that letter of complaint, for the false accusations he had made in it, for his insults and the way he had questioned Beaufort's own integrity. In retrospect, perhaps it had been a mistake to mention devil worship a moment ago, though, to be fair, he had stopped just short of making an actual accusation. The important thing was that he now had the King's absolute attention. That was all that mattered for the moment.

'I'm sure my uncle of Gloucester is innocent in all this,' the King was saying, 'but I can only pray that he is. He is away from home, I understand, so we cannot question him, but I am sure he can't have known anything about it. Otherwise, he would have put a stop to it. Immediately.'

'I'm sure he would, Your Highness. But, in his absence, the other members of the Council have been conducting their own investigations and they have been swift to act. They have apprehended all those dubious people with whom the Duchess is known to have associated. They are all in the Tower, including one woman who was actually accused of witchcraft some years ago.'

'And is she really a witch?'

'It seems so, yes. From what I understand, she sought out men of God and involved them in heretical practices. Sadly, she seems to have done the same again and it grieves me to tell you that, this time, these were men who were serving as so-called advisers to Her Grace the Duchess of Gloucester.

The King was quiet. Sitting alongside him, Henry Beaufort was not able to look directly into his face, but he heard him swallow nervously several times. He had clearly been deeply shocked by what he'd heard. At length, he spoke.

'I'd appreciate your advice, my Lord. This is truly the most dreadful news. Men of God, you say?'

'I'm afraid so, Your Highness.'

'And they were the Duchess's advisers?

'Members of her household, yes. Close advisers.'

'And where is the Duchess?'

'She has claimed sanctuary, Your Highness, in the Abbey Church of St Peter, here in Westminster.'

The King sighed deeply before he spoke. 'Then what should I do, my Lord Uncle? How do you think I should proceed from here? I cannot simply ignore the situation.'

'It seems, Your Highness, that the whole matter hinges on the fact that these people were trying to predict the date of your death by means of mirror magic, image magic and using astrolabes to cast horoscopes. I quite firmly believe that whatever results they achieved were totally incorrect, inadmissible, given the circumstances in which they were working. In my opinion, you would be wise to acknowledge the rumours, but you must not be seen to be intimidated by them because their predictions will, of course, be proved incorrect.'

'That is fervently to be hoped!' the King interrupted, allowing himself the ghost of a smile.

'So you must commission a corrected version, containing more accurate astrological calculations. An entirely new horoscope under the direction of the most trustworthy, learned men in the country, men of impeccable reputation whose word will not be doubted. That should put an end to this whole nasty business.'

'Who do you suggest? Would you be prepared to do it, my Lord Uncle?'

'I don't think I should,' said Beaufort. 'The best man for the job would be John Somerset. After all, he was your physician when you were a boy, Sire, so he knows you well. And now he is your Chancellor of the Exchequer. No one would question his judgement.'

'An excellent suggestion. And perhaps he could agree to share the work with John Langton. I met Master Langton when I visited the University at Cambridge recently. An excellent man. Moreover, not only is he Chancellor of the University but he is also a lawyer. He would be above reproach.'

'Then those would be the two best men to undertake the work, Your Highness. Shall I ask that they should be sent for?'

'I would be most grateful if you would. An alternative horoscope must be drawn up as soon as possible,' said the King. 'I must not lose the cordial love of my people. I must govern them wisely and well.'

He paused again, then turned towards Beaufort and looked directly at him.

'Tell me, my Lord Uncle,' he said. 'Why do you think my uncle of Gloucester's wife commissioned that horoscope?'

Beaufort took a moment before he answered but there was only one answer he could give and it was the truthful one.

'Consider, Sire,' he said, 'that your uncle of Gloucester is the heir to your throne. Perhaps she covets your crown.'

***

'It's not my fault. I'm innocent in all this, Jenna. Tell me it's not my fault.'

In all honesty Jenna couldn't answer the Duchess. It could be her fault or, if not directly her fault, then certainly the fault of her advisers. They stood accused of conspiring to bring about the death of the King and, by her association with them, Eleanor was in serious trouble though she protested that her concern had only ever been for the King's health. Much as she wanted to believe her mistress, Jenna doubted her motives were entirely altruistic.

'I'm sure you did what you did for only the best reasons, Your Grace.'

'Of course I did. I was deeply concerned about the health of my husband's nephew. That was the only reason I wanted anyone to predict anything, to undertake any kind of divination. I wanted to help the King. And it's the truth, Jenna. I tell you, it's the truth!'

After the initial shock of hearing what William Woodham had told her in confidence at the King's Head in Cheapside, Eleanor had taken subsequent events very calmly in her stride. Without dawdling for a moment longer than was necessary in order to keep up appearances of normality, she had returned with her noble companions in their carriages to the palace at Westminster. But, the moment she arrived there, she had summoned Jenna and told her to start packing immediately.

'Packing, Your Grace?'

'Yes, packing.'

'Packing what, Your Grace?'

'Packing everything we might need for a few days in sanctuary,' Eleanor replied, a grim expression on her face.

'Sanctuary, Your Grace?'

'That is what I said, Jenna. And please don't keep repeating everything I say.'

For the next hour, the Duchess Eleanor did little other than pace anxiously up and down her dressing room while Jenna attempted to fold some clothes and pack a money bag along with a few basic essentials into a large coffer. With no time to plan, she could only hope she was choosing what the Duchess would want.

From scraps of information given her by her agitated

mistress, Jenna was gradually able to piece together the whole story of how Eleanor had been told that Thomas Southwell and Roger Bolingbroke had been arrested on charges of treasonable necromancy and Canon Southwell was further charged with celebrating mass unlawfully. Canon John Hume was accused of the slightly lesser crime of aiding and abetting them. All in all, the accusations amounted to the very serious charge of treason.

Treason! Against the King! Jenna was horrified. Eleanor, after an initial hysterical outburst, had pulled herself together and, icily calm by now, told Jenna exactly what she planned to do.

Sooner or later, Eleanor said, those authorities who had arrested Bolingbroke, Southwell and Hume would link their names with hers. Perhaps they had already done so. But, now that she was back in Westminster, it was easy enough to move from the palace to the Abbey, to take refuge there. And she had every right to do so. Once she was on church premises, the secular authorities could not harm her as long as she remained in sanctuary. Of course, she would have to live simply and frugally, in one of the narrow cells set aside for the purpose. There was no room and no provision for a retinue of servants.

However, the Duchess would insist that one of her women be allowed to attend her and see to her immediate needs. She was a Duchess, after all, the wife of the most senior peer of the realm. And as soon as he had returned from discharging his royal duties elsewhere, her husband would command her immediate release. She should not need to seek sanctuary for long.

Wearing dark, hooded cloaks, the two women left the palace by one of the rear entrances, struggling to carry a heavy coffer between them. Within ten minutes, they had reached safety within the thick, cold walls of the Abbey and the Duchess Eleanor had thrown herself on the mercy of the new abbot, Edmund Kyrton.

During the next few days, after several trips back and forth to the palace to fetch clothes and bedding, underwear and personal necessities, Jenna had managed to make her mistress fairly comfortable. Often, she would return with snippets of gossip gleaned from what was being said among the servants at the palace. No one seemed to know anything positive so what Jenna reported back was mostly conjecture. But one thing was certain, the Duchess Eleanor would have to stay here in the Abbey where no one would dare to violate her sanctuary so she would have at least some measure of security until all the fuss died down, as it surely would as soon as Duke Humphrey returned home.

To all outward appearances, the Duchess was now calm and fully in control of her situation. Inside, she was a seething mess of worry and insecurity. Who had reported her acquaintances to the authorities? How had they got to know about the ceremonies in St Sepulchre-without-Newgate, St Benet Hithe and the other churches? Who had told them? What would happen? As the days went by, she became increasingly jittery and nervous and was growing thin and debilitated. Unable to sleep, she was grinding her teeth at night yet again and the whole of her lower jaw throbbed with a dull ache.

'Would you like me to summon a leech doctor, Your Grace,' asked Jenna, 'to bring you some relief from the pain?'

'No doctor would attend me. Not here. They dare not be associated with me now, not while I am *persona non grata*. For what it's worth, Canon Southwell is my physician and I can hardly consult him, now can I? He's under arrest and imprisoned in the Tower as far as I know.'

'Then let me ask Mistress Jourdemayne for something, Your Grace. At least she'd be able to give you some tooth tincture.'

'But I don't want you to leave me, Jenna. It's bad enough when you go back and forth to the palace. Who knows what will happen while you're away?' The Duchess, never certain whether she was being spied upon, was whispering so that no one but Jenna could possibly hear her.

'I'll be very quick, Your Grace. Eybury farmhouse isn't any further from the Abbey than it was from the palace and it never took me very long in the old days.'

With a sigh of resignation, Eleanor gave in. 'Yes, perhaps you're right. And while you're there, Jenna, ask Margery for some bishop's wort. I've got a dreadful headache this morning.'

'I'll ask her for her special headache remedy, Your Grace. I used to mix it for her so I know she always blends a little valerian root with the wood betony. That makes it twice as effective, she says.'

'Then ask her for some of that for me, Jenna, please. And make sure you're not seen. I don't want to involve Margery in all this. There's no reason to. Have you enough money to pay for it?'

'Yes, Your Grace. I think we brought enough with us for that.'

Jenna feared that Margery could already be involved, though she may not have been identified and arrested with the others. She'd soon find out. Pulling her hood around her face, she hurried through Westminster village on her way to the farmhouse.

William was in the kitchen when she arrived. So was Kitty. They both sat at the big table in the centre of the room, leaning on their elbows. Jenna's heart leaped in her chest when she saw them both together, the two people she loved most in the world. They looked deeply shocked.

'What –' she began.

'They've taken her,' said William shortly. 'She's gone.'

'Mistress Jourdemayne?'

'They came and took her,' Kitty said. 'She was in the garden and I wanted to ask her something so I went out there, but when I saw them, I hid behind the hedge. There were six of them. I counted. And they had horses.'

'Kitty says they were calling her a witch,' said William in a low voice. 'The Witch of Eye. I thought everyone had forgotten that name. But that's what they called her, so Kitty says.'

'Where have they taken her?'

William shook his head but Kitty spoke. 'The Tower,' she said. 'That's what they said. It's where they always take witches.'

'Nobody has proved that Mistress Jourdemayne is a witch, Kitty,' Jenna chided her, 'so you mustn't call her that –'

'Why not?' William said, cutting across her. 'She might as well because that's what everybody else will call her and it's the second time Margery's been accused of witchcraft. She got away with it last time, but you can wager your life they'll make the charges stick this time. They gave her enough warning.'

Still standing between the two of them, Jenna looked at William. He had his elbows on the table and his head in his hands. It was impossible to tell what he was thinking and she must know. What were his real feelings about Margery's arrest? Did he still care for his wife? The time had come for honesty: she must get at the truth of how he felt.

'Kitty,' Jenna said, trying her best to sound casual, 'how far did Mistress Jourdemayne trust you to make up medicines for her?'

'Oh,' said Kitty, brightening up, 'I used to make up lots of them if I could read the recipes. And I usually could.'

'Have you ever made the headache remedy? The decoction she makes with wood betony and valerian?'

'Yes, I made some last week for one of the ladies at the palace.'

'Then could you go and make some more, please, Kitty? I need some for the Duchess of Gloucester. She has a dreadful headache and she needs it urgently.'

Kitty, proud of being given such a responsibility in the absence of her mistress, slid off her chair and went off in the direction of Margery's room.

'That damned Duchess!' William said. 'It's all her fault that this is happening and all you care about is her bloody headache!'

'William! William, look at me!' Jenna gripped William's forearm and pulled his elbow off the table, forcing him to lift his head and look at her as she stood above him. 'William, don't ever say that again. I just needed to get Kitty out of the room. The Duchess is not my concern, she never was. For me, she is just the means of making a living. So please don't ... ever ... say that again! All I care about is you, William. I love you. You are my life. Surely, you know that?'

He was looking at her now, in exactly the way he had looked at her that other time, two years ago under the oak tree beside Willow Walk, looking into her face, as though nothing existed beyond it. Then he whispered her name.

He rose to his feet, facing her, but only for as long as it took to say her name again. Then his arms were around her and he buried his head in her neck with a muffled cry of despair.

'Dear God, Jenna, what are we to do?'

She stood for a moment in his embrace, clinging to him with her eyes closed, savouring the feel of him, the smell of him, the strength in his arms, aware of her own beating heart. Then she pulled away slightly and put her hands on his chest. His face was ashen and he was looking at her as though he was searching for answers in her eyes. But Jenna didn't have any answers, any more than he did.

'My dearest, dearest William. I don't know what we can do. I don't know what's going to happen, but as long as we face it together, we can be strong. I can't do anything on my own. I've tried but I can't … I know I can't.'

'And I've tried to forget you, Jenna. God knows I've tried to put you out of my mind. I've reminded myself over and over again that I have no right to love you, that Margery is my wife, but … oh, dear God, what am I to do?'

'William, come. Let's sit for a moment.' Jenna pulled him back towards the table.

'We have to be strong,' she said as they sat and she took his hand in both of hers. 'We must be strong for each other. Things are bad and they could easily get worse.'

'They'll burn her. They'll burn her this time, I know they will. They came close to doing it last time. I tried to save her … tried to buy them off…'

'And you succeeded. So don't give up hope. Anything can happen.'

'Jenna, we need to talk.'

'Yes. We must. But we can't talk here, not in this kitchen, it's like St Paul's Cross in here sometimes with all the coming and going. And Kitty could be back at any moment.'

'Tomorrow night. Can you come back here? We could talk somewhere, oh I don't know, I'll find somewhere quiet. Will you come, Jenna?'

'You know I will. But I'll probably have to wait until

the Duchess is asleep.'

'Then it will be dark. That could be dangerous. Can I come to you? It's a long way for you to walk from the palace.'

'I'm not in the palace. The Duchess has taken refuge in the Abbey, but it's not really any further away. So you can't come to me, not there. I'll have to come to you. But don't worry. I will come back here, but I'm not sure when or how. We mustn't draw attention to ourselves, we mustn't let people think … you know … but I must be able to find you when I do come.'

'I'll be here every evening. And I'll be looking out for you, waiting for you. But don't take too long, my sweet, please don't take too long. I'll be aching to see you.'

'Hush, William, hush. Here comes Kitty.'

Hearing the latch being lifted on the door to Margery's room, Jenna let go of William's hand and leaned away from him as Kitty came back into the kitchen, carrying a bottle with obvious pride.

'There, Jenna,' she said, putting it on the table, 'that should do the trick!'

Jenna and William smiled at each other. Kitty sounded almost grown up.

***

Adam Moleyns, Clerk to the King's Council, glanced around him, making a last-minute check that everything was in place for the meeting. Council members could be quite tetchy if things were not laid out exactly to their liking, quill pens, ink and parchment within reach, candles in position, ready to be lit at the first request. He pulled out a chair for Cardinal Beaufort as he arrived, then another for Cardinal Kemp.

Most other Council members were already here, the Earls of Huntingdon, Stafford and Northumberland, Archbishop Chichele of Canterbury and Bishop William Aiscough of Salisbury among them.

Finally, Bartholomew Halley, a valet for the Crown, brought in his charge, the man he had been told not to let out of his sight, Magister Roger Bolingbroke.

Bolingbroke was not invited to sit while the charges against him were being read out. He stood, his head bowed, his long neck protruding above his collar, listening intently as Adam Moleyns outlined each of the charges in turn. Bolingbroke stood accused not merely of sorcery and necromancy, but of treason against the King.

'Do you deny these charges?' demanded Beaufort.

'I deny them absolutely, my Lord Cardinal. I am His Highness's most obedient and faithful servant. I would never commit treason against him.'

'But you do not deny that you possess an astrolabe, Magister?'

'No, I do not deny it. I do possess an astrolabe. It was purchased for me by my patron, His Grace the Duke of Gloucester. I would never have been able to afford such a magnificent scientific instrument were it not for his generosity.'

'And for what purpose did you use it?'

Bolingbroke hesitated, but not for long. 'My colleague Canon Southwell and I used it at the request of Her Grace, the Duchess, Sir.'

'Oh, you did, did you? And I ask you again: for what purpose did you use it? To read Her Grace's horoscope, perhaps? And to divine the future?'

'Yes, Sire. It is not an unusual request. Canon Southwell had already read the Duke's horoscope more than once, particularly before he set sail for Calais five years ago.'

'Yes, and that was a very successful campaign, my Lord,' interrupted Archbishop Chichele. 'The Duke was thanked by the commons in Parliament for his part in it.' The Archbishop was keen to support the Duke and speak well of him.

'Be that as it may,' said Beaufort, 'but when it came to the Duchess's request, surely Canon Southwell should have known better than to involve himself in horoscope readings of a frivolous nature such as a woman might want, and he a Canon of St Stephen's!'

Adam Moleyns cleared his throat. 'On a point of information, my Lord Cardinal, perhaps you should know that Master Southwell is no longer a canon,' he said. 'I am informed that he was relieved of his canonry two days ago and his place has been taken by the King's almoner, John Delabere.'

That will deflate the wretched man's ego, thought Beaufort, but aloud he said: 'Very well. Thank you for informing the Council of that fact, Master Moleyns. We are grateful to you.' He turned back to the accused. 'So, Magister Bolingbroke, these are very serious charges which have been made against you. The Council will have to deliberate this case with great care before deciding what's to be done. So, for the moment, you must be returned to custody in the Tower where you will have ample time to ponder and repent your sins.'

Roger Bolingbroke made as though to open his mouth and make another denial, but appeared to think better of it. He turned quite meekly at Bartholomew Halley's command and the two left the room with four guards following behind them.

'We will have to make an example of him,' said Kemp. 'This kind of thing cannot be allowed. Everyone should see what happens to heretics like him.'

'What have you in mind?' asked Bishop Ainscough.

'A public trial,' said Kemp. 'At St Paul's Cross, where he will be given a chance to recant his heresies and renounce his sacrilege. It's the only way.'

* * *

John Virley had attended mass at St Benet Hithe on Sunday morning and, on his way home past St Paul's, he'd been intrigued to see the sheer numbers of people who were crowded excitedly around St Paul's cross in the churchyard, certainly many more than would usually attend mass in the cathedral itself. He was aware of a droning voice which seemed to be preaching a sermon in the open air, based, if Virley was not mistaken, on the Book of Leviticus.

'*But I have said unto you, Ye shall inherit their land and I will give it unto you to possess it…*'

Yes, Leviticus it was, thought Virley. Chapter twenty, if he wasn't mistaken. He wondered why that text had been chosen.

'*I am the Lord your God, which have separated you from other people…*'

Stretching his neck and standing on tiptoe, Virley strained to see over the heads of those who blocked his view and what he saw astounded him.

Next to the churchyard cross, a tall platform had been erected. On it stood a painted chair in the shape of a throne, a sword tipped with a copper image at each of its four corners. The man who sat on the chair wore a surplice and had a pair of spectacles perched on his long, beaky nose. On top of his head was a ludicrous paper crown. Tears ran down his cheeks and he was unable to staunch their flow since he was clasping a sword in one hand and a sceptre in the other. Grouped haphazardly around him were mirrors, bowls of water and several other curious objects.

At first, Virley couldn't imagine what was going on, then he saw who else was taking part in this incredible pageant. One by one, he identified them. The man preaching the sermon appeared to be Bishop Low of Rochester. Then Virley recognised Robert Gilbert, Bishop of London, and William Aiscough, Bishop of Salisbury. He was fairly sure that the two men behind them were the Earls of Huntingdon and Northumberland and there was no mistaking the Mayor of London. The men with him were probably his aldermen, thought Virley.

But he certainly recognised the two men at the front of the group. They were among the most famous and familiar faces in the city of London. Standing next to Cardinal John Kemp of York was Cardinal Henry Beaufort. Surely, nearly all the members of the King's Council were assembled here.

Virley elbowed the man standing next to him. 'What's all this about?' he asked.

Just as the man was about to reply, Bishop Low reached verse twenty-seven of the text and raised his voice.

'*A man also or a woman that hath a familiar spirit,*' he intoned, '*shall surely be put to death: they shall stone them with stones, their blood shall be upon them.*'

There was a howl of anguish from the painted chair and gasps of horror from the crowd. So, that was it, thought Virley, a public recanting. The poor man was being made a fool of and accused of heresy and witchcraft with the crowd incited to abhorrence and hatred. And all in the name of the scriptures.

His gaze was riveted to the bizarre spectacle as the Bishop closed his Bible with an authoritative snap.

'And do you, Magister Roger Bolingbroke, now confess your sins and recant your heretical beliefs?' he asked. 'And do you renounce your past involvement in the magical arts?'

'Yes, yes,' screamed Bolingbroke, 'I believe nothing of heresy. I believe in the one true, the one eternal God. And I have not sinned. I never sinned. It was not of my doing!' He collapsed back into the chair, sobbing.

Beaufort turned away in disgust. 'Oh, take him back to the Tower,' Virley heard him say.

The Tower! Just like everyone else in London, Virley had heard the rumours, but now he recognised the man who was sobbing under St Paul's Cross. He had seen him with Margery Jourdemayne and the young girl at St Sepulchre's.

The realisation that he was close enough to speak to Beaufort shook Virley, almost off his feet. Just a few yards away from him stood one of the most powerful men in the land, a man devoted to his King and known to be dedicated to ridding the church of malign influences. Cardinal Henry Beaufort had the power to send heretics and witches to the Tower, as he had just done with the pathetic, sobbing wretch in St Paul's churchyard.

This was an opportunity not to be missed. The distinguished members of the Council might well be grateful for a witness statement from someone who could verify certain aspects of the case.

Virley began to push his way to the front of the crowd. The time had come to right an old wrong.

CHAPTER TWENTY-ONE

Tuesday July 25th 1441

Normally, Edmund Kyrton discharged his duties with diligence, pleased at his promotion from Sacristan to Abbot following the death of Richard Harweden, proud of his new responsibilities as the head of the Abbey of Westminster. But he had to admit that his rather sophisticated predecessor had been far better at dealing with members of the royal family than he was ever likely to be and he was certainly not looking forward to his meeting with the Duchess of Gloucester this morning. So far, he'd had very little to do with her. What he did know about her had been gleaned from other people and, if what they said was true, she would be an intimidating woman.

As a deeply committed Benedictine, Abbot Kyrton had readily offered the Duchess sanctuary when she'd thrown herself on his mercy a week ago, but since then he'd shied away from having much to do with her while she made her temporary home in the sanctuary cell. Today however, he must face up to his responsibilities.

The Duchess was alone save for the presence of one tiring woman.

'Good morning, Your Grace,' he greeted her.

She gave him the ghost of a smile and nodded her head to acknowledge him.

'Do you bring me news, Father Abbot?' she asked.

'I do,' he said.

The Duchess Eleanor looked pale and tired. Deep shadows under her grey eyes gave her a haunted look. He noticed the tiring woman moving in to stand close behind her, as though to defend her mistress.

'I trust you don't mind the presence of my maid, Father?' she asked. 'I would prefer her to stay with me. She will help me to remember what you tell me.'

'I have no objection to that,' said the Abbot.

Despite the limitations of her accommodation, the Duchess Eleanor still wished to observe the social niceties and had asked Jenna to procure some sweetmeats to offer Kyrton or anyone else who might visit her. He waved away the pewter plate.

'Thank you, no,' he said. 'I'm afraid I haven't much time, so I think I should begin immediately.' He hesitated and took a deep breath. 'Your Grace, I have been asked to tell you that this afternoon you are again summoned to appear at St Stephen's to give account of yourself.'

'Again?'

'Yes, Your Grace. At the Royal Chapel. And ...' he hesitated, 'and, er, I understand that you will be required to answer a charge of conspiring to, er, to bring about the death of His Highness, King Henry.'

'No!' said the Duchess emphatically. 'Absolutely not! I have already sworn before Archbishop Chichele that I only ever had the King's welfare at heart. I swore on oath before all the bishops, archbishops, all those people who were questioning me yesterday, that I was concerned about the King's health. That was all.'

'That is not how it appears, Your Grace, and I'm afraid I also have to inform you that you are not the only person summoned to appear this afternoon.'

'Who else? Tell me, Father Abbot, who else!'

'Magister Bolingbroke, Your Grace.'

A loud wail escaped Eleanor and she seemed to withdraw into herself, her hands over her head. Jenna's heart bled for her mistress and she plucked up the courage to speak.

'I'm sorry, Father Abbot,' she said quietly, 'I know I have no right to interrupt you, but you can see Her Grace is still dreadfully distressed after her experience yesterday. Does she have to appear again quite so soon?'

'Yes, I'm afraid so,' said Abbot Kyrton, 'and there's nothing I can do about it. The decision is not of my making.' Then, glancing at the distraught Eleanor, he added more kindly, 'I'm afraid I can do nothing to help. Her Grace has been ordered to appear before the highest ecclesiastical court in the land so even I, as Abbot, cannot insist that she must remain in sanctuary at the Abbey.' He sighed and shook his head. 'Do what you can to comfort your mistress, but tell her the guards will be here at noon to accompany her to St Stephen's. God bless you, my child,' he said as he made to leave. Then he looked down at the Duchess Eleanor who still sat with head in her hands, the picture of despair.

'God bless you both,' he added.

Jenna did her best to help the Duchess appear self-possessed and dignified for her second appearance at St Stephen's. Overwhelmed by the thought of what she faced, Eleanor occasionally seemed to sink into herself, so helping her dress and prepare to face another ordeal was rather like trying to dress a big rag doll. There was still half a bottle of Kitty's headache remedy left but Jenna almost had to force it down her mistress's throat. Thankfully, it had the desired effect and by the time the guard came to accompany them to St Stephen's, Eleanor seemed much calmer.

Entering the chapel for the second time was just as awe-inspiring as it had been the previous day. Jenna had never seen such wall paintings, such altarpieces. Neither had she ever seen so many imposing ecclesiastical figures assembled in one place and they were all here again. She couldn't have named them individually, but their croziers, their mitres and the sumptuousness of their robes marked them out as bishops, archbishops and clerics of the highest rank.

Eleanor knew them, though. There was the hated Cardinal Beaufort, her husband's arch-enemy and his most outspoken critic. Cardinal Kemp was there, too, along with Archbishop Chichele. She liked Chichele: perhaps, today, he would be kind to her. Humphrey liked Chichele, too, but the others were all men her husband loathed and who probably loathed him equally. If only Humphrey was not away from home. If only he could be here to help her!

Bolingbroke was already on the witness stand, clutching the

rail, his knuckles white. He had the look of a man who had buckled under the weight of accusation, defeated and bent. As Eleanor was brought into the room, Henry Beaufort turned and pointed towards her.

'This is Her Grace, the Duchess of Gloucester,' he said, before he turned back to address Bolingbroke again. 'And is this the woman at whose bidding you claim that you and Southwell used the astrolabe to cast a horoscope?'

Bolingbroke hung his head and mumbled something.

'Speak up, man! The court cannot hear your reply!'

'Yes,' said Bolingbroke, louder this time.

'And for what purpose did she want you to cast a horoscope?

Bolingbroke fixed his gaze on the floor, at a point somewhere between himself and Eleanor. He would not look at her.

'Her Grace said she was concerned about the health of His Highness the King.'

'Ah, so this was the *King's* horoscope, was it? I see.' He waited several moments, rubbing his chin reflectively, then he said: 'And what did you and Master Southwell learn about the state of the King's health?'

'That he might suffer a bout of illness later this year. No more than that.'

'An illness, eh? And might that have been a fatal illness?'

'We sincerely hoped not, my Lord, and we prayed diligently to that end.'

'Very well. That is all for now, but do not imagine for one moment that we have finished with you. You may step down, but you will be called to face more questions – you may depend on it. We must get to the bottom of this. Take him away! And call the Duchess of Gloucester to the witness stand.'

'Prisoner dismissed. Call Her Grace the Duchess of Gloucester!'

Bartholomew Halley stepped forward to take charge of the prisoner and Beaufort returned to sit behind the long table with the other members of the jury. There was a buzz of conversation while four guards grouped themselves around Roger Bolingbroke and escorted him from the chapel.

Now it was Archbishop Chichele's turn to ask the questions. He watched anxiously as Eleanor stepped up to the witness stand. She looked very ill.

'Would you like to sit, Your Grace?' he asked.

'If I may,' she replied, grateful for his concern. Chichele, her husband's friend. Perhaps it wouldn't be too bad after all.

She was wrong. Archbishop Chichele's kind gesture in offering her a seat was the only one she received throughout the entire proceedings. The Duchess was accused of no less than twenty-eight transgressions and vehemently denied them all, insisting that her only concern had ever been to be a good wife to her husband and a faithful subject of the King's. And still the questions kept coming, accusation followed accusation, fingers were pointed and voices were raised. As the afternoon wore on, Eleanor became increasingly exhausted.

The questioning was too clever for her tired brain, too slick, too sly. The answers she tried to give were distorted by her questioners and fired back at her. Once again, Cardinal Beaufort rose to his feet and moved to stand in front of the table where the other council members were sitting. He walked towards Eleanor and she struggled to hold her head erect and look at him. He paused until he was certain he had the full attention of everyone who was present in the chapel.

'You say you wanted nothing more than to be a loyal subject of the King's and a devoted wife to your husband?' he began.

'Yes, my Lord, that is so. I wanted nothing more than that.'

'Very well. Now let us, for the moment, make the assumption that you were, as you say, solicitous of the King's welfare, anxious that he might not be well. How did you express those anxieties? Did you pray regularly for His Highness?'

'I prayed every day that if His Highness was ill, he would be restored to good health. The King was always in my prayers, day and night.'

'And your husband, did you pray for him, too?'

'Always.'

'You said a moment ago that you wanted nothing more than to be a good, dutiful wife to your husband. Yes? Correct?'

'Yes, that is my dearest wish.'

Rounding on her and pointing an accusing finger, Beaufort barked his next question.

'Then why did you not give him a child?'

'I did!' Eleanor was indignant: the question had thrown her entirely off balance. 'I did! No, no, I didn't give him a child, that is true, but I prayed with all my heart that I might conceive one. I pleaded with God, I asked holy men and nuns to intercede on my behalf.'

'And did you take any medicines, any pills or potions to help you?'

'I did, I did. I did everything I knew how to do.'

'And still you were barren?'

'Yes.' Her anguished reply seemed to have been torn from her. 'I was still barren.'

'And where did you procure those pills and potions you admit to using?'

'From ... oh, from several places, from various people.'

'From wise women and the like?'

'Sometimes. If I thought it would help, I would try anything.'

'Village wise women are often known to practise witchcraft. Were you aware of that?'

'I ... I don't know ... I know nothing about that. I was simply doing my best. I meant no harm by anything I did. But I did, desperately, want to have a child. I admit that. My husband had no legal heir and I longed to give him a child. I longed to! It was the greatest gift I could ever offer him.'

'But you failed him.'

Dumbly, Eleanor nodded. There was nothing she could say. She had failed. There could be no argument with that. She was close to tears and exhausted under the verbal battering. In her befuddled mind, she was aware that she had somehow been forced into the confession that she had used the services of a wise woman. And Henry Beaufort hadn't finished with her yet.

'And did you ask a wise woman for potions and lotions and perfumes to make you attractive to the Duke your royal husband, before you were married?'

'Well, I ... yes, perhaps I did. But we were married many years ago. I don't remember clearly.'

'But you admit to having taken medicines and drinks to make him love you?'

'Well, perhaps, as I said. But many women do that. I was certainly not the only woman at court who used the services of Mistress J ... er...'

It was a trap. She bit her tongue but too late.

'Mistress Jourdemayne, perhaps?'

'Yes, my Lord, Mistress Jourdemayne.' Eleanor nodded, then looked up at her tormentor. 'But she supplied many ladies of the court with such things.'

'No doubt,' said Beaufort. 'No doubt. Very well, that is all for now.'

Archbishop Chichele held up his hand. 'My Lords, gentlemen, Her Grace the Duchess has endured several hours of questioning this afternoon and still admits to only five of the twenty-eight charges made against her. I am going to suggest that this court should now adjourn so that we may decide how best to proceed with this very vexing case. It has been decided that, in due course, there will be another hearing, which will be conducted under secular conditions so that certain aspects of the case will be better judged. I must tell you that I have already discussed some of the issues raised with His Highness the King and he is anxious that things be brought to a swift conclusion for the common good, with just and proper punishment meted out in due course. But for the moment, Her Grace the Duchess may return to her sanctuary in Westminster Abbey. This court is now dismissed.'

'Court is dismissed! Be upstanding!'

Rising to her feet, the Duchess staggered a little and Jenna, sitting close behind her, moved quickly to put her hand under her elbow, fearing she might faint.

There was a scraping of chairs being pushed back as the distinguished members of the council stood up from the table, stretching their cramped legs and collecting their belongings. Making his way out of the room with everyone else, Cardinal Beaufort manoeuvred himself closer to Archbishop Kemp.

'A word before we leave,' he said quietly, falling into step beside his friend. 'I thought it interesting that she was prepared to implicate the witch, didn't you?' he asked. 'And therefore herself, of course, by association. Do you think she realised what she'd said?'

Archbishop Kemp raised his eyebrows and gave a slight shrug. 'Whether she did or didn't is immaterial,' he said. 'Because we have a confession that she used the woman's services. And that's all we need. The Duchess has all but admitted to using sorcery and the black arts to get Gloucester to marry her.'

Cardinal Beaufort smiled. 'Then we shall have to have Mistress Jourdemayne called to defend herself,' he said, 'but the case against her is water-tight. According to a fellow I met at St Paul's Cross a week or so ago, she is well known around Westminster and there are those who still openly call her the Witch of Eye, ever since a case was brought against her several years ago in which he himself had been mistakenly implicated.'

'Might that not be sour grapes on his part?'

'No, not at all because he told me that he also saw her quite recently at St Sepulchre's where she was meeting Bolingbroke. He recognised him. So it's high time she was dealt with, once and for all. You remember what the Book of Exodus says about women like her, don't you?'

'Chapter twenty-two,' said Kemp with a knowing smile.

'Indeed. God gave the Laws to Moses and those laws are laid down in Exodus, so there can be no argument. The instruction in chapter twenty-two, verse twenty-seven is very clear. *Thou shall not suffer a witch to live.*'

'And who are we to disagree with the Bible?' said Kemp with a look of wide-eyed innocence.

***

Abbot Kyrton was waiting to meet the Duchess when she returned. Whereas he had been led to believe that she was little but a shallow personality with insufferable pride in her clothes, her jewels and her possessions, he had seen her earlier in the afternoon for the vulnerable woman she was. And he had pitied her. Realising that she was exhausted and deeply upset, he resolved to show her a little human kindness this evening. After Vespers, he would offer her a modest supper in his own rooms, he decided. She might appreciate a gesture of friendship.

'Why, Father Abbot!' she exclaimed, 'how very kind of you. But really, you must not trouble yourself. Besides, I'm weary. I would like to retire early to my bed.'

'You must, of course, if you so wish, Your Grace, but I thought perhaps you might enjoy a civet of hare with me this evening. I eat only modestly at supper time, but I imagine this would be better fare than you have been accustomed to in the last few days. It might take your mind off your troubles for a few hours. You might sleep the better for it.'

The Duchess glanced at Jenna, almost as if she was incapable of making a decision for herself and needed someone to do that for her. Of course, a servant would never be invited to sit down with her at the Abbot's table but she would feel quite nervous without her. Jenna smiled encouragingly.

'I'm sure you'd enjoy that, Your Grace,' she said. 'It would be a change for you and perhaps it would help you to relax a little. And, as it happens, I would very much like to have a few hours off this evening, if I may. I haven't seen Kitty for some weeks. You remember? She's the little girl I mentioned to you.'

'Oh, yes … well in that case,' said the Duchess. 'But … but I would still like to retire to bed at a reasonable hour.'

'I will be back here at the Abbey before sundown, Your Grace, to help you prepare for bed.'

'Very well, then.' Eleanor nodded, turning away towards the main door of the monastery, with Abbot Kyrton attentively at her elbow. Hardly had the great door swung shut behind them than Jenna began to walk as quickly as she could without drawing too much attention to herself, through the village and into the demesne of the Manor of Eye-next-Westminster. Then she broke into a run. For once, she didn't care whether she saw Kitty or not, but she had to see William.

***

At first glance the Abbot's private rooms at the Abbey appeared austere, there were no tapestries on the walls and the floors were covered only with strewing herbs but the furniture was of an excellent quality, the chairs comfortably upholstered. A beautiful oak table in the centre of the room was set for two diners though there would have been room for at least another ten on the long benches to either side of it.

Eleanor was glad of the warmth from a small pile of logs burning in the hearth because although the incessant rain of recent weeks had finally stopped, the air was unseasonably cool. She gave an involuntary shiver.

'Are you quite comfortable, Your Grace?' Abbot Kyrton inquired. 'Are you warm enough? I can always call for more logs for the fire.'

'No. No, thank you,' Eleanor replied. 'I'm not really cold, just upset by the events of this afternoon.'

'I imagine it was a very distressing experience for you, Your Grace, to have been accused of crimes of this nature.'

'It was, very distressing. But what troubles me, perhaps more than anything at the moment, is … is the fear that I have unintentionally implicated someone else.'

'Really? And might I enquire who that is? Only if you wish to tell me, of course,' he added hurriedly. Then he smiled at her. 'I assure you, Your Grace, I will respect your confidences equally as much in my dining room as I would in the confessional!'

Eleanor waited until her porringer had been filled with a helping of civet of hare from a large tureen. The tantalising aroma of onions in the stew made her realise how very hungry she was. While the Abbot was being served, she took a slice of bread and buttered it generously.

He looked enquiringly at her. 'Would you like to tell me who it is?'

Eleanor waited until she was sure that the young novice who was serving at table was safely out of earshot. 'She is the wife of one of your tenants on the manor farm, a man by the name of William Jourdemayne.'

'Ah, yes. I know him, of course. A most conscientious tenant. He seems to run the place very well. I know of his wife by reputation, but I haven't met her since I inherited responsibility for the manor farm from Abbot Harweden. She has not been much in evidence on those occasions when I have visited La Neyte.'

'Her name is Margery. She is a clever woman, skilled at making cures for all manner of ills. Her tinctures and decoctions are most effective and the ladies of the court very often buy her creams and lotions, too. And not only the ladies: she often sells small items to the gentlemen.'

'So she's by way of being what you would call a business woman, then, rather than discharging her duties as a good wife to her husband?'

'Well, yes, in a way. Yes, I suppose she is.'

'And how is she involved in this case?' he asked.

With a sigh, Eleanor answered. 'I have made the mistake of buying some of her wares in the past and now the King's Council is trying to prove she's some sort of wise woman and that I am in league with her.'

Abbot Kyrton looked enquiringly at her over the rim of his spoon. 'And is she?'

'Is she what? A wise woman? Well, perhaps.'

'And are you, Your Grace? In league with her, that is?'

Eleanor thought very hard before replying. 'As I said, I have purchased some of her lotions and so on in the past. Oh, and a little tooth tincture. It's not such a dreadful thing to have done. And I have admitted it.'

Thoughtfully, the Abbot chewed on a mouthful of bread. He needed to choose his words with care. The Duchess was upset enough already. He had no desire to make things worse.

'The problem as I see it, Your Grace, is that wise women are very often accused of being witches. And if the Council can lay that accusation at Mistress Jourdemayne's door, then not much can be done to help her.'

'But they'd have to prove it!'

'If they want to prove it, they will. It won't be difficult. As I say, I know of Mistress Jourdemayne's reputation and the accusation of sorcery that was once made against her. But if she is still known in the village as a wise woman, it's only a short

311

step to a second accusation of witchcraft. And she won't be shown much leniency a second time.'

'But I still don't see how they can prove ...'

'Believe me, Your Grace, I have read the scriptures in great detail during the course of a lifetime of study and I can think of at least two Biblical references which could be quoted in support of that accusation. You must resign yourself to that, Your Grace. I'm sorry.'

Eleanor put her spoon down on the table beside her porringer. She had lost her appetite.

***

Jenna didn't expect to find William immediately. The whole demesne extended for well over a thousand acres, from the boundary of Knightsbridge village in the north to the Westbourne stream in the west, and south to the banks of the Thames. He could be anywhere, but since the working day was all but over, the chances were that he'd be in the farmhouse kitchen. He was, but he was not alone. Robin Fairweather was with him.

William was on his feet the moment he saw her.

'Jenna! Thank God! My dearest girl, I've been so worried.'

Surprised at seeing Robin, Jenna instinctively shied away from William's embrace. He glanced back over his shoulder at Robin.

'It's all right. Robin knows how it is. He's known for a long time. I had to tell someone, Jenna. I'd have gone mad if I hadn't.'

'And I think it's high time you two had some time to yourselves,' said Robin, smiling as he got up from the table. 'You have a lot of catching up to do. Jenna, how are you? It's good to see you.'

'Hello, Robin, it's good to see you, too. But you're late with this drove, aren't you? You're usually earlier than this.'

Robin shrugged. 'Weather's been bad,' he said.

'I've had to let the wheat crop stand for the same reason,' William added. 'It's been too wet to cut.'

'But now,' Robin said, hooking his finger in the collar of his jerkin and swinging it over his shoulder, 'I have to go and make sure the girls are properly milked and bedded down for the night. So I'll leave you to it. C'mon, Mallow. Work to do!' The old cattle dog, dozing under the table, struggled a little in getting to her feet yet still wagged her tail in anticipation.

'You've never worried that much about them before!' William laughed, his arm tightly around Jenna's waist.

'Who? The girls? I always worry about them! Jenna knows that. Besides, if I don't go and join the other men in the barn, they'll have finished the ale before I get there.'

'Could be there's a bit of a barn dance going on,' said William.

'Oh, yes, there will be. And you can sometimes meet a nice class of girl at a barn dance,' he added, with a broad wink at Jenna.

As the door closed behind Robin, she let herself relax within the circle of William's arms, her head against his shoulder. After a long moment, he raised her chin and looked into her face.

When he bent his head and kissed her, it was the most overwhelming, melting moment of her entire life. He had kissed her before, of course, fleetingly on Twelfth Night with a kiss as light as thistledown. Under the oak tree beside Willow Walk, when he confessed his love for her, he had kissed her with desperation, urgency, every muscle of his lean body tensed in the moment. Then, the last time they were together in this very kitchen and realised the gravity of their situation, their kiss of pure despair had changed, somehow, into a mute declaration of solidarity, each with the other.

Now the kiss was one of recognition, of new beginnings, of assent and avowal, the first real kiss of the rest of their lives together. They both knew that and, equally, they both knew what must happen next. It was as inevitable as dawn after darkness.

'Come,' said William, 'it can't be here.'

Taking her hand, he led the way towards the stable at the far end of the farm yard and up the stone steps to the hay loft. A few late bees still droned among the cornflowers in the wheat field and from the big barn came the muted sounds of music and laughter, all but drowning out the distant, plaintive call of a curlew from the river.

'Will anyone find us up here?' Jenna's eagerness was tinged with anxiety.

'No, they're far too busy enjoying themselves in the barn,' he said, pulling her down onto the warm hay, still fragrant after the heat of the day. 'Come, my sweeting' he said. 'We can't wait any longer.'

She responded to him joyously, loosening her kirtle and her shift, pulling the coif off her head and letting her dark hair cascade freely over her bare breasts. Lying on her back in the hay, she smiled up at him as he leaned on his elbow, gently brushing her hair away from her face. Suddenly he frowned.

'Dear God, Jenna, what happened to your ear?'

Instantly, her hand flew up to cover her puffball ear. She rarely thought about it these days unless she occasionally misheard something someone said. She felt her skin reddening.

'Oh, it's nothing … it's just…'

'Did someone hit you?'

'Yes, but … but it was a long time ago. Really, I hardly remember…'

'Poor Jenna, my poor, poor girl. But don't worry, my sweet. No one will ever hurt you again.' William held her close, making soothing, crooning sounds, conscious of her bare breasts against his chest.

So, Robin had been right when he said there'd been a cruel husband in her background and here was the proof of it. But if Jenna chose not to tell him that, then he couldn't tell her she was a widow. And in any case, he himself still had a wife. Sometime, some day in the future when they had come through this nightmare together, there would be time for explanations, for forgiveness and for forgetting. But that time was not now. Now he stood on the threshold of something he had long dreamed of, something wondrous and beautiful. He wanted to make love to this woman as he had never wanted anything else in his life but, savouring the moment, he kissed her just once more before he did.

CHAPTER TWENTY-TWO

August 1441

'You two are getting to be my most regular customers!' Annie the alewife called out as she spotted John Virley and William Woodham coming through the door of the tavern. Annie, wearing her usual greasy apron, was standing behind a table with two other women, dispensing ale from a tall jug.

'You're not complaining, are you, you old quean?' William Woodham roared over the heads of a few dozen noisy drinkers.

'No, of course I'm not!' she replied with a raucous laugh as they pushed through the crowd towards her. 'Your money's the same colour as everyone else's. What'll it be, boys?'

'The usual,' said Woodham. 'But make sure it's your best ale this time, Annie, not the cat's piss you gave us last time.'

'Cat's piss!' cried Annie indignantly. 'Well, you drank enough of it as I recall, so it can't have been that bad!'

'Sorry, my sweet,' Woodham teased her, blowing kisses in her direction. 'I meant nectar of the gods, not cat's piss. Come on then, hurry it up.'

Once they'd been served, the two men took their ale over to a bench near the small window overlooking Fleet Street and sat down.

'So, where does having Canon Hume locked up in the Tower leave you?' Virley asked when his fingers were contentedly curled around the handle of his tankard. 'Are you having any time to yourself?'

'Not on your life's breath! I never seem to stop going back and forth, fetching and carrying everything he needs,' said Woodham. 'He's a bad-tempered fellow at the best of times and he's bringing a new meaning to the word "demanding". He's always demanding something, his books, a change of clothes, a new quill pen … anything you can think of. Seems to spend most of his time writing letters.'

'So he's allowed visitors?' asked Virley, genuinely interested.

'Only one. And that's me. Someone has to take things in for him, food mainly. The food in the Tower is disgusting: slops and frumenty. You wouldn't feed it to the pigs. Actually, I have to look after all the poor bastards,' he added. 'Bolingbroke has no one to visit him and neither does Canon Southwell.'

'He's just plain Master Southwell again now, isn't he? At least, that's what they're saying in Westminster.'

'Oh, yes, he's lost his job all right. Seems to have broken him completely. He'll never be a bishop now.'

'Aye, he was always ambitious,' said Virley. He was silent for a moment, recalling the familiar sight of Thomas Southwell strutting around the monastery at Westminster with his rotund stomach preceding him, treating the likes of Virley with barely concealed distain and yet fawning sycophantically over anyone more senior in the church hierarchy. There was a pitiful transparency about him.

Virley had never liked Southwell and yet he felt sorry for the man. Though he himself had never cherished any serious ambitions within the church, he could well understand someone who aspired to wear a mitre. A bishop was someone with great authority, someone important, to be looked up to and respected, and if that's what had motivated Thomas Southwell, then was it such a bad thing?

'Perhaps I'll come with you the next time you visit Southwell,' he said to Woodham. 'I do know him and I know how it feels to be a failed cleric. We're two of a kind in that. So I feel a bit sorry for him.'

'Please yourself,' Woodham said. 'I'll be going there tonight. You're welcome to come with me if you want to. By the way, you never told me what was the cause of your fall from grace. Women, was it?'

'Aye, mostly. One in particular. She's involved in this case, too. That's why I'm interested.'

'Not Margery Jourdemayne?'

'Yes, the Witch of Eye. And she really is a witch. I hate the woman. Did you never hear about our extended stay at Windsor Castle?'

'You and Margery Jourdemayne?'

'Yes. In the dungeons. Imprisoned. The Jourdemayne woman, me and a Grey Friar called John Ashwell. A nice old man. Ashwell thought we could all learn from each other about aspects of healing and we did, to start with. She turned out to be a right bitch, though, if a damned attractive one. Could have given a man a good time.'

'And you wanted her to?'

'Yes. Oh yes, at one time. She was a good-looking woman. Clever, too. There's not much she doesn't know about plants and that sort of knowledge is always useful. She'd have made a good apothecary.'

'But she's a woman.'

'Exactly. She was good at image magic, too, and thief magic. And she'd find anything you'd lost. It was uncanny. Ashwell was fascinated by her.'

'So were you, by the sound of it.'

'Only to the extent of getting her into bed.'

'But you never managed…'

'No. Never. And now I wouldn't touch the bitch with a barge pole. But she'll pay for getting me into trouble, you can bet on it.'

Startled by the venom in Virley's voice, William paused for a moment, then said: 'Tell me about her image magic. Did she make wax models?'

'She was very skilful at it. She could fashion anything out of wax – flowers, manikins, poppets, you name it, the Witch of Eye could make it. And she often did.'

Woodham was thoughtful for a moment. That would explain the lump of wax in the willow basket he had found on Bolingbroke's shelf. He wondered whether it was time to share the information.

***

317

The King was pleased to see that sunlight dappled the waters of the Thames outside the Palace of Westminster, in stark contrast to the howling wind and rain that had greeted his last visit to London.

He recalled with horror his meeting on that occasion with his great-uncle Cardinal Beaufort and he still felt overwhelmingly grateful for his advice. It had been a great shock for the King to realise that not all his subjects viewed him with the loyalty and cordial love he had been led to expect of them. More than anything, it upset him to think that one of his least loyal subjects was his uncle's wife, the woman he had been happy to call his aunt, though he'd always felt slightly unnerved by her coquettish mannerisms and her studied allure.

During the past three weeks at Sheen, he'd had a chance to consider the situation and, though he could now only think of the Duchess of Gloucester with something akin to dread, he knew he would be expected to judge the situation impartially. He must mingle firmness with consideration; that was what a wise king would do. He was grateful for the support he was being given by the members of the Council, but what he really wanted was their approval.

He looked at them now, solemnly convened in the big meeting room in the Palace of Westminster and was comforted by the presence of Cardinal Beaufort, who always seemed to him to be the voice of wisdom and authority. Seated next to him was Cardinal Kemp and here too were the earls of Huntingdon, Northumberland and Stafford, who had been part of the earlier investigation into the case. Lords Hungerford and Fanhope were sitting together while the Mayor of London, Robert Clopton, sat with a group of aldermen. All eyes were watching the King intently, waiting for him to address them.

'My Lords,' he said, 'we live in trying times. So let me begin this meeting by giving you some good news. As you already know, it appears that my uncle's wife, Her Grace the Duchess of Gloucester, commissioned her advisers to read my horoscope because, she claimed, she was concerned for my failing health. Naturally, I was more than a little alarmed by this, particularly since they predicted that a terminal decline,

318

during the months of May and June this year, would culminate in my death from melancholia.'

The King looked up and scanned the impassive faces around the table. Not one of the noble lords looked likely to react until he had said something positive. He swallowed nervously before he began to speak again.

'Today, my Lords, is the ninth day of August – and I am still alive!'

There was a gale of relieved laughter and some spontaneous applause. Smiling now, the King held up his hand.

'Moreover, I am in the best of health and I would like to thank you all for your support.' The atmosphere had lightened considerably.

The King went on: 'I am also grateful to my own learned advisers, Sir John Somerset and Master John Langdon of Cambridge from whom I commissioned an alternative horoscope, on the advice of my esteemed great-uncle Cardinal Beaufort. These two learned gentlemen have put their extensive knowledge to work on my behalf. Their expertise is clearly greater than the poor skills of the Duchess's advisers and I am told that, with God's blessing, I will be among you for some considerable time to come.' He bent his head and crossed himself with due piety. All the other men present did the same and a quiet rumble of approval rippled around the table.

Straightening up, the King went on: 'I am anxious, therefore, that this deeply troubling case should be conducted in the proper manner and, importantly, that it should serve the interests of both Church and government. To that end, I have been advised to request that Archbishop Chichele, representing the Church, should preside over what might otherwise be seen as a secular hearing, because it is to be held at Guildhall. The date for this hearing has provisionally been arranged for the twenty first day of October, just over two months hence, which will give all those concerned ample time to consider every aspect of the case.'

The King disliked making long speeches in public but he sensed he had the sympathy of everyone in the room and that was a great relief. He took a sip of wine to clear his throat before going on.

'My Lords, it pains me to learn that there are people in our fair city who pursue the dark arts of necromancy, magic and witchcraft. I hear alarming reports about a superstitious sect of necromancers and persons charged with witchcraft and incantations.' Again, he paused briefly to cross himself. 'So I have agreed that a considerable sum of money, some twenty pounds in total, should be set aside in order that a committee of learned clerks, doctors and notaries can be commissioned to carry out a thorough investigation. Until that committee has produced its report, it has been decreed that all the persons thus far accused, both men and women, are to be kept in the Tower and securely guarded at all times. As far as my ... er ... my uncle's wife is concerned, I understand that she has been claiming sanctuary in the Abbey at Westminster. I'm afraid that this can no longer be permitted. Henceforward, she will be held in royal custody and will be committed to Leeds Castle to await her trial.'

The King looked across the table to where Cardinal Beaufort was watching him intently, nodding as his great-nephew enumerated every point he had been told to make.

'Perhaps, my Lord Uncle, you would like to say a few words before I bring the meeting to a close?'

'Thank you, Your Highness. In fact, I have very little further to add except to express the Council's gratitude to you for your balanced view of the whole sorry situation and your clearly expressed determination to arrive at the best and fairest judgement of the case. I also speak for the other members of the Council in thanking Archbishop Chichele for agreeing to preside over the secular trial in October. It will not be a responsibility to be taken lightly. I would add only one more thing, which is that anyone hindering the Archbishop in the performance of his task, or anyone making any attempt to approach the Duchess or, indeed, doing anything else to obstruct the legal proceedings in any way, will be severely punished. And please ensure that this warning is disseminated as widely as possible. We must, at all times, abide by the rule of law.'

'Thank you, my Lords,' said the King, rising from his seat. 'You will be given final details of the arrangements being made for the hearing at Guildhall as soon as they become available.'

'Be upstanding!'

The assembled Council members shuffled to their feet and inclined their heads respectfully as the King left the room.

***

'No straw in your hair this time, Jenna?'

The Duchess asked the question in a very arch tone of voice with her eyebrows raised exaggeratedly.

Jenna blushed. Admittedly, she was late again and panting slightly but surely, after three weeks, her mistress had forgotten the evening when she'd given Jenna permission to visit Eybury Farm as long as she was back in good time to help her to bed. But Jenna had arrived back at the Abbey sanctuary long after the bell had been rung for Compline, hot and dishevelled after running all the way. Ecstatic in the moment, she and William had clung to each other in the hay loft, not wanting that moment to end, dreading having to face the chasm of anxiety which lay outside their newly expressed love for each other, not wanting to part.

A hastily concocted story about Kitty needing her seemed to mollify the Duchess until she noticed the straw in Jenna's hair. Then she turned on her, spitting like an angry cat, demanding to know the name of the man. Jenna protested that there was no man: it was a lie, of course, but there was nothing to be gained by telling the Duchess the truth, that the man in question was none other than the husband of Margery Jourdemayne.

They reached a deadlock from which neither would step down when, to Jenna's astonishment, the Duchess burst into tears and sobbed that no one cared about her and even her maid would rather lie in the hay with a man than look after the needs of her poor, poor mistress. And where was her own husband, Duke Humphrey? Why hadn't he come to her aid?

Ever since then, Jenna had done everything she could to please her and, slowly, Eleanor's hostility melted until she eventually began to behave as though there had been no confrontation between them. For Jenna, the urge to run back to Eybury farmhouse had been almost insurmountable but she knew she must bide her time until something tangible happened. In her new-found confidence, she knew William would wait for her.

The Duchess kept up her own spirits with the conviction that everything would be all right as soon as her husband returned to London. Humphrey would take charge of everything, she knew he would. He would inform the King of the true situation, the way in which Cardinal Beaufort and Archbishop Kemp were manipulating the Council, telling lies for their own benefit. Her husband would come to the Abbey and demand her release, then take her away from all this to La Pleasaunce. There, after a few weeks at their lovely home in Greenwich, she would begin to relax and forget this nightmare. Then everyone would be sorry for the way they'd behaved; they would have to apologise to her. They'd see that she was not just any woman to be manipulated and pushed hither and thither. She was Her Grace the Duchess of Gloucester. Everything would be all right in the end. And that end couldn't come soon enough.

But the days dragged by and, apart from the occasional visit from Abbot Kyrton, they saw no one. Jenna would go out, to the palace to fetch some item of clothing or into Westminster village to buy their few necessities and she'd return with whatever gossip she could glean.

The caustic remark about straw in her hair took Jenna by surprise because this time, she was breathless only because she had rushed to tell the Duchess the news.

'There was a big meeting at the palace this afternoon, Your Grace,' she said. 'All the members of the Council were there.'

'How do you know?'

'I saw John Solers and he told me.'

'Who is he?'

'He's an esquire of the King's household, Your Grace. He said –'

'He's not your man in the hay?'

'No, Your Grace! As I said, he's an esquire of the King's Household. He … he told me that they've been questioning him about Magister Bolingbroke.'

'Bolingbroke? Why? What did they want to know?'

'He said they asked him if Magister Bolingbroke had told him that the King would die.'

'And had he? Did he?'

'He didn't say, Your Grace, but he said they're questioning everyone in the palace, all the servants. No doubt I'd have been questioned, too, if I was still working there instead of being here with you.'

Eleanor's mouth was set in a grim expression. 'This man Solers is an esquire of the King's Household, you say? And you know who is Steward of the King's Household, don't you, Jenna?'

'The Earl of Suffolk, Your Grace.'

'Exactly. William de la Pole, the Earl of Suffolk, a friend of Henry Beaufort and as devious as the day is long, he and his wife, the frightful Alice. I wouldn't trust either of them further than I could throw a pig by the soaped tail. They hate me, they hate my husband and – Oh God, where is Humphrey? Why doesn't he come?'

The Duchess was becoming agitated. Disinclined to upset her further, Jenna almost refrained from telling her the next piece of news, but she knew she had to.

'John Solers said he'd heard you were to be taken into royal custody, Your Grace.'

'Royal custody? What did he mean by that?'

'I don't rightly know, Your Grace. I imagine that means they're going to take you away from here and … I don't know … I really don't know.'

The Duchess was on her feet now, kneading her hands together anxiously, beginning to pace up and down.

'Leeds Castle! It will be Leeds Castle, I know it! That's where they put prisoners of the King. I won't go there, Jenna, I won't! It's in the middle of a lake in Kent, miles from here. There is no escape. Once I go there, I'll never come back! I won't go there, Jenna, I won't go there!'

'Hush, mistress, hush,' Jenna found herself soothing the Duchess as she would have soothed Kitty in a moment of terror.

'Hush, hush, my dove, you'll make yourself ill. I'm sure you won't have to go there. The Duke –'

'So where is he? Where is my husband? Have they killed him? Why doesn't he come for me?'

'I'm sure he will, Your Grace. You have to be strong. He won't want to see you like this when he comes –'

'I must get away, Jenna, I must escape! I can't go to Leeds Castle, I'll never come back again, I know it. I know it!'

The Duchess was pacing the small room, the way she always did when she was upset, her arms half-folded in front of her, her right hand balled into a tight fist under her chin while she thought.

'I must escape, Jenna. I'm no longer safe here. They will violate my sanctuary and there will be nothing that Abbot Kyrton can do about it. He'll be powerless. So I must escape and you must help me. Tonight, as soon as it's dark. No one will see us.'

'No, Mistress. It's too much of a risk…'

'We'll put on our dark cloaks and hoods and we'll slip out, down to the river. We'll find a boat and somehow we'll get away, even if we have to row ourselves. We'll go to Greenwich. We'll be safe there.'

'But, Your Grace, I'm sure you'll be looked after, even if you are taken away from here. The King will not see you in need. His Highness will make sure you're –'

'No, Jenna. You don't know my husband's enemies. Beaufort, Suffolk, Kemp. They'll do anything. They're powerful men. They will stop at nothing. You don't know them as I do. Perhaps they've imprisoned my husband already. Dear God, perhaps they've killed him! So I must get away, I must.'

By now she was clawing at Jenna, clutching her arms, and Jenna was trying to back away.

'Very well, Mistress. I'll get a few things together. We can't take much. D'you think we could borrow some horses –'

'No, a boat, it must be a boat, Jenna. We'll find a wherryman to take us to Greenwich and we'll hide there at La Pleasaunce until my husband comes home. Go and make everything ready. We must get away as soon as possible.'

Still pacing up and down, back and forth, totally distracted and with her shoulders hunched, the Duchess muttered oaths and threats under her breath while Jenna packed their belongings.

Within the hour, as twilight approached, the same two hooded figures who had taken refuge in the Abbey just a few weeks ago slipped out again and moved stealthily towards the Thames.

Near the Westminster steps lay an empty wherry with its oars shipped. The little boat was moored by its painter to a wooden pillar, river water slapping quietly against the hull. In the moonlight, it was just possible to make out the dark shape of the wherryman. He appeared to be relieving himself against a nearby oak sapling.

'Now, Jenna, now.'

With a frantic whisper, the Duchess broke into a run in the direction of the boat. This was madness. Jenna had little idea how to row and the Duchess probably had even less. But she had no option but to follow her.

'Hey, you! Hey, you women! What in God's name do you think you're doing? Stop, I tell you! Stop at once!'

At the sound of his master's voice, a huge dog which had been curled up and dozing inside the boat suddenly leaped up and, with its front paws on the prow, started barking. Still lacing up the front of his braes, the wherryman gave chase. Running towards them with an alarming turn of speed, he caught the two women with ease, grabbing each of them by the forearm.

'Let me go, this instant!' said the Duchess. 'Do you know who I am?'

'I don't know and I don't care,' the man replied. 'You were going to steal my boat and that's all I care about.'

'But I am the Duchess of Gloucester and I wish to go to Greenwich!'

'Aye, and I'm a donkey's uncle and you two women aren't going anywhere. Not Greenwich nor anywhere else.'

The dog, a big, brown, shaggy-haired creature, had continued to bark loudly throughout this exchange. In no time at all, there were shouts and whistles as people seemed to come from everywhere, running towards the riverbank where the wherryman still held his two captives in an iron grip. The Duchess stood her ground.

'You'll pay for this, my man. My husband is the King's uncle and when he finds out what you have done, he'll have you clapped in irons. Now, are you going to take us to Greenwich or not?'

'This man is not taking you anywhere, Your Grace. You're to come with us.'

Eleanor struggled to turn around to see who had spoken with such firmness. In the mêlée, neither she nor Jenna had realised that a barge, moored some fifty yards along the river bank outside the palace, was flying the royal pennant.

'I'll take charge of this,' said the deep voice of authority.

Jenna recognised two of the men in royal livery. One of them was Sir John Steward and the other Sir William Wolff. A dozen or so household servants stood behind them.

'Let her go,' commanded Sir John and the wherryman let the Duchess's arm fall to her side. 'Her Grace is coming with us.'

Sir William Wolff turned towards Jenna. 'And who are you?' he asked. 'Are you the Duchess's maid?'

'Yes, my Lord,' she whispered, thoroughly frightened by the turn of events.

'Then you will accompany us to the palace. Your mistress will be undertaking a journey tomorrow and will be in need of clothes, shoes and … and, er, so on. Women's things. You will pack them for her.'

'A journey?' Eleanor demanded. 'A journey? Where to?'

This time it was Sir John Steward who spoke.

'To Leeds Castle,' he said.

***

There hadn't been much sleep for either woman that night.

With two guards stationed outside the main door to the Gloucesters' apartments in the palace, Jenna had spent several hours in her mistress's dressing room, assembling every item of outerwear, underwear, hose and shoes, plus jewellery, cutlery, silver and plate she thought would be needed for Eleanor's stay at Leeds Castle. Jenna had been told in no uncertain terms that she would not be accompanying her mistress to Kent: Her Grace's every need would be met by a group of women chosen by the Earl of Suffolk's wife, Alice de la Pole.

Eleanor herself had spent the hours of darkness on her knees at her *prie-dieu*, fervently praying for Humphrey's return, alternately weeping, telling her rosary beads, and cursing her husband's enemies then praying forgiveness for having done so. In her more lucid moments the Duchess knew she was facing harsh imprisonment. Jenna's heart bled for her, but all she could think of was that, at last, she could return to Eybury Farm and William's waiting arms.

The following morning, after initially feigning illness and refusing to leave the Abbey, the Duchess was callously ordered to make herself ready to leave for Kent immediately, no matter how ill she claimed to be. Then, following a tearful farewell to her maid, she was taken away by her captors in a noisy eruption of bellowed commands, whinnying horses, jangling harnesses and rumbling carriage wheels.

After the departure of the cavalcade, the silence had been almost deafening. Jenna, standing alone in the middle of the Duchess's dressing room, was trying to come to terms with the turmoil of her emotions, an unfathomable mixture of elation and loss. She didn't quite know what she felt. The moment had finally come when she could fly to William: she ached to see him. And yet, having lived with the Duchess for so long, she felt strangely unnerved by the fact that, suddenly, she was answerable to no one.

Dithering between wanting to leave for Eybury Farm immediately and her ingrained instinct to tidy up Her Grace's apartment before she left, she wandered from room to room, folding and re-folding clothes, dusting some surfaces, trying to leave things as her mistress would want to find them on her return.

Indecision was her undoing. She hadn't expected to be disturbed so when the knock thundered on the door, she jumped out of her skin.

'Open, in the name of Her Grace the Countess of Suffolk!'

Jenna knew of Alice de la Pole's reputation as a manipulative, hard-hearted woman. The Duchess had hated Alice as much as she hated her husband the Earl of Suffolk. What could she possibly want?

Nervously, Jenna opened the door to admit the Countess of Suffolk, a tall, intimidating woman in her late thirties, her back ramrod-straight, her long, narrow face a mask of disapproval. Jenna curtsied deeply.

'Were you the Duchess of Gloucester's maid?' The question was direct, without preamble.

'I am, Your Grace,' answered Jenna, straightening up.

'You were,' corrected the Countess. 'You are no longer in her employ. You were her maid. You are her maid no longer.'

'Your Grace?'

'You have been dismissed.'

'Oh. Er, yes, Your Grace.'

'So what will you do henceforward, eh?'

'I … I don't rightly know, Your Grace. Perhaps … perhaps I will be able to return to my previous employment at the Monastery farm.'

'The Manor of Eye?'

'Yes, Your Grace.'

'So, it's true. I was told you worked at the Manor of Eye before you came here to the palace to work for the Duchess of Gloucester. And I understand she took you on immediately as her maid, with no training. That is highly unusual. Is that the case?'

'Yes, Your Grace. I worked at the Manor of Eye for some two years, in the dairy and … er, and elsewhere on the farm.'

'It's as I thought. You are in league with the Jourdemayne woman.'

'In league … Your Grace? What do you mean in league?'

'I mean exactly what I say. You know the woman Jourdemayne. You can't deny that?'

'No, Your Grace. I do know Mistress Jourdemayne.'

'*Mistress* Jourdemayne,' the Countess snarled, her voice heavy with sarcasm. '*Mistress*, indeed! The woman is a witch.

It has been proven once: it will be proven again. And you knew, didn't you, that she and the Duchess of Gloucester were as thick as thieves, fellow conspirators.'

Alice de la Pole was slowly circling Jenna as she spoke, poking at her chest and her arms with a bony forefinger. Jenna was very frightened though she stood her ground.

'You knew,' the Countess continued, 'that the Witch of Eye practised the black arts, sorcery, necromancy, magic in all its vile forms. Did you ever perform magic with her? Did you? Did you, eh? Answer me!'

'No, no, Your Grace. I know nothing of that.'

'Do you deny that you ever saw the Hand of Glory?'

'The what, Your Grace? The hand of … of what?'

'Don't pretend. Witches love the Hand of Glory, the mandrake root. They revel in it, they burn candles in it. Don't deny that the witch grew mandrake in her physic garden. It's widely known she had one.'

Jenna didn't know whether she was expected to say something. She remained silent as the onslaught continued.

'Well, did she or did she not have a physic garden?'

'Yes … yes, she did.'

'And did she grow mandrake in it?'

'She might have done, to aid sleep, it is said to be effective…'

'And did you hear the root scream and groan when she pulled it from the ground? Did you? Well, did you?'

'No … the Mistress grew all manner of things in her physic garden, borage, marjoram, heartsease … all the usual herbs.'

'So, you're denying that she grew it?'

'Yes. No … I don't know … she might have. No, I don't think so. No … I don't know.'

Alice de la Pole turned away and beckoned two men into the room. Jenna had seen them before and remembered that she had been advised to avoid them at all costs when they'd been pointed out to her as the Earl of Suffolk's notorious henchmen, Sir Thomas Tuddenham and John Heydon. They took up positions on either side of the Countess as she pointed at Jenna.

'This woman is a known associate of the Witch of Eye.

Accompany her to the Westminster steps. There is a barge moored there which is bound for the watergate entrance to the Tower. See her to the gangplank and make sure she is taken aboard. She is never to be admitted to the Palace of Westminster ever again. Not under any circumstances; not unless she is brought here under armed guard for further questioning.'

To Jenna she said, 'You will be taken to the Tower and you will remain there and repent your sins while you hold yourself in readiness for the Court hearing into the activities of the Duchess of Gloucester and her associates. As a known associate of the Witch of Eye, you are a key witness in the proceedings. You will stay in the Tower until you are called. And rest assured – you *will* be called.'

CHAPTER TWENTY-THREE

October 1441

'I've thought a great deal about it,' the Archbishop said, 'and I've come to the conclusion that, with the best will in the world, I cannot go through with this trial.'

The two old men had known one another for many, many years. In some ways then, it came as no surprise to Cardinal Beaufort to hear Archbishop Chichele's decision.

'Can I not persuade you?'

'No, really, you cannot. I'm tired, Henry. I passed my allotted Biblical lifespan nearly nine years ago. I'm an old, old man. I should be in my bed, slobbering milksop down my nightshirt, not tottering around with this wretched stick – I cannot walk without it.'

Beaufort nodded in sympathy. Though he was well over ten years younger than the Archbishop, he often wished he had no need to outwit and outstay men two decades younger than himself. They both sat quietly for a moment, staring into the fire-basket in the hearth where, with the approach of yet another winter, a pile of crackling logs gave out a welcome warmth for old bones.

'I'd like to think,' said Beaufort, 'that you could manage one more attempt to stamp out heresy once and for all, because we have so very nearly succeeded, you and I. We have both given a lifetime of devotion to the Church and to the Crown, and God only knows how hard we've both worked to eliminate the heretics and the Lollards from our midst.'

'Believe me,' Chichele said, 'I have not taken this decision lightly. Henry, consider if you will, that I have served under three monarchs – our young King, his father and his grandfather before him.'

'Then, surely –'

'No, let me finish. The reason I have made this decision is because I have become very close to the House of Lancaster and I have also come to know the immediate families of each sovereign. During the last year or so, I have worked very closely with Humphrey of Gloucester.'

Beaufort's jaw clenched involuntarily at the mention of his nephew's name but his face gave nothing away. Archbishop Chichele continued his explanation.

'Gloucester and the King are both dedicated to the concept of learning. The Duke has been telling me about some exciting developments which will enable the printing of books by mechanical means. He is keen to see more and more people being encouraged to read, to acquire an education. That is why he has donated much of his own personal collection of books to the university library at Oxford.'

'Generous of him,' observed Beaufort, with a slight curl of his lip.

The Archbishop didn't appear to notice the sarcasm and went on. 'I share his passion. As you know, the King honoured me with an invitation to join with him in establishing a new constituent college of the university at Cambridge. Our vision is for a foundation which will not only enlighten the lawyers and theologians of the future, but will also commemorate those brave men who have fallen in battle in France.'

'Ah,' Beaufort sighed, 'if only we could guarantee that there would be no more English deaths in that wretched country. I want to see us withdraw.'

'Perhaps, now that the Duke of Orléans is to be returned to his homeland, things will change for the better. When are the indentures to be signed, Henry? Do you know?'

'They are in the course of preparation, from what I understand. Orléans will be required to give certain undertakings before he sets sail for France, of course.'

'Of course. That's only to be expected. But I would hate to upset the delicate political balance at this precise moment. That's why I cannot sit in judgement of the Duchess of Gloucester. I am too well-known as a friend of her husband.'

It all made perfect sense to Henry Beaufort. If only he himself could step down. He was tired, too, but he knew he must dig out this canker in the royal household, this taint of witchcraft and heresy. It was dangerously close to the throne and he would do anything in the world to protect the Lancaster dynasty. He had devoted his life to it.

The frightful Cobham hussy and her associates had to be called to account for their behaviour. It was treason, pure and simple, treason against their King. It must be treated as such and dealt with. And it would reflect badly on his egotistical nephew, too – enough to effectively remove him from the Council. Beaufort offered up a silent prayer of gratitude that Charles of Orléans would be on his way back to France very soon.

***

Using the south entrance into the Tower of London, John Virley ran the gauntlet of intimidating, heavily armed guards who could have refused him entry on a whim. But several of them knew him as the man who often made deliveries to the office of the Lieutenant of the Tower, Sir Robert Scott, and they greeted him cheerfully enough.

The Tower was a daunting place at the best of times, but with a biting easterly wind gusting up the Thames, it was enough to strike terror into the strongest criminal heart. High, forbidding walls of grey Kentish rag-stone rose sheer towards Heaven, relieved only by arrow-slits for windows. From within, the croaking calls of ravens seemed to bode nothing but evil.

It seemed entirely appropriate to Virley that the Witch of Eye was now incarcerated within this prison, probably with several other women, because there had been a witch-hunt of alarming proportions in recent weeks. The authorities were determined to rid London of any women who might be suspected of indulging in sorcerous activity. The Sheriff's men patrolled the streets, the markets and the taverns, and several perfectly innocent women had been arrested and locked up on the merest suspicion of having practised the black arts.

This time the Witch would get her just deserts, Virley was

sure of that. Her punishment was long overdue and she could contemplate her destiny from the squalid confinement of her cell within this grim prison.

Virley was visiting Thomas Southwell. He had seen him three times in recent weeks. He'd been with William Woodham the first time but, since then, Virley had found his own way into the Tower and had become Southwell's only visitor – not that the man showed him any gratitude.

No longer the rotund, strutting, pompous figure of old, Southwell spent his days sitting on a bench in the cell he shared with two other prisoners, a murderer and a cutpurse. Iron manacles hanging on the wall were a reminder to the inmates that they could be restrained while unbearable pain was inflicted upon them, if their captors so wished.

The first time Southwell saw his visitor, his expression barely changed. Virley wondered whether he remembered him at all.

'Master Southwell,' he greeted him. 'It pains me to find you here, imprisoned like this.'

'Not nearly so much as it pains me, Virley,' muttered Southwell.

Ah, thought Virley, so he did remember. 'I wondered, Master Southwell, whether there was anything I could do for you. As perhaps you remember, I supply inks and parchments to several establishments in London. The Tower is one of them, so I come here quite frequently. I could bring in anything you needed. It would be no trouble.'

Southwell's face was a blank. 'No,' he said, in a hollow voice, 'I need nothing. I'll be here until I rot or die of melancholy. I want to die. I have no future.'

'Oh, come, you must not talk like that. Perhaps you will be proved innocent. You must have faith in the justice system.'

'Justice system? Faith? Virley, I lost my faith when I lost my canonry. I have nothing to live for.'

'Then I could bring you some books, perhaps, to help you rekindle that faith. Would you like something to read? I could ask at the monastery if –'

'Read? In this environment? Impossible.'

The murderer who shared the cell sat, facing the blank wall, saying nothing, but the cutpurse lolled on the bench, listening to the conversation with interest.

'Tell you what, mate,' he said, 'you could bring us all something decent to eat – or drink. The food in this damned place is disgusting. Even swine would turn up their snouts at it. It might as well be poison.'

Southwell's expression changed. 'Sometimes,' he said, 'I would that it *were* poison. That would solve a lot of problems, don't you think, Master Virley?'

Virley glanced at him in alarm. Was the man serious? No, surely not. Then again, it might be the least painful way out of an impossible situation. Avoiding Southwell's meaningful gaze, he bent to gather up his belongings.

'I'll come again soon. And next time, I'll bring in some cheese at least. And a flagon of decent ale, if I can get it past the guard. That should cheer you all up.'

As he rose to take his leave, an insincere smile fixed on his face, he wondered whether Southwell had meant what he'd implied.

***

Margery Jourdemayne sat on the floor of the cell with her back against the wet wall. The wall always seemed wet, even on the warmest of days, but there was nowhere else to sit. She was forced to share the cell with half a dozen other women, their faces grey from lack of sleep and a poor diet. They looked up as the door opened and another woman was shoved roughly in to join them. When the cell door had been bolted behind her, Margery realised who she was and scrambled to her feet.

'Jenna! In God's name, what are you doing here?' The other women crowded round, demanding to know who Jenna was, why she was there, how she knew Margery.

Jenna was still reeling from the events of the last few hours. With her hands tied behind her back, she had been roughly shoved up the gangplank and onto the waiting barge by Thomas Tuddenham and John Heydon, whose presence terrified her throughout the journey to the Tower. Once through the watergate entrance, she was taken to the guardroom then, after the most minimal formalities, brought to the stinking cell.

'Well?' Margery demanded again. 'What are you doing here? Have they accused you, too?'

'Yes, mistress. It seems I am accused of witchcraft by association, because … well … because I know you.'

'Every woman is a witch, if they say so,' said one of the others. 'All you need is a physic garden, or a bit of a reputation as a midwife or a wise woman, and you're in here. They bang the door on you and leave you to rot.'

There were snorts and noises of disgruntled agreement from the others. Jenna looked at Margery Jourdemayne. She hadn't seen her for several months. She had changed, grown thinner, more wrinkled. But she must have been beautiful once, Jenna thought, she must have had some quality that had made William desire her.

'How is –' Jenna began and then stopped herself. 'How is, er, Kitty?'

'Kitty! Why do you concern yourself about Kitty? You're in trouble, Jenna. You ought to be worried about yourself.'

Jenna was silent. She'd really wanted to know how William was, but then she'd realised that, in fact, she had seen him since Margery last saw him. And on that night she had committed herself to him in the most fundamental way, with all her heart and all her being. She crossed herself and silently asked God to grant her patience and forbearance if she was to remain locked up for any length of time in this fetid little cell with her lover's wife.

***

The stone facade of London's newly built Guildhall glistened in the pale sunshine of a late October morning. At one time, Eleanor reflected, she would have been driven in state up to the imposing entrance to the fine new building, alighting from her carriage with a smile, extending her hand elegantly to the Lord Mayor who would bow low before making a speech of welcome. Over the last few years, particularly on her excursions to the King's Head in nearby Cheapside, she had watched the great building take shape, imagining the lavish entertainments she and Humphrey would grace with their presence when it had been completed, extravagant receptions for dignitaries, diplomats or foreign royalty who would be enchanted to meet her.

Today, she was ignominiously bundled into the crypt, where she would stay until she was summoned to face her inquisitors.

This would be the last trial. Eleanor had already appeared at one ecclesiastical tribunal, held at St Stephen's Chapel and conducted by Robert Gilbert, the Bishop of London, who had frowned at Eleanor as she stood on the witness stand, not even inviting her to sit. Archbishop Chichele wouldn't have done that. She wondered where he was: during the long weeks of her banishment to Leeds Castle, she had pinned her hopes on the probability of Chichele's leniency. After all, he was her husband's friend.

The huge room at the heart of Guildhall was crowded as Eleanor entered. Hard-pressed at first glance to take in the sheer splendour of her surroundings, she was dimly aware of stone archways and statues, stained glass windows and all the trappings of magnificence. Enormous wealth pertained to the London guilds and it had been spent here without stinting.

The room was noisy with the eager sounds of people pressing closely together, straining to see her as she passed. Eleanor was shocked to catch a glimpse of Jenna among the witnesses who were penned in one corner, like so many animals. Then she realised, of course, that anyone associated with Margery Jourdemayne was likely to be called as a witness, and a proven association with her was almost certainly tantamount to an outright accusation of witchcraft.

Then her attention was caught and riveted by the sight of the three people who were lined up to face her as she took her place on the witness stand: Roger Bolingbroke, Margery Jourdemayne and Thomas Southwell.

They had each changed considerably since she had last seen them. Bolingbroke looked more cadaverous than ever, his back stooped and his long neck strangely vulnerable, as though already offering itself up to the hangman's noose. Margery had a defiant look about her, but she, too, had lost a considerable amount of weight and her hair, pushed carelessly under a wimple of dingy linen, looked coarse and unkempt. But the one who had changed the most was Thomas Southwell: Eleanor hardly recognised him. A man who had always relished his food, he now looked as though he hadn't eaten for months.

All three stood behind a table on which were exhibited several items which Eleanor recognised. Here was the astrolabe: Bolingbroke had been so proud of that. There were several books, too, including the Arabic text from her own library which she had never understood, but always thought she might study one day. Next to it was a paper crown, a crystal ball, some silver images she didn't recognise and the root of a mandrake, the 'Hand of Glory', next to what might actually have been a shrivelled human hand. Eleanor felt the bile rise in her throat at the sight of it.

Prominently, in the centre of the display, a half-melted ball of wax lay in a small wicker basket. It was all that remained of what she had so strongly believed would one day become her baby. That was when she broke down.

Impervious to her tears, Adam Moleyns began the proceedings, banging his lectern with a gavel, demanding silence before reading out the charges.

'You stand accused, madam, of twenty-five counts of sorcery, felony and treason.'

'No!'

Eleanor's cry of denial was ignored. 'It is alleged,' Moleyns went on, 'that at various times during the past year, you and the three malefactors who stand accused with you, did, on consecrated ground in the parishes of St Martin-in-the-Vintry, St Benet Hithe and St Sepulchre-without-Newgate, use magical vestments, effigies and instruments to invoke demons and evil spirits to bring about the death of our noble sovereign, His Highness King Henry the Sixth. This is an act of the highest treason. How plead you?'

'Not guilty. I'm not guilty. It was never my –'

'It is further alleged that while these vile experiments were being undertaken by Magister Roger Bolingbroke and the woman Margery Jourdemayne, the erstwhile canon, Thomas Southwell, who now stands in disgrace before this court, used a book of necromancers' oaths from which he chanted protective masses.'

Moleyns turned to the table and continued his litany of allegations.

'Furthermore, you see here on display before you, a wax figure of His Royal Highness the King. This effigy, it is alleged, was left near a source of fire during the course of these dire ceremonies, melting a little more each day and thus precipitating the King's death from melancholy, from black bile, a death which was calculated to occur in the twentieth year of his reign, towards the end of May or at the beginning of June in this, the year of Our Lord fourteen hundred and forty one. This is treason at its greatest extreme. How plead you?'

'No, it was never the King. It was to be my baby! I so wanted a baby! I wished to give my Lord a child. I never meant to harm the King. I only wanted to conceive a child. It was my dearest wish, it is every woman's fervent prayer. That was the only reason why Margery fashioned the waxen poppet ... it was not –'

'Silence, madam! You do not help your case by babbling about babies!'

His words seemed to echo around the hushed court. All eyes watched as Adam Moleyns gestured to Cardinal Beaufort, an invitation for him to take up the questioning from this point. Beaufort rose to his feet.

'Your Grace,' Beaufort said, 'the Jourdemayne woman is known to be a witch, she was accused of witchcraft a decade ago. I know that. Every member of the Council knows that. And you knew that. So you, as a member of the royal family, should surely have known better than to use her services in any capacity.'

'But I –'

'Because it is widely known that you bought potions and decoctions from her, for the sole purpose of enticing His Royal Highness the Duke of Gloucester into your bed, despite the fact that his lawful marriage to another woman was sanctified in the eyes of God.'

'No! I did no more than many other women –'

'Madam, your behaviour in this regard has been well attested by many witnesses.' He paused and turned towards the witness enclosure in which Eleanor now recognised many more faces. She saw Canon John Hume's assistant, William Woodham, as well as at least half a dozen palace servants whom she recognised. Could they have testified against her? Surely not!

Beaufort picked up a sheaf of papers and brandished them at her. 'With sworn witness statements like these, you can offer little argument that will convince the learned members of the Council that you are anything other than guilty. Now, I wish to call another of the accused in this sorry case.'

He turned away from Eleanor and moved towards Roger Bolingbroke.

'Magister Bolingbroke, you too have made an oath before many witnesses, including myself. You stated some months ago, under the cross in St Paul's churchyard, that you recant your previous beliefs. You claimed at that time to have renounced all interest in fortune-telling, casting horoscopes and predicting the future by using false means such as this astrolabe and other devices. That is commendable. But, tell the jury if you will, why did you undertake these experiments in the first place? Was it, perhaps, at the behest of the woman who stands before you, Her Grace the Duchess of Gloucester?'

'Yes.' Bolingbroke's reply was barely audible.

'We cannot hear you, Magister. Speak up!'

'Yes!' Bolingbroke lifted his head and gave Eleanor the most malevolent glare she had ever experienced. Then he started to shout, pointing at her agitatedly. 'Yes, it was her fault! She asked me to do it. I would never have –'

'Thank you, Magister. You make yourself perfectly plain. That is all for the moment. Have any of my learned colleagues any questions they would like to ask?' Beaufort stepped to one side and beckoned to the other senior clergy who occupied the bench behind him, indicating that they might like to carry on the interrogation.

One by one, the bishops rose from their seats and moved to up take Beaufort's position in front of the witness stand and the trial began in earnest. They proceeded to pummel Eleanor with accusation after accusation, question after question. They wanted to know why she had encouraged her advisers to use their black, demonic arts in her service, how they had gone about their satanic practices, which churches they had used, who had facilitated the use of those churches and, crucially, what the conspirators had hoped to achieve with their dark practices. As each of these senior clergymen gradually lost his impetus and retired to his seat on the bench, another was ready to take his place.

After hours of interrogation and impassioned denial, the exhausted Eleanor had admitted to five of the twenty-five charges, but clung pitifully to her claim that she had only done what she was accused of doing in order to conceive a child by her husband. By the time they had finished with her, she could barely stand and when, at last, she was told she could sit down, no one came to her aid. No final verdict had been arrived at and no formal decision had been taken about her likely punishment. She would be taken back into custody while her fate was decided elsewhere by her accusers.

Bolingbroke was subjected to a similar barrage of questioning and staggered down from the witness stand at the end of it. Then Thomas Southwell was summoned to reply to another bombardment of cross-examination against which he seemed to shrink further and further into himself, saying almost nothing in his own defence.

Finally, Margery Jourdemayne was summoned to face her accusers but they gave her short shrift. Her appearance at this hearing was largely a formality: she was here simply to be told the final verdict of an ecclesiastical court, which had met the previous day in St Stephen's chapel. As a proven heretic, Margery had been found guilty of sorcerous practices. Once a witch, declared the court, always a witch. She had been warned a decade ago that if she transgressed again, then she could expect the harshest penalty. And she had transgressed. Now, all that remained was the requirement for a signature on the death sentence.

Margery Jourdemayne, the Witch of Eye, was to meet her death by burning. Bolingbroke and Southwell were both condemned to suffer the agonising death of a traitor. They would be hanged, drawn and quartered.

Given her past relationships with both Margery Jourdemayne and the Duchess of Gloucester, Jenna had been on tenterhooks throughout the entire proceedings, expecting that at any moment she would be called to give evidence against one or both of them. Anxiously, she'd watched every single step of the trial, riveted by every question asked and every answer given. As the final verdicts were read out by Adam Moleyns, she had felt shocked beyond belief, her heart in turmoil. She didn't claim to know either Bolingbroke or Southwell other than to open the door to them occasionally when they came to see her mistress, but her heart bled for them.

Margery Jourdemayne was different, though. Jenna knew her very well. She knew her deviousness, her weaknesses, her vulnerability. She also knew her husband. Intimately. How would William take the news of Margery's death sentence? And how could she help him to accept his wife's fate?

Once the court had pronounced its verdicts on everything except the fate of the Duchess, the condemned prisoners were escorted back to the Tower. The witnesses, no longer needed to testify, were released from their big pen in the courtroom like so many animals and Jenna's first instinct had been to run, to get away, back to the farm, back to William. But though she desperately wanted to see him, she hesitated now, not knowing what to do for the best. After all, he was facing the most extraordinary ordeal. She had no way of knowing how he would be, how she herself would be when she was with him, whether he would want to talk about Margery or keep his feelings to himself. It would not be wise to rush back to Eybury. It was after Margery's death that William would need her and even then it might take him some considerable time before he could come to terms with what had happened.

If it would help him, perhaps she would be able to tell him about Margery's last days, her stoicism and resignation when she finally accepted her fate. But she could never describe for him the hysteria, the screaming, the crying, the desperate pleading and the despair that had gone before. Margery would be burned: it was a gruelling prospect to face.

Margery had recanted, of course, though much good did it do her. And she had sworn a solemn oath that, when the time came, she would face her Maker with a pure heart. In the confessional, she received the blessing of a priest and had begged him to be the one who would read her the last rites.

It had been a deeply shocking and distressing time, not only for Margery, but for Jenna and the other women who shared the same cell, perfectly decent women, persecuted simply because they knew Margery.

They, too, had been held in readiness to be called as witnesses and their relief at their sudden release after so long in captivity was tinged with uncertainty. Shivering, they all stood huddled together in the street outside Guildhall, rubbing their arms in a fruitless effort to keep warm. It wasn't long before they said their farewells and went their separate ways.

For Jenna, the chilly walk from the centre of the city all the way to Eybury Farm seemed never-ending, but she had nowhere else to go. She wouldn't be welcome in either the palace or the Abbey, and the farm was the only other place she knew. Besides, what she wanted more than anything, was to feel near William. Yet she also wanted time to think, time to plan, time to herself. So when she reached the farmyard, she moved as silently as a shadow between the farm buildings, easing herself around corners and hiding behind tree trunks, at great pains not to be seen by anyone, intending to make a run for the steps up to the hay loft.

Then she saw a girl crossing the yard towards the dairy, two milk pails suspended from the yoke across her shoulders, and realised with a slight shock that it was Kitty. But how quickly she had grown tall enough to carry a yoke! Jenna took the risk of sidling along the wall to follow her to the open door and waited until she'd seen Kitty put the pails down safely near the skimming bench.

'Kitty!' she whispered hoarsely.

Kitty nearly jumped out of her skin. Turning, she saw Jenna in the doorway and her face lit up in a huge smile. She ran towards her.

'Jenna! Oh, Jenna, thank God! We've all been so worried about you.' The two hugged each other delightedly. 'Wait until I tell the Master you're back home. He'll be so –'

'No, Kitty! No, not yet. Don't say anything to him yet. He's got a lot of problems. We need to give him time to … well, to come to terms with them in his own way. You know, do you, that Mistress Jourdemayne has been … has been on trial?'

'Yes, we all know. But we don't know what to do to help the Master. He's been looking so worried. Robin Fairweather is with him and now that you're here –'

'No, Kitty, please. It won't help him just at the moment, so you mustn't say anything. Don't tell him I'm here. Don't tell Robin either. Can you keep me a secret, Kitty? Hide me? Just for a couple of days. It's for the best, but you'll have to help me.'

'Yes, Jenna. Anything. What do you want me to do?'

'Please find me something to eat. I'm starving. And I must sleep. I'm so tired, I can't think. Can you fetch me some bread and cheese, perhaps? And a blanket, anything to warm me up a bit. Then tomorrow, perhaps, a pail of water to wash the stink of that cell off my skin. Ugh! But tonight I'll go and hide in the hayloft and sleep. There's no one else sleeping up there, is there?'

'No, not these days. You'll be safe there. I'll find some food for you. Oh, Jenna, it's so good to see you. I want to tell everyone you're back!'

Jenna pressed her finger to Kitty's lips, just as she used to do when Kitty was a little girl.

'Hush, Kittymouse,' she said. 'Let this be a secret between the two of us, just while I work out what to do for the best. For all of us. You understand?'

'Oh, yes, Jenna. Our secret. Of course I understand.'

Jenna hugged her again, but couldn't lay her cheek on top of Kitty's head, the way she always used to. She smiled: her little Kittymouse was nearly grown up.

Mercifully, the hayloft was empty and peaceful. While Kitty scuttled off to find some food and a blanket for her, Jenna was alone with just the gentle memory of William's being, his warmth as he lay beside her, holding her tenderly in the sweet aftermath of love.

Dropping to her knees in the hay, she muttered a fervent prayer of thanks for her deliverance from imprisonment in the Tower and from the shackles of her old life at the Palace of Westminster. She had a strong feeling of having come home. She knew that tonight she would sleep as she had not slept for many, many weeks. Then tomorrow, and for the rest of her life, she vowed to do everything in her power to help William.

***

Robin Fairweather hesitated with his hand on the latch before opening the door to the kitchen. In a bid to help William, he had been to the alehouse, but more to learn the latest gossip than to slake his thirst. He'd found out what he needed to know but now he had to break the news to his friend and William was distraught enough already. Still, he'd have to tell him.

William looked up as Robin closed the door against a draught of cold autumnal air.

'Well? Did you find out anything?'

'They've passed sentence,' Robin said. 'The two clergymen were condemned to preach at Tyburn Cross.'

William nodded silently. He knew that meant the gallows for them. He couldn't bring himself to ask the next question but he didn't have to.

'I'm sorry,' Robin said, 'but I heard she's to burn tomorrow.'

A huge sob escaped William. It came from somewhere deep within him and rose up through his body to end in a great shudder. From where he sat at the kitchen table, he looked up at the ceiling, partly out of the instinct to turn to his God and partly to prevent his brimming tears spilling over. Closing his eyes, he shook his head slowly, back and forth.

'Such a waste,' he said. 'Such a waste of a life.' Putting his elbows on the table, he dropped his head into his hands, his fingers laced in his dark hair.

Lowering himself onto the bench next to him, Robin put his hand on his friend's back in a gesture of solidarity and let it remain there. Expressions of sympathy and affection between men were always difficult, he thought. Had William been a woman it would have been easy to hold out his arms, embrace him and let him weep, but perhaps that would not be a welcome gesture. So he moved his hand to William's shoulder, rubbing it awkwardly while his friend regained control of himself.

Eventually, with a deep sigh, William straightened up.

'I've been expecting this day,' he said, still shaking his head. 'I've been expecting it for ten years and now it's here. And I won't be able to buy them off, like last time.'

'You mustn't blame yourself,' said Robin. 'God knows, you've done your best to get her to change her ways, to stay away from the palace and accept her lot in life.'

'Ours could have been such a good marriage,' William said, 'if only…'

'Margery was always a determined woman. She wanted things her way, so don't torture yourself with thoughts of what might have been. Look to the future. It might seem very bleak just now but, after tomorrow, there'll be new beginnings, new opportunities. Let the past lie, William. You can't change it.'

William was quiet for a moment while he seemed to consider this. Then he had to ask the next question.

'Have they said wh … where it's to be done? Do you know where?'

Robin had been dreading that question. There could have been several places where Margery might die but they both knew which would be the most likely.

'It's Smithfield, isn't it?'

Robin nodded. Smithfield. A place they both knew so well, the biggest cattle market in London, where they'd both been countless times to sell neats for slaughter. Now the slaughter would be of an entirely different kind. This would be where William's wife would meet her end in the flames. The thought was unendurable. Robin didn't know what to say, how to distract him, without sounding dismissive.

But he must try.

'From what they were saying in the tavern, they'll only be able to hang one of the clergymen. The other one is already dead. The Canon. They say he died of sorrow in the Tower.'

William roused himself and turned to look at Robin.

'Sorrow?' he said. 'Sorrow doesn't kill men. Not that quickly anyway.'

'Well, melancholy was what they said, but I reckon he couldn't face the kind of death they reserve for traitors. Being hanged, drawn and quartered isn't much to look forward to. He must have poisoned himself.'

'How?'

Robin shrugged. 'He was a physician, wasn't he? Not just a canon of the church. He'd have known how to do it, given that he could get hold of some means of doing it.'

'An accomplice, perhaps? Someone to smuggle poison into the Tower for him?'

'Who knows?'

William was silent for a moment, then said, 'Margery hasn't got that.'

'No. No, she hasn't. She won't even have henbane, or mandrake root … nothing to dull the pain. She'll have to face it without help. We must pray that God gives her strength.'

The long pause that followed was heavy with questions. And yet those questions were left unasked because there were no answers. The candle at the centre of the table burned down almost to its holder.

'Will you go there tomorrow, William?'

'Yes,' said William. 'I have to. She is still my wife. I don't know if I can bring myself to watch her die, but I must try. I must. I owe her that much.' He drew a deep, deep breath. 'But God knows how I'm going to face it.'

Gently, Robin clapped his hand on his friend's back once again.

'I'll come with you,' he said.

***

347

Friday, the twenty-seventh day of October, the Eve of St Simon and St Jude, dawned much like any other on the manor farm of Eye-next-Westminster. With first light, the muffled scrape of leather boots on the cobbled yard, muttered curses and the creaking door of the byre mingled with the lowing of cows, anxious to be relieved of their milk. In the hay loft above, Jenna lay on her back, listening to the dear, familiar sounds she hadn't heard for so long. Now, after a night of deep, dreamless sleep, she felt able to face whatever the day might bring.

In London, the sun rose on the Priory Church of St Bartholomew the Great just outside the city wall. William Jourdemayne and Robin Fairweather had not even had to think about how their day should begin; the need for solace in prayer before the onset of their almost certain distress had drawn them naturally to this ancient church. Cattlemen had always had strong links with St Bart's and many of those who made their living as drovers, cowherds or butchers chose to attend early morning mass there before going about the business of the day.

Inside the nave, the sounds of the marketplace and slaughterhouses of Smithfield were muted, but as the bell rang the hour for the Divine Office of Terce, William and Robin glanced at each other and rose to their feet.

'It's time,' Robin said.

'Yes. I must face it. God grant me strength.'

'And God have mercy on Margery,' Robin added. With his head bowed, he crossed himself. Then, straightening up, he began to steer William towards the door.

They stepped out and into the wall of sound that was Smithfield. Men with withy sticks and whips were herding cattle, sheep and pigs into dozens of small pens, slamming shut the wooden gates behind them. Their shouts and the excited barking of their dogs mingled with the cries of hawkers and street traders against a cacophony of bellowing, lowing, bleating, grunting, and squeaking. Frightened animals jostled each other, stumbling and kicking out with their hind legs, their hooves churning up the mud, their eyes rolling in alarm at the whiff of blood in the air. And over it all hung a powerful miasma, the sharp stink of animal dung.

The market was even more busy than usual, as it always was when there was to be a burning, though William could never understand why anyone would willingly watch the suffering of another human being. Yet a substantial crowd had already gathered, eager to get a good view.

In the corner of the market field, four men in the Sheriff's livery were adding the last few faggots of sticks to a bonfire they had built under a raised platform. At the centre of the structure was a tall wooden stake with a length of rope lying coiled at its base.

William swallowed hard. So many times he'd been here at Smithfield to sell his animals. And, yes, he'd often seen fires being built for the purpose of burning heretics, but he had never stayed to witness the horror. That was for others, for people with a blood lust.

'Make way! Make way in the name of the Sheriff!'

A tumbrel was making slow progress through the crowd. Between the shafts, the scrawny horse which drew it seemed destined for the nearby knacker's yard, but the Sheriff's sergeant who had hold of its bridle brought it to a halt in front of the platform. The excited shouting and calling of jibes grew in intensity.

And there she was. Margery. She stood in the tumbrel with her hands tied behind her back. William's jaw clenched as he watched the cart being tilted backwards with a jerk, propelling her to the ground. Unable to use her hands to save herself, she lost her footing and fell in the churned-up filth.

Two sergeants pulled her roughly to her feet, then began thrusting her forward towards the platform. A priest holding an open prayer-book followed behind them, appearing to mouth a prayer, though it was impossible to hear his words under the increasing noise of jeering, catcalling and whistling.

Instinctively, William shoved his way forward, pushing and elbowing people out of his way, with some frenzied idea of rescuing Margery by pulling her away from the fire.

'William, don't! Don't, William. It won't help her.' Robin was behind him, trying to grab at his jerkin to pull him back.

'William!' Margery screamed as she caught sight of him.

'Oh please, William...'

'Here, you – get back!' A sergeant prodded him hard in the gut with a short stave. William staggered briefly, but regained his balance.

'I told you, get back or I'll arrest you!' The sergeant prodded him again.

'Come away, William, for God's sake. They won't let you anywhere near her. Come away. You're only making it worse for her. Come on!'

William shook off Robin's hand and reached out again, frantically trying to clutch at Margery, but the sergeant brought the stave down with a hard thwack on the side of his outstretched wrist and he yelped in pain.

The man's face was livid. He pointed at William with his stave.

'This is my last warning. You make one more attempt to obstruct an officer of the law in the pursuit of his duty and you will live to regret it. Now get out of here!'

William fell back, nursing his bruised wrist and Robin made another grab at him.

'William, come on. You're only making things worse. She knows you were here and that's the important thing. Just pray for her soul. It's all you can do.'

The priest gave the two of them a warning look as Margery was lashed to the stake, then he closed his eyes, raised his voice and began to pray.

'*Domine Iesu, dimitte nobis debita nostra, salva nos ab igne inferiori...*'

The huge mob was now baying and braying for the blood of a witch. Margery's frantic screams rose to a crescendo before she subsided into hopeless tears as two lighted torches were pushed in among the dry faggots at the base of the fire. It hissed into flame. William, his gorge rising at the grim spectacle, staggered towards the fringes of the crowd, clutching his stomach.

'*Perduc in caelum omnes animas, praesertim eas, quae misericordiae tuae maxime indigent.*'

The pungent smell of fresh wood smoke was in William's

nostrils as he bent double with Robin's supporting arm around his waist.

'*In nomine Patris, et Filii, et Spiritus Sancti. Amen.*'

William was suddenly, very violently, sick.

CHAPTER TWENTY-FOUR

October 27th 1441

'Be upstanding!'

Eleanor rose to her feet as her accusers shuffled silently into St Stephen's chapel in the Palace of Westminster for what must surely be the last time. She was here to be told the result of their deliberations. Today, she would know her fate.

Their faces were impassive, hard, smug. They were so certain of their ground, these men of the Church, so convinced they were right. Of course, she'd heard the shocking news about Canon Southwell from the women who guarded her day and night and she wondered how these men felt in their hearts now that they had driven him, one of their own number, to die in despair by his own hand, rather than have to face a heretic's dreadful end. And how could they sleep in their beds at night, having burned an unfortunate, misguided woman to death in a public place?

And with Margery's death and Southwell found dead in his cell, what of the others? Canon Hume was well-connected so he would probably get away with it, she thought, but not Roger Bolingbroke. These clerics had condemned the learned magister to be hanged, drawn and quartered.

Poor Bolingbroke. For all that he had been so ready to testify against her, she couldn't help but feel sorry for him. She recalled happier days at La Pleasaunce when he'd been so naive and sincerely grateful for the gifts she and Humphrey gave him. The thought suddenly struck her that if Bolingbroke was forced to wear his precious spectacles while they hanged him, then he would be able to see the executioners drawing out his own guts as they disembowelled him. The thought of it almost made her choke on the bile rising in her throat.

And now her turn had come.

Adam Moleyns, Clerk to the Council, banged his gavel. 'Silence! Silence for His Grace, the Most Reverend Archbishop of Canterbury.'

Despite Chichele's personal misgivings, it had been decided that, at the conclusion of this crucially important trial, judgement was to be delivered in the highest ecclesiastical court in the land. This meant that it did require the presence of the Archbishop of Canterbury. But had Eleanor's heart not been thudding so loudly in her ears, she might have heard the old man wheeze painfully as he rose to his feet.

Thank God, Eleanor thought. Henry Chichele, her husband's friend, would surely do no more than chastise her and point out the error of her ways. She wouldn't get away with things completely, of course, but the Archbishop's very presence must surely mean that any penance demanded of her would not be too harsh. After all, she was the Duchess of Gloucester and her husband's name carried considerable weight. Her heart slowly resumed its normal beat. Chichele had probably been a benign influence on his fellow-members of the Council. He must have overruled Beaufort and Kemp. Those two would have wanted her head on a plate.

Eleanor began to breathe more normally and Chichele fixed his sombre gaze upon her for a moment before he spoke. He looked dreadful, his rheumy eyes sunken in their sockets, his skin parchment pale.

'You stand accused of grave crimes, my Lady,' he said sternly. Eleanor nodded her head, shamefaced, looking at the floor. 'In total, there were twenty-eight accusations made against you and you have tried to deny them all. But in the face of incontrovertible evidence, you have been entirely unable to prove your innocence in relation to five of those accusations. In fact, you have pleaded guilty to them and your guilt must not go unpunished. The Council has considered very carefully what that punishment should be.'

The Archbishop shifted his weight from one foot to another, as though he had already stood for too long. 'In your privileged position, so close to His Highness the King, you should have known better than to allow yourself to become associated with heretics and sorcerers, witches and necromancers. You do not need me to tell you, madam, that you ran grave risks in having persons such as these anywhere near your household, much less taking an active part in your life. Indeed, it has been proved that not only did you know about their nefarious activities, you positively encouraged them. That, in itself, was heresy. Heretical beliefs are profoundly at odds with the teachings of the Church and go hand-in-hand with Lollardy. And Lollardy must be stamped out at all costs. So I must now ask you this, madam: do you hereby formally renounce your heretical beliefs?'

Eleanor twisted a kerchief in her hands as she held them in front of her. There could only be one answer to that question.

'I do.'

'Very well. Then this court will accept your statement of avowed intent.' The Archbishop moved again from one foot to the other, as though trying to relieve an aching back. Eleanor could only hope he was feeling too uncomfortable to prolong the process of sentencing her.

'There has, however, been some genuine doubt among members of the Council that you really meant treason towards the royal person of the King. In view of this, the secular aspect of this case will no longer be a consideration. Before we abandon it entirely, however, we must have your assurance, on oath, that never, on any single occasion, did you ever have any treasonable intent towards his Highness King Henry. Can you now give this court that absolute assurance?'

'Indeed I can, Your Grace,' she answered with more confidence, wearing her most earnest expression. 'I have never had anything but the most cordial love for his Highness the King. And I believe that, in return, he had respect for me as the wife of his dear uncle, the Duke of Gloucester.'

'Hmmm.' There was silence for a few moments while the Archbishop moved his stick into his left hand and, with his right, gestured to Adam Moleyns. Moleyns put a single sheet of parchment into the Archbishop's outstretched hand. This was the moment, thought Eleanor. Now she would know.

'You have been tried and found guilty of five counts of sorcery and witchcraft. Any person, man or woman, high-born or of lowly estate, must be prepared to do penance for grave, heretical crimes such as these,' said Chichele, looking at her from under his eyebrows. 'Do you understand that?'

'Yes, Your Grace.' Eleanor's voice was husky.

'Very well. Your punishment will be as follows.' The Archbishop held the sheet of parchment at arm's length as he began to read it from it. 'You will be required to make three separate journeys, barefoot and with due humility, to three different churches within the city of London to offer up a lighted taper together with prayers of sincere repentance at each of the three. These three journeys will be undertaken on market days, specifically so that as many people as possible can learn from your reprehensible example and see for themselves what fate awaits those who defy the teaching of the Church.'

Eleanor stood with her head bowed, hardly able to believe what she was hearing. Walk barefoot through London? The shame of it! But it could be worse … They couldn't force her to do it, of course. No one would dare insist that the wife of a royal duke could be made to do something as humiliating as this. And the King, her husband's nephew, would be sure to intervene.

Chichele waited until Eleanor raised her head again. Then he spoke.

'As the wife of a royal duke, you would normally have a certain immunity from prosecution in a case like this. However, it has greatly troubled the Council that you achieved your elevated position by entirely nefarious means, as you yourself have attested. You have admitted under oath that you employed the services of a known witch to help you entice the Duke away from his wife by deceit, in using sorcery, magic potions and drinks to make him love you and want to marry you. This sheds an entirely different light on this case.'

The Archbishop hardly paused before he delivered the final blow.

'So, since it has been proved beyond doubt that you used

sorcerous means to entrap His Grace the Duke of Gloucester, application was made to His Holiness the Pope to have you divorced from your husband and we have recently received his written agreement that, in your case, this punishment is entirely appropriate.'

Eleanor was dumbfounded. Divorced! Dear God, divorced!

'Madam, know that you are now formally divorced from your husband, the Duke of Gloucester. You may no longer claim his support or his benefaction, and you are no longer entitled to call yourself the Duchess of Gloucester. Furthermore, to ensure that you adhere to the terms of this divorce, you will remain in royal custody for the foreseeable future.'

Divorced. The word rang hollow in her ears. Everything she had ever lived for was now denied her. She was divorced: she no longer had any rights. Naively, she had assumed that once this nightmare was over, everything would be the same as it had always been and she and Humphrey could pick up the threads of their old life together.

This was the one thought that had sustained her throughout the long months of her imprisonment, though there had not been so much as a message from Humphrey in all that time. Surely, surely he must have known something of her plight? Bad news has a habit of travelling far and travelling fast. Wherever he was, Humphrey must surely have heard something by now…

But in any case, she had been divorced and she could no longer look to a husband for protection and support. She had no husband. Humphrey had been at the centre of her universe for more than half her life, and she would never see him again.

***

Kitty had honestly intended to keep her own counsel and say nothing to anyone about the refugee in the hayloft but, during the last few nights, she had lain awake on her pallet in the dormitory over the brewhouse, wondering what best to do for her dearest friend and for the Master. Kitty was utterly certain in her own mind that what each of them really needed was the other, but Jenna had forbidden her to say anything to Master Jourdemayne. Not yet, she kept saying. No, not just yet.

So, what to do for the best? Kitty wondered whether Robin Fairweather would be able to advise her. He was still here on the farm and she knew he was worldly-wise, so perhaps he would know what to do. And Kitty knew he liked Jenna and that he was the Master's friend. She resolved to ask his advice. But first he had to promise to keep a secret.

'What sort of secret?' he asked when she waylaid him the next morning as he crossed the yard, a wicker pannier in either hand. Mallow, sensing adventure, followed close at heel, her tail wagging vigorously. Robin was making ready to return to Devon.

'It's a very important secret,' Kitty said earnestly. 'Will you promise not to tell?'

'It depends what it is.' Robin was tightening the girth on his horse's saddle as he spoke. He gave her a grave look. 'It had better be important,' he said.

'It is important. It's about the Master.'

'And how do you happen to know a secret about the Master?' She was a funny little thing, this Kitty. He knew William was fond of her, but she had some strange ideas. Of course, she might know something important – or she might not.

'You'll have to tell me, Kitty, whatever it is, because your master has had some problems over the last few weeks. He's got a lot on his mind. You mustn't bother him.'

'Yes, I know, but … but it's really, really important!'

'It had better be!'

'No, really. I mean it. It's … it's imperative!' That was a new word she'd learned recently. It had the desired effect.

'Imperative?' Robin looked startled.

'Yes, imperative. It's – it's about Jenna!' she finished in a rush.

The reaction was gratifying. Robin bent down so that his face was level with hers and dropped his voice.

'Jenna! Are you sure? What do you know about her? Where is she?'

Kitty was saying nothing so Robin straightened up and slipped his horse's bridle over a fence post before beginning to steer Kitty towards the byre. 'Come on, Kitty,' he said, 'it's quiet in there, so you'll be able to tell me your secret.'

To his surprise, Kitty drew back in alarm. 'No,' she said. 'Not in there! Jenna's in the loft! She'll hear us. She'll know I've told you and I promised...'

Too late. Robin took the stone steps to the hay loft at a bound, leaving Kitty standing open-mouthed behind him.

Hearing the commotion, Jenna was trying to take cover behind a small bale of hay, but when she heard Robin's voice calling her name, she felt a huge surge of relief.

'Robin!' She scrambled to her feet. 'Oh, Robin, it's so good to see you.'

He took both her hands in his, looking anxiously into her face.

'Jenna! The one person he'll want to see.'

'Oh, Robin, do you think so? I didn't know ... I wasn't sure.'

'I'm certain of it. You know, do you, about Margery? That they've ... they've burned her?'

'Already? When –'

'Last Friday, at Smithfield.'

'And was he there?'

'Yes.' Robin never took his eyes away from Jenna's face. 'It was difficult for him, Jenna. Well nigh impossible. I didn't know how best to help him.'

'But you were there?'

'Yes, of course. I couldn't let him face that alone. But I can't stay up here in Westminster for ever, I have to get back to Devon, back to work. That's why it's such a miracle that you're here. Oh, Jenna, wait until he sees you! You're exactly what he needs.'

With a wisdom that only comes with growing up, Kitty had disappeared, glad that Robin had taken charge, pleased that she had decided to let him into the secret. She'd make herself scarce in the dairy – and she wouldn't say a word to the other girls.

It was clear to Robin that he wouldn't be setting off for

Devon today, after all. But at least, when eventually he did go home, he was sure he'd be leaving his friend William in a much happier frame of mind.

***

Jenna hesitated outside the kitchen door.

'Is he here?'

'No, he isn't. He can't mope around the farmhouse for ever. There's work to be done. It'll be Martinmas next week so he's started rounding up the animals for slaughter. The pigs have been let loose to forage for acorns to fatten them up so he could be anywhere. Talking of which,' he added, glancing at her, 'you could do with a bit of fattening up yourself. You're like a scarecrow!'

Jenna gave him the ghost of a smile. 'The food's not very appetising in the Tower,' she said.

'Well, I can smell broth. Let's see what they've got in the pot. Look everyone,' he announced as he opened the door, 'look who's here!'

At that time of morning the kitchen was at its busiest, but everyone stopped and turned to see who had arrived. They immediately abandoned their spoons, knives and chopping boards and crowded round Jenna with little shrieks of welcome.

'Jenna! How are you?'

'Where have you been?'

'Are you going to stay this time?'

Smiling, she let herself be led towards the table where a bowl of steaming broth was put in front of her with a platter of bread beside it. For a moment, she sat perfectly still, relishing the moment, before she picked up her spoon.

Outside again, Robin mounted his horse and swung out of the yard with Mallow in pursuit, dodging the flying hooves. Now his priority was to find William and he wasn't going to waste time trying to find him on foot. If he was rounding up the pigs, he'd likely be in the oak wood. It wasn't more than a mile away: it wouldn't take long.

The kitchen at Eybury farmhouse had always been a hotbed of gossip and everyone seemed to want to talk at once.

Questions about Margery were uppermost in everyone's minds, how had she seemed in the Tower when she'd heard the verdict? Was the Tower as horrible as everyone said? When was Jenna released? Where had she been staying since then? Who had been supplying her with food? So why had Kitty said nothing?

She did her best to answer them, but all she really wanted was to see William. When the door opened and the shape of him blotted out the light briefly as he stood on the threshold, she thought her heart would stop.

'Jenna!' He moved into the room as though there was no one else in it, staring as if he'd seen a phantom. 'Jenna, I thought –'

Behind him, Robin clapped his hands loudly.

'Come on, everyone, back to work or dinner will be late.'

Kitchen maids and scullions scuttled in all directions to resume their duties and William came towards her, holding out his hand.

'Come,' he said. 'We can't talk here.'

Robin stood to one side, smiling benignly, as though he had single-handedly wrought a miracle.

'Why don't you two go up to the hay loft?' he whispered. 'It's quite empty at this time of day. You won't be disturbed.'

William looked at Jenna and took her hand, a smile beginning to tweak the corners of his mouth.

'I can't think of anywhere better,' he said, his fingers curling around hers.

'Go on, the pair of you,' Robin said with a broad wink. 'I'll be in the yard if you want me. I'll keep an eye open to make sure you're not disturbed.'

They found the loft quiet and deserted, with Jenna's makeshift bedding on the hay where she had been sleeping. William still had hold of her hand and when she turned to him, strangely hesitant, he looked at her in wonderment, as though there was something immensely precious between them, something they must approach with infinite care like a column of the finest, most exquisitely coloured glass. A sudden movement could risk shattering it into a thousand shards.

'Jenna.' William's voice was low. He lifted her hand to his

lips with reverence. 'My dearest girl. Is it really you? Are you a wraith? I can hardly believe you're here.'

'William, I've been so worried. It must have been so dreadful for you –'

'Hush, my sweet. We have the rest of our lives for talk.' He raised his eyes and looked at her again. 'We *do* have the rest of our lives, don't we?'

Jenna nodded without saying a word.

'Thank God!'

Now he reached for her. From this moment, there was no longer anything that could come between them and the most precious thing for each of them was the other. They didn't kiss, they simply stood, holding each other, savouring the sensation of nearness, of touch, of their beating hearts.

Jenna's eyes were closed. This would be her life from now on, here on the farm with William. Her world was almost complete, except for one dark shadow ... But William had talked of the rest of their lives, their future together, so there would be time to talk about Jake tomorrow ... tomorrow.

Today, they were here together and nothing else mattered.

***

The three main market days in the city of London were on Monday, Wednesday and Friday when the streets were crowded with merchants and housewives, urchins and stray dogs, loud with the cries of hawkers and street traders. The alehouses did a roaring trade and pickpockets, cutpurses and beggars took advantage of every opportunity.

Dreading the prospect of having to walk through the self-same streets where she had hitherto always ridden in the finest carriages, Eleanor was awake before dawn on the morning of Monday, the thirteenth of November. Waiting in her room to be dressed, she was surprised when Maude, one of the waiting-women, approached her holding a large pair of scissors.

'I'm sorry my Lady ...' she began.

'I'm sorry, Your Grace –' Eleanor said without thinking and immediately bit her lip. She eyed the scissors askance.

'What do you propose to do with those?' she asked.

'I'm to cut your hair.'

'Cut my hair?' Eleanor's hands flew up either side of her head in alarm, as though to ward the woman off. 'Cut my hair? Don't be stupid! And don't come anywhere near me with those things. I won't allow it!'

Maude had the good grace to look unhappy. 'I'm sorry, madam, they're my orders.'

'No!' Eleanor screamed. 'No! You shall not. You will not come anywhere near me. I will not allow it. Get away from me. Get away!'

Without warning, the room suddenly seemed full of women apparently bent on attacking her. One held her down in the chair while Maude hacked off the once-glorious glossy tresses. The woman's armpits reeked of sweat. Eleanor squirmed in revulsion.

Like a newly shorn sheep, she was then made to stand while her fine linen shift was forcibly removed and a loose tunic of black sackcloth was dropped over her head, secured with a leather girdle around her waist.

One of the women went to the door and called to a guard waiting outside.

'She's ready,' she said.

'Wait, wait,' Eleanor said. 'Am I to go out looking like this? Surely not! And where are my shoes?'

'You won't be wearing shoes,' said Maude. 'That's what we've been told.'

Tears welled in Eleanor's eyes and she blinked hard: she was damned if she was going to let these harridans get the better of her. But they had the upper hand and there was no point in making a scene so, whatever the day might bring, under no circumstances would she be seen to lose her dignity. Holding her head erect, she allowed herself to be escorted to the Westminster pier and taken aboard a barge.

She managed to maintain a proud silence during the journey rather than allow herself to give way to dread. The barge tied up at the Temple landing stage where Eleanor was helped to disembark, then given a lighted taper and told to carry it. Now, she found herself at the head of a small procession: on either side of her, two Knights of the realm were her escorts, and behind her trudged four guards and the half-dozen women who had been attending her during her imprisonment in Westminster. Bringing up the rear of the cavalcade, a small donkey-cart carried everyone's belongings, and the women took turns to ride in it when they became tired.

That was not a luxury accorded to Eleanor. She was expected to walk every painful step of the way to St Paul's Cross in bare feet. God, she was cold! The foggy November air clung damply to her skin and her bare head with its shorn, patchy hair, felt chilled through to her very skull. But the worst thing of all was the sensation of hard, cobbled streets underfoot. She had never so much as crossed her chamber floor without wearing slippers, but now she felt every stone like a knife beneath the soft soles of her feet and they soon started to bleed. Try as she would to pick her way between the slops and animal droppings in the road, the filth was impossible to avoid and her stomach heaved with revulsion at the thought of what was squeezing up between her toes.

But not a word of complaint escaped her lips. At Temple Gate, the group turned right into Fleet Street and, as word spread like wildfire, crowds of people began gathering to watch. At first, they had been totally silent, spellbound by the sight of this once haughty woman brought to this disgrace. Then one or two of the more adventurous tried some tentative jeers. Others began calling louder and, moments later, a rotten egg cracked against Eleanor's shoulder. For the first time, she stumbled.

Standing among the crowd gathered outside the alehouse at the sign of The Bush, John Virley allowed himself a gratified smirk at the sight of her. He was vindicated now and, more important than anything, the Witch was dead. It was a shame about Canon Southwell, whose major sin had been a pompous belief in his own importance but, at the end, he'd been glad to help him.

As though to draw a line under the last ten years of his life, Virley felt justified in aiming a worm-infested apple at the Duchess as she passed him. He was smugly pleased when it caught her in the small of her back.

On and on Eleanor walked, across the Fleet Bridge and into the city. By the time she reached St Paul's Cross, she was numb with shame and cold. Inside the cathedral, she offered up the still-burning wax taper at the high altar and moved her mouth soundlessly in prayer. In truth, she had no specific prayer to offer, she simply went through the silent motions of The Lord's Prayer. Nobody was listening to her anyway. The people who crowded the nave merely wanted to see this once proud beauty with her head bowed. Crossing herself as she rose painfully to her filthy, bare feet, she turned and made to leave the Cathedral, the Knights still at her side, the guards following and the women still trailing behind.

The thought of the long walk back to the Temple Steps was utterly daunting, but she was determined to do it without help.

Keeping her eyes firmly fixed on the path ahead of her, Eleanor didn't notice the tall figure of a man leaning against a wall in the corner of the churchyard, watching her intently. And even if she had looked in his direction she wouldn't have recognised Humphrey, Duke of Gloucester, because he was wearing the drabbest of plain brown cloaks and had his hat pulled well down over his eyes. After the procession had passed he straightened up and set off at a brisk walk south towards the Thames, where he climbed into a small wherry and rowed himself swiftly downriver towards Greenwich.

***

Outside the byre, Robin Fairweather was preparing to leave for Devon. Yet again he had tarried for a few days but, this time, nothing was going to stop him. He had already taken his leave of William and now the time had come to bid Jenna farewell. His horse stood patiently and Mallow was circling, ready to leave at her master's command. Robin stood tall as he took Jenna's hands in his.

'Make him happy,' he said. 'He's a good man and I know how much he loves you.'

Jenna was pleased to nod in agreement. 'I think you're right,' she said.

'I know I'm right,' said Robin. 'Now, I'm unlikely to return before the spring so, if you two marry before I come back with the next drove, always remember that my good wishes go with you.'

'Oh,' said Jenna. 'I'm not sure that we'll be able to marry. There are … well, there are some problems.'

'Well, no, perhaps you shouldn't do it immediately in the circumstances,' Robin said, 'you'll need to respect Margery's memory for a little while but don't leave it too long. There's nothing to be gained by that.'

'It's – it's not just that …' Jenna hesitated, then wished she hadn't started saying anything at all. She should have let Robin get going on his journey without complicating their farewell.

'Oh, you're worried about Jake, are you?'

Jenna's jaw dropped. She was speechless.

Robin laughed delightedly. He was enjoying this so much. He threw back his head and laughed again. 'Oh, Jenna, you should see your face! You're a picture.'

'But … but … how did you know?'

'You mean William hasn't told you?'

'Told me what? What was he supposed to tell me? What does he know about … about Jake? And how do you know?'

Robin dropped her hands and enveloped her in a huge hug. 'Oh, I'm sorry. That must have been such a shock for you. But I'm afraid I assumed that William had told you. He's been so obsessed with you over the last few days I've hardly seen him, and he's been so busy with the salting he hardly had time to bid me a decent farewell. But, no matter.'

He stepped back with a huge grin then turned to mount his horse. Before putting his foot in the stirrup, he looked at her impishly from under the rim of his drover's hat.

'Just make sure you talk to him as soon as he gets home tonight,' he said. 'Tell him I told you that he must give you some very important news. It's good news. But I won't tell you what it is. I'll leave him that pleasure as my parting gift.'

He swung himself up into the saddle and left Jenna standing in the yard, totally bewildered as he rode away, still laughing, with Mallow barking excitedly in his wake.

Maude had begun to feel very sorry for her mistress. Though by now Eleanor had completed two of the three penitential walks demanded of her, Maude had not heard her utter a single word of complaint. She was clearly a woman of great determination and Maude respected that.

She had accompanied Eleanor with her escort throughout Wednesday's journey, which was even longer and more arduous than Monday's. Alighting from the barge at the Swan Pier just by London Bridge, Eleanor had crossed Thames Street then walked north to St Magnus's Corner. From there, the route took her up Bridge Street to East Cheap, then on to Gracechurch Street, past the public granary and poultry market at Leadenhall Corner, then on to Christ Church in Aldgate on the eastern perimeter of the city, where she humbly offered up a second taper at the high altar. Again, crowds of people had gathered to see her, taunting and jeering, but she never wavered, looking ahead and holding her head high.

Tonight, back at Westminster, all she craved was Maude's attention to her feet and rest, blessed rest. Exactly as she had done after the first walk, Maude knelt before Eleanor's chair, gently washing her mistress's filthy, lacerated feet in a bowl of warm lavender water before drying them carefully in a soft linen towel on her lap. Eleanor winced as Maude applied a soothing balm of lavender and borage to her feet, then relaxed as she first massaged them, then bound them in strips of clean linen.

Dressed in a chamber robe with her bandaged feet resting on a stool in front of her, Eleanor found her eyelids beginning to close. Just one more of these damnable journeys on Friday and then … what? She had not been told. The only certainty was that she was destined to spend the remainder of her life imprisoned, but she had no idea where that would be. She wasn't even sure that any decision had been made. The Council would soon lose interest in her. Out of sight, out of mind. No one cared.

'Excuse me, Madam.'

Old habits died hard but, no, she mustn't correct the woman. 'Madam' would probably be the most polite form of address she could expect from now on. 'Yes, Maude, what is it?'

'The Abbot would like to see you, Madam, if that is convenient. Shall I ask him to come back tomorrow?'

Abbot Kyrton. He had been kind to her. He'd invited her to eat with him when she was in sanctuary at the Abbey. Yes, she would like to see him. Perhaps he was still compassionate and she'd appreciate a gesture of kindness. God only knew, she had few enough friends. But how long would it take her to dress to receive him? She looked down at herself, the chamber robe, the feet swathed in bandages, and she ran her hand over her shorn head.

'If Abbot Kyrton is prepared to see me looking like this,' she said, 'then I would value his company.'

Maude smiled. 'I'll invite him in.'

The Abbot had clearly been waiting outside the door because no sooner had Maude opened it than he was in the room.

'My Lady,' he greeted Eleanor. She smiled. 'My Lady' was infinitely preferable to 'Madam' and she'd settle for that.

'Father Abbot,' she said. 'It is kind of you to call on me when I am proved to be such a sinner.'

'We are all the same in the eyes of God,' he assured her. 'The Good Shepherd does not differentiate between his flock.'

Eleanor gave a rueful smile as she lifted her hand self-consciously to her hair. 'Then perhaps I will be forgiven for looking as though I am fresh from the shearing bench.'

The Abbot, unsure how to react to her brave attempt at humour, hesitated for a moment before replying.

'He might well forgive the sin of vanity, my Lady, if you confess it.'

'Then I will be certain to,' she assured him. 'But come, Father, and be seated. To what do I owe the pleasure of your visit?'

'I was concerned for your welfare,' he said as he took the chair opposite hers. 'You have been kept here at the Palace for some considerable time now and I imagine your stay will shortly come to an end.'

'Do you know what is to happen after that, Father? Because no one has seen fit to tell me.'

'Well, I understand the third day of your penance will be two days hence, will it not? On Friday?'

'Indeed. I will be required to offer up my last prayers at the high altar of St Michael's in Cornhill. That is all I know.'

'You must be exhausted, my Lady.'

The expression of genuine concern on the Abbot's face made Eleanor feel suddenly tearful. She could be strong as long as she was required to do battle, but sympathy weakened her resolve. Mutely, she gestured as though to brush away his concern. The Abbot wasn't fooled for a moment.

'I have a suggestion to make,' he said, 'and I hope it will please you. When the time does come for you to leave Westminster, I would like to offer you the hospitality of the manor house on the monastery's estate, should you need it. As abbot, it is within my gift. While decisions are made about your future, you will at least be able to relax in comfort as you recover from your ordeal. La Neyte is well appointed. In fact, several members of the royal family have stayed there in the past for various reasons.'

'That is the manor house on the Eye estate, is it not?'

'Indeed, my Lady. As I say, it is quite luxurious. To be honest, it's largely wasted on me. I rarely go there except to collect the rents when they become due. I would genuinely prefer to be near the daily routines of the monastery here at Westminster.'

'Is Master Jourdemayne the tenant farmer in charge of that estate?'

'He is, my Lady. Oh!' The Abbot's hand flew to his mouth in alarm and his eyes widened. 'Oh, of course, my dear Lady, I'm so sorry. That hadn't occurred to me. I should have remembered ... I hope I haven't embarrassed you in any way...'

'Please, Father Abbot, don't give it a moment's thought. Master Jourdemayne's wife is no longer a part of my life. That was all a dreadful mistake on my part. And I'm more than grateful to you. The thought of spending a little time recuperating at La Neyte will give me something to look forward to. Thank you, dear Father Abbot, thank you for the suggestion.'

'God's blessings upon you, my Lady.'

Eleanor thought about Kyrton's kind offer for a long time after he had left. La Neyte. Yes, the association of the manor house with Margery at the manor farm would bring back some very painful memories, but it might be a way for Eleanor to find the one person who had proved herself a friend rather than an enemy, the woman in whom she had confided so much over the last year or two. She suspected that Jenna would have gone back to the farm because she had friends there, people she had occasionally talked about, like that little girl ... what was her name? Kitty. Yes, that was it, Kitty. Jenna would be sure to go back to the manor farm at Eye-next-Westminster, for that was where Kitty was.

***

They had fallen into the habit of escaping to the hay loft of an evening, just after the fires had been covered and before Jenna retired for the night to the women's dormitory above the brewhouse and William went to his own bed. It would have been unseemly for her to move into William's bedroom so soon after Margery's death, so the hay loft had become the place where they chose to be together, away from prying eyes.

Here they had re-ignited that flame which had first burst into being in that very place and, since Jenna's return, they had made love here almost every night. At first, it had been enough to come together to satisfy an urgent passion, but now they had begun to savour their new-found knowledge of each other's bodies, delighting in their discoveries of what gave each of them the most pleasure. They lay together afterwards in each other's arms, their passion spent, their legs entwined, feeling part of one whole being rather than two separate people.

As Jenna climbed up to the loft to keep their tryst on the evening of Robin's departure, she found William waiting. He had been lying on his back in the hay, expecting her to come and lie down next to him before he took her in his arms, as he always did, and told her for the thousandth time how much she meant to him. So it was the most natural thing in the world to reach for her as she sat on her heels beside him but, to his surprise, she drew back.

'Jenna, my sweet, is anything the matter?' He scrambled to his knees and she regarded him sternly in the half-light.

'I've been talking to Robin,' she said.

'But he left for home hours ago.'

'Yes, but before he went, he told me that I was to ask you to tell me the news.'

'News? What news? What was he talking about?'

'He said you'd know.'

'I'm sorry, my sweet. I can't imagine what –'

'He wouldn't tell me what it was, but I believe it has something to do with … with my … well, with something that happened before I came here.'

'Oh, you mean Jake!'

'That's exactly what Robin said,' Jenna responded indignantly. 'How do you know about Jake? I never said anything about him. What are you both keeping from me? Come on, William, I must know. Jake is my husband. I never told you because –'

'It wouldn't have mattered anyway.'

'But how did you find out?'

'I didn't. Robin did. He knew how I felt about you because I'd had to tell someone. So he made it his business to find out a bit about your background. He couldn't understand why a lovely, capable girl like you wasn't married.'

'And how –'

'He happened to find himself somewhere near Kingskerswell and made some discreet inquiries. He had a chat with the parson.'

'Parson Middleton!' Jenna's face brightened. 'Oh, I wonder how he is after all these years!'

'You must ask Robin next time he's here. Anyway, the parson told him that Jake, your husband…'

'Yes?'

'He told him Jake had died. A cut with a sharp scythe. An

accident, apparently. I'm sorry, Jenna.'

So Jake was dead. As she kneeled in the hay, Jenna held her hands together in her lap. Jake was dead. Curiously, she felt nothing: neither grief nor elation. She had suddenly been relieved of a burden she'd carried for the last six years, something she had kept locked away in a dark place at the back of her mind. But now she had no further need to worry about it. Relief was what she felt, an overwhelming surge of relief. Jake no longer had a hold over her. Whereas she had once thought she loved the man with a great passion, she knew now that her feelings for Jake had been based on little more than physical attraction. Jake was dead and Jenna felt nothing except, perhaps, a twinge of regret that she couldn't feel any deeper emotion than that. Jake was dead. And at last she was free of him.

She looked at William. 'So,' she said quietly, 'I'm a widow.'

'Yes, you're a widow. I'm sorry I had to be the one to tell you –'

'And you're a widower.'

'Yes.' He paused. 'And you know what that means, don't you, my sweet?'

They had both been kneeling awkwardly, but as he reached out for her they fell back onto the hay, embracing, knowing with certainty that at last they each had what they longed for, and could take complete possession of it. A sudden thought struck Jenna and she laughed delightedly.

'Kitty will be pleased,' she said. 'She's been trying to marry me off for years!'

'Then she shall be your bridesmaid,' said William's muffled voice from somewhere between her breasts.

EPILOGUE

January 1442

It was proving a difficult letter to write. The ultimate decision about the fate of Eleanor Cobham lay with the King and the King felt ambivalent towards her. She had often been entertaining company and yet he had always felt slightly intimidated by her determined efforts to charm him. Now, she had been exposed for what she really was, a scheming, manipulative heretic who had bewitched his uncle. So she must be sent away, as far as possible, even if only as a means of protecting his uncle of Gloucester from her malevolent influence. Chester was suggested.

Adam Moleyns, his quill pen poised, waited respectfully for the King's dictation. 'Once Your Highness has made a decision about who should take responsibility for her,' he said, 'your mind will be relieved of the problem and you can cease to worry.'

'Sir Thomas Stanley,' said the Earl of Suffolk with the air of a man who had known the answer all along. 'He is, after all, Controller of the Household and has plenty of experience in such matters.' There were grunts of agreement from the other Council members around the table.

The King breathed a deep sigh. 'Very well,' he said, 'Sir Thomas Stanley it shall be. I can think of no one better and I'm grateful for the suggestion. Master Moleyns, please notify the Chancellor of my decision and inform him that he should make immediate arrangements for the lady's removal to Chester in the care of Sir Thomas Stanley.'

There, the decision was made. It seemed to the King that everyone had existed in a cocoon for the last two months, since the end of the trial in November. His own birthday celebration had been a very low-key affair, Advent had come and gone, Christmas and Twelfth Night had been curiously muted. But with the New Year came new beginnings and the need to make decisions.

The sensational treason trial of Eleanor Cobham and her associates had taken the whole country by storm and the King had heard tell of the extraordinary scenes on the streets of London where she had enacted her three penances. He knew, too, of Canon Southwell's suicide in the Tower and the release of Canon Hume with no more than a caution.

In looking back on the startling events of the last six months, one of the things that troubled him most deeply was that Roger Bolingbroke, a respected Magister in the University of Oxford and a man of great learning, had seen fit to put his knowledge to heretical use. Throughout the trial, the King had demanded reports each night on how the prosecution was arguing its case. When judgement was finally made and sentence pronounced, he was deeply saddened that a magister, a servant of the Church, had come to this. But Bolingbroke had been found guilty and the King thought it only right and proper that the man should suffer a traitor's death, however dreadful. After all, an example must be set. Any person who might be contemplating either treachery or heresy would surely have been deterred by the sight of Bolingbroke being dragged through the streets on a hurdle to be hanged at Tyburn then cut down, only to have his belly ripped open and his entrails drawn out while he was still alive. The four quarters of Bolingbroke's corpse had been sent to Oxford, Cambridge, York and Hereford which must surely have spread the message far and wide. That, without a doubt, would discourage Lollardy.

All in all, it had been an unspeakably upsetting case, one he could hardly bring himself to think about. Treason. Why would anyone want to kill him? As King, he wished no one any harm, he simply wanted to live in peace and harmony and enjoy the cordial love of his subjects. Sadly, that was not the way of things, so he must do what he could to change the attitudes of his people and encourage them in learning, in worship and scholarship. His school at Eton had already begun taking in poor scholars and his plans for the College Royal of Our Lady and St Nicholas at Cambridge were well under way. He himself had laid the foundation stone last Passion Sunday.

Having passed his twentieth birthday, King Henry felt daily more confident in his own judgement. The final decision to send the Duke of Orléans back to France had been his and he had never regretted it. The Duke of Gloucester, on the other hand, had made his disapproval embarrassingly obvious. The King had been pleased to attend a solemn service in the Abbey on All Saints' Day to give thanks for the new accord with the French. The service began with joyful hymns of gladness and thanksgiving, but no sooner had Mass begun than Gloucester got to his feet and marched out with his cronies, making no attempt at quietness, slamming the great west door in an unforgivable fit of pique. After that sensational departure, he had summoned his barge and left immediately for Greenwich, remaining there ever since. Nevertheless, the indentures for repatriation were signed two days later and, before leaving for home, Orléans had given his personal assurance that he would never take up arms against England. For the King, that was enough.

Moleyns interrupted his reverie. 'Perhaps, Your Highness, you would be kind enough to sign this instruction.'

King Henry looked quickly through the document then signed it and dated it the nineteenth day of January 1442. He pressed his signet ring into the warm wax of the seal. There, the deed was done. Eleanor Cobham would be sent to Chester.

'It will take a few days to arrange, of course,' said the Earl of Suffolk.

'Does that present a problem?' Having made a difficult decision, the King had no wish to concern himself further. He would never see his aunt again, neither would her former husband. It was for the best.

'No, not really, Your Highness. She has been kept in custody at Westminster since her trial ended and the council is anxious that she is moved elsewhere. Since his return to London, His Grace the Duke has been staying in Greenwich, but he cannot remain there indefinitely. He wishes to return to Westminster and that could cause him embarrassment. So Abbot Kyrton has suggested that the lady might like to sojourn at the monastery's manor house on the Eye estate for a few days while arrangements for her future are being made.'

'Abbot Kyrton? Oh, that is kind of him. Very well then, the problem is resolved very neatly. Thank you, my Lords.'

The King inclined his head to dismiss them.

***

William and Jenna were in their favourite place, holding hands and talking quietly. There was to be no lovemaking for them tonight, they were both content to wait until they had taken their vows on the morrow.

'How is Kitty?' William asked. 'Is she very excited about it?'

'Oh, what do you think, William? Of course she is! She has a new kirtle and a new pair of shoes and her two favourite people in all the world are getting married. Of course she's excited.'

Jenna studied his face in the half light. 'You've been very quiet these last few days,' she said. 'You're not having any regrets, are you? You don't think perhaps we're doing this a little too soon after Margery's ... Margery's death?'

William took a deep breath before replying. 'No,' he said. 'I hated seeing Margery die in the way she did, of course, but if I'm honest, I'd been half-expecting it for years. The sad thing is that she loved mixing with clever, superficial people, but she never saw how ruthless they could be in using her for their own ends. I always thought she was tempting Fate. So no, Jenna, I can't see that there's any reason why you and I should wait too long before we marry. I want to spend the rest of my life with you, my sweet, and tomorrow, my most cherished wish will be granted.'

He kissed her, not with passion, but as though to seal a bargain. She drew back with a smile. 'Good,' she said. 'But I know something's wrong. What's really worrying you?'

William leaned back against the hay. 'There's something I

must confess. In fact, there are two things I must tell you, and I think they'll both surprise you more than a little.'

Facing him, Jenna sat with her knees drawn up to her chest, her arms around them. 'And are these things you should have told me before?'

'Maybe,' said William. 'But you're right. I've been worrying about how best to commemorate Margery's death. I have felt very bad about her since ... since that day at Smithfield and I didn't know what to do for the best. Margery was burned as a witch, so she could never have a Christian burial, nor any recognised period of mourning.'

Jenna was quiet. The same thought had occurred to her but that was how things were. There was nothing to be done about it.

'I wanted her to have some presence in the churchyard,' William went on, 'despite the fact that she has no grave. And Robin suggested a way around the problem.'

'We have a lot to thank Robin for.'

William caught hold of her hand and kissed it. 'I thank God daily that he brought you here.'

'So what did he suggest?'

William didn't reply immediately. He sat up and reached behind him until his fingers found a small coffer. He brought it round to show to Jenna.

'What's in it?'

'Just some ashes,' said William.

'Ashes? What sort of ashes? From a fire, you mean?'

William nodded. Slowly, Jenna realised what the little box contained.

'Ah. They're ashes from the fire in Smithfield, aren't they?' William nodded again but said nothing.

'And is Margery ...?' She left the question unfinished.

'I don't know,' William said. 'They're just ashes. There may be something ... well, something of Margery in them. I really don't know. There is no way of knowing. But Robin went back to Smithfield the next morning, after the burning. He said there was almost nothing left of the fire, just a heap of ash, and no one stopped him from putting a small shovelful of it in a box.

He thought it might help me to have it.'

'And does it help?'

'Oddly, yes. And since there was never a funeral, I'm going to scatter the ash in the churchyard very early tomorrow morning before there's anyone about. It's only a gesture but it … it makes it easier, somehow. And Jenna…'

'Yes.'

'I'd like you to come with me. Will you?'

'Why?'

'To …' he shrugged, 'to seal some sort of bargain, I suppose. Margery and I meant nothing to each other by the end, our marriage was a sham. But she was a human being. We only had the word of those clever lawyers and clergymen that she was a witch. I think she just over-reached herself. That's why I'd like to scatter these ashes in the churchyard to bring the whole sorry business to – to some sort of conclusion. And I'd like to do that before you and I take our marriage vows tomorrow, so that we can make a fresh start. Will you help me?'

Jenna leaned forward and took his face in her hands.

'I don't think I deserve you, William Jourdemayne,' she said. 'You are a wonderful man and I love you with all of my being. Yes, let's draw a veil over our past lives, so that we can begin again. Of course I'll come with you. I think that would be the right thing to do.'

Again, they didn't kiss. There didn't seem any need to. Jenna, her hands still on either side of William's dear face, laid her forehead against his and let it rest there for a moment while she closed her eyes.

Then she opened them again.

'And what was the other thing?' she asked.

'Oh! I almost forgot. I had a message earlier, from the steward at La Neyte who asked to see me. He wanted to let me know that he is expecting a royal party to stay for a few days. They will arrive tomorrow.'

'A royal party! How exciting!'

'But I'm afraid you might be upset when you know who it is.'

Jenna gave him a questioning look. 'Why?'

'Because the principal guest will be that damned duchess woman.'

'The Duchess of Gloucester?'

'A duchess no longer, it seems. She has been divorced from the Duke and is to be banished, imprisoned somewhere far away. She and her escort party will stay at La Neyte for a few days while final arrangements are being made. You won't have to see her,' he added, looking anxiously at Jenna.

She said nothing for a while, she merely shook her head occasionally while she thought over everything he had told her. Eventually, she took his hand.

'That's not important now,' she said. 'Come, my love. We need to be awake before cockcrow tomorrow. As soon as the bell rings for Prime, I'll meet you outside the churchyard. Come, we'd be wise to go to our own beds now. Tomorrow will be a busy day.'

***

The two met again, shortly after Prime.

'You brought the coffer?' Jenna whispered.

'Yes, of course. It's under the lychgate. Come.' William took her hand and they entered the churchyard through the main gate, stopping only for William to retrieve the coffer from its resting place. Then they moved silently through the dew-soaked grass without disturbing those who slept for eternity.

'Here?' he asked. 'Would this be an appropriate place?'

'Under the rowan tree? But doesn't that protect against…'

'Against witches? Yes, it does, but who says Margery was a witch? I never did.'

'No, William. You didn't. You were the most loyal husband. And you're right. Let's scatter the ashes here, then.'

William removed the lid of the coffer. He hesitated for a moment, then he said simply, 'God rest you, Margery, and grant your soul eternal peace.' He shook out the contents of the coffer, around the base of a fine, tall rowan tree. Stepping back, he crossed himself, bowed his head in prayer for a moment then reached for Jenna's hand and together they left the graveyard. They didn't look back.

Five hours later, they stood together again in the church porch, hand in hand, as man and wife. William had on a new leather jerkin for the occasion and Jenna looked charming in a woollen cloak trimmed with miniver over a simple blue gown. Kitty was wearing a brand new kirtle of red wool and trying her best to look solemn. Bride and bridesmaid both carried nosegays of early snowdrops and winter herbs bound with ivy.

Stepping outside the porch at the end of the ceremony, Jenna and William were surrounded by a small crowd of well-wishers, farm hands, dairymaids and scullions. Seth and Piers the cowherds were there with their wives, Hawys and Sarah. Geoffrey the carpenter was there too, with Tom the shepherd and his boy, Jack, throwing handfuls of grain in a time-honoured gesture of goodwill. There were tears in Jenna's eyes when they all gave three rousing cheers for the Master and the new Mistress.

The big barn, scene of so many celebrations in the past, was decorated for the wedding breakfast with garlands of greenery which had remained in place since Twelfth Night. The floor had been swept and strewn with clean herbs and fragrant dried lavender and trestle tables were set up against the walls.

The top table, where the bride and groom were seated, was groaning with wedding fare. Though food was scarce in January, the larders had been raided for salted beef and cured ham, and dried mackerel was served with a delicious sauce of creamed leeks. There were baked turnips and sweet parsnips in abundance and for those who still felt hungry, two different kinds of bread with the best salted butter and plenty of cheese.

Ale was flowing and tongues were loosening while two fiddlers and a piper began to tune up their instruments. Then a tabor player started beating out a rhythm as a sign for the groom to lead his bride and their guests in the dance. William helped Jenna to her feet, but just before they took to the floor he turned back to the table, lifted his goblet of Lamb's Wool and gazed over the rim of it into his new wife's sparkling eyes.

'This is very like the moment when I first fell in love with you,' he said, proffering the goblet so that she could drink from the other side of it and share the toast.

'Ah,' said Jenna, 'yes. Mind you, I was very busy at the time, falling in love with a king.'

His eyebrows furrowed for a brief moment then he smiled. 'You and your royal connections,' he said. 'I trust you mean the King of the Bean?'

'Of course. Who else?

They had been so immersed in their conversation, they failed to notice that the music hadn't started and the barn had become oddly hushed.

'Jenna!' Kitty's urgent shaking of her arm brought Jenna back to earth and she looked round.

'There!' Kitty whispered dramatically, with a jerk of her head.

The door had opened to admit a new group of people, some half dozen in all, not wedding guests, at least no one who had been officially invited as far as Jenna could see. She scanned their faces with a frown until…

'Your Grace!' she said, nearly dropping the goblet. William took it from her, muttering something under his breath as he set it down on the table behind him. Eleanor Cobham was walking towards them with a small, regretful smile on her face.

'I'm afraid you can't call me by that title any more,' she said. 'I'm not allowed to use it.'

'I'm … my Lady, I'm … I'm not sure what to say. I had heard that you … that…'

Eleanor, well aware of the stir her arrival had caused, stopped in front of them. Two guards and a group of three women positioned themselves behind her.

'I am staying here at the manor house for a few days,' she said. 'No, let's not mince our words. In truth, I am being held in captivity at the manor house for a few days before being banished to the north of England.' She jutted her chin forward, as though daring anyone to react in any way to what she had said. 'When I arrived at La Neyte, I enquired after Master Jourdemayne and was told that he was to re-marry. And when I learned who was to be his bride, I asked if I might be permitted to come and offer my sincerest good wishes.'

William mumbled something which could have been an

expression of thanks, but might equally well have been an expression of irritation. Whichever it was, Eleanor ignored it. She kept her gaze on Jenna.

'I have brought a wedding gift,' she said. She gestured to one of her waiting women who handed her a small leather case. Eleanor held it out towards Jenna.

'Take it,' she said. 'It comes with all my good wishes for a long and fruitful marriage.'

'But ... but, my Lady...'

'Take it,' Eleanor said again. 'It is for you both. Almighty God has seen fit to give you both a second chance for happiness and that's something not given to many.' She reached forward and kissed Jenna on the cheek. 'Goodbye, Jenna. Thank you for your friendship. You will never know how grateful I was for that. Just pray for me once in a while, if you remember.'

With that, she turned and moved towards the door, her retinue of women and guards following close behind her. Everyone else in the room watched in wide-eyed silence until they had left but, once the big barn door had closed behind them, the whole place erupted with exclamations and nervous laughter.

'Oooh, Jenna! What is it? Can I see?' Kitty could hardly contain herself. She was bouncing with excitement.

Tentatively, Jenna opened the leather case and took out a writing tablet contained between two covers of exquisitely carved ivory. Everyone crowded around, wanting to catch a glimpse of this marvellous gift.

'What is it?' Kitty wanted to know.

'It's a writing tablet,' Jenna said. 'It's beautiful.'

'Yes, but what's it for?'

'You use it when you're writing, silly Kittymouse,' Jenna said.

'Can't see that it's much use to us,' William said, taking it from her as she showed it to him. 'We're farming folk. Don't have much time for writing and such. Mind you,' he added, running his hands over the ivory, 'this is a lovely piece of carving. Is this some kind of bone?'

'I don't know,' said Jenna, 'but it's beautiful. And a very

generous gift. The Duchess sets great store by learning and scholarship. She used to say that, according to the King, the future belongs to those who are willing to learn. Perhaps, one day, Kitty will be able to write well enough to use this. I'd like to think so.'

William gave her a quizzical look. 'And if not Kitty,' he said, 'there could be other little scholars?'

'There could,' Jenna smiled back at him. 'It's up to us to do something about that.'

She turned to Kitty and handed her the writing tablet.

'Look after that please, my dove. It will be yours one day.'

With that, William gave her his hand and led her out to join their friends in the dance.

THE END

Historical Footnote

All the major characters who appear in the book you have been reading were real people – with one exception. It is a recorded fact that William Jourdemayne re-married after the death of his first wife, though his second wife's name is unknown. William's own name ceases to appear in the manorial accounts after the year 1450-51 but it seems that his widow went on to run the farm very capably. I have given the second Mistress Jourdemayne a name and she has done me the great favour of becoming the 'mortar' which holds together the many, many building blocks of this extraordinary true story. But Jenna Harding exists only in the pages of this book.

Naturally, a great deal more is known about the fate of the House of Lancaster.

Humphrey of Gloucester remained a popular figure among Londoners, even after his wife's disgrace, but he was just as much of a thorn in the sides of his old adversaries as he had ever been. They had succeeded in discrediting him but he was still next in line to the throne, so he must be got rid of: and he was. In February 1447, a session of Parliament was convened at Bury St. Edmunds, well away from London. Humphrey was summoned to attend it and did so, only to run straight into a trap. He was placed under arrest. Three days later, he was dead and the manner of his death has been the subject of conspiracy theories ever since. Was he murdered? Was he poisoned? Did he die of natural causes? No one will ever know. What is indisputable is that a great deal of trouble was taken to display his corpse publicly, thus putting paid to rumours that he had been tortured.

Humphrey is now chiefly remembered as a considerable man of letters and a patron of the arts. His gift of books to the

University of Oxford still forms a part of the Bodleian Library and is known as 'Duke Humfrey's Library' to this day.

King Henry VI's patronage benefitted Cambridge University rather than Oxford. The college he founded is now known simply as 'King's' and is renowned for its outstanding academic record, its chapel and its choir. The annual Christmas *Carols from King's* is broadcast to millions around the world. At Eton, the independent boys' boarding school, there are still traditionally some seventy 'King's Scholars' and these are the 'poor scholars' provided for in King Henry's original statutes. Though his legacy lives on, the King himself was destined to become the last of the Lancastrian line. The King's inept governance of his realm was one of the key elements which provoked the sporadic civil war between the rival royal houses of Lancaster and York, now known as the Wars of the Roses.

Over-pious and weak-willed throughout his life, Henry suffered regular bouts of mental collapse. It is quite probable that he inherited his unstable psychological state from his maternal grandfather, the French King Charles VI, who richly deserved the nickname of 'Charles the Mad'. Despite this, Henry married Margaret of Anjou and fathered a son, Edward. In 1471 Edward, the seventeen-year-old Lancastrian heir, lost his life in the Battle of Tewkesbury and King Henry himself, imprisoned in the Tower of London, was put to death shortly afterwards. The intermittent battles raged on, culminating in the Battle of Bosworth Field in 1485 which was won by the forces of Henry Tudor.

Tudor's loyalty was to the House of Lancaster but he was actually the grandson of Henry VI's French mother, Catherine, and her Welsh lover, Owen Tudor. He claimed the throne as Henry VII and married Elizabeth of York, thus uniting both quarrelsome factions of the royal family. The colourful Tudors remained on the throne of England until the death of Queen Elizabeth I in 1603.

Cardinal Henry Beaufort, as an illegitimate son of John of Gaunt, was a member of the royal House of Lancaster but one without a claim to the throne. Instead, he devoted the whole of his life to maintaining the success of the dynasty. Though he and Humphrey of Gloucester were constantly at loggerheads, Beaufort cannot be implicated in the plot to trick the Duke into attending the fateful Parliament in Bury St. Edmunds. That was masterminded by the Earl of Suffolk. By then the Cardinal, an elderly man in his seventies, was spending what would be the last year of his life in the diocese of Winchester, which he had rather neglected while he was a central figure in English politics. It was in Winchester, six weeks after Humphrey's death, that Beaufort himself died on April 11th 1447.

The **Duchess Eleanor** was, without doubt, a pawn in a deadly political game. History remembers Eleanor Cobham as decorative, talented and amusing, though devoid of the guile to realise until too late that she was being used to bring about her husband's downfall. Having been found guilty of the charges against her and divorced from Humphrey, she was variously imprisoned at Kent, Chester, on the Isle of Man and in Beaumaris Castle on the banks of the Menai Strait in Anglesey. It was here that she ended her days, still in captivity, in 1452. Ten years earlier, before leaving Westminster for the last time in January 1442, it is a recorded fact that she spent a few days in the care of Sir Thomas Stanley at La Neyte. In so doing, Eleanor provided me with the opportunity to give this rather gruesome story a happy ending.

Bibliography and Acknowledgments

Historical fiction can never be any more than an interpretation of events that took place a long, long time ago. So the writer who is not a fully paid-up, bona fide historian must rely on the facts as presented by those who are. I am particularly indebted therefore to several academic historians and their works:

Breverton, Terry, *Breverton's Complete Herbal* (Quercus Publishing, 2011)
– in which the author makes Culpeper's 1650s classics *The English Physitian* and *Compleat Herball* accessible for the modern reader.

Cooke, G.A., *The County of Devon* (c.1816-1820)
– a source of dialect words reproduced online by John Lerwill, a proud Devonian.

Ginn, Peter, Goodman, Ruth & Pinfold, Tom, *Tudor Monastery Farm* (BBC Books, 2013)
– to accompany the television series of the same name.

Griffiths, Ralph A., *King and Country: England and Wales in the Fifteenth Century* (Hambledon Press, 1991)

Griffiths, Ralph A., *The Reign of King Henry VI* (Sutton Publishing, 2004)

Radford, Lewis Bostock, *Henry Beaufort, Bishop, Chancellor, Cardinal* (Sir Isaac Pitman & Sons Ltd, 1908)

Vickers, Kenneth Hotham, *Humphrey, Duke of Gloucester – A Biography* (Archibald Constable & Co., 1907)

Watts, John, *Henry VI and the Politics of Kingship* (Cambridge University Press, 1996)

Various contributors to *The Oxford Dictionary of National Biography*. This indispensable work of reference is freely available to members of subscribing local libraries, in my case the Vale of Glamorgan Libraries Service.

Perhaps my greatest debt is to the authors of the following two academic papers:

Freeman, Jessica, *Sorcery at court and manor: Margery Jourdemayne, the Witch of Eye next Westminster* (© Elsevier Ltd, 2004. All rights reserved.)

Rutton, William Loftie, *The Manor of Eia, or Eye-next-Westminster*. This paper was read to the Society of Antiquaries in London on January 20th 1910.

I value the honest opinions of several friends who read the original manuscript, but I particularly want to thank my mentor, Andrew Wille, as well as my editor at Accent Press, Greg Rees, for shining a light into a few dark corners.

And, as always, thanks to Jonah for not minding my occasional neglect.

Llanilltud Fawr
2016

Root of the Tudor Rose

Mari Griffith

1421: Henry V and his young bride, Catherine de Valois, are blessed with the birth of a son – but their happiness is short-lived. Catherine is widowed and when her father, the French king, also dies, her son inherits the crowns of France and England. Just ten months old, Henry VI needs all his mother's watchful care to protect him from political intrigue.

But Catherine is a foreigner at the English Court. Lonely and vulnerable, she is held in suspicion by those with their own claims to the throne. Only with another outsider, a young Welshman named Owen Tudor, does Catherine find true friendship but their liaison must be kept secret at all costs. Catherine, Queen of England is forbidden to remarry and she is in love with a servant…

The White Ship

Nicholas Salaman

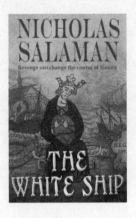

For all fans of historical fiction and especially readers of Ken Follett's *The Pillars of the Earth*

Based on a true story, this tale of passion and revenge brings the past vividly to life.

Normandy in 1118 is a hotbed of malcontent barons kept in fragile order by their duke, Henry I, King of England. Fresh from early years in a monastery, Bertold - the bastard son of one of these barons - meets Juliana, a countess and daughter of the King.

He falls in love, or lust (he isn't sure), but sees that his chance could come with work in her small court. Soon, though, he finds himself caught up in a ruthless feud between Juliana and her father. Juliana's daughters are offered as hostages for a strategic castle, and even love is not enough to allay a tragedy that will change the course of history.

Swordland

Edward Ruadh Butler

Robert FitzStephen is a warrior down on his luck. Arrogant, cold, but a brilliant soldier, FitzStephen commands a castle – yet although his mother was a princess his father was a lowly steward. When a Welsh rebellion brings defeat and a crippling siege, his highborn comrades scorn him, betraying him to the enemy. A hostage of his cousin, Prince Rhys, FitzStephen is disgraced, seemingly doomed to a life of obscurity and shame.

Then King Diarmait arrives …

Diarmait is the ambitious overlord of an Irish kingdom. Forced to flee by the High King of Ireland, he seeks to reclaim his lands by any means possible – and that includes inviting the Normans in. With nothing left to lose – and perhaps a great deal to gain – FitzStephen agrees to lead the Irishman's armies, and to drive Diarmait's enemies from his kingdom. His price? Acceptance, perhaps … or perhaps a kingdom of his own?